By the same author

Dear Amy

Everything is Lies

Night Falls, Still Missing

HELEN CALLAGHAN

PENGUIN BOOKS

PENGUIN BOOKS

UK | USA | Canada | Ireland | Australia
India | New Zealand | South Africa

Penguin Books is part of the Penguin Random House group of companies
whose addresses can be found at global.penguinrandomhouse.com

First published by Michael Joseph 2020
Published in Penguin Books 2021
001

Printed and bound in Great Britain by Clays Ltd, Elcograf S.p.A.

The authorized representative in the EEA is Penguin Random House Ireland,
Morrison Chambers, 32 Nassau Street, Dublin D02 YH68

A CIP catalogue record for this book is available from the British Library

ISBN: 978–1–405–93559–3

www.greenpenguin.co.uk

For Mum and Dad

Prologue

Langmire, Grangeholm, Orkney, January 2020

The TV blares away in the background in the little living room at Langmire.

Madison slouches on the sofa, dressed only in an oversized blue pullover, draining her glass of Sauvignon Blanc. She is barely watching it – if anything, it is simply white noise to keep her company in the endless restless quiet.

The silence here is a strange thing. It is beautiful during the late red dawns and early darknesses, almost holy, punctuated only by the cries of water birds and the murmur of the sea. When she lies in her bed, woken from the deep sleep that the constant physical labour on Helly Holm brings upon her, the thought of going home to the roar and clank of London and leaving this place behind causes her an almost physical pain.

But there is something about this particular hour – eight, nine o'clock on a Saturday night, when a house should be full of post-dinner chatter, contented binge-watching with friends, a glass of wine or two before winding down for bed – that makes her lonely, melancholy.

Well, she thinks ruefully, biting her full bottom lip. *Melancholy is perhaps one way to describe it.*

It is more like a subtle dread. But she is not frightened, no. Not yet. Madison never admits to fear.

She stands up, about to move off to the fridge and recharge her glass, when, glancing through the window, out across the water, she sees the tiny flicker of a white light.

She pauses, squinting out into the darkness. The light isn't steady, but bobs about like a tiny firefly over the sea, until it is momentarily consumed in the flash of the lighthouse.

Except this light can't be on the sea. It must be on Helly Holm, which she cannot see in the moonless night until the lighthouse flashes awake, once every twenty seconds.

Madison purses her lips, puts her glass down on the window sill, picks up her phone.

Yep, she sees after a quick check on the tide tables, the causeway is out from under the water now, as it is twice every twenty-four hours.

There's nothing to stop anyone from crossing it and poking around the dig. Though, that said, why anyone would be foolish enough to attempt such a thing in complete darkness on a tidal islet with no phone signal is a mystery. Most of the tools and all of the samples are taken home in the boat at the end of the work day, and everything else is locked in the storage boxes. There will be nothing out there worth stealing.

Perhaps it's someone with a metal detector, who's seen the archaeologists there, and now with them gone for the night they want to try their own luck.

Madison sighs, a little huff of annoyance.

Part of the reason that someone is posted out in Langmire cottage (ostensibly, at least – Madison has her own views on why she has been isolated out here at the last minute) is to act as watchman for the site.

Madison scrolls down her phone to Iris's number, calls her. After just a couple of rings it goes straight to voicemail.

Hmm. Now what?

For a second she considers calling Jack, but just as she is about to she pauses. No, not Jack.

Through the cold glass, lit for a moment by the tower with

its blazing electric lantern, Helly Holm looms like a dark mountain against the starless sky.

Then it all vanishes, back into blackness.

She narrows her eyes, considering it.

Why doesn't she swing by in the car and take a look from the shore?

Friday

I

Caithness, Scotland, January 2020

It was only three o'clock but the sun was already slung dangerously low on the horizon, a bright, burning orange. Small lakes reflected its failing light, and looked filled with molten gold.

Fiona Grey leaned in with the petrol nozzle, careful not to let her new red coat brush against the thick caking of mud and road salt smeared all over her little car. She already suspected that her boots were a write-off.

She was heading north.

Her breath steamed before her, a fragile plume, as the old-fashioned pump grumbled and pulsed and the stink of petrol was everywhere. Apart from this everything was silent, hushed by the snow – only the occasional splashing of a passing car through the slush on the nearby road intruding. The lively wind was fresh against her face, as though it was slapping her awake, and she was grateful.

She would be more grateful for a hot coffee, however.

She had set out from Inverness after breakfast and stopped to shop for some suitable cold weather gear – there had been no time to do this in Cambridge as Madison's summons had been too urgent, too peremptory – and this, she thought, eyeing the sinking sun, had been a tactical error. It would be long dark before she reached the ferry port at Scrabster, and the drive, which had followed a perilously winding cliffside road through towns with evocative names like Golspie, Dornoch and Dunbeath, had been beautiful but hair-raising in equal measure.

The car filled, she went inside to pay a large, pleasant blonde woman, who looked in danger of being crushed to death at any moment by the enormous number of boxes, cardboard stands and groaning baskets full of car fresheners, almost-out-of-date chocolate bars and window scrapers festooning the shop.

'That'll be thirty-nine pounds six, hen,' she said. 'Is that all you're after?'

Fiona took her card out of her pocket. 'Actually, I wondered if I could get a coffee . . .'

The woman shook her head, sighing at the panoply of goods surrounding her, as if mourning the lost opportunity Fiona presented to be rid of some. 'Ah, sorry. The machine is broken. Are you heading out for the ferry?'

Fiona admitted she was.

'Sailing for Orkney tonight?'

'Yes,' Fiona said, her mouth growing a little dry.

'Where are you from?'

'Cambridge.'

The woman nodded. 'You on your holidays, then?' she asked, putting the sale through before offering Fiona the card terminal.

'Um . . . well, I've been asked to go up and visit a friend who's working there. She . . .' Fiona stilled, having caught herself just in time. 'She says she needs my help with something.'

The woman raised an eyebrow while Fiona keyed in her PIN. 'That's a long way to come to help someone.'

Fiona had only shrugged.

Before getting back into her car, she took out her phone and captured a quick photo of the magnificent melting sunset.

She texted the photo to Madison, with a quick message – *Getting closer! Fx*

She was not expecting a response at this time of day – about now the dig was probably still in full swing.

Hi hows it going? Mx

4

Fiona, surprised, tapped in her reply, smiling.

Hello stranger — all good here! Not long now . . . Already bought some fizz! x

She buckled herself into the car while she waited for the reply.

Sounds good! Missed u sooo much! Be great to see u! Mx

Relief flooded Fiona. Madison had been cagey throughout this journey northwards, and they hadn't spoken since Fiona had left Cambridge.

You too! How are you? Are you okay?! x

There was a long pause before the reply came.

Yeah, why wouldn't I be? Sry gotta run. See you when the ferry gets in! Mx

Fiona frowned at the screen, her cheeks heating as though she'd been slapped.

If everything was fine, what was she doing here?

Before she knew it, Fiona had hit the number and was calling her friend.

Almost immediately, it was answered.

'Oh, hi Mads, I just wanted . . .'

'The person you are calling is not available,' interrupted the answerphone message. 'Please hang up and try again later.'

Madison had disabled her voicemail months and months ago, on the advice of the police after the court case, and then never reinstated it.

Fiona sighed, dissatisfied, then shrugged, throwing her phone on to the empty passenger seat next to her.

Doubtless all would be revealed, she thought, attempting to put it from her mind, despite the coiling disquiet in her belly.

* * *

'What do you need me on Orkney for?' Fiona had asked. She'd been in the bath, her phone resting on the tiled border next to her beeswax-scented candles.

5

Her heart had leapt when Madison had called – she'd missed her, she realised, missed having someone to share the minutiae of her life with, missed her spiky sense of humour, missed that communion with someone who really knew her.

They had been friends since they were little girls, growing up in the same village together, fascinated by the same things, but actually living worlds apart. Fiona had been raised by her alcoholic father, after her mother had abandoned them both. There had been an Aunty Lisette, busybody and virtual stranger, who'd occasionally visit and cluck over Fiona's ragged clothes and her dad's collection of empty lager cans that rolled about under his bed, but after she'd died the extended family had promptly dropped the pair of them. Perhaps they'd had troubles enough of their own.

Madison, in contrast, had lived in the biggest house in the village, a sprawling seventies concoction on the very top of the hill, bookended by ugly extensions. It was presided over by Madison's American father, Gulf War veteran and self-made man, a distant and dark creature who somehow managed to make the whole family fall into nervous silence the minute he entered the room, and Judy, Madison's fragile, impeccably turned out English rose mother who, without ever saying as much, had always made it perfectly clear that Fiona was not welcome.

It had made no difference. From the day they'd started at Blackdown Hill Preparatory, they had become inseparable – Madison the bold, ballsy agent of chaos who feared nothing, and Fiona her studious, long-suffering antithesis, picking up the pieces.

And it had seemed to Fiona that she could foresee no time that this would ever change.

How little Fiona had been able to foresee, in the end.

'What? I can't ask my bestie to come visit me?' Mads had been mulish, almost sulky, and Fiona felt her heart sinking.

'You can . . .' she said, dipping her toes back under the cooling bathwater. 'But you know it's difficult for me in term time . . .'

'It's not term time.'

'It *is* term time,' said Fiona, trying to be conciliatory but firm. 'Term starts on January the fourteenth . . .'

'Oh, so at most you'll miss a day or two. And you can pass it off as research. You know,' said Mads, warming to her theme, her voice becoming silky and persuasive, 'it's this big exciting dig, in this beautiful part of the world with a celebrity archaeologist, potentially going to make everyone's careers, with lots of fab metalwork . . .'

'Yeah,' said Fiona, before she could stop herself. 'An uninhabitable Scottish island in the middle of darkest winter. I'm sure the digging is *fabulous.*'

'There's no need to be sarky,' snapped Madison, her charm offensive abandoned.

Silence.

Then, a tiny, contrite voice. 'Are you still there?'

Fiona let out a stiff little sigh. 'Yes.'

'I'm sorry,' said Madison, and for the first time in the phone call she sounded like her genuine self. 'I'm just . . . I can't tell you what I think is going on. But I don't feel safe here. Not at all.'

'Hang on.' Fiona eased upright in alarm, the water swirling around her. 'What do you mean, you don't feel safe? Has someone threatened you?'

'I . . . no. Well, maybe. I dunno.'

'What does that mean?' Fiona's thoughts leapt forward. 'Is Dom back?'

Silence again, then, 'I told you, I don't know.'

'What?' Fiona was stunned. 'Who else could it be? What's that twat doing now?'

'Oh, the usual. Someone's tweeting bollocks at me. Whoever they are, they're on Orkney.'

'He's up there on *Orkney*? How do you know?'

'It says so. On one of the tweets.'

'Have you spoken to the police yet? What did they say?'

'No, I haven't spoken to . . . I don't know it's him. You know. Dominic.'

'What?' Fiona's jaw dropped open. 'Who else could it be?'

'I don't know!' snapped Madison. 'You know, this isn't my fault!'

Fiona took a deep breath, tried to calm herself. 'I know. I'm sorry, I'm just worried about you.'

'I know you are,' said Madison, with a sigh. 'And it's not like I don't love you for it. But you need to relax.'

Fiona stared at the phone. Madison's attitude didn't make any sense. 'Why do you think it's not him? Why aren't you worried he's on the island with you?'

There was a pause, Madison's breath hissing softly as she thought.

'I can't explain it. But it's just different this time.'

'You need to go to the police again,' said Fiona urgently, trying to rein in the desire to reach through the phone and shake Madison. 'Isn't that why you want me to come up, because it's bothering you?'

Now it was Madison's turn to be quiet.

'I don't understand,' said Fiona, frowning at the phone. 'You're out there in that cottage on your own and he might be . . .'

The silence expanded.

'Madison?'

'Yeah?'

'What's going on?' asked Fiona. 'I mean, *really* going on?'

'I . . . Look, I just need you here. I need to show you something. The only way you will get a chance to see it, to see what I mean, is to come up here.'

'Mads, it's not that simple.' She tried not to sigh again, caught between the competing impulses of frustration and alarm. 'Whatever it is, you must be able to talk about it . . .'

'Fee, I . . . no. I can't. Not right now. I don't even know what I think is going on. But I need you here now. I'm freaking out.'

'Mads, it's not that . . .'

'You never fucking believe me.' Madison sounded angry, and close to tears again. 'You think I'm crazy, I know!'

'Calm down. Yes, I do think you're crazy. It doesn't mean I don't believe you.'

'Then *come*,' she said, and Fiona heard her blatant, exposed need. 'Please come. I have never been so fucking miserable. I'm losing my mind . . . Please do me this one favour. Please come. *Please.*'

* * *

'Oh hi there, Nanook of the North,' Adi said, his voice pleased. He'd answered almost immediately. 'I was just thinking about you. How's it going?'

All was darkness, except for the sodium orange light of the harbour. Through the windscreen of her little car she could see the ferry approaching the terminal, and against the black sea and black sky it seemed to be a tiny floating island of light, trapped between heaven and earth.

'I'm okay.' She'd smiled, feeling herself relax against the driver's seat, letting the warm chocolate of his voice melt over her. 'Got to the ferry port in one piece. Just waiting to drive on.'

'How are things?'

'Things are freezing.'

He snorted. 'It's Scotland in January. What did you expect?'

'I dunno,' she said. 'That they would be freezing.'

He laughed. In the background music was playing – Amy Winehouse's 'Tears Dry on Their Own'. 'When's your ferry?'

'It leaves here in forty-five minutes.'

'I bet the views will be gorgeous.'

'They may be, but it's too dark to see anything, and anyway, they'd be wasted on me,' she said. 'You know I get terrible sea-sickness and I'm frightened of boats.'

'But you've put the patch on, haven't you?' he breezed.

Her hand drifted up to the little plaster behind her ear. 'Well, yeah, but it just takes the edge off . . .'

'You'll be fine. Most of motion sickness is just psychological anyway.'

'I dunno, Adi.' She shifted in the car seat. She'd managed to put off thinking about the boat for most of the day, but this discussion was stirring unwelcome feelings. 'It doesn't seem "just psychological" when it's happening . . .'

'Hmm,' he said, but there was something distant in it, as though she was being deliberately obstructive. 'Never mind. What are you up to right now?'

'I've been sat in the car brushing up on my Early Norse metalwork, since there is a very real danger celebrity archae-ologists might attempt to have intelligent conversations with me about it.'

'Ah yes,' he said, then loudly performed the trumpet-driven theme music from *Discovering the Past* in the form of raspberries, eliciting shocked laughter from Fiona. '"And now, the glamor-ous Professor Iris Barclay fills us in about an exciting discovery from Britain's mysterious prehistory . . ."'

'Philistine,' she hissed in mock contempt.

'Yeah, yeah, yeah,' he said. 'Anyway, I hope your meeting with the great woman goes well. Make sure you put some lippy on. And laugh at her jokes.'

'What do you mean?' asked Fiona, confused.

'I mean,' said Adi with barely concealed surprise, 'Iris Bar-clay would be a great contact for you. Obviously.'

'I suppose. She's really highly thought of in feminist archaeology at the moment – her paper on gendered grave goods in the Tpaletske Roman-period cemetery was astonishing . . .'

'What? No, I don't even know what any of that *means*, you ludicrous creature. I mean a *media* contact. You know, for getting on TV.'

'What? Me?' Fiona rolled her eyes. 'That's an adorable idea, but . . .'

'No . . . well, yeah, it is adorable, true, but that would be a brilliant move for you right now.'

'You say the sweetest things.' She laughed again, but she was blushing with pleasure. 'No point making much of that, anyway. I'm here for Mads, and I'm pretty sure she isn't going to want me hanging around her boss much.'

'Hmm.' Adi sighed, a tight little exhalation of breath.

'What is it? What's wrong?' she asked.

'Fiona, you should *make* Madison show you the dig. You should *make* her introduce you to Iris Barclay . . .'

'Well, she *will*, of course she will . . .'

'She will on her terms.' Adi's voice was tinged with strain, frustration, and ultimately, pity. 'She should introduce you properly, put you together. It's the very least she could do.'

'What do you mean? Why should she?'

'Because you've dropped everything and come all that way for her? Because it could be good for you, professionally?' He snorted. 'If Madison was a real friend, she'd make a point of helping your career.' His voice was cold. 'She never lets you in on anything if there's any danger of her having to share any glory.'

She felt herself flush. 'That's horrid. Why would you say that?'

'Because it's true.'

Fiona tried not to sigh. Adi did not like Madison, and he wasn't being fair.

Madison wanted something of her own. Fiona's career had taken off in ways that Madison's never had and Fiona knew she felt it. Iris's patronage was the best thing that could have happened and, rationally or not, Mads was nervous and insecure about losing it.

Fiona understood Madison, even if Adi could not.

'If it makes you feel any better,' she said, 'I'd rather be going to Zurich with you tomorrow.'

He made the *hmm* noise again, as though she had not really answered him.

'To be fair, it could all be worse, you know,' he said, relenting. 'Beautiful Scottish islands and dead Vikings and *buried treasure*,' and at this last his voice grew low, mimicking a pirate's. 'Arrr! It sounds awesome.'

'I wish you were here instead of me, then,' she said. 'My feet are blocks of ice right now.'

'You miserable cow. You don't know you're born. Do you want to know what I did in work today?'

She grinned despite herself. 'What did you do?'

'I gave a presentation on international insurance legislation as it relates to investment banking,' he said, full of mock annoyance. 'And it was every bit as exciting as it sounds.'

She giggled, shifting her phone to her other hand. 'How thrilling.'

'Nail-biting. Absolutely nail-biting.' He yawned.

'You know, I just wanted to . . .' She was reluctant to begin again on this subject. 'Well, about Mads . . .'

'What about her?' His tone was suddenly short, brisk. 'Has she told you what she needs you for yet, or is she still being mysterious?'

'No,' Fiona admitted. 'But it will be about that ex of hers — Dominic Tate. I know it.'

'But something's bothering you, isn't it?'

Fiona sighed, looking out at the sea and the distant lights of the ferry.

'No. Well, maybe yes.' She scratched her temple.

'Which is?'

She bit her lip. 'It's probably nothing, but it just stuck with me. She said something in a text. I asked her if she was okay and she said, "Why shouldn't I be?" It just – I dunno, I thought it was strange, since she'd asked me to come up at such short notice. Like she'd no idea what I was talking about.'

'Yeah?' Now there was cool anger mixed in with the pity. 'A tenner says you get all the way up there, and all this ex-stalker drama she needed you for is over and your trip's been for nothing. It's just that she didn't want to tell you.'

* * *

The ferry was called the *Hamnavoe*. With its blue cloth seats and polite safety announcements delivered in a soft brogue that was almost Scottish, almost Scandinavian, it was deceptively comfortable at first.

Fiona sat in one of the lounge chairs, the rain pattering gently against the darkened windows. Her fingers drummed on the armrest next to her. She was too anxious to read, to look at her phone – to do anything.

In the beginning she thought she would be all right as they pushed through the flat sea, but once they pulled out of Gill's Bay and joined the tidal race of the Pentland Firth she could feel it, that sickening tug and rock, as though giant hands were pulling and pushing the boat up and down. She sat blinking and swallowing her excess saliva, fighting the dragging current of her nausea while her coffee cooled in front of her, untouched.

Through the window the vanishing harbour lights appeared and disappeared with the rolling of the ship. Somewhere below in its bowels, a car alarm started to wail, like a squalling child.

You have the patch on. And Adi is probably right. It's just psychological . . .

Madison hadn't responded to any of Fiona's more recent texts. This was normal, she reminded herself, as there was no signal out on the islet the dig was on. But as seven became eight, then eight-thirty, Fiona had found herself growing uneasy, and not just with seasickness.

On an impulse, she jabbed Mads' picture, lifted the phone to her ear. This time it went straight to her recorded message.

Hi Mads, where are you? Just tried to call. Are you meeting me at the terminal still? Fx she texted instead.

A pause before the phone chimed once.

Sorry – not ignoring u! Things r MAD here! BIG BIG FIND on site here at Helly Holm!!! Can't talk now but SO MUCH catching up 2 do! See u in 30 mins! MXXX

Wherever Mads was, there must be signal of some sort.

Sounds exciting! What did you find?

Another pause, then the chime.

Take 2 long 2 text. Tell u when I see u!

Fiona sighed.

All right – keep me in suspense! See you soon. Fx

* * *

As Fiona rumbled out along the steel plates of the ferry on to solid earth, she was greeted by the sight of a picturesque stone town built into the side of a hill, the restless dark sea lapping at its edges. This must be Stromness, she realised, and the street-lights illuminated intriguing sandstone buildings threaded with narrow flagged streets, and a harbour full of boats, their masts a thicket streaked in moonlight. The stars above were hard, sharp and impossibly numerous, like sugar grains spilled across the sky.

Despite her journey, her doubts, she felt a little flicker of excitement, now that she was back on dry land. Fresh sweet air swept in through the open crack in her car window, tasting of salt.

Madison must love it here, she thought.

A great longing rose in her then to see Madison, and in that moment she realised how much she'd missed her these past two months. The reasons for their quarrel, which had made her so furious, evaporated in her mind as though they'd never existed.

They would have a few drinks and talk, and Madison would tell her why she had summoned her all the way to the very northernmost tip of the country, and together they would solve everything – whatever it was.

First, she had to find the terminal office, where Mads was going to meet her. She pulled slowly in front of the ticket office near the car park, gulls wheeling above it by the lights of the harbour.

And waited.

* * *

'Are you all right there?'

Someone was tapping on the driver-side window.

Miserable and furious, Fiona was still sitting in her car, in the dark.

She pressed the button, lowering the window, letting the cold in. An earnest man with a heavy, jowly face was now leaning over her, his hooded jacket zipped up to his chin and striped with hi-vis markings. The battering wind seemed to have no effect upon him.

'I . . .' Fiona wanted to cry, was aware of this as a building pressure. 'I'm waiting for my friend – she's meant to meet me here, but she's not answering her phone . . .'

The other cars had rumbled away, one after the other. A small knot of foot passengers in weatherproofs – men, women and children – had waited patiently at the flat terminal building, new cars arriving to drive them away in twos and threes.

Soon all were gone, even the gulls, except for three men locking up the offices, who must be making their way home for the night.

And Fiona.

By then she'd been there for over an hour, with no word from Madison, and no answer to her numerous frantic phone calls.

'Meet you here, aye?' The man had kind eyes and a low, lilting accent – an Orcadian. Around him, through the gap in the window, the cold sea air blew in, stirring her unruly hair and the forgotten shopping bag with its celebratory bottles of fizz.

'Yeah,' said Fiona, already feeling calmed by the man's measured manner. 'She's called Madison Kowalczyk. She's an archaeologist, over at Helly Holm . . .'

'Oh aye, they're doing some work out there, aren't they? Do you know where she's staying?'

You know, thought Fiona, *I do*. 'Yeah, it's . . .' She thumbed through her phone. 'Langmire. The village is Grangeholm . . .'

'Aye, I know it. It's on the other side of the island. If your friend doesnae show, you can head out that way yerself. You'll probably meet her coming,' he said, scratching his head under his bright orange hood.

'Oh, thank you. I don't know what I thought. I just haven't heard from her since before I got on the ferry.'

He nodded. 'They do work some late hours out on Helly Holm sometimes. Are you one of them, then? An archaeologist?'

Fiona demurred. 'Yeah. But I'm not here to dig . . .'

'No? I hope you packed warm anyway. Ye've picked the time of year for it,' he said placidly.

* * *

After he'd delivered his directions and gone, she rolled up the window, letting the car's heating once again flood the interior. She was overreacting, she realised, and making a fool of herself – if the others had found something at the site, no wonder Mads was delayed.

You're just tired, she told herself. *You've been travelling for two days, after all, and you're missing Adi. A couple of glasses of Prosecco and a good laugh and a good night's sleep in a warm bed will set you as right as rain.*

Fiona picked up her phone again, tried to push down her annoyance. However busy Madison was, she should have let her know she'd be late. Fiona knew she was being treated in a cavalier – in a (let's be honest) *Madison-like* way.

Say something, murmured a voice in her ear. It sounded like Adi's. *You're here at her request.*

But what would the point be? And why start fighting with Madison again, before she had even arrived at the house? Why spoil everything now and possibly ruin the whole week?

Fiona sighed, staring out across the blackness of the sea lapping at the harbour.

Check her social media.

Of course. If there was something going on at the dig, the team might tweet it.

Almost without realising it, she had gravitated to @Helly-HolmDig, the Twitter feed for the dig Madison was working on.

Madison did not appear publicly on Twitter, Facebook or Instagram, and had not done so for some time. Fiona knew that this had been hard for Mads, who treated all forms of social media with the narcissistic enthusiasm pundits on the television were endlessly warning the world against.

There were only two pictures today, all taken at least four hours ago in full daylight. Fiona tried to batten down her disappointment.

One showed the excavated end of some tapering shadow in

the earth. This must be the Viking boat they'd found – the wood had wholly rotted away, leaving only its dark ghost in the soil.

Above it stood a man in a grey woollen hat, perhaps in his late thirties, adjusting some surveying equipment – squinting through the sights, unconscious of the camera. His eye, focused on the device, was a very pale blue. This was Dr Jack Bergmann – site supervisor and Iris Barclay's right-hand man.

The second image was of a tray of rubbly pieces of decayed iron, little more than black nuggets of rust, being held up by a woman, her head uncovered despite her hair being tugged at by the wind, her smile wide and gleaming.

This was Iris Barclay, Madison's famous boss.

@HellyHolmDig: A lovely surprise! @ProfIrisBarclay shows off rivets from rescue of 10th-century Viking boat burial! Rare survivals. #HellyHolm #Archaeology

Fiona thumbed through both pictures again while the wind shook the windows in her little car. She frowned into her phone, trying to make sense of things. The recovered rivets were nice – interesting, true, especially to an expert on ancient metals like herself, but hardly show-stopping. Even a professional like Madison would not have described them as a *BIG BIG FIND!*

Madison must be referring to something else.

Idly she tapped Madison's Twitter handle in the search box: @MadsKow.

She knew there would be nothing from Madison herself, but there was a new tweet from a stranger, someone that had tagged her.

It was from @BH9JTqwwx – a fake account, Fiona realised, doubtless attached to some fake email address. The profile icon was a drawing of a sinister smiling man, his eyes whirling.

Fiona's breath stopped in her chest. She felt cold and sick.

It was happening again.

@*MadsKow* YOU CAN GRUB IN THE DIRT TILL THE ENDS OF THE EARTH BUT I WILL FIND YOU AND CUT YOUR FUCKING TITS OFF CHEATING WHORE. #*golddigger* #*youllgetyours*

2

Grangeholm, Orkney, January 2020

Fiona's mood ratcheted between anger and alarm as she drove, the road vanishing beneath her wheels, her radio fading in and out into clouds of static. The asphalt gleamed faintly with what looked like gravel before she realised, with a little start, that it was road salt. According to the car dashboard, it was -1C outside. The cold radiated in through the windows, barely held at bay by the little heater.

The digging must be lovely right now, she thought ruefully to herself, as *Grangeholm 7m Helly Holm 2m* appeared on a nearby road sign.

Before she knew it she was passing a tiny, neat little car park with an information board, which then narrowed into a single concrete track. This continued for about three hundred metres before vanishing beneath the bible-black sea.

It was a road to nowhere.

She found herself braking, slowing down.

Further out, beyond the car park, there was nothing except for the rush of the waves, the sighing of the wind against her windows, and high up, perhaps half a mile out, the flare of a slowly revolving lantern – the Helly Holm lighthouse. It illuminated nothing. It was merely there to shine a light on itself.

Above the car park was a single sign:

Helly Holm – Please read safety instructions

This was it. The dig site.

She pulled into the car park, feeling the sea winds gently buffet the car as she pulled her coat on and crushed down her woollen hat before climbing out.

The cold was staggering, the wind throwing it into her face like a rain of tiny daggers. She pulled up the collar on her coat, quickly fastened it, her fingers already numbing around the buttons before she could thrust them back into her pockets. She'd left her gloves in the car. It was not a mistake she'd be making again, at this rate.

But still, she walked briskly up to the small concrete track, looked out to sea, peering into the velvet darkness. The islet was not visible, as the cloud was a series of thick, fast moving bands, but somewhere beyond the sea was Helly Holm.

She waited for a few minutes, feeling cold and disconsolate, hoping to be rewarded with a momentary clearing of the skies, a glimpse of the island, but there was nothing, nothing but the gleam from the lighthouse, lancing out then vanishing, teasing her.

Fiona sighed, then reluctantly returned to the car.

It was obvious that whatever had been happening on the island, it was over for the night. If so much as a torch had been shining out there, she would have seen it.

* * *

Fiona nearly missed Langmire House, which would, in daylight, have been difficult to do, as at first glance it seemed to be the only dwelling for miles around. It was a small white house set in a neat square enclosure of drystone walling, closed off with an ornate cast-iron gate.

It rested at the foot of a big sloping hill, strewn with massy boulders, separated from it by the asphalt strip of the road. Up on the hillside itself she could see twinkling yellow lights and big shadowy buildings – a farm of some sort, with a pale narrow track leading up to it, glistening with ice.

But on the other side lay the cold, murmuring sea, which she was starting to realise was never far away from her here. The rutted driveway ran off the road, past the cottage and out towards what she could see was a small quay, with a single moored boat swaying restlessly on the moving waters.

At some other time, she might have been charmed by it all.

Fiona pulled up on to a rectangle of gravel before the gate and got out, this time prepared for the bite of the freezing wind with the addition of her scarf.

A bottomless anger and anxiety was growing within her.

There was clearly nobody home.

All of the lights in the cottage were out. The windows were pools of darkness. As she opened the little gate and let herself through, following the icy flagstones to the front door, there was not even a porch light on.

Stepping up, she pressed the doorbell, the only illuminated thing, and stood back.

Within the house there was an upbeat double-chime, but no answer.

Her gloved hands balling into fists against the cold, she moved to the window, peered in. The curtains were open, which was strange at this time of night, but then she supposed privacy wasn't a problem for people around here. She leaned close, squinting into the darkness. She could make nothing much out – a sofa that might be leather, the silver rim of a flatscreen TV, the vague shadow of an open door into another room.

Ringing the bell again achieved nothing. Neither did calling Madison herself several times more once she'd retreated to the comfort of her car.

Am at Langmire House – where are you?

She debated for a moment whether she should add her signature kiss, decided against it. *No. Let her see how annoyed you are.*

Because that was it. Madison was being feckless again. It wasn't that anything had happened to her, Fiona told herself, despite feeling a kind of dull nausea, like seasickness, only composed of worry.

But somehow this sick feeling didn't stop her just closing her eyes, resting her head against the car window, using her bunched coat as a pillow of sorts, as the stereo played gently and the chugging engine warmed the interior.

The sea journey had taken it out of her, and she was simply exhausted. The patch for her travel sickness sometimes made her drowsy, and despite the lonely location, the darkness and her own uncertainty, her eyelids were beginning to flutter.

Don't fall asleep, Fiona told herself. *If she calls, you'll miss it.*

But somehow, within minutes, the muffled thump of the wind, the roar of the sea and the hot breath of the car had combined to pull her under.

3

Grangeholm, Orkney, January 2020

The next thing Fiona knew, she was shocked awake.

She didn't know what did it — it felt as though someone had passed close to the car window and she wondered for a moment whether it was Madison — though as she came to, drowsy and disoriented and her neck stiff and one foot gone to sleep, she wondered if it had just been the wind, which had gotten high and angsty. She could feel the car judder beneath her with each blow.

Her phone said it was now 1:54 a.m.

There had been no messages from Madison. No missed calls.

She sat there, stunned, trying to make sense of this.

Fiona glanced out of the window, peering at the house. All was still darkness. There was no sign of another car.

What the hell?

For a second she paused, considering, then thought *sod it*, and switched on the flashlight on her smartphone.

It was time to take a look.

Once again she forgot to fasten her coat up before she got out of the car and was nearly blown over, and swore as she tried to gather the stray ends together, to get the zip to align, the scent and sound of the sea everywhere.

'For fuck's sake, Madison,' she hissed as her hair lashed into her eyes. In the darkness, waves crashed and the fittings on the boat jingled like ringing bells. 'Where are you?'

She approached the house, opening the gate against the wind, and shone the phone into the front window, and while she saw everything a little more clearly, there was no more detail. It was a sparsely but pleasantly furnished rented house, tidy (hard to believe with Mads staying in it, but still) and possibly cosy if anyone had been about to let her in, or even switch on a light.

'Fucking hell,' she swore aloud.

Walking around the house, she found herself squinting into a spotless kitchen with an empty drying rack and an open dishwasher, likewise empty, and with a feeling of increasing unease passed on to the back, and once again shone the light in.

It was the bedroom.

This was when she realised.

The bed was completely stripped and the wardrobe door hung open, showing only a collection of hangers.

The heating dial, an electronic panel on the wall near the door, had been switched to OFF.

Fiona blinked, trying to make sense of all this, fighting to find a different conclusion to the obvious one. Madison would absolutely not tolerate the heating to be off in the middle of winter. On Orkney.

No matter how Fiona looked at it, there was absolutely no doubt.

Madison didn't live here any more.

In fact, nobody lived here.

She circled the house again, her mind trying to deny the evidence of her eyes, but no matter where she looked, the conclusion was inescapable. The bins, in their shed at the back, were empty. The curtains were pulled wide – there was nobody within whose privacy required protection.

She was trying to hold on to her annoyance, to the sense that this was Madison being typically Madison, but it was deserting her, stealing away in pieces to be replaced by fear. Something was badly wrong.

Once again she was in the car. She fired the engine up into a low purr and turned up the heating to full blast, rubbing her frozen hands together.

She lifted the phone, called Madison's mobile. It was a hopeless gesture, she realised – it was no more likely to be answered than any of the other times, but she was gratified to see that there was signal.

Again, no answer.

Madison had pulled some real tricks in her time, it was true – but nothing like this. Nothing like urging her to come up to visit her at the edge of the world, in her most pleading and anxious tones and despite Fiona's obvious, palpable reluctance, and then vanishing before Fiona had arrived.

She wanted to be angry, because that was much more comfortable than being frightened, but nevertheless a creeping chill hung around her throat and the back of her neck that the blasting car heater could do nothing to allay.

She was remembering that tweet: YOU CAN GRUB IN THE DIRT TILL THE ENDS OF THE EARTH BUT I WILL FIND YOU . . .

The clock in the car read 2:05.

Taking out her little Moleskine, she scribbled a quick note in a shaking hand.

MADISON

I WAS HERE UNTIL 2 A.M. AND NOBODY WAS HOME – WHERE ARE YOU?! I AM GOING BACK TO THE PORT TO LOOK FOR YOU. IF I DON'T FIND YOU SOON I AM CALLING THE POLICE!

PLEASE RING ME – I AM VERY WORRIED!

FEE XXX

She got out of the car once more, made for the front door. She tucked the paper into the letterbox, its crumpled, desperate capitals visible even from the path. Though the wind shook it ferociously, the bite of the letterbox held firm.

She was just turning to go when, on an impulse, she tried the door handle.

With a click, it went down, and the door opened.

4

Grangeholm, Orkney, January 2020

'Hello?' Fiona called out.

She stood in a windowless porch, with a thick welcome rug and the walls lined with hooks for coats. There was no sign of any coats, nor any of Madison's prodigious collection of shoes, though the carpet was dusty, crusted with bits of dried mud that showed that somebody's boots had been here recently.

Her breath steamed before her, like a ghost.

She pushed open the glass door into the darkness of the house proper. It was chilly, but at least it was out of that biting wind.

She switched on the light.

'Madison?' she called out, more for form's sake than any other reason.

The kitchen was big, tiled, with a dining table and chairs under the window facing out to the sea. The fridge freezer was completely empty except for half a bag of ice cubes.

Her mind groped for logical, prosaic explanations. There was some mistake in communications, perhaps. Was this the right Langmire? Was she even on the right island in Orkney?

Don't be stupid. Of course you're on the right island. And this is where the satnav led you, isn't it?

Call that silly cow again, she told herself crossly. *And if she answers, give her hell for mucking you about and . . . and . . .*

Scaring *you like this.*

She picked up the phone, swiped Madison's number again.

There were a few seconds of delay before the ringing started. Then a few more.

Then a single long beep, and the message Call Failed.

She decided to phone Adi instead, realised that it was late – too late. He was in Zurich now, anyway, probably still socialising with his firm's clients if previous form was anything to go by.

So what? This is an emergency. You are stuck on an island in the middle of the night. You have no idea what has happened to Madison . . .

What has happened to Madison . . .

She glanced uneasily over her shoulder, towards the other rooms.

You should have a closer look, she told herself.

* * *

The bed was stripped, as she had seen from the window, the bedding lying in a pile on the far side. All the drawers were empty, the mirrored wardrobe doors shut.

But something was wrong.

One of the mirrored doors was cracked, as though something had hit it hard.

The bedroom lighting was dim, ambient, so she pulled out her phone and turned the flashlight on again, leaned in close to the crack.

In one of the jagged seams was a tiny smear of blood.

She gasped, her heart missing a beat.

And then suddenly it was pounding, as though to catch up, and Fiona knew she would not stay here for a second longer.

She had to get out. She had to get *out* . . .

She dropped her phone into her pocket and was just turning to go when she heard the front door swing open.

'Hello?'

It was a man's voice, with the low music of an Orcadian accent.

Fiona froze.

'Hello, is anybody here? I saw your car . . .'

And suddenly they were both there, framed in the bedroom doorway, blinking at her. It was a tiny house – Fiona would have been easy to find.

They appeared an unlikely pair of malefactors, hardly sinister: a middle-aged couple, the woman with vast brown eyes and mid-length dark hair secured in a ponytail, and a broad barrel of a man, bald, with a ginger moustache and neat beard. Both wore puffer jackets and wellington boots, and looked, if it were possible, as frightened of her as she was of them, drawing together anxiously; a tiny, telling moment.

'Oh . . . hello . . . sorry, I'm looking for Madison. Madison Kowalczyk.'

There was no response. They simply stared at her.

'Um, I . . . sorry. She's supposed to be staying here. I caught the ferry over and waited and nobody came and she wasn't answering her phone. So I drove over and then I waited some more . . . And, well, I must have fallen asleep and then when I woke up she still wasn't here . . . I was going to leave a note, and then when I pushed it in the door it opened and I thought I'd look for her and . . . and . . . and . . .'

Fiona could hear the rising hysteria in her voice.

'It's all right,' rumbled the man, who could doubtless also hear that hysteria. 'We saw the lights on in here. We found your note.' He lifted up her scrap of paper in one meaty hand. 'Is this you, then? Are you Fee?'

'Yeah, that's . . . I'm Fiona Grey . . . sorry,' she said, moving towards them, and trying not to notice that they recoiled, just slightly. 'Look, I'm so sorry about this. I'm not a burglar, usually.' She pulled her phone out. 'See, this is the email from my friend Madison. She said to come to this house – this is Langmire, isn't it?'

The man exchanged a significant look with the woman. 'It is,' he said slowly.

'And do you know what's happened to her? This is very unlike her. She's stopped answering her phone . . .'

'Madison moved out,' said the woman, stealing a glance at the man, as though looking for confirmation. 'She moved out Wednesday night.'

'She did a flit,' said the man.

'Oh, don't say that, Douggie,' said the woman, trying to be charitable, but without much enthusiasm.

'No, she did,' he remonstrated mildly. 'There isnae any point denying it, Maggie.'

Fiona blinked at them. 'I don't understand. What do you mean, a "flit"?'

'She left,' said the woman. 'She moved out – in the middle of the night, too. First we knew of it, I got up out of bed to go to the loo and the lights were all on and the car idling outside. I thought, this is late even for her . . .'

Fiona caught a sudden whiff of disapproval and realised that Maggie and Douggie were having a much easier time believing this of Madison than she was.

They didn't like her, for some reason.

'You saw her leaving?'

'Oh, aye. Well, it was her car.' Maggie must have caught Fiona's confused look. 'Oh, sorry, we're the owners. We rent the cottage out. Normally folk only come in the summer, but they're doing this archaeological dig . . .'

'Helly Holm,' Fiona said instantly.

'That's right!' Maggie said, warming up a couple of degrees. 'Are you one of them, the archaeologists?'

'I am an archaeologist – well, an archaeological scientist,' Fiona said. 'But I'm not with the dig. I'm Madison's friend. She asked me to visit her out here. She wanted . . .' Fiona paused, wondering how much she should share with these people. She didn't know them, after all. 'She wanted some company.'

'Hmm,' said Maggie, raising an eyebrow at her. 'She never seemed short of company to me.'

'Now, now, Maggie,' said her husband, his mouth compressing in displeasure.'

Fiona was too impatient to pursue this for the moment. 'Are you saying she just got up and left? The night before last? With no word?'

'Oh no,' Douggie said. 'We got an email from her, yesterday morning, saying she had to go back home. Her mother was sick.'

'Judy was sick?' asked Fiona, stunned. If something had happened to Judy, who was chronically ill, things made a little more sense, but still – why would Madison text her all day yesterday and today as though she was still on Orkney?

'Aye, she said so. She'd packed everything up, and if she owed us any money, we were to write and tell her and she'd pay it. So we were like, ah well, that's a shame and explains the lack of notice – though where she thought she'd get to at that hour on Wednesday I've no idea. There'd be no ferries or planes off the island till dawn.'

Fiona blinked.

'But anyway,' he continued, 'Maggie here went down to check the place out yesterday morning.'

'That's right,' said his wife, recognising her cue, 'and while I was here, Madison's mother rang on the landline, looking for her.' She shrugged. 'Her mother knew nothing about it. Said she was in excellent health, considering – I think she's got heart problems, has she no?'

'Yeah, that's right,' said Fiona.

'Anyway, I felt a peedie bit guilty afterwards. I think I worried her when I told her, and she seemed like a nice lady.'

'So Madison lied to you?' Everything suddenly felt very unreal. 'About the reason she was leaving?'

Maggie wrung her anxious hands together. 'Did she say nothing to you?'

'No.' Fiona shook her head.

And now her exhaustion, her anxiety, could no longer be controlled. This was some nightmare. Madison had left in the middle of *Wednesday night*. It was now the early hours of Saturday morning.

All the while she'd been driving up from Cambridge, while she'd been in that hotel room in Inverness, while she'd been on the ferry, Madison had already vanished from here.

Her horror must have been obvious to the owners.

'And you came up today?' Maggie asked, sounding almost as bewildered as Fiona felt.

'I . . . I came up from Inverness today.' She blinked at them. 'I drove up from Cambridge yesterday morning . . .'

Douggie waggled his eyebrows at her. 'Have you naewhere to stay, then?'

'I . . . I was supposed to be staying here.' Fiona looked around, at a loss. Why hadn't Madison mentioned any of this in her messages? What was she playing at?

Had it even been her? No, it must have been. She was talking about the dig . . .

Meanwhile, the couple exchanged another look.

'Oh, you can't stay here,' said Maggie. 'There's no heating on . . . you can stay with us up at the house tonight, and tomorrow morning Douggie'll run you back down to Helly Holm. Maybe they know more about what's going on with your friend at the dig.'

Douggie grunted in assent.

Fiona flushed in embarrassment. 'Oh no, I couldn't possibly. I'm sure I could find a hotel . . .'

'No, no, no. None of that.' They were both shaking their heads at her, Douggie with the heavy solidity of all Scottish patriarchs, and it seemed useless to resist. 'We've got a spare room up at the house,' he said. 'It's nae trouble. And it is all very strange,' he rumbled. 'Very queer indeed.'

'It is that,' agreed his wife.

'Come on now,' he said. 'Have you got a bag with you, at least?'

* * *

The owners, who Fiona quickly learned were called the Fletts, ushered her in. Maggie showed her into a small, neat room with posters of footballers lining the walls, and that faint but unmistakable smell of hormonal teenaged boy. ('This is Lachy's room,' Maggie told her. 'He's just gone back to college on the mainland now.') A towel was quickly found and placed at the foot of the bed.

'I'm so sorry to put you out like this. It's practically morning . . .' stammered Fiona.

'Not at all.' Maggie waved this away. 'We're glad we found you. Sleep tight.'

And she was gone, the door gently closing, leaving Fiona alone with the footballers who gazed down upon her, larger than life, like Greek gods.

She lay on her back, staring at the ceiling. According to the little alarm clock on the nightstand, it was 2:54 in the morning.

Any prospect of sleep seemed unthinkable. Through a gap in the curtains, the stars of Orkney were white and impossibly numerous.

Glancing up at them, she felt a sharp tug of loneliness. She wanted to talk to somebody, anybody, about these shocking developments, but what she was realising, with a kind of bleak hopelessness, was that the go-to person she would call about this was . . . Madison.

You could call Adi. I mean, I know it's late and he's been travelling and got clients and all . . .

She sighed.

For a little while now she'd been growing aware that it was always she that called Adi, and not the other way around – and that in the four months they'd been together, this had rapidly become the pattern.

Of course, once she had registered this, she could not stop noticing it. She told herself that perhaps she was being too needy, he was too busy at work, he was simply not the chatty type.

They were both hard-working, overachieving people, and how could she expect him to understand her desire to succeed if she didn't give him free rein to be the same way?

He was happy enough to ring you all the time when you first started seeing him, Madison had observed shrewdly as they met up for drinks in her tiny Clapham flat.

Madison had been excited then, almost ecstatic – she'd been selected to dig with Iris Barclay's team on Helly Holm in Orkney, and it promised to be a very important, perhaps career-defining excavation – a Viking ship burial. She was to be Finds Manager, cataloguing and tracking all of the on-site finds and samples.

Of course, Fiona had heard of the site director, Iris Barclay, who like herself had started out in ancient metallurgy. Iris had shot to fame after finding a fabulous golden necklace while supervising her first-ever dig up in Northumberland – the dig had been an unpromising couple of ploughed-down Bronze

Age barrows, reputedly foisted on her when her boss had been too busy to bother with the site himself.

The find, a priceless artefact now named the Jesmond Hill torc, had ended up in the British Museum. Fiona had often found herself in front of the case containing the torc – a kind of necklace made of solid twisted gold, open at the front, with exquisitely detailed decorated ends – whenever she had business at the museum. She could never resist stopping there for a few moments, just to admire its gleaming beauty.

Iris herself, in the resulting media frenzy, had been discovered as a feisty, charismatic personality during interviews about the find, and as a direct consequence had been offered the job of fronting *Discovering the Past*, a big-budget, location-based archaeology television show that was now in its third series.

She had, in short, *arrived*, and Madison was hopeful that some of that glittering luck might rub off on her. Iris had a reputation for trying to help women's careers. Rumour had it that this was because of how her old boss had treated her. It was said that her ex-supervisor, Professor Hearst, who'd fobbed the job of excavating Jesmond Hill on to Iris, was now unable to hear her name mentioned without throwing objects across his office.

Fiona remembered that night at Madison's. They'd toasted each other with flutes of chilled Krug. It was a brilliant opportunity, perhaps a sign that Mads' luck was changing at last.

She'd been so happy, thought Fiona with a pang. Things had been going well for her on a personal level, too. Her surgeon boyfriend, Caspar, had bought her a Bulgari bracelet that flashed in the candlelight.

Madison affected to despise his wealth and status, but her cat-like green eyes glittered with suppressed excitement while she did so, almost as brightly as her new jewellery.

At any rate, with this success under her belt – the first relationship she had had in years that had lasted longer than six months – Madison was now inclined to view herself as something of a love guru. *You know, Fiona,* she'd said, tilting her head with a mischievous smile, her lips painted a deep carmine red, *if I was you, I'd give Adi the chance to miss you.*

Fiona sighed, resting her hands beneath her head on the pillow.

Now her panic and bewilderment were receding, but they were being replaced with something else – a nameless dread, the sense that something was desperately wrong with her best friend.

Why would Madison not tell her anything of what had happened? Why had she fled? And why not tell Fiona? Was she embarrassed over the money Fiona had spent on ferries and hotel rooms in response to her begging, her need?

But then, how embarrassed would she be when Fiona got here and found her gone?

The more Fiona looked at it, the more she couldn't understand it. They were friends, best friends. Why would she just keep texting and leading Fiona on? Was Madison still furious at her for some reason, and this was all some elaborate revenge? Why would she do this to Fiona?

Indeed, *had* she done this to Fiona?

Madison had not answered the phone in person since Wednesday, before her supposed flight. All Fiona had had was a series of slightly off messages.

This is crazy, Fiona told herself. *These people said that they saw her packing. Whatever you are imagining, you are being over-dramatic. She's done plenty of more thoughtless things in her time, though, admittedly, usually to men and not to you.*

When you get over to the dig in the morning she'll be there in her wellies being snappy and defensive and trying to make out this is all your fault.

Fiona shut her eyes, tried to sleep.

Tried to squeeze out her memory of that smashed mirrored door, and her growing fear that something terrible had happened to Madison.

And that Dominic Tate had had something to do with it.

Saturday

5

Grangeholm, Orkney, January 2020

There was a tentative knock on the door, startling Fiona awake.

'Hello, love, are you awake? Did you sleep?' It was Maggie. 'I've brought you up a cup of tea.'

'Oh, thank you!'

She was in Lachy's bedroom in the Fletts' home. A pale light had replaced the stars, but it was not quite morning. That meant nothing, though. It was January, and this far north daylight kept office hours.

A kind of panic came over her as she remembered. *Madison*.

That cracked mirror with its blood-laced edges . . .

Maggie, fully dressed, set the cup on the bedside table next to Fiona.

'Thanks,' she said. 'I'm getting up now . . .'

'There's no rush,' Maggie replied. 'Douggie's just gone to see to some jobs, and when he gets back we'll have some breakfast.'

'Oh, thank you, you're too kind, but I think I need to speak to Mads' colleagues on the dig straight away . . .'

'Maybe you do, but you'll need to wait till low tide to get over to Helly Holm, and that's not for another hour,' Maggie said, pausing on the threshold. 'You may as well have breakfast first.'

'Oh, I see. Thanks, then. That would be lovely.'

Maggie nodded. 'The shower's at the end of the corridor.'

After she'd gone, Fiona snatched up her phone, which she'd

41

left charging overnight, and tried Madison again, fruitlessly. The desperate text she'd sent last thing was still unanswered.

Now she'd slept on the matter, she realised that none of this would do. Something was very wrong.

There was one more call.

'Fee?'

'Hey. Sorry to call at work. It's just – well, I don't know how to . . .'

'Listen, I'm presenting to the client in ten minutes . . .'

'I know, I know, but there's an emergency. Madison's missing.'

'She's *missing*? What do you mean, she's missing?'

'Got here last night, and the cottage was empty. I'm at the landlord's house. They tell me she moved out in the middle of the night. *Wednesday* night.'

She could almost hear the cogs in his brain working, his confusion mirroring her own. 'Wait – she *moved out*? And didn't tell you?'

'Yeah. And it looked like there'd been some kind of fight in there. Someone had smashed the wardrobe mirror . . .'

'A *fight*?'

'Yes.'

'And you've heard nothing from her?'

'No. Nothing since last night.' Fiona sat back down on the bed, the cup of tea at her elbow.

'But you said people saw her moving out?'

'Yes, so it seems.'

'So, is she in trouble or not?' asked Adi, incredulous but distracted.

'I don't know! Part of me thinks I should talk to the others on the dig first – who knows what she's said to them? And the owners here too,' she lowered her voice, glanced towards the door. 'They're definitely leery of her. They're holding back on something they know about her.'

Adi's only reply was a low whistle.

'Bloody hell, Fiona.' He seemed to be thinking. 'Look, I have to go in now. Phone me the minute you find anything out.' There was a pause. 'I'll be worrying about you until you do.'

'Sure,' she said. 'Bye.' She nearly said, I love you.

But she didn't.

Then he was gone.

She scrubbed her teeth, bracing herself for the day ahead, and washed quickly in the surprisingly luxurious shower.

Maggie was frying not only eggs, but Scottish square sausage, bacon and potato cakes when she came down the stairs to the kitchen. This hissed and spat on the stove, and Fiona's mouth started watering at the smell. 'Sit down,' Maggie said placidly, waving away Fiona's offer to help out. 'Did you sleep?'

'A bit, as well as I could. I've got to be honest, now I've thought about it, I'm really quite worried about my friend. None of this makes any sense.'

'Hmm,' said Maggie with a sharp, thoughtful inflection that told Fiona instantly that something was wrong.

'What is it?' she asked.

'Well,' said Maggie, turning the sausages in the pan. 'Douggie and I were talking about this last night, and we're not entirely sure that we could swear it was herself packing the car. Someone was there, but you know, we're halfway up the hill here, and it was the middle of the night.'

'What time?' Fiona asked, feeling sick.

'One, two in the morning. The wind was low. I could hear the car idling up here, which is why I looked – it's very quiet.' Maggie popped white bread into the toaster. 'You notice things out of the ordinary.'

There was something about this phrase, *out of the ordinary*, and the clipped way it was spoken, that again had that shadow of disapproval. Maggie, though she was being perfectly nice, had had some kind of problem with Madison, so much was clear to Fiona.

'Did Madison owe you rent?' she asked, aware she was being cheeky.

Maggie looked slightly uncomfortable. 'Well, she didn't owe us any rent. The company – the archaeologists – pay us for that,' she said, putting a teapot on the table, just as Fiona heard the back door open behind her, the sound of masculine huffing, boots being scraped on the mat.

Again, that sense that this house was run like a well-oiled machine.

'But she did owe us for the wardrobe door in the bedroom. Not much, mind, it's easy enough to put a new one in – but himself had to order it in from the mainland.'

'So Madison had already broken the mirrored door?'

'She says she did,' replied Maggie, shrugging.

'It was just that I saw a bit of blood in the cracks last night and thought . . . I don't know what I thought . . .' said Fiona, knitting her fingers together on her lap. Relief flooded through her.

'Bless your heart,' said Maggie, with a little laugh, before she moved forward to the stove again. 'Oh no, no, no. That happened Monday. She told us about it straight away,' she said, then added after a moment, 'To be fair to her, she was always good that way.'

It was an accident, thought Fiona. *Just a random accident.* Her shoulders unknotted a tiny fraction.

'Is breakfast ready?' Douggie was standing in the doorway.

Turning to greet him, Fiona saw that he had a slightly hard expression, as though displeased, and she instantly subsided, wondering what she had done wrong.

But he wished her a cheerful good morning as he pulled up a chair at the table, without acknowledging his wife, and asked her again how she had slept, and Maggie dispensed fried meats

44

and potato cake with a spatula, adding in an almost rebellious little flip of the utensil each time.

Somehow, Fiona had wandered into one of those silent rows married people occasionally conducted, and she wondered what it was that had caused it as she tucked into her sausages. Had she done or said something wrong?

But neither appeared to bear her any personal ill will, asking her polite questions about where she lived and what she did for a living.

'Oh, I'm a scientist and a lecturer. I work with metal.' She sipped her tea, feeling more fortified, ready to face the archaeologists. 'My specialty is the construction of ancient weapons. Swords, mostly.'

'Swords?' They exchanged a look, and instantly she saw the tension between them ease in their shared curiosity. 'You don't look the type. Is that what you're here to do? At Helly Holm?' asked Douggie.

She shook her head. 'No, not at all. Madison asked me up for . . . for a holiday.' The Fletts didn't need to know that Madison had been in trouble of some sort. 'Though I was hoping to have a look at the dig too. They say it's a great site, from the sounds of it.'

Maggie nodded, dispensing more tea. 'The boatmen were saying that it was all a lot grander than anyone was expecting.'

'Yeah, it's a really nice Viking boat burial. There was a person in it – a warrior, they think, or at least someone buried with weapons, that kind of thing.' Fiona bit into her toast and marmalade.

'So tell us, Fiona,' Douggie had bent once more to his breakfast, 'do you ken how to fight with a sword, like? Do you do that reconstruction stuff?'

Fiona laughed, despite herself, despite her anxiousness. 'Not at all. I'm not very *fighty*.'

'So you just dig the swords up?' Maggie offered her more bacon, and Fiona shook her head.

'No, thank you. And I don't even dig them up. The metal-work arrives at the lab pre-dug, and I just analyse the wear patterns.' She grinned. 'I love the past, but I don't really do the outdoors if I can help it.'

Husband and wife looked at one another then and laughed, their tiny spat forgotten.

'You've come to the right place, all right. And you'll love Helly Holm,' said Douggie, mopping up the last of his egg yolk with a slice of buttered bread. 'There's outdoors, and there's *outdoors.*'

* * *

Douggie drove her back to the house and her car, waving away her protestations. The house was only ten minutes away on foot, if that.

This felt very strange to Fiona, and she wondered about it as they trundled down the farm track to the main road. The Fletts had been very generous – so much so it made her uneasy in some strange way, and she glanced sidelong at Douggie's face, trying to read something into his laconic expression.

At the hill's foot, Langmire in daylight seemed very small and bleak, surrounded by waterlogged fields on three sides, and on the other, the sea.

The little quay, its sides padded with old tyres, stretched out into the dark blue water.

However, the boat was gone.

'They've gone out, I see,' Douggie growled suddenly, breaking the silence.

'I'm sorry, who?' asked Fiona, distracted. She'd been checking her phone. No messages from Madison.

He flexed his eyebrows at her. 'The archaeologists. They use a boat to get back and forth to the site.' He pointed to a muddy white Ford Transit parked on a patch of tyre-churned earth near the quay. 'That's their van.'

'Oh, of course.'

'You see, if they sail,' he sighed, scratching delicately at his bald head, 'rather than using the causeway, it means they can take advantage of all the daylight.' He smiled briefly at her. 'Or what passes for daylight around here. It's a funny time of year to do a dig.'

'It was an emergency, Douggie,' said Fiona. 'There was a huge storm a few weeks ago, and it knocked off some soil, exposing human bones and part of a boat.' She shrugged. 'They had to contract someone to dig it. Or they'll lose it.'

He nodded, gazing fixedly out to sea.

'I remember that storm,' he said.

Silence fell between them.

'You were probably wondering,' he said eventually, 'what Maggie and I were at odds about, up at the house.'

This was such a perceptive remark that Fiona visibly started. 'I . . .'

'Don't bother pretending you didnae notice,' he said, with a sideways glance at her.

'Well, I . . . I did wonder . . .'

He offered her a small, decisive shake of his head. 'It's good to be interested in your neighbours. You need your neighbours out here.'

Fiona didn't know what to reply.

'Whereas for me, well, sometimes you can be a little too interested in what folk around you are getting up to. In things that are nain of your business.' He tilted his head at her. 'And you're wondering why I'm telling you all this, I suppose?'

She had no idea but could take a guess, from the morning's clues. 'It's about Madison, isn't it?'

'Aye.' They had reached Langmire now, and he pulled up next to her little car. 'I wouldnae be telling you this if . . . if this strange thing hadnae happened. It was a little bit embarrassing. Embarrassing for Maggie, certainly.'

Fiona waited, not understanding, but with a feeling more would soon become clear. This was why he'd insisted on driving her back here, she realised. It was so they could have this conversation alone.

'So, Maggie gets quite friendly with your girl Madison. And she'd mentioned a boyfriend, some lad named . . .'

'Caspar,' Fiona supplied, wondering. Where was this going?

'*Caspar*. Yeah, that sounds right. Anyway, we see that she's started bringing a fellow to the house.' He held up his hands. 'All well and good, we think. He must have come up to visit her.'

Fiona listened with growing astonishment. Madison hadn't mentioned Caspar on the phone, and she'd certainly not told her he was coming to Orkney.

'Douggie, are you sure about this? I mean, she had some legal problems with an ex-boyfriend . . . could it have been someone turning up and spying on her?'

'Oh no.' He waved this away. 'She let him in. One morning, early it was, she stood at the door and saw him off in her dressing gown.'

Madison has said nothing of this.

'And then, it would have been . . .' He paused, thinking, one beefy finger tapping on the wheel, 'last Monday night . . . she calls and says, sorry, Douggie, I've broken the glass on your wardrobe door.

'So I says, never mind, it's not that big a deal, let me come and have a wee look at it. She says fair enough, so I tell Maggie and then Maggie says she'll come and visit too. So down we come, and everything's very friendly, and there's the mirrored door broken — she says she's done it in the night, tripped and fell, and I'm taking a note and a measure of it and we're all having a peedie laugh about seven years' bad luck, when this car pulls up and the doorbell rings.'

'It was him,' Fiona said, dazed at this revelation. 'The guy.'

'Exactly. So he comes in behind her and Maggie, bless her, she's got as much tact as a sledgehammer, she says, "Oh, you must be Caspar, we've seen you about," and . . . so, the temperature drops about ten degrees while they both go red and somehow I get my measurements and we get out of there and were glad to leave. I didnae care, but I think Maggie felt like she'd been taken in – d'you see what I mean? – and hasnae had it in her to forgive her.'

Fiona didn't know what to say to this. She felt poleaxed.

There was a man. She shouldn't be surprised, she realised. With Madison, there was always a man.

But Madison had never mentioned him. Clearly there were huge parts of her story she was not sharing with Fiona.

Had Mads run off with him? And hadn't dared tell her?

She felt a faint stirring of sympathy for Maggie. Madison had taken her in, too.

For Madison to throw up her career and her boyfriend like this, and to not . . . to not even hint to Fiona what was going on, after luring her up here, was desperately cold and selfish.

A little splinter of ice was working its way into the heart of her anxiety, her bewilderment, as she climbed out of the truck.

Did Dominic Tate know about this man too? Was that what had brought him out of the woodwork now?

'Did you ever find out his name?' she asked Douggie.

'His name? No. I just found out it wasnae Caspar.' He looked about to laugh, but something about Fiona's expression must have made an impression on him. 'No, no name. Not that I remember.'

'I . . .' Fiona didn't know what to say. 'Thanks for letting me know.'

'I thought you ought to. Anyway,' he said, 'the car park for Helly Holm is just a few miles that way down the road. The tide's out now so the causeway will be open. Make sure you dinnae get stuck there.'

'Thanks,' she said, meaning it. 'Not just for this, but for everything – the bed for the night, breakfast – I mean, I . . .'

He waved this away. 'Listen now – Maggie meant for me to tell you – if you find you're stuck and need somewhere to stay for a couple of days, you're very welcome to use the cottage. It's all paid for, after all. You just come up to our house and get the keys from Maggie. We'll switch the heating on for you when I get back.'

'Thank you, Douggie,' she said, touched by this kindness.

'Anyway, I'd better get back to work,' he said. 'Good luck finding your friend. I hope it was all something and nothing in the end.'

'Yeah,' Fiona said with feeling. 'Me too.'

And with that, and a wave, he pulled out and was gone.

6

Helly Holm, Orkney, January 2020

The road was different in daylight. The twinkling ice was gone and the tarmac was dry, the sky eggshell white, the sea on her left grey and frothy, breaking against pale sand and neat rows of washed up seaweed. The heating in her little car roared gamely away.

The island of Helly Holm itself stood out against the luminous horizon, rising out of the sea like a pedestal, its edges crinkled with crumbling red sandstone columns. The tide was out, and in amongst the damp boulders and cracked slabs of rock, a single concrete track was visible – this must be the tidal causeway everyone had told her about. It led straight as an arrow out from the car park to the islet, a white road through the sea.

On the island itself she could see the square and rectangular cuts of archaeological trenches, brown wounds in the vivid green slopes, and people in hi-vis jackets moving back and forth across them, like bright yellow ants.

Fiona stood for a long moment, thinking. Then she pulled out her phone. There was a tiny signal – perhaps two bars – but it was enough.

She dialled the number.

It rang and rang and then Judy's voice; clipped, formal (and fake, realised Fiona for a rebellious second, before ruthlessly quelling this train of thought): 'I'm sorry I cannot reach the phone at the moment. Please leave a number and I will get back to you.'

'Hi, Judy – it's me, Fiona. It's kind of urgent. Can you call me back, please?' She rattled off her mobile number, twice, and then hung up, sighing.

Trust Judy not to be in when you needed her. Still, despite her need, Fiona was faintly relieved not to have to speak to her.

It was time to talk to the archaeologists instead. Maybe Madison was there.

Maybe.

The air was chill, stinging her cheeks, and laced with salt and sea wrack. Ahead of her, the white road to Helly Holm stretched out into the sea, and, thrusting her gloveless hands deep into the pockets of her inadequate coat, she set off towards it.

* * *

At the top of the steps heading down to the beach was a yellow and white warning sign:

BEWARE – HELLY HOLM IS A TIDAL ISLAND!
This causeway is only exposed during low tide.
CHECK tide tables for safe visiting hours to avoid being stranded!
At high tide the island is surrounded by extremely strong currents and there have been numerous fatalities in previous years.
DO NOT attempt access to the island out of low tide!

Well, thought Fiona, miserable and lost, *that just sounds perfectly lovely*.

The causeway was set concrete, too narrow for a vehicle of any kind. It was lined with grooves in places to provide a grip, but nevertheless the stone was slimy with algae and in her thin fashion boots she nearly slipped a couple of times. Everywhere was the salty, fishy stink of the drying shore. On either side of the causeway, broken slabs of dark sandstone stuck out of the exposed seabed at strange angles, like shards of smashed glass. In the interstices between them, worn sea pebbles and white sand lined rock pools like tiny aquatic gardens.

It would have been beautiful, she realised, striking, had she been in any other frame of mind.

The sea had retreated into a liquid glimmer on the horizon, hissing and muttering quietly to itself in the distance. Ahead of her, Helly Holm rose towards the whey-coloured sky, its misty edges making it appear like a mirage, or a bad dream.

The wind stung the tips of her ears, her face.

Hopefully, she would not be here long enough to have to invest in a proper hat.

Hopefully Madison was at the end of this long, straight road.

She glanced at her phone. No messages and no signal. Madison hadn't lied about that, she thought, then gritted her teeth. At least.

On the island, she could see four people sitting and kneeling in the muddy trenches. None of them looked like Madison, but swathed in their hoods, hats and bulky jackets, it would have been hard to spot her anyway. Measuring poles in red and white had been driven into the soft loam and twitched in the sea wind. The causeway was rising, and with a sense of relief she realised that she was back on dry land.

Encouraged, she quickened her pace, eager to get on with her mission, but the concrete was still green and slippy with seaweed, and suddenly her feet shot out from under her and she fell backwards, crashing into the pebbles, a searing pain lancing up through her buttock, her thigh, her left arm . . .

'Whoa, whoa! Are you all right?'

A man in a hi-vis jacket stood at the top of a flight of stone steps into the side of the island, his figure etched against the sky for a moment before he was scrambling down towards her.

Fiona let out a groan, then rolled on to her side. Nothing

was broken, she realised, but it had been a very lucky thing. And she was going to have spectacular bruises.

'Here, do you need a hand?'

'No, I'm fine . . .' Her leg twinged. 'Actually, you know what . . .'

Without further prompting he reached down and bodily picked her up and righted her. She was astonished by his strength.

'Are you all right?' His accent was English, southern. He towered a good foot over her. 'Can you stand?'

'I'm fine,' she said again, as though willing it to be true. She was mortified. She set her foot on the ground, tried tentatively to bear weight on it. It complained, all the way up to her back, but it would do. 'Sorry. It's the shock more than anything.'

'Way to make an entrance.' He smiled. 'Ah well. So long as you're all right.'

He was bulky as well as tall, muscular rather than fat. Faint dark-blond stubble was apparent on his upper lip and chin, and above the three deeply scored lines on his forehead. His eyes were a striking cold blue. He wore a grey woollen hat and leather jacket and a gold ring in his ear, with a tiny axe dangling from it – but his hands were bare, crusted with brown dirt, jammed even beneath the fingernails, the knuckles prominent.

'You're Jack,' she said. 'Jack Bergmann. I recognise you. From the dig's Twitter feed.'

'Lucky me,' he said, with a rakish grin. 'What can I do for you?'

'It's, well, it's complicated. I'm looking for Madison Kowalczyk.'

His face stilled. 'Madison? You're not the only one.'

Fiona's heart fell. Of course Madison wasn't here.

'Are you all right? You're very pale. Sorry, you're right, I'm Jack, the site supervisor. And you are?'

'I'm Fiona. Fiona Grey.'

'The Sword Lady!' he said instantly, grinning. 'Madison told us about you!' His expression clouded. 'She didn't mention you were coming to the site this morning, though.'

'It was a spur-of-the-moment thing,' said Fiona, because this was almost true. 'I'm . . . well, I don't know how to explain it, but Madison was supposed to meet me in Stromness last night, and she wasn't there. And when I went to the house she was renting, it had all been cleared out.'

His brow contracted dangerously. 'What? *Cleared out?*'

'Yeah, all her things were gone . . .' She swallowed. 'I was hoping you might know where she is. Well – really I was hoping I'd find her here, just caught up in the dig.'

'She's not here. We've not seen her since Wednesday night,' he said. 'She told us she had flu, but she'd be back this morning.' He stared at her, as if amazed. 'As far as we know, she's at Langmire.'

'Oh,' said Fiona. 'I . . . well . . .'

And it was only then, at that moment, that she realised how desperate she'd been to believe that this was a trick, a misunderstanding, that Madison was here. She felt nauseous suddenly, and gripped with icy panic.

'You need to sit down somewhere,' said Jack, with a firm hand under her arm. 'You don't look right. Can you make it up the steps? We've got a tent. You can tell us all about it.'

* * *

She was led upwards, grabbing Jack's arm the better to stabilise herself as she was hauled up the rocky steps. Her leg and back hurt, but more than anything she was confused and frightened.

Of course Madison wasn't here. Why would she be?

Somehow she found herself in a little polar fishing tent that had been set up on the grass, and urged on to a folding stool. She was vaguely glad to be out of the snapping wind. Faces surrounded her, and murmurings — seemingly a crowd, but there were only three of them.

Jack had gone to fetch a Thermos of coffee and press a cup into her hand, and in the meantime news had spread.

Everyone fell silent as a woman entered and eyed Fiona keenly. Her rich dark hair was bound in a wind-tousled French plait and covered under a blue headscarf, tied at the back of her neck, and her hands and wrists were encased in thick, dirty gardening gloves.

Even without the trademark bright red lipstick she wore on television, Fiona recognised her instantly: Iris Barclay, now the face of *Discovering the Past*, finder of the Jesmond Hill torc.

The only difference was that the Iris Barclay on television was always beautifully dressed and smiling. This version appeared considerably more dour and preoccupied.

'I'm the Site Director,' she said without preamble. 'Jack tells me that there is a problem with Madison?'

Fiona paused, her mouth open, her train of thought derailed.

A problem with Madison.

Yeah.

Perhaps there had always been a problem with Madison.

7

Saxon Street, Cambridge, December 2018

'Hiya!'

Madison stood on the cobbled street outside, slightly unsteady, her eyes bright with drink, but she looked tired to Fiona — no, not so much tired as drained. Dominic stood next to her, one arm possessively threaded through her own.

'Oh my God! You're here! Come in, come in!' Fiona hiked up her smile and stood back from the front door, trying to paper over her annoyance with an excess of brittle enthusiasm.

She had been planning her Christmas/housewarming drinks for the past month and the details had obsessed her — cooking the food, choosing the right wine, inviting the guests. Her excitement fizzed like champagne. She had never been sole hostess of a party before. She had never even lived alone before.

Madison was now three hours late, and furthermore, she'd promised she was coming alone.

'Hi, Fee!' Madison sang out, shaking herself free from Dominic's hold in order to embrace her, enveloping her in the cold arms of her red swing coat, and her hug was sudden, quick, very hard, as though she was being rescued from a sinking ship rather than greeting a friend she'd seen less than ten days ago. She looked around the flat's hallway — 'Oh, isn't it *cute*?'

'Thanks — I really love it.' Fiona brushed off her sense of misgiving. 'It's college accommodation, usually for visiting academics. I was lucky to get it.' She opened the bottle bag, smiled.

'Ooh, fizz, thank you . . .' She paused, aware that Dominic hadn't spoken or moved. 'Hi, Dom, how's it going?'

In the six weeks he'd been dating Madison, Fiona had quickly realised that she and Dominic Tate were never going to be friends. She'd discovered that any conversation she raised provoked cutting, sarcastic responses masquerading as friendly banter.

It wouldn't ordinarily have mattered – Madison had always had idiosyncratic tastes – and usually Fiona would have simply avoided him, made plans to see Madison on her own. But it wasn't working out that way, because lately, whenever she made arrangements to meet with Madison for drinks or a curry and a catch-up, somehow he was always there.

The last time she had met Madison at her Clapham flat, he had called by unannounced with a bottle of wine and flowers; claiming to have forgotten Mads telling him that Fiona was coming over, dominating the conversation and starting to yawn heavily around nine o'clock, a cue for Fiona to leave.

When they'd met at Fiona's place in Cambridge, he'd called Mads' mobile, with some story about his grandfather having collapsed and his car breaking down – he needed Mads to meet him in Essex and take him to the hospital.

'There's no one he knows within a hundred miles that can drive him? He can't get a taxi?' Fiona asked, astonished. She'd only just opened a bottle of wine.

Madison shrugged. 'Well, yeah, but he probably needs support.'

'Is he close to his grandfather?'

'I dunno. Probably.'

She should have let it go. Mads liked him, Mads wanted to be there for him. It was none of her business, she thought, watching Madison pack up her overnight bag and head back out the door to her car.

But a hint of suspicion persisted. The next morning she rang and asked Mads how the sick patriarch had been.

'Oh, I never saw him. They'd discharged him by the time I arrived and taken him home. Dom says it turned out to be nothing.'

'Is that so?'

By the time she and Mads ran into him 'accidentally' in the bar at the South Bank Centre after a concert, her suspicions had hardened into hostility.

Madison affected to take these overt manipulations at face value, but Fiona wondered. She suspected, in her heart of hearts, that Mads didn't believe them either, not really, but somehow the idea of being *contested*, of feeling fought over, did something for her on a fundamental level that no considerations of friendship or common sense could allay.

'Hello, Fiona,' Dom ground out through gritted teeth, as though being gracious in the face of some offered offence.

'Let's go in,' Madison cut in, steering Fiona back into the hall. 'I need a glass of something.'

They emerged into the little living room, where a dozen or so people stood around or sat on the bowing sofa or mismatched chairs while low music played. Some of them, like Anneka, Fiona's old roommate, and Ken, a senior lecturer at the Archaeology department, knew Madison quite well already and greeted her, and Fiona left them there, though not before asking them what they wanted to drink.

'A beer,' said Dom shortly. He stood ramrod straight behind Madison and did not look at Fiona.

'I'll have a glass of white, please,' said Madison. 'Where should we put our coats?'

'Just throw them on the bed,' she called back from the kitchen, busying herself pouring out a glass of Sauvignon Blanc.

She thought Mads might follow her into the kitchen, so

was not surprised when she stole in behind her after a few minutes.

'Anything to eat?' she asked. Her voice was slightly slurred. She had gravitated to the open back door and was peering out into the foggy yard.

'Yeah, there's crisps and dips,' said Fiona, bent over the beer bottles chilling in the fridge. 'There might still be some crusty bread and cheese left out on the table.'

Madison frowned. 'I thought you were cooking.'

'I *did* cook,' said Fiona, trying to keep her voice even. Madison's defection had hurt her. 'I cooked hot food earlier. It all got eaten.'

Madison let her back rest against the wall, her eyes downcast. 'Sorry, Fee. I know I said I'd come by and help. I just couldn't get away. I had to . . .'

'So, the party's in here?' Dominic had appeared behind Madison. He still wasn't smiling. In fact, watching him, Fiona had the sense of a prison guard escorting a criminal to a court hearing.

'Apparently so.' Madison rolled her eyes, seemingly indifferent as to whether he could see this or not, as Fiona passed out the drinks.

'I'll be back in a minute,' said Fiona, suddenly unable to bear either of them for a moment longer. 'Need to go and do the hostess thing.' She raised a half-hearted smile and scurried out with a bottle of wine in her hand.

'Fiona!' said Anneka, her face flushed with alcohol, gently clasping her hand in passing and pulling her down next to her on the ancient sofa. 'Stop rushing about. Sit down for a minute and relax. You are making my head spin.'

'We've hardly seen you,' said Liam, her partner.

'Sorry, I know, but I've been so . . .'

'But all is done. Everyone is fed, everyone has a drink. Now you can join the party. Where is your drink? Please tell me you have something to drink.'

Liam had stood up and sourced a clean glass for her, lifting the wine out of her unresisting hands. 'She does now.'

'Oh, thanks, guys . . .'

She glanced sideways, through the open kitchen door. Within, Madison was hissing loudly at the stone-faced Dominic, gesturing and pointing sharply into his face with her wicked purple gel nails.

'Leave them to it,' murmured Anneka.

Liam merely scowled, scratching his ginger curls. 'I'm getting a bad vibe off that guy,' he muttered.

'How's work?' asked Anneka, keen to change the subject.

'Oh, really good! I've been asked to present a paper at . . .'

Suddenly Mads was in the hallway, catching Fiona's eye and jerking her head towards the door with the emphasis of a command, gesturing with her vaper. Her coat was back on.

'Excuse me,' Fiona said, feeling bullied and defeated. 'I'll be back in a minute.'

She followed Madison out on to her own front step. After the warmth of the house, she felt cold in her thin blouse and wrapped her hands around her arms.

'Yeah?' she asked Madison. She felt a hot flare of resentment. Already her first party in her new home was being bent and warped into another platform for Mads' dysfunctional relationships, for her . . . for her *grandstanding*. 'This had better be good.'

Madison was silent for a long moment, as though wondering how to proceed.

'I'm sorry, I really am,' she said. 'I know I'm being a rubbish friend. I meant to be here hours ago, I did, but he . . . he was waiting for me at the house after work, wanting to talk about our relationship, and I just . . . I just couldn't get rid of him.'

She darted a look at Fiona, and in the darkness her eyes were little more than tiny points of light. 'He's . . . so *intense*. I don't know what to do.'

'Finish with him,' said Fiona. 'Obviously. He's stalking you. I *told* you this.'

'I tried . . .' said Madison. 'That's what I've spent my whole fucking evening trying to do in the pub. But he just won't accept it . . . it was all, *I'm running away from our problems, from my issues* . . .' She shot Fiona a glance. 'I know you've never liked him . . .'

Fiona shrugged helplessly. 'He's never liked *me* . . .'

'. . . but he was different in the beginning . . .'

'No, he was always the same, he just hid it better.' Fiona sighed in exasperation. 'He's a proper psycho. How do you get in these situations, Mads?'

Madison didn't answer, instead putting her vaper in her mouth and inhaling.

And the Yeats quote that Madison herself often used came into Fiona's mind: *It's certain that fine women eat/A crazy salad with their meat.*

For Mads, crazy salad always seemed to be the dish of the day.

'What do *you* want to do?' asked Fiona.

'I want us to turn the music up,' said Madison. 'And have a proper dance.'

'I can't play the music any louder.' Fiona cast an apprehensive glance up the brick wall, to where yellow light glowed out from an upstairs window. 'I'm not supposed to have loud parties, annoy the neighbours, you know . . . they're very strict about it. It's the only downside about having college-owned accommodation.'

'That doesn't sound much fun.' Madison gestured contemptuously, then overbalanced and staggered backwards against the wall, giggling. Fiona realised she was quite drunk. 'Fine.'

She turned her head, gave Fiona a misty smile. 'You know, I just wanted to say congratulations, Fee. It's a lovely flat. Just perfect for you.' She lifted the vaper to her lips, sucked in, and then reached into her coat pocket. 'Listen. I'm going to call a taxi.'

'You don't need to leave, Mads. You know, if you want *him* to leave . . .'

'Hello, ladies,' said Dominic, appearing not out of the front door, but instead out of the narrow alley at the side of the house.

Fiona flinched, startled. What had he been doing back there?

The answer came to her instantly. He had come out of the back door and lingered in the little alleyway in order to eavesdrop on them both.

'What do you want?' asked Madison coldly, turning to glare at him. 'I already told you, you're leaving or I am. Since you're not leaving, I'm going home. Don't try to stop me.'

Dom turned to Fiona. 'You know, could you give us some privacy, please?'

The request was perfectly neutral, almost civil, but radiating out of him there was a sense of stifled, barely controlled rage. Fiona threw an alarmed look at Madison.

'It's all right,' said Madison, with a weary wave. 'Go back to your party. I'll ring you when I get in.'

'I'm asking *nicely*,' said Dom to Fiona.

Fiona ignored him. Who the hell was he to order her around outside her own home? 'Are you sure?' she asked Madison.

Madison nodded. 'Yeah.'

Reluctantly, with a last warning glance at Dominic, she went in – but she didn't shut the door after herself.

Her guests were inside, but as she passed back into the living room, she heard a man's voice coming from outside.

'GIVE ME THAT FUCKING PHONE!'

It cut through the music, and everybody seemed to freeze.

'Fuck off!' screamed Madison. 'Fuck off before I call the police!'

With a sudden crash the living room window shattered into pieces, glass falling on to the little table with its burden of nibbles and drinks. Anneka shrieked, and Alex, a friend of Fiona's from work, leapt up, his hair and back full of sharp slivers.

Fiona was running outside, a couple of the men with her, including Liam. Mads was alone, sobbing, her coat ripped, her phone clutched in her shaking hand.

Dominic Tate was already running, his back retreating up Saxon Street into the darkness. From upstairs, Fiona noticed with despair that the neighbours were opening their windows, peering down to see the source of the fracas. The disapproval in their lined faces was intense.

Oh my God, she thought. *Am I going to get kicked out of this flat now?*

She had to pull herself together. Her own fears would have to wait. Madison was in trouble.

'Mads, are you all right?' she asked. Liam was already calling the police, talking urgently into his mobile.

Madison nodded, still tearful, but composing herself. 'Yeah. He didn't want me to get the taxi.' She sniffed. 'He grabbed my phone and I pulled back and he went to punch me and his fist went into the window.' She brushed her fallen hair out of her eyes. 'He ripped my coat, the bastard.'

Her mascara was running down her face, and she swiped at it with her fingers. 'Still, I think he got the message. I reckon I'm rid of him now.'

Fiona bit her lip, her eyes searching out the top of the street. She wasn't so sure.

8

Helly Holm, Orkney, January 2020

There were four of them now, two women and two men, standing around her as she sat on the stool, all of them buttoned up against the cold in arctic jackets and thick work boots.

In contrast to Jack, the other man, Callum, was dark, with pale skin and white teeth that seemed to be slightly too big for his face. His waterproof jacket and trousers looked expensive. He was staring at Fiona in brooding silence.

The girl, Becky, short, freckled, with fizzy brown curls and big square glasses on her small square face, stood slightly apart from them, at the back of the tent.

Fiona smiled weakly at her. She did not smile back.

'What are you saying?' Iris demanded. 'Madison's *run away*?'

Fiona, her stammered explanations over, felt a hot blush rise up her cheeks.

'I'm sure she's not run away,' she said, though an internal voice murmured, *Are you completely sure about that?*

What if something had frightened her enough?

'Madison *left*?' Becky asked.

Callum twitched out a shrug. 'She told us *she* was sick, not her mother,' he said, while Iris shot a look at Jack.

Fiona had the sudden sense that something about this development pleased Callum.

Becky raised a suspicious eyebrow at Fiona. 'Are you *sure* about this?'

'She's been texting me since I set off on Thursday. In the

texts she claimed to be at the dig here . . . to have found "something big" and that's why she was so hard to reach.' She sighed. 'Certainly nothing about leaving.'

'Found something *big*?' asked Becky. 'That's weird.'

The others exchanged looks, and Callum gave Becky a theatrical glare, before seeming to realise that Fiona could see this.

How very interesting.

'Well, I can tell you that we've not seen her since we finished up here on Wednesday afternoon.' Iris's lips compressed as she rubbed the back of her neck. 'Then she was in touch first thing Thursday, saying she had a sore throat and a fever. She was going to take a couple of days off and hopefully be back today. I tried to phone yesterday, and this morning, and got no answer. And as Becky says, she seemed fine Wednesday night.' She tightened her folded arms.

Something struck Fiona then. 'Did she call you, or did she send a text? When she told you she was sick?'

'She . . .' Iris opened her mouth, then closed it. 'You know, I can't remember. But thinking about it, I think she texted.' She sighed, gestured helplessly. 'I'm embarrassed to admit it, but I remember being annoyed. We were all very annoyed with her. She can't help being ill, I know, but with the terrible weather and the dig running late, her timing was abominable.'

There was an eloquent pause, as though Iris was reviewing her next words carefully.

'And, well . . . it wasn't the first time we'd noticed that Madison had something on her mind.'

'What do you mean?' asked Fiona, struck by her tone.

Callum let out an embarrassed little cough. 'There'd been some problems with the finds. And bagging up the samples.' He threw Fiona an apologetic look, in a *I'm just the messenger* way. 'Mads was the Finds Manager here on the dig – it was her responsibility to prepare them . . .'

'Oh, don't labour the point, Callum,' said Iris. 'There were, admittedly, a couple of mistakes . . .'

'Expensive mistakes,' Callum replied with gloomy emphasis, though it seemed once more to Fiona that saying this gave him a measure of inexplicable satisfaction, as though watching Madison fail had pleased him. 'Hundreds of pounds a throw.'

'Callum, this is *not* the time . . .'

'Blew up her own laptop, too – expensive little MacBook. We had to lend her one of ours . . .'

Fiona glanced at him. Madison had loved that laptop.

'I think the point Iris is trying to make,' Jack interrupted quietly, but both Iris and Callum nevertheless fell silent, 'is that it was very out of character for Madison. She'd always been one hundred per cent reliable.'

Fiona wasn't sure why, but knowing Madison as she did, this assessment struck her as unlikely. And yet it wasn't, really. However chaotic her personal life was, Madison worked hard and was very smart – people told her this, time and time again.

She had a tiny flash of self-insight then – *you don't believe in her, do you?* Then a pang of guilt. *Does Madison know that you don't believe in her?*

She shook her head, dismissing the thought. It didn't help any of them now.

'So none of you have actually physically spoken to her since Wednesday night?' she persisted.

They looked around at one another, shook their heads.

'No,' said Jack. 'I don't think so.'

Fiona bit her lip, her hands clasped around her cooling coffee.

'Um, I don't want to . . . well, I don't want to alarm anybody . . .' she began.

Iris's head came up again, and that intense gaze was on her once more. Fiona could feel how nervous it made her.

'What?' Iris asked. 'What is it?'

Fiona swallowed. 'I'm not convinced that Mads would do this – any of this.' She took a deep breath, rallied her wandering thoughts. 'I don't believe that she'd bail on an important dig. That she'd leave without telling me after I travelled two days to get here. There were – I dunno – I got a strange feeling from some of her texts, and from what you've said, and the Fletts, it seems that nobody has seen her since Wednesday night.

'And I don't know if you know this, but Madison had a stalker.'

'A stalker?' squeaked Becky. 'What kind of stalker?'

The others merely stared at her, shocked into silence.

The only exception to this was Iris. From her still, thoughtful expression, Fiona realised that this was no surprise to her.

Fiona looked out through the tent flap. Beyond, she could see the trenches, three big rectangular storage boxes, the causeway leading back to the mainland. Across the strait, she could see a couple, little more than stick figures from here. Around their feet played a couple of large yellow dogs.

If someone had been watching Madison while she worked, she realised, they would have to do it either from very far away or very close up.

And if Dom Tate had come to Helly Holm, Madison would have recognised him.

'Did you . . . I don't know, happen to see anyone hanging around here?' she asked. 'Someone unusually interested in Madison, or did she mention anything to you?'

They all looked at one another, shook their heads. They seemed genuinely at a loss.

'People – locals and tourists – know that we're digging here. Sometimes they watch from the mainland, sometimes they come over the causeway and have a nose around,' Callum said slowly.

'Callum handles our IT and does our social media out here,' said Iris. 'It's his job to show people the dig, answer questions.'

'Really?' asked Fiona, seized with an idea. 'So . . . sorry, hang on a sec,' she was digging for her phone, swiping through her pictures. 'So, Callum, have you ever seen this guy around here?'

She held up the phone. It was the picture Madison had sent her prior to that disastrous Christmas party at Saxon Street the year before last.

Dominic Tate stood there, with his unsmiling narrow eyes and grin too wide for his face and his neat brown hair, one arm possessively tightened around Madison's waist. She too wore a loose smile, her head cocked, her cat-like eyes vacant in drink. One hand rested gently on his shoulder.

With a little start, Fiona realised that Madison was wearing the forest-green mohair cardigan, loosely gathered under her breasts, fastened with little copper toggles. It was one of those expensive, arty pieces that Madison had an infallible nose for. Fiona had loved that cardigan and told Madison so. A week later, it had arrived in the post, wrapped in a gold ribbon with a card tucked in. *'This is for you. I know you liked it. The colour will be better with your hair anyway. All my love, Mads XXX'*

She felt sick with dread.

But now was not the time to cry. Now was the time to get on with it.

They all circled her, peered into the screen.

'No . . . no. Not ringing a bell,' said Callum, nibbling at his thumbnail with those big teeth. He looked around at the others. 'Anyone else recognise him?'

They shook their heads regretfully.

'Um, you're sure no one's seen him?' she asked, hearing the desperate note in her voice.

'What's he supposed to have done?' asked Becky, and again,

she sounded scornful, as though Fiona was trying to pull the wool over their collective eyes.

'He slashed her tyres. He threatened to throw acid over her. He was convicted of criminal damage and sending malicious messages eight months ago. They put a restraining order on him,' said Fiona, and the widening of Becky's eyes gave her a tiny measure of selfish satisfaction.

'Oh,' she said.

'Shit,' Iris simply hissed after a long moment. 'What do we do now?'

'We contact HES, I guess,' murmured Callum, sticking his hands into his pockets. 'Get them to send someone out to replace her . . .'

Becky made a contemptuous tutting noise. 'For fuck's sake. Way to miss the point . . .'

'No, Callum,' said Iris, sounding like a woman struggling to stay patient. 'I meant what do we do about Madison?' She rubbed her temples. 'Something's *happened* to her.'

The next move was obvious to Fiona.

'I think I need to go to the police,' she said. She felt weepy suddenly. This was all turning into a nightmare.

'I've got Mads' next of kin details on the laptop,' said Callum. 'Whoa, no, I don't mean it like that.' He must have seen Fiona's face grow pale. 'I mean, her contact in an emergency. Do you want me to go find it?'

'Yeah, thanks, that would be great.'

He bustled out, while the others exchanged looks.

'Where are you staying, Fiona?' asked Jack, peering into her face, his thumbs hooked into his pockets.

'I'm – I'm in Langmire, for now. The Fletts offered to let me stay on at the cottage,' she said. 'Just for a couple of days.'

'That's nice,' said Iris. 'They're nice people.' She was distracted, thoughtful.

'I mean,' said Fiona, suddenly flooded with embarrassment, 'I think you guys are paying for that house, so if that doesn't suit, I'll get a hotel room in Kirkwall. I'm heading out to the police station there anyway . . .'

'No,' said Iris, raising a quelling hand. 'Don't give it another thought. It's fine.'

'Be good to have someone at Langmire, anyway,' said Jack, rubbing his chin. 'Just in case she comes back there. Yeah. You'd be doing us a favour.'

Iris nodded in agreement, still lost in thought. 'Fiona's right. I think the police are the logical first step,' she murmured. 'I mean, how do we know Madison didn't phone in sick under duress? Didn't text you under duress? No, I don't like it.' She raised her dark eyes to Fiona. 'And you'll keep us informed if you find out anything?'

'Of course.'

'Do you need one of us to go with you?' Iris asked.

'No,' said Fiona. 'Thank you. But I don't think so.'

'You're sure?'

'I think you're probably needed here more.'

Iris shook her head in impatience. 'This is just a dig.' She flapped a hand in the direction of the excavation. 'The person buried here is going nowhere.'

'Well, they might be going somewhere,' said Callum, returning with a bulky laptop open in his hands, and once more his voice was both gloomy and yet self-satisfied. 'There's a big storm coming on Monday night and if it hits the site while it's exposed . . .'

'Callum, that is *enough*,' snapped Jack, suddenly ferocious, his blue eyes cold and furious.

Everybody froze.

'It's fine,' said Fiona into the silence, taken aback by this explosion.

Jack nodded, but his face was red, closed, his mouth tight. He stalked out of the tent.

Callum blushed, bent back to the laptop.

'So this isn't very helpful,' he said. He seemed almost breathless, trembling. 'Her emergency contact is Dr Fiona Grey on Saxon Street in Cambridge, who I'm guessing is . . .'

'Me.' Fiona was stunned, and oddly touched.

Of course she was Madison's emergency contact.

9

'Caspar?'

Fiona was back in her car, her thigh and back aching from her stumble on the causeway path, the phone in her hand. Her face was pink and warm with windburn. Despite the cold, the sun was high and bright, the sea a cobalt blue.

She'd been passed to various people, some speaking English, some speaking French. The line had sounded staticky and distorted – well, she was calling Sierra Leone. Caspar was out there with Médecins Sans Frontières, and had been there for the past month.

'Yeah, yeah, this is Caspar,' came the heavily accented voice. 'Who is it?'

'It's Fiona Grey,' she said patiently.

'Who?'

Fiona had spoken to Caspar numerous times in the previous year. He was an Austrian surgeon based in London. Madison had started dating him almost immediately upon finishing with Dom. Fiona had had dinner and drinks with them both at least half a dozen times, but he always seemed incapable of recognising her over the phone.

Years ago, an ex had said to Fiona, 'I think you're Madison's friend. I don't think she's yours.'

Those words seemed to haunt Fiona right now.

'Fiona Grey,' she repeated, gritting her teeth against her irritation. 'Madison's friend.'

There was a long pause, so long that Fiona wondered if they had been cut off.

'Caspar?'

'Yes? What do you want?'

Accented English or not, there was no mistaking the hostility in his voice. Fiona was taken aback by it.

'We're looking for Madison . . .'

'I don't know where she is.'

'Oh. It's just that . . .'

'She told me she no longer wishes to be in a relationship with me. Just told me over the phone, a week after I arrived in Freetown. She couldn't even wait to tell me in person, when I got back to the UK. She cancelled our holiday this year and paid nothing back for the deposit.' He let out a little huff of displeasure. 'It is nearly five hundred euros . . .'

'Ah, I see . . .'

'All with no explanation . . .'

'Ah. *Ah*. I'm so sorry to hear that, I didn't know.' Fiona felt she was fighting an uphill battle to get the conversation back on track 'But listen, Caspar. She's gone missing. She seems to have left her job and . . .'

'I told you, I do not care. I haven't spoken to her for three weeks and have no idea where she is or who she is with.' It seemed to Fiona that he was breathing hard. In the background, she could hear raised voices in French, the sound of a crying child. 'I am sorry, but I am very busy here. This is nothing to do with me. I have to go.'

The call clicked off.

Fiona stared at the receiver helplessly.

'Shit,' she hissed to herself.

* * *

Kirkwall was a bustling hive of activity after the empty quiet of Grangeholm. The police station was in a tiny industrial estate, on the banks of a small, placid marine inlet. The tall grey building oddly resembled a chapel and was bordered by that flat, jewel-green Orkney grass that looked as though it had just been mowed, but was in reality a product of the endless wind that kept it shorter than any lawnmower could.

Fiona had managed to organise all the texts and emails Madison had sent to her, both before she'd set off and then after, compiling them all into an attachment that she'd send to the police once she'd spoken to them. This seemed the easiest course, as she didn't have access to a printer.

As she'd read through the texts she'd been sent since Wednesday, she felt increasingly sick at heart. Something was wrong, particularly with the texts – brushing her off one minute, overly charged with exclamation marks and textspeak the next. How had she not seen that something was wrong?

She'd known, she realised, but had been too distracted by the journey, by missing Adi, by work, by – and she had to be honest with herself now – the low-lying resentment she felt at being asked to put her own life aside to come up here on such short notice.

She'd played the martyr, but it seemed clear to her now that Madison had possibly been in real trouble, and Fiona, for all her protestations, had just not been there for her. True, Madison had been cagey, and keeping a frightening number of secrets (*she dumped Caspar over the phone? And didn't even mention it when we talked? Wow. Just . . . wow*).

That said, in the cold light of the blue morning with its whipping wind shaking the car windows, Fiona realised it was very Madison. She was a creature of impulse. If she woke up one morning and decided Caspar should be gone, phoning him up and dumping him was in no way unexpected behaviour from her. She was not sentimental and never hesitated.

Particularly if she'd met someone new.

I should have asked the right questions. I should have wheedled more out of her. She shut her eyes, buried her head in her hands. 'For fuck's sake, Madison, where are you?'

10

Kirkwall Police Station, Orkney, January 2020

'My name's Fiona Grey. I want to report a missing person.'

'I see,' he said. The detective was an older man, perhaps fifty, hatchet-faced, as her mother might have said, and tall and thin with a slight stoop. Fiona hadn't thought about her mother in months, and this remembered phrase — 'hatchet-faced' — unsettled her.

Where was her mother now? she wondered. She'd been back in Croydon the last time they'd spoken, three years ago, when Uncle Jamie had died.

She should look her up, find out if she was okay, but the thought always appalled her. She was terrified by what she might learn.

'If you could just follow me.'

He held open the door as she scurried through it, passing into a corridor lined with offices. He walked in front of her now, opening one of the doors.

She was in an interrogation room, she realised, with mint-green walls and a cheap Formica table. She felt subtly intimidated, as though she was being confronted with some criminal act.

'So I'm Inspector Linklater,' he said. His voice was friendly enough, but there was something faintly chill in his grey eyes. 'I just need to ask you a few questions about this missing person.'

'Um, yes,' said Fiona, trying to put a smile on. 'Naturally.'

She was questioned thoroughly, on Madison's age, name,

and once again she told the strange story of being stood up at the harbour after her stream of texts. All of this was typed with great care into a laptop.

'Was your friend on any medication, do you know?'

'Um, like drugs?' Fiona asked in alarm.

There was a short pause and his typing fingers stilled. 'Well, I'll get to that. I was thinking more of medicine – like insulin for diabetes, say . . .'

'Oh no, nothing like that. She was fit as a fiddle, usually.'

'Was she having any other problems, do you know?'

'Hmm,' said Fiona, offering him a weak smile and shrugging. 'I guess. But you'd know about that.'

He frowned at her. 'I'm sorry, I don't follow you.'

'Well,' said Fiona, 'I mean – Dominic Tate reappearing again.'

Inspector Linklater became very still. 'Who?' he asked.

She looked at him for a long moment. 'You don't know what I'm talking about, do you?'

'I'm sorry,' he said. 'Should I?'

'Um . . .' She was blushing again. *Oh, Madison. You promised me you'd tell them.*

His grey head had dipped to the screen in the meantime. 'I understand there were some problems – ah yes, I see, he was convicted last March. Criminal damage and malicious messages. Six months' suspended sentence . . .' He glanced up at her. 'So why don't you tell me what happened?'

Fiona laced her fingers together on her lap. 'Um, sure. So Dominic Tate. Madison was seeing him briefly. They only lasted about seven weeks.'

That steady gaze did not leave her face.

'It was this whirlwind romance that ended badly.' Fiona shrugged. 'I was, well, I was never that keen on him, to be honest.'

'Why not?' he asked her.

Fiona crossed her legs.

'He . . . well, there was something controlling about him from the very beginning. He was super-charming until you disagreed with him, even if it was over something trivial. The first time I met him we were all at the bar in this little arts theatre my college friend Carys worked at – she'd introduced them – and we'd all seen this new play together that Carys was raving about.

'I thought it was really great, really thoughtful, but he hated it. There was no, "let's agree to disagree". It was this embarrassing, borderline aggressive thing, and he was getting red in the face so in the end I just yielded. He was Mads' date and I don't like confrontation. Carys did the same.'

'I see.'

'I mean, I didn't say anything, it wasn't me going out with him, but I thought it was a red flag. But at first Madison didn't get it. She just thought I didn't like being challenged, that he was entitled to his opinion. That I had misjudged how hostile he was because I was oversensitive. But then . . . she started to experience it herself.'

Fiona fell silent for a moment. 'The more controlling he got, the less she wanted to see him. They had a big fight at my house, at my housewarming party, and he broke my window. I thought that would be it. But then I think they got back together briefly.' Fiona felt that sharp lance of betrayal again when she'd heard – *what do you mean, you're giving him another chance?*

'Yes? When was that?' asked Linklater.

'I dunno. About a week before Christmas the year before last. She was always cagey on the details.' Fiona swallowed.

'Anyway, she finally finished it with him on New Year's Eve after this big row, and it was really nasty this time, apparently – he wouldn't physically let her get out of the car and was yelling at her, punching the door.'

'That must have been very frightening for her.'

79

Fiona opened her mouth to agree, then shut it again. 'You'd think so. But she's fearless. It was me that had to persuade her to contact the police about Dominic – and by then he had already slashed her tyres and was posting all these vicious things on social media about her.'

'What sort of vicious things?'

'Oh,' said Fiona, gesturing into the air. 'She was a cheat and a liar and she'd get hers. And worse – in one of them he threatened to throw acid over her, in another he threatened to give her an "ISIS haircut". Then he'd send over big bunches of roses to her work and cry on her voicemail for forgiveness until she disabled it. She's very difficult to faze, but even she was getting alarmed by then.'

'He was posting these things under his own name?' Linklater was mildly incredulous, those grey eyes narrowing.

'No, not the threats. He was cunning. He actually worked in IT – but he'd told Mads he was a theatre producer – this compulsive lying thing was one of the reasons she finished with him. The messages were posted on these anonymous accounts, tied to fake email addresses and pay as you go phones. He had access to all kinds of test phones through his work. But it didn't matter. We all knew it was him. It was just that we couldn't prove it.'

'I see. But he was caught . . .'

'Yes. One of the Instagram pictures was of her front door – she was living alone in Clapham, in this ground-floor flat with big picture windows, really close to the street. It wasn't very safe.

'That was when I persuaded her to put CCTV in. Watching it back was the scariest thing.' Fiona gave a little involuntary shiver at the memory. 'When they arrested him for the tyres he admitted posting the threats. I don't think they would have got him for that otherwise.'

'And where was he posting this?'

'Twitter, mostly. And tagging her on Instagram. Some fake

accounts tried to friend her on Facebook but she didn't accept. Anyway, these posts would only be up a day or two and then they'd be deleted and the account closed. Madison ignored them until the picture of her door appeared on Twitter. She worked for an archaeological unit in London at the time and she'd already had a nasty shock, because that same day her boss had had an anonymous phone call claiming Mads was stealing artefacts from work and selling them on eBay.

'It was a complete fantasy, of course, and nobody ever believed it, but Mads was alarmed enough to do something by then, so we set up the camera, and . . .'

'I see,' said Linklater. 'So that was the end of the matter?'

'Um, that time, yeah.'

'That time?' He leaned forward. 'There was more?'

'Yeah. It started again, out of the blue, about two weeks ago. The threats started being posted online again. On Twitter.'

'What kind of threats?'

Fiona opened her mouth, closed it again, intimidated by his frank, cool stare.

'I . . . don't know. I only saw one this time, the one on Friday night – they were gone by the time she told me about them. But it was the same as before – horrible messages calling her sexual names and threatening to hurt her. The exact same language as before. One came last night, and I managed to get a screenshot.'

'Hmm,' said Inspector Linklater, as she showed him the image she'd captured on the phone. 'Charming.'

Fiona moved to withdraw her phone, but Linklater kept peering quizzically into it, his pale, lined brow contracting. 'And this came the night you discovered she was missing?'

'Yes.' Fiona swallowed, lacing her fingers on top of her lap, unable to shake the feeling that somehow he did not believe her. 'She promised she was going to report all this to you.'

'Did she say that?' His thin fingers tapped briefly on the table, as though he was thinking. 'She might have mentioned it to one of my colleagues, but looking at this,' he glanced at his own screen, 'I don't see any record of it.'

Oh, Madison, thought Fiona, feeling the sting of embarrassment. *You only had to do one thing.*

'So,' asked Linklater, 'was she seeing anybody?'

'Well, she was until recently. A guy called Caspar Schmidt.' She crossed her arms over her belly, remembering that embarrassing phone call.

'A long-term partner, then, aye?'

'I suppose – they'd been dating for about a year. But he wasn't always about. He goes abroad for his work, places like Liberia, Sierra Leone, for three months at a time.'

Linklater folded his arms. 'So, she must have started seeing him quite quickly after this relationship with Dominic Tate ended?'

He was sharp, she realised.

'Um, yes.'

'How quickly?'

'Um, well, almost immediately.' Fiona could feel herself flushing scarlet. 'To be honest, I think there might have been an element of . . . crossover.'

'Hence the ugly row in the car on New Year's Eve?'

'Yeah.'

'Did this Caspar know about the stalking?'

'Um, he did the first time it happened. He didn't seem to when we spoke just now. She'd finished with him about three weeks ago and he seemed quite upset about it. Angry.'

'Is that so?' He looked interested.

Fiona bit her lip. 'Yeah. She finished with him over the phone and didn't give him an explanation.'

'Angry, you say?' He tilted his head at her. 'Angry enough to do something about it?'

'I . . .' The memory of that call lingered. 'I don't think he was that type of guy. On the phone, he sounded annoyed because she stiffed him for half a five-hundred euro deposit, but not heartbroken. And anyway, he couldn't do anything even if he wanted to.'

Inspector Linklater shot a look at her. 'Oh yes? Why not?'

'They sent him to Sierra Leone in December and he knew he wasn't going to get any home leave until March.' She played with the little silver ring on her pinky. 'He wouldn't have left without permission. He's pretty passionate about his work. Possibly the only thing he was passionate about, Mads used to say.'

'Is that why she ended the relationship?'

'I don't know,' Fiona admitted helplessly. 'I didn't even know she had, and he said she never told him why.' She knitted her fingers more tightly together. 'I suppose – there might have been someone new on the scene, perhaps – and I think it's been quite . . . intense on the dig. She told me they worked every day except Christmas and Boxing Day, because the site is in such danger from erosion and the sea, and I know she was exhausted . . .'

'Is that why you came all this way to see her?' asked Linklater, watching her carefully.

'Well,' Fiona licked her dry lips, 'yeah, I guess. I mean, she said she had something she wanted to show me that was important, but to be honest, I think that was an excuse. I think it was to do with Dom. I know she was having a difficult time at the dig, and they seemed to think she wasn't focusing properly. She was desperate for me to come up, so . . .' Fiona held out her hands. 'I did.'

'And when did you last have contact with her?'

'Personal contact? Wednesday lunchtime, the day before I left Cambridge. We spoke on the phone. She'd walked off Helly

Holm to the car park to get a signal, to say she was looking forward to seeing me. There were texts afterwards, but I didn't – I didn't speak to her in person after that.'

'Do you have these texts?'

'I do. I put them all together, and her emails, and the tweet, into a ZIP file. I can send it to you if you give me your email address.'

'You know the drill then?' he said, raising a cynical eyebrow.

'Yeah,' said Fiona. 'From the first trial.'

'Well, that would be very useful, thank you. Now, do you know if there is anyone other than this Dominic Tate that might wish Madison harm?'

Of course, Fiona realised, this was where it was all tending. Someone had wanted to hurt Madison. It was one thing to be perpetually exasperated with her high-handed and reckless ways, but talking about it here in this interrogation room with Inspector Linklater and his cold grey eyes made a chill sink through her.

This was happening. This was real.

'I . . .' A panoply of Madison's furious exes was suddenly before her. 'She had relationships that had ended,' she said, 'but I can't think of anyone else that would be angry enough to pursue her up here. At least,' she qualified again, 'not that she mentioned to me.'

'I see,' he said, bending back down to the screen, carefully typing everything in with two fingers.

She watched him, pressing her lips together. 'There's . . . there's something else.'

'Oh yes?'

'She . . . well, the owners of Langmire caught her with another man. They assumed it was Caspar so it was a bit embarrassing for them when he . . .'

'When you say caught her with another man . . . ?'

84

'They'd seen him coming and going. And they met him once.'

'Did they know his name, the owners?'

'No. He wasn't introduced to them.'

'And she never mentioned him to you?'

'No.'

He held her gaze. 'Would you say she was a secretive person, then?'

Fiona shrugged helplessly. 'No. Not before now. I'd always thought she was completely frank with me, no matter what light it cast her in. I knew she was no saint.'

'Has she ever vanished before?'

A moment of thinking, and she was aware of him noticing it. 'No. Never like this.'

But in that room, Fiona felt how weak and tenuous her connection to Madison must look. There was so much that Fiona couldn't answer for, and she had a sense of how unreliable she must appear. Practically anybody on Orkney could have told him more about Madison's state of mind, her romantic arrangements, her secret fears.

She felt shut out, judged almost, but also a growing, furtive anger. She had been put in this position, come up all this way, despite her better judgement, and Madison hadn't even felt that she'd owed her the truth about anything.

She felt her jaw ache and realised she'd been gritting her teeth.

'Well, thanks very much, Ms Grey.' Linklater was pulling his things together and now standing up. Clearly they were done. 'We'll look into this and be back in touch very soon.'

11

Fontarabia Road, Clapham, London, January 2019

'What are you doing?' asked Fiona, astounded. 'Are you making *popcorn* right now?'

She sat at the dining table in Madison's shabby-chic open-plan living room, squinting into her laptop.

'Yeah, of course,' called Madison from the tiny kitchen, shoving the microwave door shut and hitting the button. 'Aren't we watching a movie?'

Fiona chuckled despite herself. 'C'mon, Mads, this is serious.'

Madison loomed over her shoulder, pulling her face into a solemn rictus. 'Is that any better?' she said, in her best impression of sepulchral bass.

Fiona burst into laughter. 'Stop that, you mentalist.'

'All right . . . Hey, do you want butter on yours?'

'No thanks, I probably shouldn't.'

'Oh, don't be like that. I'm having butter and look at me, I'm gorgeous.' Madison plumped herself down on her big blue squashy sofa, spread out her arms and stretched languorously, like a cat. 'Live a little. Have butter.'

Fiona sighed. 'Are you ready to look at this yet?'

'No.' Madison rolled to her feet. 'Give me a minute.' From the kitchen came the erratic snap of popping corn. 'Do you want a glass of wine?'

'It's early, isn't it?'

'It's after five.'

Fiona, surprised, glanced up. 'Oh God, so it is.'

The sun had sunk while she had been setting up the feed. Through the big picture window returning Saturday shoppers, wrapped in coats and boots, strode through the slush of Fontarabia Road, their heads bowed and shoulders hunched against the sleet. Soon they would be heading out again, to the bars and clubs of London.

'Time flies,' Madison called back gaily. 'Hey, d'you want to put it on the big TV?'

'Sure. Why not? It might be clearer on there anyway.'

'White or red?' asked Madison, coming out to set two glasses on the table.

'Either.' Fiona stood up, the laptop under her arm.

There was a sharp ding from the microwave. 'Is this going to be very boring?' Madison asked.

'I'm hoping so,' muttered Fiona, connecting the laptop to the TV and fiddling with the remote while the smell of melted butter filled the air. 'That's what we want.'

'If you say so.' Madison reappeared in the doorway carrying a huge bowl of popcorn and a bottle. She set both down, switching on a lamp that bathed the living room in a soft glow. 'Thanks for sorting this out for me, Fee.'

Fiona snorted out a laugh. 'Well, let's see if it's worked first.'

They sprawled on the sofa, the laptop on Fiona's thighs. 'Okay,' she said, as Madison applied a handful of popcorn to her face. 'This is the beginning, which is Tuesday morning.'

'So what's the plan?' asked Madison.

'Seeing if we can spot Dom on the video.'

Madison glanced up at the miniature CCTV camera nestled discreetly in the valance above her dark red curtains. It pointed through the gathered fabric out at Madison's driveway and the street beyond. 'Tuesday? Shouldn't we just start now and go backwards?'

'I don't know how to do that,' said Fiona, somewhat stiffly.

'Oh,' said Madison, in an offhand way that managed to both judge Fiona's incompetence and simultaneously forgive it. 'And what are we doing here?'

Fiona tried to rein in her impatience. 'So this "anonymous guy" who we know is Dominic Tate has taken pictures of the house and posted them on Twitter and Instagram, right?'

'Yeah . . .'

'And he must have been stood directly outside to do it, right?'

'Well, yeah . . .'

'So this camera should have filmed him if he's done it again this week. And if it's Dom, like we suspect, we'll have footage of him we can take to the police,' Fiona finished.

'Right,' said Madison slowly, as though this had all been Fiona's idea rather than her own. 'But is it illegal to do that? To just hang around outside my house?'

'No. But it is illegal to threaten to chuck acid over you, Madison.'

'It is?'

'Yeah, it's harassment. You can report him. You can even sue him.'

Madison's lip curled.

'What?'

'To be honest, Fee, if I ignore him he'll probably fuck off on his own eventually. It's not as though he's getting any encouragement.'

'Mads, I keep telling you, these stalkers, sometimes they don't need encouragement. They can encourage themselves.' They'd had this conversation at least three times in the last twenty-four hours.

'I don't think he's crazy, though,' said Madison. 'I just think he's an arsehole. I really think you're overreacting.'

Fiona silently counted to ten. 'Trust me, Mads, it doesn't hurt to be sure.'

'Yeah.' Madison settled back into the couch. 'I'm sorry. I know you're only here to help.' A pause. 'Hey! Shall we get a curry in later on?'

'Ooh, yeah!' said Fiona. She was starving, she realised. 'King Prawn Battari for the win.'

'Sounds good.'

The picture was very clear on Madison's big screen TV, and in colour, which Fiona had not been expecting for some reason. In it the ground was laced with clumps of melting snow, and little white divots lingered on the top of the hedge in the front yard. Madison's old blue Renault Megane rested against the kerb, a neat cap of square snow on its roof, another on its bonnet.

The screen read 21-01-2019 10:26:13, and this time ticked faster as Fiona sped up the feed. Mads poured her a glass of wine.

Fiona took a sip. 'This is lovely, ta.'

Madison smiled. 'I'm glad you came round,' she said, rubbing Fiona's arm. 'I feel like I've hardly seen you lately.'

'Yeah, your evil ex is bringing us together. It's a heart-warming Christmas tale.'

This time Mads' laughter was uproarious, full-throated. She raised her glass in a toast. 'Cheers, Dom!'

In the footage, yummy mummies with pushchairs jiggled past, cars swooshed by like flickering phantoms, and the melting snow began to be replaced by a fresh downfall that whirled like a kaleidoscope in speeded-up time. The sky darkened, the flow of people and cars passing by swelled as rush hour began.

'What does Caspar think of your postage stamp-sized micro-flat?' asked Fiona, her eyes still focused on the jittering sprites on screen.

'It's "charming",' said Madison, in a good imitation of his accent.

'What are you going to do when he works out you're not slumming it ironically and this is, like, your actual home?'

Madison grinned. 'We can cross that bridge when we come to it.'

'That's . . . wait.' Something had caught her eye.

'What?' asked Madison, peering at the screen. 'I don't see anything.'

'That car opposite . . .' Fiona paused the feed.

'There is no car opposite the flat.'

'On the other side of the road, see? The silver one?'

'Yeah?'

'There's somebody in it and they've been sat there for hours now.'

Madison squinted. 'I can't see . . . oh yeah, there is someone in there.' It was impossible to make anything out of the occupant, who was nothing but a shadow on the very far edge of the picture, obscured by falling snow. She shrugged. 'Doesn't matter. That's not Dom's car.'

'You're sure?'

'Yeah,' she said. 'That's a Ford Focus. He drives a Beemer. Black. A Seven Series.' She took a slug of the wine. 'It was the best thing about him, frankly.'

Madison's ability to identify cars was one of the many surprising things about her.

'Hmm,' said Fiona. 'They've been there for . . . five hours, and you can only park for four.'

'They might have a resident's permit.'

'If they were local,' said Fiona, starting the feed again, only this time on normal speed, 'why would they just sit in their car? I mean, you'd sit in your house if you lived nearby, right? It's *freezing* outside right now . . .'

'Hmm,' replied Madison. 'Maybe.' She smiled, cocking her

head at Fiona, as though seeing something in her for the first time. 'You're really good at this, aren't you?'

'What? What do you mean?'

'You missed your calling,' said Madison. 'You should have been a spy.' She raised her brow, as though something had just occurred to her. 'Maybe you are. After all, you went to Cambridge . . .'

'Har har.'

'You know, I . . .'

But then the silver car suddenly came alive. The lights flashed on, and it was pulling out, in some haste, nearly slipping in the dirty slush.

It drove past the front of the house, and in that single glimpse there was no doubt – Dominic Tate's face leered through the driver's-side window, staring directly at the house, and in those brief seconds of visibility, the expression on his face – a combination of rage and hunger – struck Fiona with a vivid sense of fear.

Even Madison was shocked.

'What the fuck was that? What was he doing there?' she asked.

Fiona shook her head. 'I don't know. Waiting, probably.'

'For what?'

'For *you*.' Fiona tapped Play again. They waited together, and then a uniformed figure appeared into the picture from out of the left side of the screen.

'Parking enforcement!' Madison tried on a hearty laugh, did not quite succeed. 'He didn't want a ticket.'

'I'll bet he didn't want a ticket,' said Fiona, not joining in, a certain grim dread settling over her. She felt ill. 'It would have had the name of your street on it. And I'll bet you any money that that's his real car.'

'What?'

'Oh, come on, Mads. He's a compulsive liar. He lied about his job. He lied about his past. Ten to one he borrowed that big car, or it's some company car he has access to. How many times did you see it, anyway?'

Madison's mouth opened, then snapped shut. 'Shit,' she said, after a moment.

Fiona fast-forwarded the feed again.

And now on screen there was a sudden presence, a person in a big coat swinging around the hedge, walking briskly to the front door, phone in hand. Fiona realised, with a start of relief, that this was Madison herself, returning home after a day at the offices of the archaeological unit in London, her furry trapper hat with its earflaps framing her face, her boots high-heeled and impractical.

She raised her head, offered a beaming grin and knowing wink to the hidden camera, and after moments fiddling with her key let herself in and vanished.

Behind her, a silver car was slowly rolling back in the direction it had come from, now little more than a shadow in the gathering dusk. At the wheel, Dominic Tate gazed after Madison, his eyes shadowed and filled with that terrible, inexplicable hunger.

There was no more talk of takeaways. The silver car parked in the space it had recently vacated, and now the timeline read 17:41:35. No matter how Fiona rewound, paused or tried to focus the screen, she could see nothing of the licence plate.

Madison sat next to her, her arms now folded tight around her waist, silent and mulish.

The silver car did not move.

More time passed.

At 01:19:20 one of its doors opened and Dominic Tate

climbed out. He looked scruffy, in a pale jacket and worn sneakers not suitable for the weather.

He did not approach, not straight away. He stood next to the car, looking up and down the street, and when a man in a trench coat passed across Madison's side of the road, he stepped backwards, into the shadows.

When the man was gone, he reappeared.

Another quick look from left to right, and then he was hurrying across the road, for the front door, and his urgency, his furtive glances around for witnesses, made Fiona and Madison reach out and tightly grip each other's hands.

Dominic Tate stood on the steps, at the front door, shrinking against the porch, obviously trying to avoid being observed from the street. He peered into the frosted glass panel above the door knocker, rising up on tiptoes, his eyes luminous, darting here and there, and then he moved towards the picture window. The angle was such that it was not possible to see his face, just the crown of his head, though his jaw was working, his hands shaking.

He had something in his fist, something thin and sharp that glinted.

'What's he holding?' demanded Madison.

'I don't know,' lied Fiona, her heart in her mouth.

He backed away from the house, keeping low, and in turning to look at the street again he bumped against Madison's car, its tyres now buried in a couple of inches of snow.

He paused, his ungloved hand resting for a moment against the passenger-side window, where it dislodged a thin flurry from the bonnet.

Then he bent down, and with quick, careful movements, jammed whatever he was holding into the gaps in the treads of the tyres, his arm levering up and down with enormous restrained force each time. The car sank a little further into the slush, unevenly, causing the powdery snow to shift and tilt on its roof, its bonnet, its windows, until he had slashed all four tyres.

He stood upright, then paused, hands on hips, as though surveying a job well done.

Then, without a moment's hesitation, he strode out, back to his own car, and got in. The lights came on again. He pulled out and drove off, slowing only once, as he passed Madison's house, and his white face was stretched into a horrible, satisfied grin.

Then he was gone.

'Holy fucking shit,' breathed Fiona.

Mads did not reply, but her hand clutched Fiona's own.

'Have you driven that car since . . .'

'No,' said Madison. 'Not since Saturday.'

'We need to check the tyres.' Fiona rubbed her eyes. 'We need to call the police.'

There was no answer.

Fiona turned to Madison. She was white and shaking.

'Mads, don't worry,' said Fiona, though Madison's fear, a thing so alien to them both, was making her afraid. She strove to appear confident, blithe. 'We have all of that on tape. He's not going to get away with . . .'

'Fee . . .'

'What?'

Madison's green eyes were saucer round. 'Is he out there now?'

Fiona stilled.

'I . . . I dunno.'

'Fee, will you go and look?'

'Will I . . . ? Um, Mads . . .'

'Fee, it has to be you. I can't go. He's been wandering around the place, peering into the windows, with a knife. Do you see?

94

He'd go for me. If you go out, he won't get into it with you. Just see if that silver car is there . . .'

'I don't know, Mads . . .'

'I am not going to be able to sleep tonight if that psycho is out there!' Madison was nearly in tears. 'Please, Fee. Just *look* for me.'

12

Fontarabia Road, Clapham, London, January 2019

It was dark and the street was quiet, though the wind was high and shook the empty branches. The snow of a few days ago had all but vanished now and the streets shone with new rain. On any other night it would have felt mild, fresh.

Fiona stepped out of the door, her hands thrust deeply into the pockets of her coat, her phone grazing the knuckles of her right.

Shit, Madison, she thought. *How do you talk me into these things?*

The plan was for her to walk to the Tesco Express on Cedars Road. It was only five minutes away. If Dominic Tate's car was on the street or there was any sign of him, she would act as though she had forgotten something and then return immediately to the house.

Madison would then call the police.

She tried to school her face into an unconcerned expression as she stepped out of the yard, attempting not to notice Madison's mutilated car as she turned into the street. She paused, looking from left to right, but in the darkness car colours were almost impossible to spot and a third of them could conceivably have been silver.

She realised she was shaking. She wanted to go back in.

But she'd promised she'd do this, so she would. She struck out, walking slowly, making way for a young couple talking animatedly about a movie they had seen. ('It was *sick*,' the boy kept saying with passionate admiration. 'Those cars were *sick*.'

'It was fucking rubbish,' said the girl, her voice rising in contempt. 'Next time *I* choose the film.')

Their quarrelling voices grew fainter as Fiona pushed on. It was Saturday night so every space that could be parked in was taken, cars bumper to bumper. She trod slowly past them all, her eyes gliding over drivers' seats and through windscreens, as if in passing. *That's right*, she said to herself, *just look like you're not looking at anything in particular* . . .

When she walked past a tree and saw him there, sitting in his car, mere feet away from her, she should have been prepared, and yet somehow wasn't. He looked straight at her, making no attempt to hide his presence, nor did he seem embarrassed. His mouth was a flat white line, his chin unshaven and speckled with grey.

She hesitated, nearly stumbled, fixed to the ground in shock.

They stared at one another.

The plan was that Fiona should now look as though she had forgotten something, turn back to the house, but this was ridiculous. He had clearly seen her reaction to him.

She did not know what to do.

Long seconds passed. The fighting couple were gone, and the streets were empty. From nearby, the faint scratchy sound of a TV came from a neighbouring house.

She had to move. She couldn't just stand here. This man had threatened to throw acid over Madison.

And then, as she remembered this, a little flicker of rage woke within her.

Who did he think he was, the big bully? Just because he'd been dumped? Fiona had been dumped before, but had never dreamt of destroying someone's property or threatening to hurt them.

Sometimes relationships just didn't work out.

What was the matter with him, the spoiled, entitled arsehole?

Before she knew it, she was rapping hard on the car window, her bare knuckles stinging against the glass.

Slowly, with an electronic whine, the window rolled down.

'Can I help you?' he asked coldly.

'What are you doing here?' she demanded. She could hear the crack of fear in her own voice. 'Leave right now, or I'm calling the police.'

'This is a public street,' he said, and his voice was loud, as though calling attention to the crazy woman harassing him in his car. 'I can be wherever I want.'

'You can't slit Madison's tyres, though. And threaten her.'

A thin smile moved over his face, like an eel. 'I have no idea what you're talking about.'

'You didn't slash her tyres?' She persisted, everything in her wanting to run, and yet somehow, finding she could not. 'You didn't park over there,' she said, gesturing to the place on the street, 'for all day Tuesday, then sit there all night, then come over at 1:19 a.m. and peer in Madison's windows?'

That smile seemed to freeze in place.

'You're on CCTV.' The spark of an idea shot through her. 'You're on CCTV right *now*.'

The smile did not flinch, his mocking eyes didn't blink, but she had the sense then that behind his malignant, contemptuous front, something was retreating, fleeing in rout.

She realised he was a coward at heart.

That said, it didn't mean he wasn't dangerous.

'You fucking bitch,' he breathed. 'You and that filthy cheating cunt better watch your fucking backs . . .'

But Fiona had seen that flash of weakness.

'Fuck off, Dom,' she said, standing upright, turning on her heel, marching with purpose back to Madison's flat.

There was nothing as she did so, just silence, apart from the wind in the branches, the measured tread of her boots on the pavement.

Then suddenly his engine roared to life. She didn't look round, filled with relief that he was finally going.

And then he screamed alongside her, and at the last moment swerved in, just a fraction, as the wall of cars lining the street opened up in a gap. She froze, petrified, as his car lights lunged for her.

Then he swerved back again, tore along the road, and she had a final flash of his desperate, malicious eyes as he drove away, vanishing as he turned right.

For a long time she stood there, shaking, as though she had run a long race, her breath pluming in the thin air. It had been years and years since anyone had offered her the threat of physical violence — not since her mother had left home — and the shock of it was visceral, all-consuming.

She felt absolutely fragile and hollow, as though if someone came up and touched her, she would crumble slowly into a pile of glass shards.

A window opened in a flat across the street. A man in a kufi and beard peered out, his expression quizzical. He had been drawn, no doubt, by the roar of engines.

The spell was broken.

She could move again, though her breath was laboured, and as she headed off towards Madison's flat, she started to run.

13

Kirkwall, Orkney, January 2020

'Hi, Judy . . .' Fiona's throat was dry.

'Who is this?'

'It's Fiona. Fiona Grey. I left a message earlier.'

'Oh, sorry, I haven't listened to my messages yet,' Judy said airily, her voice breathless with its perpetual slight wheeze.

She didn't sound very sorry.

Judy, diagnosed with chronic heart failure, had moved to Majorca shortly after Rob, Madison's dad, had died in a car accident. His Jaguar XJ had skidded off a country road while Mads was still at university, and collided head on with a tree.

Since Rob had not been alone but with his thirty-year-old personal assistant when this happened, and they had been heading for a country hotel in Sussex rather than a previously attested sales conference in Slough, Judy had been inclined to completely reappraise her life and marriage. The move had been the opening step. She had felt that the hot, fresh climate would be 'just the ticket'.

And maybe she was right. She'd been holding on for the last ten years. Whether that was a result of the change of air or her kicking her twenty-a-day smoking habit was up for debate.

'So, um, Judy, I just got out of the police station . . .'

'What?' Judy snapped. 'What did you do?'

Fiona paused for a moment, stunned.

'I didn't . . . sorry, *I* didn't do anything.'

'Oh,' said Judy.

Fiona was silent, speechless with sudden humiliated fury.

You know, she thought, *I can outgrow my past, and I have. I can recover from my untreated bipolar mother and my father who drank himself to death, and our life in a shabby little ex-council house where we're all on first-name terms with the police and the bailiffs. I can get my doctorate, build an academic career, meet a nice boy . . .*

But it will never make a lick of difference to Judy. To her, I'll always be Madison's Unsuitable Friend.

And she'll never knowingly miss an opportunity to remind me of it.

Fiona's jaw clenched. She fought to keep her temper in check, to calm her racing emotions.

Have pity. You are, after all, about to give her some bad news.

'It's not about me, Judy.' She could hear how fragile she sounded. 'It's Madison.'

'What?'

'She's missing.'

As Fiona explained the last couple of days, then the last couple of weeks, Madison's mother remained silent.

Oddly silent, Fiona thought.

'So where is she?' demanded Judy at the end, as though Fiona had somehow concealed Madison somewhere.

'Well,' Fiona said, 'they're not sure Mads didn't leave the house herself under her own power for some reason, especially since she seems to have contacted people, but they're going to look into it. They've taken your details. You'll probably hear from them very soon.'

Judy did not reply.

Fiona swallowed, leaned against the wall of the police station. 'And you know, it very likely could be something or nothing . . .'

'Yes. You said that already.' Fiona heard the tiny intake of her laboured breath. 'But what do *you* think?'

'I . . .' Fiona was once again shocked, but for entirely different reasons. She realised that Judy had never once asked her opinion on anything before today, and that she should do so now signalled how worried she was.

She owed Judy the truth.

'I'm sorry, I think it's really strange.'

'Oh. Oh God,' said Judy.

'But, you know, on the other hand, people say they've had texts and emails from her, giving different excuses. So I don't know what to believe. It could be nothing.'

Silence – no, not silence, for there was always the hitched sound of Judy's breathing, that high, shallow sighing in her lungs.

'Judy,' Fiona asked cautiously, 'are you sure Madison was okay? That she wasn't having any problems?'

'Well, you know, I'm not sure . . . we weren't speaking. We had a row.'

No change there, thought Fiona. 'But still . . .' she began.

'No, a real row, Fiona.' A pause, as though bracing herself. 'We hadn't spoken in weeks. About, well, legal things.'

Another tight little pause.

Fiona frowned, waited. Madison had not mentioned a row, but then Madison always spoke about her family in exasperated terms anyway. In many ways, it was a constant, ongoing row – it was just that the volume was louder or quieter depending on personal circumstances and the mood of the participants.

'I'm flying over,' said Judy. Her tone was flat, no nonsense.

'You are?'

'Yes. And Hugo is coming up too. I'll phone him now.'

Oh no. Hugo, thought Fiona, scratching her neck nervously. *I'm not sure I could cope with Hugo right now.*

'Is he not there with you?'

'No.' A pause. 'He moved back to England with Tara.'

Fiona frowned, puzzled. The idea that Madison's brother would willingly leave Judy's beautiful house in Cala Llombards where he and his wife lived rent-free was distinctly strange.

Perhaps Madison was not the only one Judy had fallen out with lately.

'But are you safe to fly?'

'I'll worry about that,' she replied, almost snapping the words. 'I'll book it now and ring you with the details when I'm done. You can pick us up when I arrive.'

There was no hint of a please or thank you.

'Of course,' was all Fiona said.

'Right, I'd better get on. Speak to you soon.'

Judy was gone.

With a sigh Fiona turned to head back to her car, when her phone buzzed in her palm.

It was a text from an unknown number, and she poked it open furiously, wondering if it was from Madison. At last, at last . . .

Hi Fiona — it's Jack. Are you okay? How did it go with the police? Give us a call if you get the chance. J

How did he get this number? she wondered, then realised that of course she was Mads' emergency contact. The diggers must have looked it up. She gazed down at the message.

Selfish as it made her feel, she was moved by this, the first time someone had asked her how *she* felt. It would be polite to give the archaeologists a call, to let them know how it had gone.

When she tried, however, it went straight to voicemail. Of course, there was no signal on Helly Holm. Jack's message could have been sent at any time.

She glanced up into the cloudy sky with its patches of startling blue. The sun was low, very low – it was only two in the afternoon and yet sunset did not seem very far away.

She was exhausted, done in. It was time to get back to

Langmire and do the only thing she could now – sit and wait, and hope that Madison got back in touch.

She pressed the car key, was greeted by the welcome beep and flash of lights.

So Hugo moved back to England, she thought, letting herself into the car.

Now, that I did not expect.

14

Langmire, Grangeholm, Orkney, January 2020

Fiona had returned to the Fletts' house after her trip to Kirkwall, a pair of new all-weather boots in a carrier bag over her shoulder.

The Fletts were out, it seemed, but to her surprise, they had taped an envelope to their own front door with *FIONA* written on it in marker pen.

Within, there was a set of keys on a keyring with an enamelled Orkney flag dangling from it.

Fiona tried to imagine anyone doing something similar in London, or Cambridge, and laughed.

As if.

As promised, Langmire was warm when she went in, locking the door after herself. She was touched to see, as she carried her suitcase into the downstairs bedroom, that Maggie had made up the stripped bed for her in crisp blue and white linen.

She went into the comfortable sitting room, let herself collapse in a heap, switching on the wall-mounted television with the remote, putting her phone on the table.

You never knew if Madison might ring, after all.

Seduced by the louring iron-grey skies outside, the ubiquitous hushing of the sea, she stretched out on the couch, and shut her eyes. Before she knew it, she was fast asleep.

* * *

When she awoke all was darkness outside, and she was in a momentary panic of being completely lost, of utterly forgetting where she was. She had the sense that some noise had woken her, but no idea what it was, or even whether she had just dreamt it.

She sat up, scanning the room by the flickering light of the television.

Nobody was there.

Groping for her phone, she realised it was only just after five. The days were short this far north. It did nothing to cheer her anxious, restless mood.

Memory came crashing in, in a series of waves – she was on an island off the coast of Scotland. Madison was missing, and perhaps had been taken from the very house Fiona had been enjoying this unguarded nap in.

Anyone could have passed by the windows and seen her lying here, vulnerable.

She scrambled upright, rubbing her eyes, and cast an anxious glance into the glass.

She saw only the front garden wall, lit in a yellow glow from the lamp by the front door. The rest was utter blackness, but she knew that on the far side of the house, out of eyesight, lay the little pier where the archaeologists tied up their boat so they would not be wholly dependent on the tides to access Helly Holm.

Perhaps they had returned, and this was what she had heard.

There was a single text – she must have slept through its arrival. It was from Judy and merely said, *We're arriving tomorrow at 12:15. Flight No. LM434. See you at the airport.*

Fiona ground her teeth. The thought of playing taxi to the ghastly Hugo filled her with revulsion, but what could she do? Under the circumstances, with all that was going on, she could hardly refuse.

She shivered, as though she had stepped in something slimy. *Grin and bear it*, she thought. *You have no choice.*

But there was no word from Madison. No other phone calls or messages, and her emails were all marketing scurf or exclusively work-related. She didn't have the heart to read them, never mind reply.

Once more she crushed down her disappointment. Whatever had happened to Madison, Fiona was going to have to make peace with the idea that she was not going to reappear suddenly at this point, larger than life and pretending not to know what all the fuss was about.

This was going to have to be lived through; one long, grey, anxious hour at a time.

Perhaps forever.

The solitude was crushing, suddenly, and it occurred to her to go out to the little pier, and if it was the return of the archaeologists that had woken her, to say hello to them. Perhaps something had changed in the last couple of hours – perhaps there had been some news.

It would be good simply to make contact with other humans.

In the porch, she pulled on her coat, forced her socked feet into her damp boots, and reached for the door to let herself out.

It opened easily, letting in the first few flicks of cold sea breeze.

She paused, surprised.

She was *sure* she had locked it.

Had someone come in here? The Fletts, perhaps? But surely they would have knocked?

She hurried back into the living room, her heart knocking against her chest, and scanned her surroundings.

Nothing appeared to be missing in the cottage. Her purse still rested in her handbag, lying on its side on the armchair, and her laptop was poised on the bed, now fully charged.

She must have forgotten, despite the fact that she could have sworn she'd locked the front door, tested it once she was inside.

For a long moment she stood, staring at the door handle, feeling her breathing slow to normal.

Do not do that again, she told herself sternly.

The pier was only a minute or two away, but the darkness and starlessness made it hard to find without turning on the flashlight on her phone.

The boat was there, she saw, a fishing boat, perhaps thirty feet long, with the name *SAMARKAND* printed along the stern. It bobbed slowly up and down, making the ropes tying it creak, gently scuffing up against the tyres nailed to the pier. The fittings jingled together, moved by the waves, the wind.

But there was no sign of a light on it, nor any soul nearby. The white van was gone. Could that have been what she heard, the van driving away?

She found her way back into the house and drew the curtains shut. The television was still on, some show featuring young, good-looking people that she did not recognise, but who the presenters clearly thought she should. These people were having stagey, intense conversations about one another and their feelings in places pretending to be intimate settings — coffee houses and living rooms and a nightclub with all of the atmosphere of a morgue.

She had a fleeting regret that she'd put her studies and her seriousness first and never kept up with popular culture after her dad died — otherwise she too could be watching this, laughing at/with these people as the presenters did, and feeling less lonely.

Madison had always told her, *You know, Fiona, not everything has to have a point*.

She missed Madison then, spontaneously and with a yawning ache. It was not Adi but Madison she wanted to call right now, to ask her what it was she was seeing on the TV, because Madison would have known.

She wiped at her eyes with an impatient hand.

Her phone burst into melodic life, startling her. She snatched at it, not recognising the number, and this gave her a second of wild, unwarranted hope.

'Hello?' Her fingers clenched around the case.

'Oh, hiya, is this Fiona?'

It took her a second to recognise the voice, then she placed it: Jack, the site supervisor from the dig.

'Yeah, this is me. Has there been any news?'

Silence, then: 'Um, no, . . . it's not about Madison. Not directly. Listen, a bunch of us are going out to sample the bright lights of Kirkwall. Do you want to come?'

His voice was loose, rolling, as she switched the TV to mute, and she wondered if he'd been sampling the bright lights already.

'I . . . sorry,' she could feel the disappointment running through her again like a thin cold stream. 'I don't think so. I think I have to stay here and, you know . . .'

'I know you're waiting for news. You have your phone, right?' His voice was kind.

'Yeah, but I need to pick up Mads' mum from the airport tomorrow and . . .'

'You'll still be able to do that. And well, we think you should come out.' He paused, and Fiona could hear people rustling, muttering good-naturedly to one another, a peal of laughter. It made her homesick, as though for a country she'd been exiled from. 'A change is as good as a rest, they say.'

Fiona wanted to get out like she'd wanted nothing else recently. But still, she felt like a truant, or traitor. Who was she to have a good time while Madison was missing?

'I'm not . . .' she began. But increasingly she realised that she didn't want to be in this house alone tonight, being startled out of her dreams by real or imaginary noises.

And the sly thought also occurred to her – *if you go, perhaps you'll learn something. Something that will help explain all this.*

'You know what?' she said. 'I think I will.'

'You will? Great! Becky's on antibiotics and is off the sauce for the nonce, she tells us, so she can swing by in the van and get you from there. You're good for that, right, Becks?'

His voice faded out. He must have been turning to Becky.

'Yeah, right, I suppose.' She didn't sound very happy about it.

But at that point Fiona was past caring about whether Becky was happy. She was already on her feet, heading to the bedroom to switch on the light, to throw together something to wear.

'All right then,' she said. 'I'm getting ready now.'

'Brilliant. Becky should be there in about half an hour.'

'Great . . . and, well, thanks . . .'

'Don't thank me yet, Dr Grey,' he said, laughing. 'The night is still young. See you in a bit.'

Then he was gone.

She needed her suitcase, she realised, if she was going to change – she'd put a top in there, something soft and woolly that would not need ironing.

This was the first time she had seen the broken mirror in full light.

All at once that jagged crack was before her, cutting a line down the wardrobe door, bisecting her reflection into two unequal parts. And her face had vanished, almost as if it were pixilated, because about two-thirds of the way up, the crack broke into a circular crystal burst, wider than a fist, as if somebody's head had smashed into it.

And in between these tiny glass scales, as though a little brush had painted it in, the sharp edges were very lightly touched with the maroon dark of dried blood.

Pull yourself together. I know it looks bad. But remember, Douggie and Maggie said that Mads had broken the mirror.

She raised a hand to the glass, with its tiny but telling bloody traces, then stopped, just before touching it.

It was time to get ready.

Time to see what she could learn from Madison's comrades.

15

Stromness, Orkney, January 2020

It was, in fact, fifty minutes later when the van pulled up outside the house. Its headlamps flashed spookily over the furniture through the window, like the searchlight from a guard tower.

Sat alone in the dark in front of the television, Fiona had been writing texts to Madison:

Heading out with the guys from your dig for a drink. Becky Ackland is coming to pick me up. xx

Is she the one you thought was an oddball? xx

Your mum and Hugo are coming over tomorrow. xx

Please get in touch – even if just to say you don't want to talk. We're all so worried. Fxx

Snatching up her bag, Fiona headed out the door.

The van, a white Ford Transit, was idling in the little drive, its sides pelted with dark brown flecks of mud. She squinted at it – the headlights were on full beam and she couldn't make out who was behind the wheel.

Gesturing quickly with a raised hand, she turned and locked the front door, struggling with the unfamiliar mechanism.

After waking to find it open earlier, she had been unable to resist checking it once, then twice, then three times.

She gave it a final hard pull and push, and then turned towards the van. As Fiona approached the driver's side of the van there was Becky; she recognised her dark fizzy curls.

Becky didn't look pleased.

'Oh sorry,' said Fiona. 'Just wanted to check it. I'm a bit paranoid about the door. It was giving me trouble earlier . . .'

'Are you ready to go, or what?'

Becky's voice was flat, bored, but there was no mistaking her hostility.

Fiona, taken aback, fell silent, not knowing how to respond. 'Yeah, I'm ready,' she said.

'Good. Get in then.'

The passenger door of the van clicked unlocked. Becky made no further move towards it.

Clearly this was a difficult person, or someone with something on their mind.

I just have to treat her gently, be nice, thought Fiona. *Be friendly.*

'Hiya,' she said brightly to Becky as she swung the door open. 'Thanks so much for doing this . . .'

'Don't thank me,' said Becky, her eyes half-closed. She didn't look at Fiona. 'This was Jack's idea.'

'Oh, yeah, yeah.' She offered a self-effacing smile, though blushing with embarrassment at Becky's brush-off. 'But thank you anyway . . .'

Becky rolled her eyes theatrically, and Fiona fell silent, as though she'd been slapped.

She never knew what to do about rude people. Between the two of them, this had always been Madison's particular area of expertise.

Fiona realised, as she climbed up into the seat with its smell of earth and spilled coffee, Becky wordlessly gunning the engine, that she was already composing this strange journey into a story, a story she would tell Madison and they would laugh about, and then with a sick sense of recall remembered that Madison was missing and she couldn't tell her anything.

Instead she snapped on the seat belt and pulled the pale blue handbag that Mads had bought her for her birthday on to her lap.

The memory of receiving the bag stirred something in her then.

She was here to find out about Madison. Nobody had said it was going to be easy.

What would Mads do?

She squeezed the handbag, this gift from Madison, as though hoping it might lend her inspiration.

And suddenly it did.

If Madison was here, she would *persist*. She was not of a nature to take no for an answer.

Fiona glanced sideways at Becky, racking her brains – what had she been told about Becky, in those too brief phone calls before she had set off? Not much, as she guessed Madison hadn't been that interested in her.

She had been one of Iris's postgraduate students. She was an oddball. She was needy.

Fiona wasn't finding the last one, but perhaps she was looking in the wrong places.

'So, how long have you been with Iris and the team here?' she continued, as though they were chatting away like old friends.

Becky didn't look away from the windshield and the road in front of her, but her expression hardened.

There was a long pause.

'A while.'

It was clearly meant to be a conversation closer.

Persist.

'Nine months, isn't it?' asked Fiona. 'Mads mentioned you'd been with the team for a while before her.' She pretended to be busy in the handbag, looking for her lipstick.

'Something like that.'

'You were Iris's PhD student, weren't you? That must have been awesome. Would have opened a lot of doors.'

No answer.

Fiona pulled the lipstick out, slicked it over her mouth, guided by her faint reflection in the windscreen. Out of the corner of her eye she could see Becky, her expression still hostile, but this time it was tinged with discomfort.

'You know, I wondered why Mads was out in Langmire on her own. It's a lovely house – great views. And two bedrooms. Seems a shame. Do you know why?'

'I don't,' said Becky. 'You would have to ask *Iris* about that.'

Her voice, which had been curt and unfriendly, was now icy, and Fiona could not help stealing another glance at her.

Her cheeks were red, as though at some remembered slight, and Fiona realised that she was not the only person Becky seemed to resent.

For the first time she felt a flicker of alarm at this unearned ill-feeling.

'Mads said you found something nice at the dig.'

'We're not allowed to talk about it,' Becky ground out.

'Ah,' said Fiona, after an uncomfortable period of silent driving. 'So, how's the dig itself going?'

'Fine,' said Becky.

She did not speak to Fiona again until they drew up to Helgi's bar in Kirkwall, some twenty-five minutes later.

16

'Ah! You're here!' cried Jack from his seat at the table.

Helgi's was a little bar-restaurant on Harbour Street, narrow and warm inside, full of talking, laughing people despite the cold weather and searing wind outside, and sporting a glittering collection of whiskies on optics behind the bar.

Jack and Callum were sitting at a table peering through laminated menus, which they put down as Fiona approached, giving her a little wave of welcome. Jack rose to his feet.

Something flickered in Callum's eyes – not exactly enmity, but not exactly welcoming. More watchful.

Fiona didn't know what she'd been expecting after the extreme sense of awkwardness that had been the van journey up, but clearly there was a status quo here that she might be in danger of upsetting. She looked over her shoulder and noticed with relief that Becky had vanished on the way through the restaurant.

'There you are!'

To her surprise Iris stepped out, away from the bar. She looked pink and slightly tousled, with crimson lips and ruddy cheeks and big hooped earrings, and Fiona's suspicion that the party had started earlier for them all seemed to be confirmed.

Around them, Fiona could see the locals, some peering at Iris, trying to work out where they recognised her from, others steadfastly ignoring her, having recognised her and not wishing to seem too starstruck.

It must be stressful, Fiona realised, being famous – to have to forgo one's native anonymity, to have things expected of you by people who don't know you; to never really be able to relax.

But then, Iris was flown all over the world on her television show, appearing on her vintage Harley-Davidson in places as diverse as Machu Picchu and the Valley of the Kings, and was very well paid to do it.

If fame was a problem, Iris seemed to wear it lightly.

'What are you having?' she asked Fiona, only slightly slurred, her arm drifting up around Fiona's shoulders. Her light sweater was of the open-necked, loose kind, sliding off her shoulder, and she sported an ornate black tattoo that Fiona had seen somewhere before but could not, just at that moment, recognise.

'I dunno . . .' said Fiona. She had given the matter no thought.

'When in Rome, try the beer,' Iris said, with a knowing look.

'You think?'

'Iris, what does she want?' shouted Jack from the table. He was pulling off his fleeced hoodie and was now clad in a black T-shirt with tour dates for some band she'd never heard of before. His biceps were well-muscled and tawny, also webbed with tattoos.

She felt her breath catch a little, treacherously.

'I'll try the beer,' said Fiona tentatively. 'Why not?'

'Get her a Dark Island!' bellowed Iris to Jack, who nodded in response. She slipped a companionable arm through Fiona's, her voice dropping to a murmur. 'I'm glad you came. Jack's right, it's not good for you to be cooped up all alone. How are things?'

'They're . . . well, I went to the police station.' Fiona tried not to sigh. 'They say they'll be in touch.'

'Hmm,' said Iris, catching her mood. 'Jack says Madison's mother is arriving tomorrow.'

Fiona nodded. 'Yeah. I'm picking her up from the airport.'

'Could she tell you anything useful?' Iris asked.

'No,' said Fiona, aware of how uncomfortable talking about Judy made her. 'They'd fallen out, again.'

Iris's mouth twisted downwards. 'Madison did say it was a difficult relationship.' She let out a disgusted sigh. '*Family*. I know how that goes.'

Fiona cast a curious glance at her. There had been real bitterness there.

'They're always squabbling about something,' she told Iris. 'Mostly about the estate. Madison's father was a rich man, but . . .' she paused, aware that she was perhaps sharing too much. 'Anyway, I didn't think much of it.'

Iris shrugged in agreement. 'Why should you?'

Fiona shook her head. 'You know,' she said with feeling after a moment, 'I am so worried about Mads, but I could just strangle her right now. She promised me she'd tell the police about Dominic . . .'

'Hmm,' Iris said, guiding Fiona towards a quiet corner under the pretence of making way for Jack en route to the bar. 'Perhaps she meant to. We've been busy as blue-arsed flies on the dig. Anyway, presumably the police are going to be hunting down Mr Tate and asking him some searching questions. And maybe she *has* left on her own.'

'I don't know,' Fiona said, trying to control the sudden impulse towards tears. 'I know that Mads could have just left. I do. I just don't . . .'

'. . . Believe it.' Iris stood back to let Callum pass by. His gaze fell on them both, inquiring, curious, but Iris ignored him, turned in fact, showing him her tattooed shoulder.

He immediately took the hint and walked on.

'I mean, why would she do that?' Fiona asked. 'Just leave her career, her life . . .' *Me*.

'I don't know either,' said Iris, lowering her voice even

further. 'And it seems very unlikely, to be honest. But listen – I already knew about some of the . . . problems she was having.'

'You did?' asked Fiona, with a little flood of relief.

'Well,' said Iris, lowering her voice, 'she couldn't hide it from me.'

'What do you mean?' asked Fiona, surprised.

'He – well, *someone* – emailed my production company a fortnight ago, trying to get through to me. They didn't, of course – they got through to Shaheed. Part of his job is shielding me from crazy people on the internet, of which there seems to be an inexhaustible supply. Anyway, this email was all some nonsense about Madison being fired from her previous job at the London unit for dishonesty.'

'Yeah! He did that before!' Fiona was getting angry all over again. 'Made some mad phone call to Rachel Hemsworth about how Mads was stealing artefacts to sell on eBay. You know,' she snarled contemptuously. 'Like you do.'

Iris shrugged again. 'I knew it was bullshit, of course – I'm friends with Rachel, who's only ever had good things to say about Madison.

'But you know, it set off alarm bells. I'd already noticed that Madison was careful not to be in the dig pictures Callum took, so I asked her about it.' Iris's lips tightened. 'And she just told me. She seemed relieved, to be honest. I think perhaps some things had happened recently, and it had been preying on her mind.'

The timeline sounded right to Fiona. A fortnight ago. 'That's when he started tweeting at her again, I think. Or so she thought.'

'Oh, he was absolutely charming when he started in on me,' Iris said, her face hardening. 'Especially once he worked out that I wasn't going to be firing her on his say-so. "Stay away from @MadsKow unless you like being gang-raped you feminazi bitch."' She sneered. 'You know. Basic issue.'

'How *lovely*.'

'Oh, I'm used to it.' One eyebrow drew up. 'I'm a woman on television. She told me there's a restraining order, isn't there?'

'Yes,' said Fiona. 'For all the good it does.'

Her weary despair must have made an impression of Iris, who merely squeezed her shoulder, a tiny gesture of solidarity.

'I'm sorry you had to put up with that,' said Fiona. 'I just don't understand it. Why would he bother you?'

'Oh, don't worry about me. As I say, I'm used to abusive trolls on the internet. And the answer to your question is: why *not* bother me?' Iris offered her a bitter smile. 'It's a cunning strategy, when you think about it. I'm her boss. By tagging me as well as her it makes it very clear that she's in trouble, and by supporting her, I'm in the firing line too.'

Her eyes narrowed. 'It's a way of isolating your victim, cutting them off from money and support.' She sucked her teeth. 'Revolting arsehole.'

'Not talking about me again, I hope?' Jack appeared next to them, brawny arms crossed.

'Not this time,' said Iris, turning her bright smile upon him. 'Fiona went to the police station today.'

Jack stilled, flickering from amusement to concern. 'I know. What did they say?'

Fiona sighed. 'Not much. They'll be in touch.'

His brow wrinkled into three deep furrows. 'Hmm. To be honest, I hoped she might be in touch today herself, seeing as she knew you'd be here.' He paused, almost tentative. 'Um, she hasn't, has she?'

Fiona shook her head.

'Nah. Of course not. You'd've said.' His face was glum. 'Look, have you eaten yet?'

'No . . .'

'We were going to get some food. Becky, have you finished with that menu?'

'What? Yes.'

Somehow Becky had reappeared, sitting next to where Jack had been. Fiona noticed that she had had to squeeze past Callum into the booth, ignoring more convenient seats, to get that position.

Maybe she'd been sitting there before she'd been dispatched to fetch Fiona from Langmire. Judging by the flushed, slightly prim way she dropped her bag and arranged her coat over the back of the booth, it seemed more than anything that Becky was keen to claim the position next to Jack.

'I know it seems frightening to you that this creep could chase Madison all the way up to Orkney,' murmured Iris, steering her back towards the table. 'But you ought to know, despite all the horrible drama, she never once claimed to have seen him here. And after you left us this morning, we talked about it. None of us ever saw or heard anything remotely suspicious.'

'I dunno, Iris. That doesn't explain why she's not in touch with me to tell me this herself. It doesn't explain her texts to me on the way up. They didn't sound like her. They were just . . . off.'

'I don't know the answers.' Iris tilted her head. 'But perhaps the texts are strained because she had things on her mind. I – don't get me wrong – she wasn't scared. She never seemed scared. But the others are all telling me the same thing – she seemed *distracted*.'

Fiona's heart squeezed in recognition. No, Madison was never scared. Even when she should be.

'You know,' Iris offered a rueful smile, 'I can see you're worried to death. But despite everything, and I absolutely think we should do all we can to find her, I'm going to remain hopeful that Madison has left under her own power, for her own reasons that she's not ready to share yet. Because I'm just not sure we have any evidence to believe the alternative.'

Fiona blinked at her.

Madison clearly had things going on that Fiona knew nothing about, and when she'd confronted her on the phone about Dom, Madison wasn't even that interested in discussing him. Like he was a side issue.

Iris could be right, she thought with a tiny bright spark of renewed hope.

'So, let's travel hopefully, at least until we get some news,' Iris murmured.

Fiona nodded. 'Yeah,' she said, feeling close to tears again. 'Let's.'

'Come on. We'll get something to eat. You look like you could do with a good feed, if you don't mind me saying so. And we'll drink more. That's also a plan.'

Iris sat down opposite Becky, guiding Fiona to join her. Fiona let her gaze travel back over her shoulder, to the bar, as she took her seat. Callum was carrying three very full pint glasses carefully together, in a way that seemed to be asking for trouble, threading through the crowd at the bar towards the table.

'You know, one thing I did mean to ask,' Fiona said, turning to Iris. 'Why was Madison out there in that cottage on her own? It seems so isolated.'

'Ah,' said Iris, 'I thought we needed someone based near the boat in case of emergency, you know. And Madison had had sailing lessons, so she seemed the best fit. She took us across to the dig most mornings.' Iris tilted her head, thinking. 'It seemed to be working well. For a little while I thought I might send Becky over to join her, but that turned out not to be necessary. Which was for the best.'

She winked at Fiona, a gesture so tiny that Fiona wondered if she'd imagined it, while Becky, startled out of her conversation with Jack by the mention of her name, glanced around, wondering what she'd missed.

There was a heavy male sigh, a clink of glasses on the table. At Fiona's elbow Callum was setting three dark pints of stout down, each in its own puddle. He looked pink and slightly pissed, like the rest of them. He was wearing a college rugby shirt.

'Here we go, ladies,' he said, clearly oblivious to the conversation he'd interrupted, or assuming it to be unimportant. He carefully lifted one, offered it to Iris. 'This is for you.'

'Thanks, Callum. I've talked this beer up to Fiona – she'd better like it.'

'I'm sure she will.' Callum didn't even look at Fiona as he delivered her pint, his gaze fixed on Iris. Fiona understood, in a lightning moment, that either all other women were invisible to him when Iris was in the room or, alternatively, that Callum was invested in making Iris think so. 'Chin chin!' he said, raising his glass.

Iris gently tapped his pint with her own. 'Cheers. Here's to unexpected days off.'

'You had the day off?' asked Fiona.

'No, just the afternoon,' said Jack, with a wry smile.

'It was just *impossible* to dig in that wind,' said Iris. 'We couldn't even get the poles to stand up straight. We stuck it out until two and then thought sod it, let's fuck off and try again on Monday.'

'Very wise,' said Fiona. 'But then I'm not very outdoorsy.' She raised her glass, regarded the dark contents with trepidation, then sipped at it.

'Oh,' she said. 'This is lovely.'

Over the lip of his own glass, Jack, having overheard her, grinned and winked.

There was something in the way he did this that made something flutter around her solar plexus.

Stop that, she told herself firmly. *What the hell's wrong with you?*

'Well,' said Iris, raising her voice to include the whole table, 'we should enjoy it while we can. Monday is going to be a complete bastard from start to finish.'

'Oh?' asked Fiona. 'Why is that?'

'We're excavating the bodies,' said Iris, letting her voice drop almost to a whisper. 'We're trying to keep it on the down low for the moment. We're . . . well, we're not entirely sure what we're going to find.'

'Bodies?' Fiona was surprised. 'Mads only mentioned one.'

'We thought there was only one,' said Jack, 'because the grave had been trashed at some point after deposition, probably by rabbits. Anyhow, what with the bad weather and flooding they've been having here recently, the site's very badly disturbed . . .'

'But you found another skeleton?' asked Fiona.

'Well,' said Jack, his blue eyes twinkling mischievously at her, 'we found another pelvis yesterday, near the boat's midsection. Which is usually a giveaway. Like skulls, folk tend to only have one each.'

'Wow,' said Fiona. 'Have the police had a look yet?'

'They just sent the county archaeologist. Most places it would be blue tape and sirens; out here you can practically pick bones out of the shore in places, and the police are like, *yeah yeah, ancient human remains, we get it. Whatever, dude. Go wild.*'

'That is a gross exaggeration, Jack,' Iris said. 'Try not calling the police and see where you end up.'

'An exaggeration,' he said, 'but hardly a gross one.'

'Anyway, we're waiting for the licence from the coroner to excavate the bones, which should be coming Monday, with any luck.' Jack shrugged. 'We can't touch them till then. Everyone is getting proper narked off by it all. There's not much to do except surveying and cleaning in rubbish weather, and no real shelter to do it in.'

Iris reached out, put a placating hand on Jack's shoulder. It was a surprisingly intimate gesture. 'Only one more day till we start again,' she said.

'Thank God,' sniffed Becky. 'If I'm on that island freezing to death, it would be nice to have something to show for it.'

'Hmm,' said Callum. 'It should be good, though. It was a big boat, at least thirty foot. There's somebody very important buried in there.'

Fiona glanced at him. 'Thirty foot. That *is* a big boat. What's the preservation like?'

'Not great, not terrible.' He shrugged. 'The wood's gone, of course, but the rivets are still there. Just.'

'Ah, yeah, the rivets. I saw them on your Twitter feed. And definitely Norse?'

'Yeah. Mid tenth century. We've got some . . . um, coin evidence.'

A kind of strain crossed his face, as though he'd been about to say something indiscreet.

'Did you manage to get anything at all from the bones yet?' asked Fiona.

'The bones we're absolutely not supposed to be looking at until we get our licence from the sheriff's office?' Jack glanced at Iris with a conspiratorial glimmer. 'A little. Maybe.'

'Really? Like sex?' Fiona asked, her professional enthusiasm immediately kicking in.

'Why thank you, Dr Grey, but I try to avoid it too soon before a meal. Brings on my indigestion . . .'

Fiona shot him a glance.

'Sorry, sorry,' he laughed, and she saw Becky look away, scowling. 'Sorry, Fiona. But you did kind of walk into that one. So the first body is indeterminate. The second one, the one we just found, is female, we think. But DNA hasn't gone off for either of them yet.'

'Anyway,' Iris put her pint down, 'there may even be more people in there. They'll all be boxed up and sent off to the osteo folk, hopefully this coming week, and we'll get to go home before long.'

'Not a second too soon.' Becky crossed her arms.

'Speak for yourself. I like it here,' said Jack.

'Even in this weather?' asked Becky, with a slightly too loud giggle, an awkward attempt at flirtatiousness.

'Yeah, even in this weather.' His animated face grew thoughtful. 'Perhaps especially in this weather.'

'Madison liked it here,' blurted out Fiona unguardedly, and then felt anxious and self-conscious as they turned to look at her. 'She told me she loved the peace.'

'Yeah, well, she was on her own, wasn't she?' said Callum. 'I'm sure it was very peaceful out in the cottage.' He grinned at Iris. 'Jack snores like a motorbike in the TT.'

'I do *not*,' sputtered Jack. Then he offered Fiona a conspiratorial wink. 'At least, I'm never awake to hear it.'

Callum barked out a laugh, and the others joined in. Iris grinned, sitting back. 'I couldn't possibly comment,' she drawled.

Fiona smiled. *Just go along with it*, she thought. *Act as though Madison is coming back, and perhaps she will.* Though the beer tasted sour to her when she thought of Mads, perhaps dead somewhere, out there in the icy Orkney night.

'Anyway,' said Iris, and Fiona had the sense that she had been spotted wandering down this doleful mental road, 'that's for Monday.'

'Yep,' said Callum, stretching. 'And hopefully this thing with Madison will be resolved soon and things can get back to normal.'

'Callum,' said Iris with a cold crispness that made the word sound like a reprimand.

Resolved. Fiona could only stare at him, but then she caught sight of Jack, frowning at Callum, then offering Fiona the shadow of a compassionate smile – *he doesn't mean to be cold.*

They don't believe anything is wrong, Fiona realised – *well, except maybe for Iris. This is why they are nice to you. Why most of them are nice to you, anyway. Possibly even why they invited you out here.*

They pity *you.*

It implies that they know something about her that you don't.

She stood up suddenly, aware that she was about to cry.

'Sorry, just need to nip to the loo.'

The toilets were empty, and she splashed her face with cold water, tried to calm her hitching breath.

In the mirror, her eyes were red-rimmed, her skin pale.

What if they were right? What if she has done this deliberately?

But why? Why would she lure you up here? And why wouldn't she tell you why she needed you?

As Fiona walked back through the bar to the table, there was a pretty girl with a notepad standing next to it, taking their orders for food.

'She does *not* stop talking,' Becky was hissing to Callum, just loud enough for Fiona to hear. 'And she is *so* nosy . . .'

'Becks, that's enough.' Jack thrust a menu at her. 'What do you want to eat?'

Fiona had not even looked at the menu yet, so when Jack recommended the burger she quickly went along with his suggestion. The others gave their orders, the girl lingering over Jack's. She quickly withdrew, his eyes following her pert behind as she vanished.

Suddenly he glanced up, as though aware of Fiona's attention. He offered her a self-deprecating smile, blushing slightly. 'Sorry,' he said. 'But you can't blame a guy for looking.'

'Hmm,' said Iris, her eyes hard. 'That's a matter of opinion.' She stood up. 'My round. Who wants another pint?'

17

Kirkwall, Orkney, January 2020

They lingered in the bar until at least closing time, and as the barmaid took away the last of their glasses, giving Jack a final smile goodbye, they found themselves outside, the wind ruffling Fiona's hair until she quickly stuffed it inside her hood.

It was a clear night, the cold crisp and refreshing after the warm mugginess of the bar.

'Where do we go next?' asked Fiona, her cheeks flushed, hearing the slight slur in her voice.

'Mince roll,' said Jack.

'Mmm, yes,' said Iris.

'A what? And didn't we just eat a couple of hours ago?' asked Fiona.

'What can I tell you?' shrugged Jack. 'Digging is hungry work.'

'You only dug half a day.'

'But they don't sell mince rolls in halves. What's a man to do?'

Kirkwall was a mix of tall, gothic sandstone and concrete car parks, as if all the ages of Orkney had come together and then collapsed on the sides of the street. It was in the middle of one of these car parks, opposite the Lidl, that everybody came to a halt next to a small catering van.

'So the dig is at a standstill?' Fiona asked Jack as they queued up. In front of them, a quintet of young lads in jackets, wool hats and tattoos were ordering paper packets of chips – ('More vinegar pal, aye? Cheers.'). 'The Vikings are on hold. That must be frustrating for them.'

He looked down at her. With his blond hair and broad shoulders, he had the look of a Viking himself.

'It's . . . well, we're keeping it a bit schtum at the moment, but we reckon we have something quite nice going on here.'

'I can see that. A full boat burial.'

'Yeah, and the rest.' His eyes flicked away from her, to the lads at the front of the queue. 'Hmm,' he said. 'This isn't the best place to discuss this. Not really. Wait till we get back to the house.'

She followed his gaze, and at the back of the queue, her arms crossed over the chest of her thermal jacket and her gloved hands tucked in her armpits, Iris was giving Jack what could only be described as a hard stare.

As the lads moved away she found herself being guided to the front. A selection of offerings were on display – mostly meat being served in some kind of bread.

'Can I help ye?' The man at the front leaned forward towards her.

'You want a mince roll,' breathed Jack into her ear.

'I did just eat a couple of hours ago . . .'

'I know, I know. Ask for a mince roll. With chips.'

The mince roll was exactly what it sounded like – minced beef in gravy, ladled into one of the feathery, flaky Scottish bread rolls people had been serving her since she'd reached Inverness.

'Go on, eat it.' Jack was watching her, his own roll in hand. 'It won't bite.'

It was delicious, salty and meaty, but gone too quickly. She picked through the accompanying chips, now regretting she hadn't asked for gravy with them. Gravy on her chips was one of the few things she missed from the village in Yorkshire she and Mads had grown up in.

She pushed down the pain this memory brought her.

They were all walking back into Kirkwall and towards their white van, frost sparkling on the pavement under the street-lights, and Iris was leading, engaged in some earnest discussion with Callum about the gender politics of Halloween, and behind them Becky stomped on her own, her arms crossed against the cold. She seemed to be angry again.

Perhaps, thought Fiona, because Jack had fallen in beside her.

Gulls cried out at the harbour, not put off by the darkness – and beneath all was the constant, ever-present murmur of the sea.

Jack strode at her side, silent, a blocky warm presence, before saying: 'Penny for them.'

Fiona shook her head, smiled apologetically up at him. 'Sorry. They're not worth that much.' She thrust her hands into the pockets of her inadequate coat, feeling cold and self-conscious. 'I just wish I knew where she was.'

He seemed at a loss for a reply.

'Anyway,' and she tried to raise a smile, to dismiss her fears. 'There's something about this dig you haven't told me, Dr Bergmann.'

'What do you mean?' he asked, but his voice had dropped, as though he didn't want Iris to overhear him.

'You found something, didn't you?'

He smiled.

'Something you're keeping to yourself,' she persisted.

He let out a snort of laughter. 'Very well, Dr Grey. So, we're still analysing, but it looks like a really sweet classic ship burial, with at least two people in there, and a sacrificed horse cut into eight pieces.'

'Impressive.'

'There're some lovely grave goods too – a sword hilt, shield bosses, what we think is a spearhead, at least twelve arrowheads – and we're still not finished.'

'Nice.'

'Hmm,' he said, letting his head drop near hers, his voice growing low. 'There was also, rather intriguingly, a leather bag of coins and jewellery – silver coins mostly, but still a very respectable little trove of treasure. We haven't analysed or cleaned it yet, but it looks good.' He shrugged again. 'Some nice pieces.'

'Wow!' said Fiona. 'A silver hoard! That's very cool.'

He laughed then. 'It's not bad.'

'It's better than not bad.' She smiled up at him. 'I think you lot are all jaded after discovering national treasures all over the place. Jewelled boxes and that Jesmond Hill torc and I don't know, whatever you find next, the Holy Grail or whatever.'

She'd been expecting him to laugh too, but he didn't, and it seemed to her that his gaze grew distant, his smile dropped. 'Jaded. Yeah, maybe.'

She was surprised, confused. She wondered if she'd offended him somehow.

But some similar process appeared to be at work in him. 'Sorry. I'm just tired. You're right, it *is* very cool. And there's probably much more to find. The second person is lying behind the head of the first one, next to the horse, and we haven't been properly able to excavate under that body yet. There's the whole prow which we haven't properly dug yet. Who knows what we'll find?'

'It's pretty rich-sounding.'

'It's very rich. This is why we're all risking life and limb to get to it before the sea and scavengers take most of it away.'

'Mads said it was a great site.'

Jack nodded, but even though they had been speaking quietly, Iris's head seemed to swing around, her gaze upon Jack narrow and beady.

Jack offered her a cocky wave, and she slowly turned around.

At her side, Callum frowned between them, as though annoyed to be left out of some hidden communication.

'Iris doesn't want it discussed publicly.'

'Even in the street?'

'Especially in the street. Careless talk costs lives, you know.'

'She's worried about metal detectorists?'

'She's . . . she's worried about a lot. And trying to keep on top of the information is difficult and stressful for us all.'

'Right . . .'

'Iris has to fly out with the coins to Edinburgh next week. She's heading out anyway, she has some pickup filming she needs to do for *Discovering the Past*. If it helps, it explains why we were all a little guarded when you pitched up this morning. We only found the coins yesterday, last thing before packing up for the day . . . are you all right?'

Fiona had stopped walking.

'What is it?' Jack pulled up beside her.

She glanced sharply at him. Her mind was whirling.

'Oh . . . oh, nothing.'

'You sure?'

The others were slowing, having reached the van in its slot on Harbour Street, and were turning to look curiously at her.

She had to say something to them.

'I was just thinking,' she said, her voice cracking slightly, 'it's such a shame Mads missed it all.'

'Yeah,' he said, 'I suppose.' But he looked doubtful, his face suddenly shuttered, as though he suspected she was keeping a secret from him.

And she was.

The last text she had received before Madison had gone dark had said: *Sorry – not ignoring u! Things r MAD here! BIG BIG FIND on site here at Helly Holm!!! Can't talk now but SO MUCH catching up 2 do! See u in 30 mins! MXXX*

132

And on Friday they'd found the coins – the coins they were not telling anybody about.

If Madison had gone missing on Wednesday and the archaeologists hadn't seen her since then – how had she known about them?

However friendly some of them seemed, she realised she couldn't trust them.

At least one of them was a liar.

18

Nordskaill, Stromness, Orkney, January 2020

The house the archaeologists lived in was set in two adjoining fields, both empty of everything except susurrating grass and a vast bowl of sky above, liberally dotted with stars. The lights and narrow grey streets of Stromness were visible from the front gate. The *Hamnavoe*, the ferry to the mainland, was now in dock, a white behemoth lit up in orange, nestling in the port like a metal swan at rest.

Inside, everything had the clean, cheerful air of a holiday home. Fiona followed Becky and Iris into the front room, while the men vanished into the kitchen in search of more beer.

Langmire, the isolated cottage, was pretty enough, but it occurred to Fiona that Madison would have been happier here, with the company of the others.

'It's nice here,' she said, feeling her throat close with emotion, but needing to say something for the sake of conversation. She surveyed the walls and their collection of seascape prints and ornamental mirrors.

Becky didn't reply, as though Fiona had not spoken, but Iris, who had collapsed ostentatiously into one of the armchairs, making the pieces of her big necklace clatter together, opened one eye sleepily.

'It *is* nice, isn't it? It's much easier to find decent housing in the winter here.' She pulled herself upright and stretched her slender back by gripping her arms behind her head and opening out her shoulders. 'Not that I've seen much of it.'

'Why's that?'

She shook her head. 'I'm *constantly* travelling. They're filming pickups for the new series of *Discovering* in London, and of course nobody is available when you need them to be, so I have to keep popping in and out. Which is not a big deal from my office at Imperial but is an absolute slog to do from here.'

'Yeah,' said Fiona. 'But it could be worse, I guess. The site is amazing, from the sounds of things.'

'To be fair, it was Callum that found it.' Iris glanced fondly at him as he emerged from the kitchen. 'Well, he didn't "find" find it, you know, trip over the side of the boat while he was out walking or anything, but he pointed out that the emergency contract was available for digging, and its potential.'

'I'm always on the lookout for good opportunities for Iris and the team,' he said, sounding like a dog that has found a particularly juicy bone and presented it to his mistress, 'since she's so busy she never has a moment to herself.'

There was something so self-satisfied and yet obsequious about this little speech that Fiona felt herself flush in embarrassment on his behalf.

'Oh, I see,' was all she said.

Iris threw her a look that seemed to say, don't laugh. Even if he deserves it.

'So we've *you* to blame for us digging out here in January.' Jack, following him out of the kitchen, fixed the back of his head with a mock glare and a raised fist that made Fiona suppress a giggle.

'Anyway, the timing couldn't have been more awkward,' said Iris, 'but I just couldn't say no. I mean, *look* at it.'

'Yeah,' said Fiona. 'It sounds a fantastic opportunity.'

But she was thinking that there was really no need for Iris to be here in person at all. Why hadn't she made Jack the site director? Hired more help?

Obviously Iris hadn't wanted to surrender control of the dig.

And there would be consequences to that, she realised. The rest of the diggers were working round the clock in horrendous weather and conditions, and they were a woman down a lot of the time. A woman who, as site director and senior archaeologist, would be claiming the lion's share of the glory and prestige such a dig would attract.

They must all be very fed up. Well, she suspected Callum was more loved up than fed up, judging from the puppy dog eyes he made at Iris, but what about the others?

In those kinds of circumstances, who knew what stress and exhaustion might do to them all?

And as for Madison – Fiona knew that nothing about this would have sat well with her.

Iris's shoulder was exposed again, and her tattoo on display, a roundel with stylized budding branches framing it, and within, a diagrammatic horse leaping out. It was at once beautiful and alien, a design constructed by ancient minds. It was so familiar, though – and this time, the answer came swiftly to Fiona – 'That's the Altai Ice Maiden tattoo, the one preserved on her skin through the permafrost.'

'Correct!' said Iris, beaming, clearly pleased to have it recognised. 'What do you think?' She flexed her shoulder cap outwards, the lamplight reflecting off its thick dark lines, her pale skin.

Fiona stood up, leaned in to examine it. 'That's very cool.'

'Jack wasn't so sure,' Iris said, cutting her eyes towards him mischievously. 'He has a problem with the cultural misappropriation of ancient body modifications.'

'I do not,' he said, twisting his own arm forward, with its inky sleeve of Celtic knotwork. Fiona watched the play of his smooth muscles, swallowed. Was it hot in here? 'I merely observed that it's not always wise to adopt a tattoo when you don't know what it means.' He raised his bottle to his lips.

'Why did you pick that one?' Fiona asked Iris, intrigued.

Iris regarded it for a long moment. 'I picked this tattoo,' she moved it again, peering down at it, as though enchanted, 'because there was something about the burial that spoke to me. A single woman, buried in her own mound high in the Altai, in a part of the world called the Second Layer of Heaven by the locals. She's a Scythian, and Scythian women were warrior women.' She stroked the skin with a dreamy, meditative air. 'I don't know what else to say. It just spoke to me.'

Fiona fell silent. That phrase, *warrior women*, chimed in her head. And it seemed to her that she was suddenly plunged into the deep waters of ancient memory, back to a time Madison had said *we must be the warrior women now* to her, in another life when we were young and students, years and years ago.

'Are you all right?' Jack asked.

Iris was looking at her with concern, her expression soft in the low lamplight. Fiona was aware of herself with red, filling eyes.

'Sorry, yes, I'm just very tired,' she said apologetically. 'It's a beautiful tattoo.' She cleared her throat, desperate to change the topic of conversation away from herself, to diffuse this upwelling of grief. 'Do you consider yourself a warrior woman, then?'

'Of course,' said Iris, and for a second Fiona wondered if she had managed to offend her. 'Aren't we all?'

* * *

Fiona emerged on to the steps of the house, sucking in the clear fresh air, so cold it hurt her throat.

The fields and their dusting of ice spread out before her.

She just needed a moment to get herself together. That memory of Madison – she should have drunk less, perhaps . . .

But what if she's out there somewhere, alone?

'Are you all right?'

She started, gasped, but it was only Iris, regarding her mildly from the doorframe.

'I'm fine,' said Fiona, offering her a weak smile. 'I just . . . I just needed some fresh air.' She looked out across the icy fields.

'Me too.' Iris leaned back against the wall. 'Though with the storm coming this week I think we'll all be getting all the fresh air we can handle.' She tutted. 'I'm supposed to be flying out again this week as well.'

'Again?'

Iris sighed. 'I know. But it was arranged weeks ago. I've got an interview segment for *Discovering* lined up with this Texan palaeontologist and he's only in the country for a few days.' She shook her head.

'That sounds . . .'

'I know what it sounds like. It all sounds like madness.' She shot Fiona a frank look. 'I know what the others think,' she said candidly. 'Becky in particular has the subtlety of a JCB. But there was no other way to do it. I'm contracted to do the work for *Discovering*, and with the winter storms the dig here wouldn't wait.'

Fiona rubbed her chin. 'You must be busy.'

'Oh yeah,' said Iris. She came forward, joined Fiona on the step. 'I'm that all right. You spend most of your career wishing for the chance to excavate a site like Helly Holm, and I lobbied for it straight away. And I got it, too. Fair and square.'

There was something both rehearsed and steely about this short speech, and Fiona knew better than to say anything.

'You know,' said Iris, 'I . . .' She looked at Fiona then, seemed about to speak. 'Never mind. Sorry. You have enough on your plate.'

'No, go on.'

'I . . . I wouldn't be getting half of this shit if I was a man,' said Iris with passion, her cheeks flushing delicately. 'I've worked on many, many digs, and the site director frequently was off site and nobody questioned it, because they assumed, nine times out of ten, that he was off doing important work elsewhere. When I do it, I'm constantly having to explain myself and my whereabouts to this endless silently disapproving jury.'

Fiona, realising there was more, waited.

'I think the filming thing doesn't help either, you know.' Iris raised her bottle to her lips, drank. 'You're there being pretty on television, to a lot of them. Nobody takes you seriously.'

'Oh no,' said Fiona. 'I'm sure they take you very seriously, Iris. It's certainly my impression of them all.'

She sighed. 'Thanks. Nothing about this is easy, so far.' She raised the bottle again. 'And Madison . . .' she paused, let this trail off. 'Madison is missing.'

'I know.'

'Will the police contact you if they find out anything more, do you think?' Iris glanced sideways at her.

Fiona shook her head. 'I think it's unlikely that they'll talk to *me* much. Now with her mother coming over. And Hugo.' She let this hang there. 'Anyway.'

'Oh, is this the brother? Madison mentioned him. They don't get on, do they?'

Fiona marvelled at this understatement. 'Not really.' She let her gaze fall to her feet, hoping the subject would be dropped. Even talking about Hugo made her feel uncomfortable.

The memory of that night in Cala Llombards was never far away.

'Yeah,' said Iris, contemplating the *Hamnavoe* in the darkness. 'Madison mentioned that he came over here.'

Fiona shot a look at her, a wash of cold drenching her that had nothing to do with the weather. 'What? To *Orkney*? When?'

'It was a couple of weeks ago,' said Iris, shrugging. 'Near the start of the dig. She wasn't thrilled at the prospect, if I remember . . .'

'No, she wouldn't have been.'

'I don't think they'd been in touch much . . .'

'No,' said Fiona. 'As far as I knew, the last time was at his mother's house on Majorca. There was, well, kind of an unpleasant episode. She hadn't spoken to him since.'

As far as you know, she thought to herself.

Iris raised an eyebrow, but Fiona was relieved to see she had no interest in prying.

Hugo, here on Orkney?

Yet another thing Madison hadn't told her about. But unlike the rest, this had the cold jab of treason. Had Madison invited him here? He was her brother, after all. Had she been making up to Hugo behind Fiona's back, after what had happened?

Girl, she thought to herself, *you should have called the police on him.*

'Ah, there you both are,' Jack appeared in the hallway. 'Everything all right?'

Fiona, mastering herself, nodded. Iris regarded her with a cool, steady gaze, her bright necklace winking in the porch light.

'I know you don't want to . . . you know, talk about Madison's business, Fiona, but can you think of any reason why she might have disappeared?'

'Other than Dom Tate being back on the scene?' Fiona shook her head. 'No. But you know,' she said, suddenly remembering, 'Douggie and Maggie thought she might have been seeing someone at the cottage.'

'Seeing someone? Really?' asked Iris, leaning forward and clearly fascinated. 'Did they know who?'

'No. But they came in unexpectedly to fix her wardrobe and found her with a guy there, and they mistook him for her boyfriend Caspar and . . .'

'Mistook him for her boyfriend?' asked Jack, his blond brows furrowing.

'Um, yeah, it was kind of embarrassing, they said . . .'

'That was me,' said Jack.

Fiona stopped, stunned. 'It was?'

'Yeah. I remember being there. She'd smacked her head against the wardrobe door in the night. I said I'd come over and see if it could be fixed. Of course, it couldn't be fixed – the glass was too big a piece and would need shipping in from the mainland – but I remember coming round, and the mix-up where Douggie and Maggie called me Caspar.'

'But . . . oh . . .' Fiona didn't know what to say. 'They seemed to think . . .'

Jack's blue eyes widened. He was alarmed, as though he had only just begun to understand the implications inherent in this conversation. He looked to Iris. 'I don't know why they would think that.'

Iris shrugged. 'It'd be none of *my* business either way.' That said, she had blushed as well, and Fiona doubted it was with pleasure. Her mouth was a thin, hard line.

Jack glowered at her. 'I'm not sure how happy I am that they're spreading stories like that around.'

Iris sighed, let her eyes close. 'Why? What's it to do with them, anyway?'

'Because she's gone *missing*,' he said. He was growing more and more angry, the knuckles of his muscular hand whitening around the bottle. 'And, most importantly of all, it's simply not true. Lots of people could end up hurt.' His face was ruddy. 'I've half a mind to say something to those two . . .'

'Please don't,' said Fiona, growing alarmed. 'I feel terrible. I'm quite sure they're not telling other people.'

'With all due respect, Fiona, you don't know that,' said Jack.

'I'm sure they meant no harm,' said Fiona, miserable now

that she had only been on the island two nights and had already embroiled herself in a fight over loose talk.

Almost as if he had read her mind, Jack smiled briefly at her. 'You know, I can see that it's worrying you, but I have no intention of coming at them all guns blazing. That said, I'm going to let them know the truth on that score. Just so we're all straight.'

'Of course,' said Fiona, though she still felt anxious, as though she was betraying somebody. 'Especially with her family arriving tomorrow.'

'Exactly,' said Jack, nodding vigorously.

'I better get off,' Fiona said, the chill starting to seep into her clothes, 'I'm sure you guys want to get to bed.'

'You too,' said Jack. 'It must have been a long day. Becks,' he called back into the house, 'are you ready to take Fiona here back?'

'I was ready ten minutes ago,' said Becky coldly.

'It's all right,' said Fiona, dreading getting into the van with her again. 'I can always get a taxi . . .'

'Don't be silly,' said Iris. 'Becky can take you. It's not that far. And we *did* offer.'

There was something very precise and definite about this speech, and though Iris didn't look around, Fiona had the sense that it was being made to Becky rather than herself.

In any event, Becky appeared, sighing. 'Come on then. Let's go.'

'Uh, thank you,' said Fiona to them all. 'It was lovely to get out.'

'You're very welcome,' said Jack. 'And keep us posted. Good luck tomorrow with Madison's family.'

Iris smiled at her. 'Honestly, Fiona, I'm convinced it'll turn out to be all right,' and to Fiona's surprise she gave her a brief, tight hug. 'But keep us in the loop, okay?'

'Yeah, of course. And thanks again.' Fiona picked up her coat off the hook near the door, and then saw, next to it, a flash of dark grey fur, something she recognised.

'Is this Madison's hat?' she asked Iris, lifting it off the peg.

Iris turned to peer at it, shrugged. 'You know, I think it is. Madison was always leaving things here.'

Fiona turned it over in her hands. Yes, it was Madison's trapper hat, all right, with its waxed grey crown and faux-fur lined earflaps. It had always made Madison look like an adorable wolf, and Fiona had often teased her about it.

She sniffed it, and the vaguest whisper of the scent of Madison's hair came out of it. Something squeezed hard within her chest.

'Can I borrow this?'

'Of course,' said Iris gently. 'If you want.'

19

Grangeholm, Orkney, January 2020

Fiona woke in the middle of the night, curled up in her bed in Langmire.

She was groggy, disoriented and slightly hungover as the wind thudded into the windows. She had no idea what time it was, or what had woken her – she had only the sense that she'd heard something that somehow didn't belong.

She lay motionless, listening to the tiny scratch of her eyelashes against the cotton of her pillow, to the murmur of the window glass juddering gently in its frames, to the distant cry of guillemots out over the sea. On the little bedside table, her phone, upright on its charging stand, read 3:17 a.m.

Seconds ticked on into minutes, became 3:19, 3:23, but whatever had woken her was not repeated.

She must have dreamt it, she realised. Perhaps it wasn't that surprising, with all that had gone on.

Her eyes fluttered shut once more.

And then it happened. It was the most minute non-sound, a sigh of held, controlled breath, and then, next to it, the mere shadow of a footfall.

It was coming from outside her bedroom door.

Fiona absolutely froze, even her lungs stilling, leaving her alone with nothing but the hidden, racing beat of her own heart.

A few seconds more, and then another footstep, and this time there was no doubting what it was, stealthy though it had been – the floor creaked beneath it.

An unbearable panic and terror washed over her, thick and cold, drenching her in icy sweat. She could no longer even think clearly. She lay as still as the dead, waiting for the bedroom door to open, for this interloper to walk in to her room, for . . .

No. This would not do. She couldn't be discovered here like this, supine and helpless. She had to get up.

She had to get up.

Slowly, so slowly, she slid out from beneath the duvet, bare inches at a time, even the tiny sounds of her skin scraping against the linen filling her with fear. She had no plan, except, perhaps, to steal along the bedroom floor, plant her back against the door, and . . .

She glanced at her phone.

Yes. Call the police.

Her hand closed around it as, trembling, she rose to her feet.

And suddenly the whole room was bathed in white light, with an accompanying motorised roar.

Somehow, she managed not to scream. In fact, she could not have screamed, her throat closing shut, her body growing stiff.

Outside the bedroom window a car had growled awake, and the white lights, she realised, were its headlights, piercing the gaps in the curtains. They were on full beam and she was dazzled then, raising her hand to shield her eyes as the car roared again, groaning as it was thrust into reverse, and then peeling away and vanishing into the night, with a high squealing that moved away with immense speed.

It came into her head, suddenly, almost nonsensically, that whoever it was had perhaps been as startled as she was.

Despite this, and the heavy, empty quiet that descended once more over the house, it took her at least five minutes before she even dared to move towards the bedroom door, the phone still gripped in her hand. She was too frightened to raise it to her face, to even speak into it.

Out in the hall, in the living room, all was exactly as she had left it, bathed in gentle moonlight. Her handbag still sat on the couch, undisturbed. The empty coffee mug lay where she had left it on the table.

There was no sign of any intruder.

The door. Try the door. If that door is . . .

The front door was locked. Locked exactly as it had been when she'd checked it when she came in, surly Becky already gunning the van away, ignoring her called out goodbye.

She tried the handle, flexing it up and down, but it was impervious, resolutely sealed.

Had it been the van outside, just now? Was that what had woken her? Could the archaeologists, or Becky, have come back for some unknown reason at three in the morning? No, no, she didn't think so. It had sounded like a car as it drove away. A small car. So it wouldn't have been the Fletts, either – Douggie had a truck.

She searched the house, slowly, shaking still, but growing in confidence that whoever it was had now gone. All was in order. Picture frames glinted and the sofas were a soft grey in the moon's light, innocuous, waiting for her as she flicked on the light. She paused at the big picture window upstairs, looking out over the drive to the sea, the wood flooring warm beneath her feet, and felt her heartbeat returning to normal.

Out on Helly Holm, the lighthouse flared and went out, flared and went out.

She'd checked all the windows. Everything was locked.

Her phone was still in her hand, her fingers curled tightly around it, the knuckles white.

Now it was time to call the police, to tell them . . .

To tell them what?

She couldn't, she realised, swear that someone had been in the house. Yes, she'd thought she'd heard a footstep, a breath, and there had definitely been a car here, a car with no business at this address, but what if she had imagined the sounds coming from inside? After all, the wind was buffeting the front of the house, a feisty fore-taster of the gales the archaeologists were expecting on Tuesday. Of course the house would shift and creak. Tiny draughts moved through the most secure windows.

She'd been woken, perhaps, by the car noise. Yes, that made sense. There was no traffic out here, so any car would have been loud, have disturbed her sleep.

But what had they wanted?

A tiny hope flared up in her then.

Could it have been Madison?

But that was impossible. Why would Madison be skulking around the cottage and not tell Fiona?

She peered through the window: the drive was dark, the road a pale silver. No cars moved along it now.

Perhaps it was someone that was looking for Madison?

And as it occurred to her, she realised the absolute truth of it. They had been looking for *Madison*. Perhaps whoever it was had realised that this wasn't Mads' car in the driveway.

Perhaps they had peered in through the curtains, she thought with a slippery nausea, and seen her asleep in Madison's bed.

Was it the mysterious boyfriend? No, no, it couldn't be, because Jack had told her that was him. That had been a misunderstanding, a mistake.

She paused, staring still into the darkness.

Or so he had said. She should not be too quick to trust any of them, she realised. But it didn't explain why Jack would be driving out here in the middle of the night. He already *knew* Madison was not here.

Her fingers tightened on the phone, so tightly they hurt.

It could only be, it *must* be, Dominic Tate.

He wouldn't be shy about coming after Madison. About coming after *her*.

After all, he'd done it before.

20

Saxon Street, Cambridge, March 2019

The first thing that struck Fiona as she opened the door, her black sack of rubbish in hand, was how mild the night was.

It had been a beautiful day, and the low murmur coming from the people sitting outside the pub opposite was full of laughter, a barely restrained joy. Spring had come at last, and it seemed all of Cambridge had caught the scent of it.

She felt a little tug of sadness as she stood in the narrow lane that was Saxon Street – here it was, this gorgeous evening, and she was alone, buried in work, confined to barracks. Perhaps Madison was right. She should get that dating app she'd been thinking about for months.

After all, she thought, stepping out on to the cobbles, gazing up at the moon as she let the door swing shut behind her, lots of people met through apps nowadays. She didn't need to feel as though it made her a failure. Lots of people found it hard to connect in real life, not just her, and . . .

A lone cyclist let out a sudden yell and ring of his bell as he raced up the tiny cobbled lane at dazzling speed, heading against the one-way direction, and she shouted in surprise as he shot across in front of her.

'Look where you're going!' he snarled out behind him.

She bridled. 'You look where *you're* going – idiot!'

He threw back an obscene gesture, and she glared after him as he vanished into the gloaming.

'Twat,' she muttered, aware of herself breathing hard at the near miss. She hoisted the black bag higher.

The bins were in the central courtyard where the cars were parked, and as she pushed open the red gate on its swing mechanism and its strident signs saying PRIVATE, she became aware of something wet brushing against her bare calf below her pink capri pants.

The bag was leaking – it was over-full and dripping some dark stinking liquid on to her skin, on to her newish white tennis shoe.

'Oh, for fuck's . . . argh!' She could never keep anything nice for longer than ten minutes, she thought, crossing quickly through the narrow pathway in the dark. She needed to throw this in now before it split any further and she was left with a pile of festering muck on the paving stones.

Typical. And she had so much to do. Just *typical*.

The bins were full – it seemed the entire estate had had the same idea, all hours before she had – and then there was the disgusting work of swinging up the sticky lid of the skip from where it rested on the pile, before she could toss the ruptured bag on top.

The lid banged down on to its burden, closing like jaws. Rubbing her grubby hands together she turned to head back to her flat; to her half-drunk coffee and the article on Aztec goldwork she was in the process of reviewing for *World Archaeology*.

She froze.

Standing in front of her, not five feet away, was Dominic Tate.

He wore a pale T-shirt and tight skinny jeans that belonged on a younger man. In the weak streetlighting his face was shadowed, saturnine, and a faint gleam of sweat dewed his clenched forehead, his thin moustache.

She had not seen him since the court case a week ago, when

he'd been standing in the dock in his charcoal suit, glaring at her as she sat in the public gallery.

'Hello, Fiona.'

His voice was tight, neutral.

A flush of cold panic came over her.

'What are you doing here?' she asked, hearing the fear in her voice and hating it.

'I'm not here for you.' He gestured away, as though she was of no account. At least his hands were empty. He was trying to stay even, dispassionate, but he couldn't quite control the edge of his rage, his contempt for her. 'I just need you to pass a message on to Madison.'

She stood absolutely still, considering him. What she wanted, more than anything, was to tell him where to shove his message. To point out to him that she was not his courier and that after a mere six days he was already breaching his restraining order – was he insane?

But what she also felt, with knife-keen alarm, was that if he was capable of such brazenness he was also capable of more. She was a woman alone in the darkness with someone that had threatened to throw acid into her best friend's face and had knifed her car. His crazy rage, his desire, was stronger than his fear of consequences, his fear of prison.

She trifled with him at her peril.

She swallowed, her throat dry, aware that he could sense her terror.

'You need to tell her to stop this,' he said. Despite his tight, controlled words, he was breathing hard. His chest rose and fell beneath his thin shirt. 'To stop being so fucking stupid.' He licked his lips briefly with a pale tongue. 'We need to talk.'

'I can't do that,' said Fiona, her heart pounding. 'It's out of everyone's hands.' She resisted the temptation to step back from him, though she was shaking. 'There's a restraining order now. You can't talk to her. I can't take messages to her. You're not supposed to contact her, either "directly or indirectly".' She swallowed again, glancing around, hoping against hope someone would pass by. 'You need to *leave her alone*, Dom.'

His glare was suddenly hot, murderous. 'Don't tell me what to do. You're fucking loving this, ain't you, you interfering cow?'

'Dom . . .' Her throat was so dry she could barely get the word out.

'You're so jealous of her. I can practically *smell* it on you.' He was advancing on her, and the upraised finger he was pointing at her trembled. 'It's *you* that's done all this, isn't it? You've broke us up. You must be so fucking proud of yourself, you smug little bitch . . .'

'Excuse me,' shot out a nearby voice. 'Is everything all right here?'

Their heads whipped around. A tall man in a white shirt and crisp trousers stood under the streetlight. Near his feet a French bulldog sniffed the ground, her stub of a tail half-wagging, oblivious to the human drama unfolding in front of her.

He looked vaguely familiar, a neighbour. His eyes glinted with suspicion. Neither of them had heard him approach. He looked at Dom but spoke to Fiona. 'Everything okay?'

There was a pause, a mere breath, and in it Fiona understood how furious this interruption, this potential witness, made Dominic Tate. For a flickering second she saw his desire to lash out, to challenge the newcomer, but again that stymied cowardice was winning over.

Instead he snarled at Fiona. 'This isn't over, *cunt*.'

'I think you'd better leave,' the man with the dog said in a cold, still voice. 'Before I call the police.'

'Oh, fuck off,' snapped Dominic Tate, but he was already backing away. 'This is nothing to do with you.'

By way of reply, the man reached into his trouser pocket, drew out a phone.

'Call the fucking police then,' snarled Dom. 'See if I care.' But he must have cared on some level, Fiona realised, as his retreat was growing hastier. He was already halfway across the carpark lot from them, his face in shadow.

She stood rigid, breathless in the face of his hatred, watching until he had vanished under the budding trees with a final malicious leer.

Suddenly there was a cool, wet flash at her ankle and she jumped, startled.

The bulldog had edged forward, tentatively licked at the sticky dark stain on her capri pants.

'Jemima! Stop it! Sorry. She's got no manners. Are you all right?'

'I . . . yes . . . I'm fine, thanks . . .' Again that light-headed feeling, as though she was going to faint. 'I just need to get back inside . . .'

'Are you sure? Who was that?' asked the man. His voice held a mixture of concern but also a kind of judgemental and wary distance – she appeared to him, she realised, to be the sort of woman that strange men screamed 'cunt' at in public, someone with questionable relationships and perhaps guilty of dire choices. 'A bitter ex?'

She felt stung, suddenly. 'Absolutely not,' she shot back.

He recoiled. She'd offended him, she realised.

'I'm sorry,' she said, trying to get her feelings back under control. 'He's my friend's ex. She's got a restraining order against him. He wanted me to pass a message on to her – sorry, I'm in bits. I thought that would be the end of him . . .'

'Do you need me to call someone?' he asked, but there was a

pronounced drawing back in him, as though, in being not wholly grateful and distraught, she had let him down in some indefinable way.

'No, thank you. I'll be fine. Once I'm in the house . . .' She glanced down at her hand, saw it was shaking. 'I'll be fine. I only live on Saxon Street . . .'

'All the same,' he said, the French bulldog fighting against him to reach Fiona's pants cuff. 'I'll walk you to your door.' His gaze flickered over the car park. 'It looks like he's gone for now. But you never know.'

* * *

'He did what?' asked Madison, the phone line crackling with her outrage. 'What was he playing at?'

Fiona sat hunched on her faded, oversoft purple sofa. The article she'd been reviewing flickered on her laptop, forgotten. 'He wanted me to give you a message.'

'What message?'

'Oh, does it matter?' said Fiona, weary now of the whole affair. She was sick to death of Dominic Tate, she realised, of discussing and thinking about him, and had been for months. '"She needs to stop this, we need to talk." You know. The whole "I'm the victim here" shtick.'

'I'll talk to him, all right,' sizzled Madison. 'But I don't think he'd like what I had to say . . .'

'No, you won't!' snapped Fiona, alarmed. 'You won't talk to him at all! There's a restraining order, Mads, remember?'

'Well, he clearly didn't get the email,' said Madison, 'so what are we supposed to do, then?'

'We don't call him. He's breached his restraining order, so we call the police.' She flopped back on the couch, passed her hand over her face. 'They take it from here.'

There was a pause.

'Oh,' said Madison eventually.

Fiona felt a prickle of foreboding tickling the back of her neck, a presage of things to come. 'What do you mean, *Oh*?'

There was a sigh, the quick burble of a vaper. 'Listen, Fee, I know he scared you . . .'

'And?' asked Fiona, her voice hardening.

'And I know he's an appalling dickhead and all, but listen, do you really want to get into all that again?'

'But . . .'

'Fee, listen to me . . . wait, don't get angry. I'm not talking down or minimising what happened to you tonight, honest. But just listen. Say we do that, right? We go to the police. We dob him in and we can actually prove it and there's a hearing and they send him off at Her Maj's pleasure for six months . . . I mean, is it worth it? Really? He'd be out in four months with good behaviour.'

'Mads . . .' she began, boiling.

'No, you're not listening to me. You're angry 'cos he scared you and you think I'm taking his side. He's already furious, because that's the kind of entitled arsehole he is. How much more furious is he going to be if he gets sent to prison just for trying to send a message?'

Fiona could feel herself bridling. 'He's not going to prison because he tried to pass on a message, Mads. He'd be going to prison because the courts have told him to leave you alone, and he still can't control himself. He's got no self-restraint, and he's going to hurt someone someday . . .'

'Yeah, yeah, I know all that.' Again the bubbling of her vaper. 'I do, honest, I do. I am merely suggesting that we, you know, pick our battles here.'

Fiona was stunned. 'What are you on about?'

'If he'd threatened you, I'd say yeah, definitely we should get the cops involved, but the fact is he was just doing what Dom does when he's not getting his own way.' Madison had shifted away from the phone, must have been reaching for something nearby. 'And that involves throwing his toys out his pram and being a prick.'

'So what do you think we should do?' said Fiona, amazed. 'Just let it go?'

'Yeah,' Madison said. 'I'm suggesting *exactly* that – we let him have this one for free. Let's assume he didn't understand the real lie of the land, that he's not supposed to be getting to me through you. Just this once.'

'How could he not understand?' Fiona could feel her temper rising again. 'The judge, the police, the probation service, his solicitor – they would have all told him what would happen . . .'

'He didn't understand because he doesn't ever listen to things he's not interested in hearing,' said Madison with weary frankness. 'But there was a witness tonight, and he's getting no joy from you, so I don't think you'll see him again, Fee. I just don't.'

'And what if he comes back again?' demanded Fiona.

'We call the police.'

'Or he slashes *my* tyres . . .'

'Of course, we'll call the police.'

'Or he starts hanging around at my work, or . . .'

'If you catch so much as a glimpse of him, anywhere,' said Madison, with a grandiose calm, 'we'll call the police and tell them everything that's happened. I promise. But I just think going after him over this could backfire. For both of us.'

And Fiona felt it then, the real reason for Madison's seeming indifference. She was frightened – frightened of the consequences for her if Fiona pursued things further.

You picked him, Fiona thought bitterly.

All the same, she understood. Madison wanted to downplay

all this, because she had always maintained that eventually it would go away. The fact was, Fiona knew, that if it went away or not, it would be because something changed for Dominic Tate, and not anything that she or Madison did.

She could, however, see the appeal of Mads' plan.

'All right,' she said. 'One freebie. But only one.'

Sunday

21

Kirkwall Airport, Orkney, January 2020

Kirkwall's airport was a tiny building surrounded on three sides by low, flattish hills, and on the fourth there was a smudgy blue expanse of water that could have been either lake or sea. The terminal itself was warm, and dominated by a surprisingly lively café which was offering a special of 'cheese and mince baked tattie'.

Fiona, who had not slept a wink since the incident with the car in the middle of the night, was sorely tempted by this paean to carbohydrates and grease. Instead she restricted herself to a single latte and settled in one of the seats facing the large windows. From here she would see Judy's plane arriving.

She rang Adi on video chat.

'How are you feeling today? Better?'

She'd phoned him last night, waking him up in his hotel bed in Zurich at four in the morning. She'd blurted everything out to him before breaking down into large, sucking sobs that he'd been powerless to calm.

She was tired of being frightened, of not knowing, of being lost. So very tired of it.

But she felt a little surer now. She pressed her right headphone closer into her ear.

'I'm . . . I'm okay,' she said. 'I'm sorry I was so hysterical last night.'

'Don't say that,' he said quickly, almost irritably, his dark brow creasing. 'You don't have to be sorry. It's okay to be scared sometimes. If I'd been there, I'd have freaked the fuck out.'

Fiona giggled despite herself at the thought of meticulous, calm Adi 'freaking the fuck out'. She found such a thing hard to imagine.

'Yeah, yeah,' he scowled. 'Laugh away. Mock my lack of exceptional SAS butchness, why don't you? But I'm glad you seem better. I was worried about you. Where will you stay tonight?'

She paused, hearing the hesitancy in her own voice, hating it. 'I was going to stay at the cottage again.'

'What? No! Are you kidding? I thought you were going to go to a hotel?'

'I know,' she said, bracing herself for his objections. 'I said that. But I was thinking about it some more. I think I imagined a lot of it – I mean, the noises inside the house. And the door was locked anyway, so no one could have . . .'

'What? What does that mean?' he asked, his voice growing louder. 'Whoever it was could have had a key. It's a holiday home, isn't it?'

Fiona tried to rally her resistance. 'I know, but . . .'

'And the people who own it – you say they seem nice but you don't know them, Fiona, not really. Madison went missing from that house, remember. Think about that. They didn't like her and poof, she's vanished.'

She glanced around uneasily, wondering if people who knew the Fletts might be listening to this, realised that they wouldn't be able to hear him.

'I don't think they disliked her *that* much,' she countered. 'And it was only the wife . . .'

'I have *never* approved of the idea of you staying there. Not once. Who offers you their house for free the first day they meet you? Just get a hotel room.'

'Well, Adi, it's just that . . .'

'Is it the money?' he barked, and she felt her first flicker of shame, of irritation. ''Cos if it's the money, I'll pay. I'll book you a place right now, on my card. I don't want you . . .'

'No,' said Fiona, with sudden force, so loudly that people nearby turned to look at her, startled. 'Sorry, but . . . no. I *want* to stay there.'

Adi had fallen silent, shocked. She never raised her voice to him, and she felt embarrassed now, mortified.

'But why?' he asked after a long moment.

'Because what if Madison comes back there?' Fiona swallowed, her mouth dry. 'What if she comes back and there's nobody home? She could be in trouble. She could be scared, or hurt, or she might . . . she m-might . . .'

Adi sighed out, finally understanding. 'Ah. I get it.'

'You see?' she asked, aware of her sinuses flooding, her eyes watering. 'I have to be there. I have to . . .'

'Fee,' he said softly.

'I have to . . .'

'No, you don't. Listen. You really don't. I know this is hard on you. I wish I could be there for you, I really do. But you don't need to be in that house. She knows how to get in touch with you if she wants to. Just like the police.'

'But I'm just so . . . I'm just *sat* here, doing nothing . . .' She swiped at her wet eyes with her hands.

'Listen – how much good can you do her if something happens to you right now? Clearly Madison was scared. She *left*. Maybe,' he said, trying to keep his voice even, calm, 'you should follow her lead.'

Fiona fell silent. She had not considered this.

He glanced over the top of his phone, frowned again. 'I have to go,' he said, low and reluctant. 'The car's just pulled up outside.'

'What are you up to?' she asked, swallowing down her tears, trying to pull herself together.

'Oh, this stupid tour of Zurich,' he shrugged dismissively. 'Some hospitality thing. We're taking the client round the city for the day.'

'It sounds nice to me,' she said with a weak smile, trying to move the conversation back into less heated channels. 'Y'know. Zurich.'

He made a little hmph noise. 'Maybe it would be, if it was you and me doing it. But they're . . . they're so horrendous. Just a bunch of shouty spoiled toffs. Their lead negotiating guy has already started dropping heavy hints about ending up at some strip club tonight. But the business they're bringing – it's gonna be huge. So . . .' he trailed off. 'Well. You know.'

She should say something now, she realised in a lightning flash, perhaps along the lines of looking but not touching at this strip club, of not getting any ideas, but somehow the words stuck in her throat. They felt presumptuous, clichéd, vulgar.

And with that phrase *look but don't touch*, suddenly Jack Bergmann was in the forefront of her mind again, with his easy kindness and rolling biceps.

She blinked his face away. What was the matter with her?

'I guess you'll be unavailable for a while then,' she said to Adi, trying to muster a smile.

He didn't return it, and she realised that yes, she should have said what she planned to say. It had been another opportunity to cement their intimacy, one that she'd once again spurned. Neither of them ever committed, in word or in action. They skirted around each other, as skittish as teenagers, shooting jokes at one another, each waiting for the other to break first.

Completely pointless.

And yet . . .

'You can still text me, though – if anything comes up.' He

ran his hand through his velvety dark hair, before remembering to pat his neat hairdo smooth again. 'You know, if I have to, I *can* escape the Personality Vacuum. Don't let that stop you, seriously.'

She laughed then, and he did too, and for the first time that day, she felt almost normal, almost okay. Then there was a sudden rapping on wood, and he turned, startled.

'Gotta go, Fee. That's Andreas.'

'I know, I know,' she said, trying to keep smiling, at least until the call finished. 'Have fun.'

'I'll try. Look,' and he was urgent now. 'Promise me you won't stay at that cottage. Please.'

She scrunched up the napkin the latte had come with and wiped her nose with it. 'Okay,' she said. 'I'll find a hotel.'

'I'll call you tonight.'

'Yeah.'

A long pause, pregnant now with the words neither of them said.

'Bye.'

And then he was gone.

* * *

In front of her, between the two big viewing windows, the world's troubles were being blasted across the waiting area on a television – BBC news.

There was already a tiny propeller plane on the forecourt, with *Loganair* painted near its nose. From the departure board it looked as if it was heading to North Ronaldsay, and she marvelled for a moment at the idea of such a fragile thing with its feathery blades crossing those stormy seas, even if the journey was only minutes long.

'And now the weather,' said a man on the television, as though reading her thoughts. 'Deep snowstorms throughout most parts of Great Britain and Ireland, with plummeting temperatures and rising winds in Scotland and the North which are destined to get worse after the weekend. The RAC are reporting record numbers of callouts . . .'

The ghost of a thought occurred to her then, of Madison trapped somewhere in her rental car on these bleak isles, broken down perhaps, injured in a ditch somewhere, freezing to death, the petrol running her car heater having long since run out.

And she was sitting here in the warm, doing nothing . . .

She shook her head free. *Don't do this. Though they appear huge and empty, these islands are really quite small. Someone would have seen her by now if that was the case.*

You did what you were supposed to.

But still . . .

She typed in yet another text, to join the dozens she had already sent since Mads had gone missing.

I know you probably can't read this or reply to it, but if you can, please please do, Mads. I'm at the airport in Kirkwall waiting for your mum and Hugo. We're so frightened for you. Please put us out of our misery. And if you can't, then know we're looking for you. Love always, Fee XXXXX

P.S. I have commandeered your wolfy hat so if you want it back please get in touch.

None of these texts had been answered, but still, she sat with the phone loosely in her hand, as though Madison would respond instantly, the way she usually did.

The little lounge was starting to fill up – old men with white fisherman's beards, harried mums and excited children, the latter running across the concourse and looking like little starfish in their mittens and thick winter coats.

Quickly she drained her coffee, put her untouched paperback back into her bag, some crime novel – it had seemed so appealing when she bought it, but now its dark content felt too close to home. Outside, orange windsocks streamed out in the lively breeze.

The plane was arriving, right on time – a proper-sized plane this time, and after what could only be a few minutes of delay, the crushed, dishevelled passengers were emerging into the freezing wind, fastening their coats, cramming down hats and wrapping scarves around their throats. Judy would be amongst the last off, Fiona expected – or would she be the first, being in a wheelchair?

And Hugo would be with her. The thought was enough to push her anxiety almost into nausea.

Well, it made no difference. She would be civil.

Act like nothing had happened.

Be careful not to be alone with him.

She stood up, wandered up to the glass, pretending to herself that she was controlling her impatience, despite the fact her teeth were sunk into her bottom lip.

The first arrivals were reaching the glass doors, emerging on to the small concourse, some hobbling through with grim determination, others being caught up in kisses and bear hugs. Fiona could feel it all around her, this static of noise and interaction, a human sea surrounding her while she stood there, her own island of dread and loneliness.

She needed to perk up. It wouldn't do to look as worried as she felt in front of Judy.

Oh God. Please God. Don't let Hugo be with her.

The stream of passengers was dwindling away now, a few stragglers hurrying to the glass doors, the wind licking their scarf ends and free hair into swirling shapes, battening the padded material of their jackets.

She schooled her expression into something neutral, something serious but not grave, and waited.

And waited.

Fiona knew it would take a little while to get Judy and her wheelchair off the plane, so she wasn't alarmed, not really, even when the loudspeaker began to announce the flight back to Glasgow, or at least until she saw the small flurry of departing passengers crossing quickly across the tarmac through the doors, heading for the plane.

A small, sick feeling shot through her.

'Excuse me,' she asked the cheerful-faced woman in a blue shirt sitting at the information desk. 'I'm waiting for a passenger. Judy Kowalczyk. She was supposed to be on flight LM434 . . .'

'Aye? From Glasgow?'

'Yeah, that's the one . . .'

'Well, that plane's boarding again now. Are you sure you didn't miss one another?'

'No, we wouldn't have done. She would have been in a wheelchair.'

'She can't be on the plane. Are you quite sure you didn't miss her?'

'I . . .' Fiona's head twisted this way and that. Could she have missed her? It would merely have been another impossible thing after all, in a hail of impossible things. 'I don't see how. Can you tell me if she was on board? Her name is Judy Kowa . . .'

'I'm sorry, love, I can't tell you about the passenger list. Data protection. Perhaps she was late for her flight.'

'But – but she texted me from Majorca. From the airport . . .'

The woman's eyes were calm, sympathetic, but there would be no budging. 'I don't know what to tell you. Has she got a mobile? Try texting her.'

Of course. Text her. Fiona was already pulling her phone out.

'If she's missed this flight . . . ?' she asked.

The woman anticipated her, smiling, clearly glad reason was winning out over panic. 'The next flight in from Glasgow is at seven-fifteen tonight. If she's not on that, it will be tomorrow.'

Fiona thanked the woman, her fingers quickly working the screen, still peering at the boarding passengers, the plane, the concourse, as if Judy had somehow sneaked out past her vigilance, perhaps by hiding in one of the luggage trolleys.

She hit Send and waited.

She didn't even put the phone away, carrying it as she drifted through the airport, checking the toilets, emerging into the car park at the front, her nerveless, gloveless fingers clasping it, waiting for that telltale vibration, for Judy to explain what was happening.

But she didn't.

An hour later, when Fiona finally climbed into her freezing car alone and defeated, the northern clouds were falling over all like a fire blanket, and there had still been no reply.

* * *

'Her mum didn't show up.'

Fiona could hear that thin, tiny tremor in her voice, as though Judy was her own mother and had abandoned her.

Jack sighed down the line. He'd picked up Iris's phone – she was in the shower, he said. Fiona could hear a television going in the background, and Becky, her voice raised, demanding to know who had not switched the dishwasher on.

It had felt an imposition to call, especially this day, Sunday, the archaeologists' day off.

But she simply couldn't do this alone, she realised.

'Bloody hell, Fiona, you're getting no joy lately, are you?' he observed.

'Not really, no.'

'But I think you'll find this is something trivial. She likely missed her plane. She'll be on the next. She won't be able to contact you if she's in the air.'

'That's just the point, Jack – she won't be in the air yet. Her flight from Glasgow won't take off till this evening.'

'Do you know what plane she was supposed to catch from Majorca?'

'No. And she's still not texted me back, or answered the phone . . .'

She'd left Adi a text and there had been no reply, though she was not expecting one. He was probably being ushered around the Fraumünster even as they spoke.

Or not. It was as though there had been some apocalypse beyond Orkney's southern shores, and the world beyond had vanished. She imagined London empty and silent, the buses inert and abandoned, only the pigeons still going about their business. She imagined Judy's flat in Majorca, her pet parrots trapped in their cage, waiting for someone to feed them, someone who would never come . . .

She thought she was going to scream.

Somehow it seemed as though Jack sensed this down the phone. 'Where are you?'

'I'm at the hotel. The Lynnewood. I . . . I didn't know where else to go. I thought, you know, perhaps I missed her and she caught a taxi here from the airport, and . . .'

Her storm of tears caught her off-guard, sudden and sheet-thick.

'Okay, I'm going to come and get you,' he said.

'You don't need to do that . . .' She was embarrassed suddenly. Here she was, a senior lecturer at a prestigious university, a putative grown-up, weeping down the phone to virtual strangers. She was aware of herself as unhinged and needy, a growing burden.

'Of course I do. This is our problem too, remember?'

'I . . .'

'I'll be right there, okay? Don't go anywhere.'

* * *

Jack was sitting out in the car park in the dig's van, just switching the engine off, when she walked over to join him. He was back in his fleeced hoodie, his chin freshly shaved but his blond head stubble giving him a dishevelled look. It was about two o'clock in the afternoon. The sun was low, as it always seemed to be this far north, and cast an elongated version of him as he jumped out to meet her, his shadow reaching her long before he did.

'Don't tell me you've been waiting out here all this time, Sword Lady.' He reached down, gently squeezed her in greeting. 'You must be freezing.'

'No. I saw you pull in from inside. I just . . . I wanted to get out of the hotel.' She took a deep breath. 'Sorry about the drama on the phone earlier.'

He waved that away. 'Did you hear from Madison's mum yet?'

'No.'

'I'm sure you will.'

Fiona wanted to believe this. 'I hope so. Bloody hell, it's almost exactly what happened with Madison. I feel like I'm losing my mind.'

'It's always in the last place you look.' He grinned at her, as though selling his weak joke through sheer force of personality, and she found herself bursting into nervous laughter.

'I guess.'

'Come on. There's no need to panic yet. When's the next flight?'

'Seven-fifteen.'

'So we've time to kill.' He folded his arms. 'Do you want to see something very cool?'

'Oh, I couldn't possibly use up your day off . . .'

'Don't be ridiculous,' he said. 'Do you want to see something cool or not?'

* * *

She let her bag fall on to the seat first, then climbed up towards it. Jack was already starting the van, and she felt the breath of the heater, still warm. She flexed her cold fingers against the grilles, letting the hot air rush past them.

She was starting to calm down. It was a simple travel snafu. Nothing that required this level of histrionics.

'You need proper gloves,' observed Jack, startling her out of these thoughts.

She glanced down at her thin green fashion gloves. 'I need proper everything. I managed to buy boots in Kirkwall, at least. I was not really prepped for this trip, to be honest.' She offered him a sad smile. 'Is it obvious?'

'And yet you came,' he said. He regarded her thoughtfully. 'And at short notice. I suppose I'm wondering why.'

'Well, I . . .'

Why had she come? She'd come because Dom was back on the scene, and because Madison was in trouble, obviously.

And she would have said as much, but she had a sudden burst of memory then, or rather something re-remembered; a bright flash, almost as though she was watching a film. She was lying in her bath in her little flat on Saxon Street, and Madison was on the phone, and she was saying . . .

'She said there was something she needed to show me.'

As Fiona said the words out loud, she felt for the first time their real significance.

'Show you?' Jack's brow furrowed impressively.

'Yep,' she said, filled with a kind of vague wonder. Why was she remembering this now? 'That's exactly what she said.'

Of course, she had mentally scrutinised every conversation she had had with Mads since her disappearance, searching for some clue, some snippet that could help. How had she forgotten this?

You didn't forget what Mads said. You just thought it didn't matter. You thought that she was just covering for her fear, for her anxiousness that Dom was on her trail again.

She turned to Jack, who was peering over the wheel, trying to see around a blocky sandstone building into the street beyond to make a turning.

'Do you have any idea what she meant?' Fiona asked.

'No.' He rubbed his chin with his hand. 'But surely she meant the dig.' He gave her a roguish wink. 'Let's see if we can persuade Iris to let you have a little poke around the finds tomorrow.'

22

Cala Llombards, Majorca, July 2019

'I hate him,' Madison told Fiona, while they lazed on the beach together near Judy's house. Madison was leaning up on her elbow, her sunglasses pulled down low. 'I fucking hate him.'

They had arranged this holiday a few months ago, during an icy English winter while they rubbed their hands ruefully in the front room of Madison's flat and fantasised about escape – they would spend a couple of nights with Judy on Majorca, then travel on to Ibiza on spec and do some clubbing.

But somehow, the 'couple of nights' here had become the whole week, and Ibiza dropped out of the picture. Still, Fiona was happy enough – money was short for both of them at the moment, and Judy's villa was gorgeous, beautifully situated on top of the cliffs overlooking the white sands of Cala Llombards, and her guest room window was a pure piece of plate glass, giving fantastic views of the sea.

That was before they discovered Madison's brother and his wife would be here too.

Fiona, lying on her back on her red beach towel, opened her eyes, blinked at Madison.

'Are you talking about Hugo?'

'Who do you think I mean?' she huffed. Her skin gleamed with sunscreen. 'The fucking twat.'

'What's he done now?' Fiona asked.

Madison didn't reply immediately, merely shaking her head. 'He . . . well,' she said, her voice crisp, 'I think he's "borrowing" money off her.' Madison waggled angry little quotation marks with her fingers.

'Off who?' asked Fiona.

'Mum.' Madison threw down her sunglasses on to her towel, as though they disgusted her.

'Is he? But I thought his business was doing so well . . .'

'Told you that, did he?' Madison didn't look at her.

'He's always dressed in the best, got the newest car . . .' Fiona ventured. 'Always off skiing with Tara . . .'

'Yeah,' said Madison with real bitterness. 'He's got looking the part of the successful financial advisor right. That's down pat. What he doesn't have is any "free capital", apparently. Or talent. Or investors.'

Fiona pulled herself up, concerned. 'What has your mum said?'

'Nothing to me. But I came downstairs early this morning and I could hear Mum whispering to him, "Now, Hugo, I'll need all of this back by the end of January. *Please*. Don't let me down again." Then I walked in, pretending I hadn't heard anything, and they both started up this false, chatty "Did you sleep all right, Madison darling?" thing.'

'"Let me down again?"' asked Fiona.

Madison replied with an ominous nod. 'Caught that, did you?' She sighed. 'I've had a feeling that something's been going on for a while.'

They both fell silent, Madison staring out to the crystal blue sea.

'I'm sorry, Mads. What are you going to do?'

'What can I do?' asked Madison. 'It's her money.' She rolled over on her towel. 'And if he has his way, it will be *his* money.'

'Well, if he's borrowing off her . . .'

'Not just that,' said Madison, with a decisive slice of her

hand. 'He keeps making all of these noises about wanting power of attorney if she gets too sick to make decisions.'

'How do you mean?'

'You know she's got a bad heart. He wants to be able to control the money if anything happens to her.'

'I don't . . .'

'Why's he moved over here so suddenly?' hissed Madison, though they were the only people around. 'I think he's lost his house. Not that Mum will tell me anything.' She let her head drop back to her towel with a furious sigh. 'He always was her favourite.'

'Since he's the oldest, wouldn't he get power of attorney anyway?' asked Fiona.

Madison had simply smiled. 'No. He might be my mum's favourite, but she's not completely stupid.' She closed her eyes. 'If anything happens to her, the power of attorney goes to *me*.'

* * *

The sea bream was undercooked and glassy, the vegetables had barely seen the water. The anchovy crust was little more than mush. The whole thing could have done with at least another ten minutes in the oven, but nobody pointed this out, or had the opportunity to, as Tara, Hugo's wife, chattered on and on, in the strain of a pre-emptive conversational strike.

'I think nothing ruins a fish more than overcooking it, don't you? Losing all the vitamins and micronutrients, you might as well just throw it in the bin.' Her face was flushed in the rising Mediterranean heat, her messy blonde ponytail flicking from side to side as she set the tray and its contents on the table.

'Oh yes, dear,' said Judy, her breathy voice sweet. She liked Tara. 'I'm sure you're right.'

'It makes no difference to me,' said Hugo, who sat at the table, his pink shirt rolled up his forearms and collar open, with a glass of Grenache in front of him that he never let get less than half full. 'I just eat what she puts in front of me, isn't that right, love?'

He turned to Tara, who was quickly spooning the fish and the vegetables on to plates, and offered her a vague smile, as though she was an amusing pet.

'It's lovely,' said Fiona, accepting her portion and managing to smile. 'Thanks very much.'

'You're so lucky, Judy. They do such nice fish here,' said Tara, who never seemed to know what to do with Fiona, and so found it best to ignore her. 'Fresh straight out of the sea!'

'Well, that is how fish work,' muttered Madison, seemingly engrossed in her smartphone and not seeing or choosing not to see Judy's warning raise of eyebrows.

'Bon appétit!' said Tara, sitting down and not eating, but instead staring owlishly at them all while they tucked in, as though daring them.

'Mine's fresh enough, at least,' said Hugo dolefully, poking his with a fork. 'This is still wriggling.'

'Oh . . . do you want me to put it back in the oven for a little while?' asked Tara, who appeared to have picked up a slight tremor.

'If you wouldn't mind.' He threw down his fork and turned from the plate as his wife removed it, reaching over for his phone.

Fiona waited hopefully, but nobody else was offered the opportunity of a refiring and requesting one seemed socially impossible, so after a second or two she resumed eating.

'So how's work, Fiona?' asked Hugo suddenly.

Fiona stilled. Hugo had never made small talk with her, even when they had all been children together. Still, it was a good sign. In the interests of social amiability, she should give a polite response.

'Um . . . good, thanks. I've applied for a senior lecturer's position. I'll hear in a few weeks whether I've got it or not.'

'Yeah? That's great. I guess you have to stop being a student and living off my taxes sometime, right?' He offered her a wolfish smile.

'Fiona's a lecturer, on a contract. She's not been a student for years.' Madison's voice was flat with displeasure, and she did not look up from her phone. 'And for her to live off your taxes you have to pay them first, Hugo.'

'Calm down, Sis, I was only having a little joke.' He was refilling his wine again, and grinned and shrugged at Fiona, as though they were complicit together. 'Did they not let you take your sense of humour through customs, Madison?'

'Could you both stop it, please?' asked Judy sharply. 'You're giving me a headache.'

The siblings subsided, Hugo with a superior and slightly drunk smirk, while Judy bent to her raw fish and Tara hovered around the oven wringing her hands in unconscious anxiety, as though this would make Hugo's dinner cook quicker.

Fiona felt stifled, uncomfortable, her sundress clinging to her. She had the sense that Hugo was watching her, and once again felt like that little girl who had come to play with Madison, the girl with the drunk father, the girl that everyone viewed with suspicion.

Don't let them do this to you, she told herself.

'We're out of wine,' announced Hugo to the room, pushing the empty bottle away.

Fiona saw her chance for a moment's escape. 'That's all right,' she said, waving back Tara, who had already darted towards the door. 'I'll get some more.'

* * *

The wine cellar was down the stairs in a cool alcove in the foundations, the bottles racked against the dewy limestone walls. The damp and chill felt good against Fiona's bare sunburned arms, her flushed face, almost as good as the respite from the hostilities upstairs.

We should have gone to Ibiza, she thought to herself.

'All right there?' rang out a voice.

It was Hugo.

'Yes,' she called back, trying to keep the frustration out of her voice. What was he doing here? Making sure she didn't steal the wine?

She could hear him coming down the stairs, the rhythm of his steps erratic, and she suspected he was a great deal drunker than she'd previously thought.

She selected another couple of bottles of the Grenache she and Mads had bought in town a couple of days ago and hastily started back towards the stairs.

Hugo had reached the bottom and stood on the final step, one fat pink hand wrapped around the wrought-iron rail, the other resting against the wall, blocking her way.

'Hi, Hugo. Excuse me, please . . .'

'What's that you've got there? Is it the good stuff?'

'It's just the Grenache. Can you let me through? Our dinners will be getting cold.' She was hard pressed to keep her voice polite.

'Our dinners are already cold.' His watery eyes settled on her.

'Hugo, would you mind . . . ?'

He didn't move or acknowledge her, and her feelings were sliding from awkwardness to confusion. 'Hugo . . .'

He stood, swaying faintly, and his hand rose from the railing and drifted up towards her face.

She stepped smartly back, nearly dropping the bottles in her haste and horror. What was he thinking of? 'Hugo, get out of my way, please.'

'What's your rush?' he slurred, and came at her.

There was a ghastly moment of his thick arms pressed around her, him pressing his hot, hard crotch against her own, his plump, wet lips being mashed against her face. The fingers of his right hand were suddenly digging into her buttock, massaging it.

The shock at first was so great that Fiona was stunned, numb and nerveless, the bottles in her hands trapped against her breasts, crushing into them.

'Get off me!' she hissed at him. 'Get off me, or I swear I'll scream!'

His wide left palm was instantly against her mouth, silencing her. His breathing was hard, heavy. 'Quiet, quiet,' he sighed. 'You know you want to . . .'

But he had created an opening for her, and gripping the bottle in her own hand tightly, she swung it up and between his legs.

She had expected him to fall over, to fold, as people did in the movies, but it only seemed to slow him a little, make him bend in the middle with a low *oof* sound.

Still, it was enough. She pushed hard, running for the stairs, and over he went. One of the bottles fell to the stone floor, shattering.

At the top of the stairs Madison appeared, a frown on her face.

'What's . . . what's wrong?'

* * *

The 23:45 to London Heathrow had been full except for a couple who had missed their flight, so there was room. It was just getting ready to board by the time Fiona had made her excuses to Judy, and Madison drove them both off in the rental car.

It must have been kismet.

Fiona sat back in her plane seat, gazing out at the stars over Majorca as the plane circled, rose, her stomach bottoming out with the rising acceleration.

Next to her Madison had been silent.

'You should have called the police,' she said eventually, though without much enthusiasm. 'It's what you would have nagged me to do.' She folded her arms.

Fiona could not deny this. It was exactly what she would have nagged Madison to do. She shifted against the cutting weight of her safety belt.

'I just – I just wanted to be gone. To go home.' She felt weak, hollow with the shock of what had just happened. 'He didn't hurt me.'

'Still,' said Madison.

'I just can't.' Fiona let her hands balls into fists. 'His wife was there. And his *mother*. I'm in this foreign country. I just . . .' She paused, trying to gather her wandering thoughts. 'I mean, we've known each other since we were kids. What the *hell*?'

'I know. You know, it's up to you what you do about him. Don't feel pressured, even if he is my brother.' Madison rolled her eyes, and then gently patted her arm. 'I *told* you he was a twat.'

23

The Ring of Brodgar, Orkney, January 2020

'Wow.'

'What do you think?'

Fiona nodded, and despite herself, felt better. 'You're right. It's very cool.'

Next to them, on a small rise, was a huge ring of massive rectangular slate megaliths, standing to form a broad, irregular circle containing scraggy heather. All around, the landscape functioned like a bowl, or an auditorium, as though the surrounding hills were paying attention; as though the stones were actors on a huge outdoor stage.

They regarded the stone circle in silence for a long moment from the front seat of the van, marvelling at its enigmatic beauty, the ancient, unanswerable riddle it represented.

'They're amazing,' she said, moved. 'I mean, I've seen pictures, but nothing like the real thing.'

'Yeah,' he said, nodding. 'It would be criminal to come all this way and miss them.'

It was kindly meant but it put her in mind of her real purpose here. She was not a tourist, and the howl of the wind from outside the car was cold, desolate.

She needed to calm down, she told herself firmly. This was a mere travel hiccup, as Jack had told her while they drove, a road bump. If Madison's disappearance hadn't put her on panic stations, she'd realise this.

These weird highs and lows were happening because she was all alone out here.

And it was then that she felt those first, prickling notes of resentment towards Adi. She could appreciate that Adi had a busy job and important people depended on him, but at what point did she become important? When her best friend went mysteriously missing? When her friend's *mother* did?

Was it when Madison's corpse was discovered in a ditch somewhere?

Somehow it had fallen on to strangers to offer her comfort.

She shook her head. It would do no good to dwell on it now.

'How long have you been digging out here on Orkney?' she asked. 'With Iris and the team?'

'Me? This is the first time I've dug on Orkney with Iris. But this is where I trained, back in the day. Came out here every summer during my degree, volunteering.' His eyes widened, as though at a happy memory. 'Good times.'

'Oh.' She considered that sense she'd had, that they were old hands together. 'You and Iris seemed to know one another really well.'

'Ah,' and it seemed to her that he blushed. 'I mean, I do *know* her. Obviously. We were students together. We reconnected workwise a couple of years ago, at Jesmond Hill.'

Fiona glanced at him in surprise. 'You dug at Jesmond Hill? Wow.'

She had read about the dig as it happened. It had, like the story of Tutankhamun's tomb, a ring of legend about it.

The dig itself was a simple rescue excavation before the building of a supermarket, a box-ticking exercise for the construction company, a legal obligation.

The archaeologists had been exploring what they suspected were a trio of late Bronze Age round barrows – ancient graves for important people that had originally been tall mounds in the soil, but which had been ploughed flat in the intervening three thousand years.

Two sealed urns of cremated remains had been found, hidden in small stone cists, but nothing else.

It had been almost the final day of the excavation, and after digging for two weeks, in mud and flies and with the bulldozers mere hours from crashing in, the team were in the final exploratory trench, which was a little way from the barrows and would ultimately end up directly beneath the fish counter at the new Asda.

One of the team, scraping out the bottom of the muddy trench, had run his trowel over the panel of Northumbrian mud, and suddenly, beneath him, bright gold had gleamed through.

That famous necklace – the Jesmond Hill torc – had been discovered.

Fiona remembered admiring the finds on the BBC website when the discovery first become public. She'd felt a little stab of jealousy – how amazing would it be to make such a discovery yourself, to be the first to uncover such exquisite treasure after thousands of years?

It was a find that would have satisfied any other archaeologist for the rest of their career, but there had been others for the team, though less spectacular. Iris had a gift for knowing what sites to choose and how to excavate them.

'So what was that like? Finding treasure like that?' she asked Jack.

He looked away then, and she had the sense she'd embarrassed him somehow. 'Memorable.'

'Sorry,' she said. 'You must get that all the time, you must be bored to death talking about it.'

'No, not at all . . .' But there was no enthusiasm in it.

'But it must have been amazing, to see that beautiful torc come out of the ground – there's just something about gold, isn't there?'

'It was . . . something else.' He nodded, offered her a little self-deprecating shrug. 'You can dig your whole life and never see finds like that. But ultimately it's luck rather than talent. Well, certainly not my talent. Whether it's Iris's talent is another question. She certainly has a great nose for these things.' He cocked his head to one side, as though thinking. 'And she comes across so well. It's how she got the *Discovering the Past* gig.' He sighed. 'She's a force of nature.'

'I'm sure she wouldn't get far without a good team behind her,' said Fiona politely, wondering if she was intruding on some private resentment, some jealousy. There were a lot of reasons to envy Iris – her luck, her instincts, her career. It was surprising, she supposed, that Madison had not seemed to.

'Hmm,' he said. 'I'm not so sure. She was something else back in the day, even when she was a student.' He smiled fondly at the memory. 'She came from filthy rich people – I forget what they did, something in soap – but she never really got on with them. She had a weird, distant relationship with her father. At home, she had to call him "sir".'

'Really?'

'Yep,' continued Jack. 'Well, I say that. I think once she discovered marijuana and motorbikes that all went out the window. She was the Wild Girl when I knew her at uni. I don't know how she found the time to graduate. She organised raves most weekends. Made her own jewellery and sold it at festivals. I came off the back of that first bike of hers more than once and nearly broke my neck.' He scratched at his chin, grinning. 'It was only years later I discovered that she didn't have a motorcycle licence.'

Fiona laughed. Perhaps jealous Madison had not envied Iris

because, as the children of distant, grandiose fathers, they understood each other better than most.

She glanced at Jack.

'You know, I did think when I first met you that you guys might be an item . . .'

'What do you mean?' he asked quickly, as though she had offended him.

'You know,' she said, colouring uncomfortably. 'You and Iris.'

His guffaw of laughter was sudden, shocking. 'Oh no. Or at least not any more. We tried the, uh, Girlfriend Experience and it didn't really work out. We're better off as mates. Soulmates, really. But we don't – we want different things.'

So they're not actually together. The thought flashed through Fiona's mind like a treacherous darting fish. *That'll please Callum,* she thought, with a tiny touch of glee.

'I would find it difficult to work with an ex,' she said. 'But then maybe that's because I never manage to stay friends with them.' She gave a small laugh, embarrassed. 'It's a failure in adulting properly, I expect.'

'Hmm. I dunno,' he said, keeping his eyes on the windshield, and she had the sense that she'd touched a nerve. 'Sometimes there's a lot to be said for a clean break. I don't think that Mairead and I would still be in touch if we hadn't had Brand in common.'

'Brand?'

'My son.' He cast a sideways look at her.

'Oh, right. And how old is he?'

'Ten.'

'Do you get to see him often?'

Jack shrugged, a stiff, almost ashamed gesture. 'Not as often as I'd like. Mairead and I – well, it's still a bit frosty. I . . . to be honest, I wasn't a very good boy when we were together.' He sighed. 'I'm not a very good boy generally.'

'You surprise me,' she replied archly.

He snorted in amusement. 'I'm not sure I do,' he said. 'But I wouldn't want you to get totally the wrong idea about me.'

'Or totally the right one,' she said with a grin, and he laughed again.

You are flirting, said a grave voice in the back of her head. *Which is not like you.*

She ignored it.

'Shall we get out?' he asked.

She nodded – she was eager to see the stones, stretch her legs. Though the sky was blue she knew that when she got out, the wind would knife through her new red coat and ruffle up her sleeves.

But she'd come all this way. It was time to engage.

They got out of the van, him walking around the front to help her down as she splashed into the mud, her new boots already starting to rub her heels.

'This way.'

The stones themselves were deserted, the wind making a thin screaming as it tore through the low-lying heather.

'They're expecting a gale,' she said, as he walked her up. 'I wonder if they'll cancel the flights soon.'

'Probably. They cancel the ferries pretty regularly.'

'Where are the others today?' Fiona asked, oppressed by the silence, broken occasionally by the mournful cries of water birds.

'At the house,' he said. 'They're either in front of the internet or down the pub.'

She laughed. 'Can't say I blame them.'

'Well, you know, it's not like any of us can complain about not getting enough exercise and fresh air.'

They were about to approach the first stone when, before she could stop herself, she asked, 'Jack, what do you think happened to Madison?'

The question wrong-footed him, literally – he seemed to almost stumble.

'Me?'

'Yeah. I mean, you must have a feeling.'

'I . . .' and she saw to her disappointment that he was looking away, frowning, thinking, and she recognised the expression.

She understood that he was not going to give her an honest answer but the one that would make her happiest, or at least most quiescent.

She grasped instantly that this was probably part of why he didn't stay friends with many of his exes. From her fleeting acquaintance with Iris, the warrior woman, she suspected that this would have got old for her very quickly indeed.

But then she thought of that line of Yeats' that Madison always quoted at such points: *It's certain that fine women eat/A crazy salad with their meat.*

There was no knowing what a woman might refuse to put up with, until you saw her refusing to put up with it.

'I . . . I honestly don't know where Madison is.' He shrugged at her, a quick little twitch. 'Whatever the circumstances, if I knew, I would tell you. It would only be fair. But I don't.'

She studied his face for a long moment, sighed.

'I mean,' he went on, as though sensing her dissatisfaction with this answer, 'at first, when you mentioned the stalker, I suspected something had happened to Madison.' He thrust his hands into his pockets. 'But now I wonder.'

Fiona widened her eyes at him. 'Wonder what?'

'Well, think about it. Why's her mum not here, or texting?'

Fiona was bewildered. 'I don't understand what you mean.'

They had reached the megaliths, with their long, thin shadows. They were cut out of some slate-like stone which made them straight as scalpel blades, towering over both of them. The heather quivered in the wind, a tiny tremor which made it look possessed of oddly mobile life.

'Perhaps,' and he seemed to choose these words carefully, 'her mother's not come because she already knows Madison isn't here.'

'*What?*'

'I mean,' he said, 'perhaps Madison's been in touch with her.'

Fiona didn't know what to say. What on earth was he driving at? 'But . . . but that's ridiculous. Why wouldn't they tell me?'

He took a moment before speaking again, his clenched jaw making his chin jut out a little. 'Secrecy? Embarrassment? I'm sorry, Fiona. I just don't know. None of this makes sense.' He shrugged. 'It's just an idea.'

She let the pieces of this fall through her mind.

Perhaps Madison was safe and sound somewhere, and Judy knew it.

It might possibly be true. They'd fallen out – they were always falling out over her dad's money, because Judy always favoured Hugo (*Hugo* – for a second she was lost in the memory of his blubbery wet lips pressing themselves against her face and shuddered).

Judy had been funding his various unsuccessful business ventures, leaving Madison, who she perversely considered a failure, out in the cold.

But Hugo constantly schemed to be named as power of attorney and executor if Judy died – Judy was a wealthy woman with a bad heart and Hugo was constantly short on funds. If, as Iris had suggested, Hugo had visited Madison on Orkney, it would be in connection with this and nothing else.

And while Judy might be a fond and foolish mother, she wasn't completely stupid.

What if, somehow, Madison found out that her sick, frail

mother was catching a plane out to Orkney in response to her disappearance? Hugo would be left in charge . . .

She might decide things had gone far enough, break cover to tell her mum.

Madison could be difficult, there was no denying it, but she and her mum did love each other, in their own dysfunctional way.

But why not tell me?

Stop it. Stop it, she told herself. *You don't know this. This is just Jack guessing.*

She glanced up at him. *Or is he guessing?*

Does he know something?

24

West Orkney, January 2020

When Milly had seen the tiny woman lying out on the rock, with her round eyes and grooved hair and carved wings, she had known that she was special.

She was not beautiful, particularly – not like the rose-gold Swarovski locket that Alicia Sutherland had been given for Christmas and never shut up about or stopped fiddling with – this pendant was too odd, the woman's expression too neutral, her little disc-like eyes almost creepy. But even so, there was some hidden magic in her – the soft way her gold glowed against the wet rocks, how heavy she had been in Milly's hand despite her tiny size – it was like how Milly imagined a bullet to feel. Her first impulse had immediately been to snap a picture of it on her phone and share it, and her second impulse, accompanied by a flash of alien cunning, was to absolutely not do this. She had a feeling it was not something she would be allowed to keep to herself, and so it proved.

'What's that you got?'

'Nothing,' Milly said, shoving the precious thing roughly in the pocket of her jeans and standing up from where she had been crouching on the rocks.

'No, you found something.' Tom, her younger brother, gave her a gimlet stare, his eyes narrowed. 'Show us.'

'It's just an old necklace.' She pulled her hood up to protect her thin fair hair from the sea spray.

There was the skitter of flying pebbles, claws scrabbling on wet stone. Slobber the dog, freed from the back of their parents' car, came racing over towards them, his pink tongue lolling out of the side of his mouth. He barrelled into Milly, his muddy paws hitting her square in her chest.

'SLOBBER!' yelled Dad. 'GET DOWN! Milly, don't let him do that!'

'I didn't ask him to!' she shouted back, aggrieved at this unfair blaming. 'Stupid dog!'

But Slobber was not put off by this, and licked her face a few times, braced against her on his hind legs, until she giggled.

'Bloody hell, Jules,' her dad said. 'She's only just got out of the car and she's filthy again.' He snorted, slamming the boot shut. 'She takes after *you*, you know.'

'Milly, come away from that cliff edge!' Mum called out, with that annoying edge of fear that always entered her voice whenever Milly was about to do or say something interesting.

'I'm *miles* from the edge!' she shouted back.

'You too, Tom, both of you come here,' said their dad. 'Help me get a lead on the beast.'

Milly sighed, and looked around as Slobber let her go. No new fossils today, just the slippy broken rocks and the rage of the sea, the very tops of the waves coming up over the cliffs.

In fact, the rocks looked very broken today, their edges fresh, as though something big and heavy had come through and smashed them. In the algae near where Milly had made her find, there was the splendid sharp print of a tyre mark, though, Milly supposed, that made no sense.

There was nowhere to drive up here.

They trudged back to the car, Milly zipping her coat up as Dad fastened the leash on Slobber. It was time for their Sunday walk. They would hike along the headland, out past Yesnaby Castle, which wasn't a castle, just a stack of slumped stone standing proud of the ocean like a tower. This was to get some 'fresh air', which Milly understood to mean 'become absolutely freezing and have no phone signal', and then go into Stromness for a late lunch of macaroni cheese and chips in the little café near the harbour, where the owners let Slobber sit under the table if he was good and not too dirty.

'Milly found a necklace,' said Tom.

'Shut up,' said Milly.

'What did you find, Milly?' asked her dad.

'Just a mucky old necklace.'

'Show me,' said her dad.

'Why? It's only a . . .'

'Milly, show it to me now,' he said, in his I'm Not Messing Around With You Any More voice.

And that was that. The game was up.

'What is it?' asked her mum. 'Isn't it strange? Is it meant to be an angel?'

Her dad dangled the little woman from her yellow chain. 'Ooh, look at that. She's got a sword.'

'That looks like gold,' said Milly's mum, picking up the pendant and peering at it thoughtfully. 'You know, I think we ought to hand this in.'

'What?' snapped Milly. 'Why? It probably came from the sea.'

'I don't think the sea would have got it up here on its own, Milly. Someone's dropped this while they were out walking . . .'

'It's not fair! I never get to keep anything! It doesn't belong to anyone and I found it!'

'Now, now, Milly – if we hand it in and the police don't find the real owner, you'll get to . . .'

'I hate you!' she declared. 'Keep the stupid necklace!'

She sulked all along the cliffs while the skuas screeched above them, her own little black storm cloud – constantly texting in speedy, jagged little tics, just to make absolutely clear to her family that yes, she was complaining about them all on social media.

She kept the secret of the tyre marks to herself.

But her cheesy, carby lunch raised her spirits a little, and by the end she had recovered enough to grudgingly accept the offer of a hot chocolate with marshmallows from her parents, along with a promise that if nobody really owned the necklace, then of course it would be hers.

And after lunch, on her way to the Tesco in Kirkwall, she and her mum handed the necklace in at the police station, explained where they had found it.

The police had seemed extraordinarily interested.

Gratified by their attention, and the respectful way they questioned her, Milly went on to explain about the mysterious tyre marks on the cliff edge, which seemed to interest them even more.

25

Kirkwall Airport, Orkney, January 2020

'This is the last flight from Glasgow tonight, yeah?'

Fiona was back at the airport with Jack in tow, but once again Judy hadn't been on the plane. She realised, with a little start of shock, that she had never expected her to be. Already she was tapping on the number, lifting the phone to her ear, prepared for the futile ringing.

When it was answered, her shock left her stammering.

'Who is this?' a male voice asked peevishly.

Hugo. Why was Hugo answering the phone? Where were they?

But wherever he was supposed to be, he had hold of Judy's phone now, and he sounded furious, as though she had interrupted something important. In the background she could hear voices and movement, the droning rise and fall of someone talking hurriedly in Spanish, being answered in the same language.

Judy must still be on Majorca.

'Hugo? Is that you? It's me, Fiona Grey. I'm here at Kirkwall waiting for you . . .'

'Well, she won't be arriving any time soon.'

'What? I don't understand . . .'

'She's had a heart attack,' he said, clearly enunciating each word, as though Fiona was an imbecile. 'She collapsed in the taxi on the way to the airport.'

'What?' Fiona's fingers were numb around the phone. 'Is she all right? Where is she now?'

'In hospital, where else would she be?' he snapped. 'Look, I have to get back to her . . .'

'But Hugo, wait,' she said, stumbling over the words. 'What happened, exactly?'

'She had a shock. She got a call from the police in Scotland,' he said. 'Apparently they found Madison's car in the sea up there.'

'*Madison's* car? You mean the rental car?'

'I haven't time for this. They're taking Mum in for a scan now.'

'But did they find Mads?'

'I don't know. They say it was driven off some cliffs into the ocean.'

'What . . . ?'

It was too late. He had hung up on her.

Fiona didn't really remember much of what followed. She stumbled backwards from the inquiry desk, staring at the phone, too bewildered to speak.

'Fiona, what do you want to . . .' Jack re-emerged – he'd gone to the bathroom. 'What is it?'

'Mads . . .' She merely stared up at him, her eyes huge. 'They found her car. In the sea.'

He stood there, stock-still, utterly silent. His blue eyes were unreadable.

'You know what,' he said after a long moment. 'Let's just sit you down before you fall down.'

* * *

Her car, she kept trying to explain to Jack as he drove the van back towards Stromness through the rough winds and buffeting rain, she had to get her car. She had left it in Kirkwall, at the hotel.

'Forget about your car. It'll be fine. I'll call them when I get in.' Jack leaned low over the wheel, and the grey cast had not left his face. He snorted. 'I don't think you're in a condition to drive, anyway.'

He was speeding, at least twenty miles over the limit, and with the bad weather and the thickening darkness she was growing afraid. It wasn't clear to her that he should be driving either. This news appeared to have greatly affected him.

'Are you okay?' she asked.

He blinked at her, surprised.

'*I'm* okay,' he said, then made a little disparaging twitch, as though aware how much his appearance belied his words. 'I mean, it's a lot to take in. Oh fuck, Madison. She was . . . but never mind that. We don't know the score yet. We need to talk to the police. The others are going to . . . shit, Fiona,' he ran a big hand over his stubbled head. 'This is really heavy.'

'Yeah,' said Fiona in a small, distant voice.

She had stopped crying now, and instead felt empty, loose, like a kite in the middle of a windstorm.

Oh God, there is no way Madison would just abandon a car, not for any reason. Something has happened, something has definitely happened, something big and bad, and is it, in some way, my fault? Did I not push her hard enough to report Dom to the police once the tweets started up again? I know how she is. I should have guessed she'd procrastinate, try to blow it off as nothing even as she begged me to come up here.

Should I have nagged her about it more?

Oh God, Madison. Please don't be dead. Please, please *don't be dead.*

As they approached the house, the front door swung open, and Callum was standing in the doorway, oblivious to the rain.

'Iris, it's them, they're back!' he yelled.

They climbed out of the van, Jack coming to her side to support her as they hurried in through the door. Iris and Becky stood in the hallway, and Fiona realised instantly that they, too, had had news.

'What is it?' she asked Iris.

Iris looked from Fiona to Jack, then back to Fiona again. 'I think you need to come in. Becky,' she barked. 'Put the kettle on.'

Becky vanished, without demur this time, and this, more than anything, sent a chill through Fiona.

'What is it?' she asked again. 'Judy isn't coming. She had a heart attack. They found the rental car in the ocean.'

'Yes,' said Callum. 'Off the west cliffs.'

Fiona's heart was pounding. Her mouth could barely form the words. 'Where is that?'

Becky had reappeared, and her face was absolutely expressionless. 'It's the local suicide spot.'

26

Grangeholm, Orkney, January 2020

They wouldn't hear of Fiona leaving. There was a sofa in the living room and she was welcome to stay there. Iris would drive her out to Langmire and together they could pick up her things. Fiona was clearly in no fit state to drive herself.

Tomorrow they would take her back to her own car in Kirkwall before they started work on the dig.

Fiona assented to all of this, with the numb misery of being trapped in a nightmare. She was given a cup of tea, which she did not drink.

It had been Callum who spotted the bulletin on the local news, but Iris who had spoken with the police and somehow managed to garner a few more details. The GPS on Madison's rental car had led the police to it (how did Iris get the police to tell her these things? Star power, Fiona supposed. Iris had that in spades) after there had been reports of tyre tracks going off the cliffs by a member of the public.

The others discussed this in hushed, shocked voices while Fiona sat silent, thinking.

Dom would know about GPS. He understood GPS and phones and emails and hacking texts and being a disgusting creepy inadequate bully, all right.

If he's hurt her. Oh God, if he has . . .

Then somehow a decision about Fiona had been reached, and she was shepherded into Iris's rental car, a white Taurus with leather seats. They were going to Langmire, to collect her things.

She supposed she should text Adi, tell him all this, but somehow the thought appalled, seemed to make it all more real, and the effort involved to do it, to explain it all again, was more than she could face.

She was relieved when Iris did not attempt to make small talk on the journey to the cottage or try to cheer her up with platitudes. Fiona simply stared out of the window into the darkness until it was time for her to get out of the car.

'I'm going up to the Fletts',' Iris called out to her from the driver's side window once they arrived. By the swimming lights of the dashboard, she looked drawn, older than her years, her jaw heavy and blunt. 'I need to tell them what's happened, and that we won't be needing the cottage any more.' She shook her head, her eyes huge. 'I can't believe this is happening.'

'Me neither,' mumbled Fiona.

Iris simply reached out, squeezed her arm. 'I'll be no more than ten minutes. Did you have something to eat today?'

Fiona shook her head. 'I'm . . . I'm fine. I'm not hungry.'

Iris gave her a thin-lipped smile. 'Ten minutes, Fiona.'

Kind though Iris had been, Fiona felt a little flare of miserable relief as the red tail lights of her car retreated up the hill to the Fletts' house.

She wanted to be alone, to think; just for a few minutes.

Though now she was alone, staring out across the sea to the lighthouse blooming then vanishing on Helly Holm, she was not sure what she wanted to think about.

All seemed hopeless. Madison's car was at the bottom of the sea. She was not answering her phone or emails.

And most damning of all, Fiona understood why there had been no more of the horrible messages on social media. It was because whoever was sending them must have known that Madison was dead and would not be reading them.

Dom Tate had probably killed Madison, perhaps after

forcing her to send out her final texts to put everyone off the scent. Then he'd driven her car off the cliffs, with any luck with himself inside.

You knew this. You worked that out days ago.
You just didn't want to acknowledge it.

The cottage was in darkness, except for a faint yellow glow from the back of the guest bedroom upstairs. Fiona had showered in there that morning. She must have left the light on.

The light wind ruffled her hair as it poked out from underneath Madison's trapper hat while she produced the key for the cottage and let herself in. The smell of the sea wrack fluttered in and out over the quiet murmur of the waves.

She breathed it in, closed her eyes, tried to pull herself together. She needed to pack, and quickly. As desperate as she'd been for a little peace, Fiona had no real desire to be alone tonight. She would stay with the archaeologists, and in the morning try to come up with a plan. Perhaps the police would need her.

And tomorrow she would steel herself to try to approach Hugo, find out how Judy was doing.

Find out what the police intended to do about Madison's car.

Find out if they had caught up with Dom Tate yet.

She let herself into the little house, quickly switching on the hall lights, throwing her jacket on to a chair in the hallway, swiping off Mads' hat.

The bedroom was exactly as she had left it – strewn with clothes and books, the striped blue duvet hastily pulled over the exposed sheets. The mirrored wardrobe doors with their shattered central panel greeted her as she let herself slump down on the bed, suddenly unable to move, to act.

The spiderwebbed cracks threw her reflection into a thousand splinters.

You know, a cozening voice murmured to her, *you don't know*

Mads is . . . is gone. She might be being held captive somewhere. That crazy, fucking, obsessed bastard may have her trapped. He may have got rid of the car because he couldn't hide it or take it off the island.

There still might be a chance she was not gone forever, gone into the deep, vanished into the roaring abyss of the Atlantic.

Some faint, impossible chance that she was alive.

Fiona looked down at Mads' hat in her hands. The soft feel of the dappled grey fur beneath her fingers, the smoothness of the leather, seemed to throw wide some ancient doors of undisclosed grief that held back a vast, impossible tide.

She did not even attempt to resist the tears, letting her anguish rage through her like a river in spate, wet and ugly and with jagged, painful sobs – grief for her lost father, grief for her absent, stunted, inadequate mother, and finally grief for this, her one constant, Madison – who despite her reckless selfishnesses and little storms of envy, had always been there for her when it truly mattered.

The men in Fiona's life had come and gone. Even now she and Adi shifted uncomfortably around one another, like teenagers at a dance. But she had never once doubted that Madison loved her.

And in the wake of her grief came fury, molten-red and hot like the iron she worked with, and it pulsed through her like hammer blows.

He is going to pay for this, she thought, her fingers scything into the furred hat on her lap, her teeth clenching, the backs of her hands soaked with her own tears.

He's going to pay, and how.

And then, above her, the floor creaked.

She froze.

Utter silence reigned. Not even the weather or the sea was audible.

She dropped the hat beside her, stood up. She strained to listen, but the sound was not repeated.

What was up there? Just the guest bedroom with its stripped beds, and the en suite shower which she'd used that morning, before rushing out to meet Judy's plane.

All of that seemed a lifetime ago, to have happened to another Fiona.

She'd been sure she'd switched everything off when she left.

She swiped at her hot, wet face with her sleeve, still listening, but there was nothing more. A velvet quiet lay over the whole house like a cloak.

But Fiona was not fooled. Her breath hitched in her chest.

Get out, she told herself. *Get out and wait for Iris. Better yet, start running up that hill to the Fletts'. I don't care how it looks. I don't care how dark it is. Just do it. Grab your phone out of your jacket as you go.*

Yet she felt a terror, a reluctance – within the house she was in the light at least, but outside there was only freezing darkness, the nearest building at least ten minutes away.

Whoever was up there had not confronted her. They must know she was here, have heard the front door being opened, but they hadn't moved.

At least not yet.

Could it be Madison? she wondered suddenly, with a throb of hope.

Do you want to bet your life on that?

She swallowed hard, thinking, trying to be rational in the face of her rising panic. There was nothing in the bedroom that could remotely function as a weapon – even her aerosol deodorant was upstairs, lying on one of the guest beds where she'd thrown it after her shower.

Through the open bedroom door, the hallway was exactly as she'd left it, with its innocuous carpet and pale walls, the chair half in shadow, her jacket lying over it. But the stairs were dark.

She had an impulse to change this and she raised her hand to the light switch, dropped it again.

Better to just go. Go *now*. Just walk, quickly and quietly grabbing the jacket, and head out of the front door, and then the minute she was out to start running. She'd be halfway up the hill by the time they – he – realised she'd flown.

Because that was the answer. It could only be Dom up there.

That was it. *Walk, don't run. Do nothing that will set him off. Not until you get outside, at least.*

She never made it as far as the hallway. Sudden, clumping footfalls, someone heavy, someone coming down the stairs fast. She knew it was him before she even saw his face.

He was running at her.

A spike then, of hatred, of pure adrenaline. She screamed as she lashed out at him, backed into the bedroom, stumbling over the edge of the bed and falling gracelessly on to her back in her shock and terror.

'Fiona . . .' he shouted.

'Stay the fuck away from me!' she shrieked, scrambling backwards over the fawn-coloured carpet, until her head struck the little oak night table by the bed.

'Fiona . . . Fiona, stop screaming . . .'

'People are coming!' She was hysterical, gibbering with fear. 'Iris is going to be here any minute – don't you dare come near me!'

'Shut up! FUCKING SHUT UP FOR A MINUTE!'

He stood at the foot of the bed, his hands raised high, but his palms outwards, as though she was the aggressor, as though she was about to shoot him. His face was mottled, pale, and his eyes red. His thin hair was greasy and he had not shaved in days.

'CALM. DOWN!'

Silence. Nothing but the sound of both of them breathing hard in the little room, as Fiona wrestled with her growing confusion.

And then he said, the whites of his eyes shining with terror: 'I have to talk to you.'

27

Grangeholm, Orkney, January 2020

'*Talk* to me?'

Fiona sprawled on the bedroom carpet, staring up at him.

Dominic Tate looked terrible. Also, he stank like an unwashed animal – of sweat and damp clothes, his sneakers filthy and stained, his eyes wild and bloodshot. If she had had to conjure up the picture of a deranged murderer, Dom Tate would have fit the bill.

His hands were still raised – a gesture almost of supplication, at odds with his wild appearance.

'Dom,' she said, swallowing, trying to keep her voice even, but incapable of leaving the question unasked. 'What have you done to Madison?'

'Nothing!' he wailed. 'I don't know where she is! I swear to God! On my little boy's life, I don't know!'

Fiona blinked, in the midst of everything still astonished that she had the capacity to be surprised by how despicable he was. *You have kids?* she wanted to hiss. *Pretty sure Mads didn't know that.*

But no, no. It was irrelevant right now. It was merely a reminder that she had to remember, no matter what, that he was a compulsive, manipulative liar.

She mustn't believe a single thing he said.

Somehow she had to calm him down, persuade him to leave, before Iris arrived. Who knew what he would do if he felt threatened?

Oh no, what if he hurts Iris? We're alone out here. We're . . .

She tried not to look in the direction of her jacket where her phone nestled. It might as well have been on the moon.

Instead, she focused on him, despite her loathing and dread. 'Dom, they found Madison's car in the sea.'

'I know they did! It was on the news here. I swear to God I had nothing to do with it!'

'Dom,' she said again, her mouth dry, aware that she was treading a very thin line here, 'you must know you're going to have to hand yourself in to the police. They're going to want to talk to you . . .'

'DON'T TELL ME WHAT TO DO!' he bellowed suddenly, his teeth bared. She shrank back against the carpet. He loomed over her as she cowered on the floor, his finger pointing into her face. 'This is ALL YOUR FUCKING FAULT!'

Fiona fell silent, paralysed with fear.

He had begun to pace back and forth in front of the bedroom door. She watched him, a cornered animal.

'I mean, it looks bad . . .' he trailed off. 'I'm not thick. I know how it looks.' He was shaking. 'I should never have come back here. This was such a fucking *mistake* . . .'

Fiona did not speak, terrified of angering him any further.

'I should have stayed away like I promised. Oh fuck,' he said, dropping his head into his hands, his shoulders heaving. 'Oh *fuck*. Oh, Madison. *Madison.*'

He seemed about to weep.

She swallowed. 'What do you mean, you promised?'

'What?' He raised his head, peered at her.

'You promised not to come back here?'

He blinked at her, as if she'd confused him. 'I was staying here.'

'You were staying *here*? In this house? With Mads?'

'Yeah.'

Her face must have made an impression on him.

'Don't fucking look at me like that! It's true. I was going to come back after you'd gone. She said I had to stay hidden. That you'd never understand.' His eyes turned cold, and he stilled. 'You're not very understanding, apparently.'

All of this story was palpably untrue, though she was unsettled by the realisation that Dom appeared to know of her arrival. An idea shot through her mind, then, and with it, a tiny cinder of hope. 'Wait – why did you come back now? Did you hear from Mads?'

He shook his head miserably, but there was something taut and suspicious in his expression, as though she was laying a trap for him. 'That was just it. I didn't. After Wednesday night she stopped answering the phone. I just got these texts – these texts that weren't like her. All . . . I can't describe it. Just not . . . her. At first,' he said, and that coldness was back in his grey eyes. 'I thought it was you, trying to give me the runaround.'

Fiona merely stared at him, her spine crawling. When he focused on her, all of his jittery, anxious animation stilled into menace.

She stirred again, aware that she had to get off the floor, out of this vulnerable, subservient position.

The moment had passed, though, and he was back into his story.

'So I thought, "No, I'm not getting messed around like this. I'm going over there and that judgemental little bitch Fiona is just going to have to live with it." ' His eyes narrowed at her. 'So I caught the ferry over yesterday. I know she said not to, but she should answer her fucking phone, then, shouldn't she? I'm already breaching my restraining order. I've been nothing but nice . . . I *helped* her. I came all the way up here, took time off work – you know?'

His gaze searched hers constantly, looking for cynicism, treachery, doubt.

'Helped her?' she asked, puzzled.

'Yeah, helped her.' He drew himself taller. 'With her stalker.'

Fiona could not restrain the amazement that flitted across her face.

'You . . . *you* helped her with her stalker?' she asked, managing at the last minute to make the final word sound less accusatory, less surprised.

'Yeah. See, she texted me. Out of the blue.'

This was, on the face of it, so absurd, that Fiona could make no reply. She was about to be told some vacillating, self-justifying story, she saw, and that was fine, so long as she didn't anger him. With any luck, Iris would see him through the undrawn curtains, and know to call the police.

Fiona just had to keep her head.

But there was something in his expression, a hard glint of triumph, as though he knew he was surprising her with knowledge about Madison that she did not have.

It gave her pause.

'She texted you,' said Fiona, neutral and straining for calm.

'Yeah.'

'Why?'

'She was all annoyed at first. She said that if I didn't stop being vile on the internet about her, she would go back to the cops and tell 'em I violated my order.'

Fiona did not speak, waited.

'I had no idea what she was going on about. None. I thought she was trying to stitch me up, trying to get me to message her back and get me into trouble. So I ignored her at first.'

From his pacing, jittery agitation, it was clear he wouldn't have been able to ignore her for very long.

'Apparently it was tweets, and since I knew she went off

Twitter and Facebook after the court case, I didn't get what her problem was.' He held up his palms, helplessly. 'And then I thought later, well, maybe she's thought better of it all.'

'What do you mean?'

'Maybe she's looking for a way to make friends, now the dust has settled some – who knows?'

'Friends?'

'Yeah, you know. Get back together.'

Fiona bit her tongue against the acid sense of contempt this filled her with.

'So I texted her back, saying that whatever problem she was having, it was nothing to do with me. Then she sent me this – well, a link to this tweet that got sent to her work's account, and said, "Well, who sent this? Sounds like you." And it was pretty nasty stuff. I mean, I know I said some bad things to her earlier in the year when I was angry, like. Only I'd never sent this.' He held up his hands again, as if appealing to Fiona to see reason. His face was shiny with sweat. 'I mean, it had been six months! Why would I suddenly be sending this stuff to her work out of nowhere?'

'What did it say?' asked Fiona.

'What did it say?' He gestured dismissively. 'It doesn't matter what it said. Not nice things. Like about throwing acid on her and . . . look, it doesn't matter.' He grew angrier, as if the acknowledgement of the link between this and his previous behaviour infuriated him. 'It doesn't matter what it *said*, all right?' He was almost shouting, a little drop of spittle landing on his lip.

Change the subject, thought Fiona. *Now.*

'So what happened?' she asked.

He paused, derailed, and then seemed to remember where he was, what he was saying.

'Yeah. So I said it wasn't me. But I was – whoever this was, right, was obviously trying to pretend to be me, to get me into trouble, right? But they'd made a mistake. They forgot to switch the location data off on their phone when they sent the first couple of tweets – so I knew it was someone on Orkney doing it. And I was eight hundred miles from Orkney and could prove I was. So I texted that to her, and told her it was her problem and not mine.'

Fiona waited, gripped despite herself.

'And?'

'Then she rang me, you know, didn't text, and we properly talked about things. And she told me, I swear on my son's life, Fiona, that she'd had a feeling it wasn't me. That there was someone here who'd got it in for her. Someone who was jealous of her.'

'What? Who?'

'She wouldn't say. She said she wasn't sure. But would I look into it for her? I mean, she didn't ask it like a favour – I knew she still had the hump with me a little.' He smiled, as if at a warm memory. 'But she also knew that this was, like, my area of expertise. And you know, I could tell she'd missed me. That old flirty spark was back.'

Oh, Madison, thought Fiona. *You idiot. You charmed him to get him to do what you wanted.*

But you've never quite mastered the spell for un-charming any of them.

'You looked into it for her?'

'Yeah. But I didn't get very far. Whoever it was didn't make the same mistake twice.' He shrugged. 'And in the UK anyone can buy a phone and a SIM, and if they pay cash . . .' His face was thoughtful now, matter-of-fact, and she had a glimpse of what he was like in normal life, what most people saw. 'They can track the phone itself through mobile phone towers, but they have to catch you with it if it's not registered to you. Anyone can get a burner phone.'

Fiona considered this, stunned. Someone was pretending to be *Dom*? Here on Orkney? That was an absurd lie, obviously. Obviously.

Wasn't it?

'She wouldn't say who she thought it was?'

'No. She reckoned it would be more effective if she didn't "lead me", if you know what I mean – give me clues. Anyway, I looked into it, and I thought, you know, it would be too complicated to explain over the phone. I needed to see her in person.'

You explained it to me in a couple of sentences, thought Fiona, feeling her face harden, but she said nothing.

'I decided to surprise her, you know, come up rather than call. I got her address out of someone at her office . . .' he paused, as though editing his memories before he offered them, and she sensed that this acquisition of Madison's whereabouts had involved some kind of fraud. 'She was so happy to see me – once she got over the surprise, like.'

Fiona schooled her expression into neutrality.

'I had a hotel booked but they'd made a mistake, and I'd nowhere to stay, and she said no worries, you have to stay here.' He gave Fiona a defiant look, face flushed, and Fiona recognised it from the court hearing. It was the one he used when he was mixing a lie with truth. 'Before long we was just like we used to be.'

He smiled at Fiona, both beatific and triumphant.

She glanced away, unable to control her feelings for a second. *Oh, Mads, how did you not see it coming? He's obsessed with you and you gave him an in. Then he was off and running.*

If it was true, Madison must have been astounded to see him on the doorstep. Why hadn't she sent him packing? Was it because, like Fiona, she was here in this remote corner of the world, alone with him, and she hadn't wanted to get him angry?

Or, once she got over her shock and annoyance, had she been flattered by the attention? Fiona had seen the way he shook when he mentioned her; his desperate, ensorcelled adoration, strengthened rather than vitiated by his rage. For Madison, raised by her distant, unapproachable father, such proofs of love and emotion, however toxic, would have exerted an irresistible call.

She'd unceremoniously dumped Caspar, after all. Could it be because she wanted to take things up again with Dominic?

Fiona might be repulsed by him, but to Madison, Dominic Tate had always exerted a bizarre appeal.

Perhaps he had again, after a year's break.

It's certain that fine women eat/A crazy salad with their meat.

Could it have happened this way? Did Madison feel threatened, and contact him?

Or was this some romantic embellishment, some white knight fantasy, and even now he knew where Madison was lying, dead and rotting?

At this thought, it seemed to her that knives were digging into her heart every time she breathed.

He's a liar, she thought firmly to herself. *Never forget that he is a liar.*

'So I ended up staying,' Dom was saying, 'and then she told me the landlord had seen me and wasn't happy. She wasn't allowed to have any guests, like, and he'd threatened to kick her out and tell her work on her.'

Could *Dominic* have been the person who Maggie saw on Madison's doorstep? From a distance he could look similar to Jack.

'And nobody else knew you were here?' she asked.

He shook his head. 'No. I wanted us to go out, you know?' He glanced at Fiona then, and there was something furtive and vulnerable in him, something pathetic. 'I wanted to go to the

213

pub and do things, you know, together. But she said that it was a bad idea. Considering all that had gone on.'

'So, you left . . .'

'Yeah. On Sunday last. You were coming up on Friday anyway so I couldn't be here. She said she'd call me when you went back.'

'Did she say what she needed me to come up for?'

He shrugged. 'I only know what she told you that night.'

'What?' Fiona was confused, thrown. 'What night?'

'When she rang you last week. You remember – you were in Cambridge. I think you were in the bath at the time. She said to come up.'

Fiona could only stare at him for a long moment.

'You were here? When we had that conversation? You were here in this *house*?'

'Yeah, of course I was.' He offered her his thin, unpleasant smile, which was somehow worse than his rages. 'You were a complete fucking bitch to her, as I recall. Going on about it being "term time" and being "too busy". She always said that you were all about your career.' His eyes were flinty in that instant. 'You made her beg for you.'

Fiona did not answer. This was at once so accurate and yet so unfair she had no reply. She felt sick.

She had made Madison beg. It was true.

He gave her a mocking shrug.

'But you don't know what she needed me for?' asked Fiona.

'No. Moral support, maybe?' He smiled again. He was enjoying her discomfiture, her despair. 'She was going to tell the others, her work pals, that you were coming up to see the metalwork.'

She was terrified, she was furious, she was grief-stricken, but, as she realised with a little jolt, she was also thinking. Yes, he'd heard their conversation that night. She remembered how evasive Madison had been when she'd talked about him, and she remembered how surprised she'd been when Madison wouldn't directly accuse him.

Yeah, he'd been in the room with her, all right.

Such an enormous number of emotions moved through her then that she was paralysed. Rage, grief, fear, and yet one was first and foremost, one pricked her sorest, one tipped in poison – betrayal.

Her words, when she spoke, felt like powdered glass in her mouth.

'So you left Langmire a week ago today, and then you came back yesterday. And she was missing.'

His smile faded. He must have been recalling that he had nothing much to smile about.

'Yeah. I wanted to talk to Madison and thought I'd get her after you'd gone to bed. I had the key . . .'

'She gave you a key?' asked Fiona incredulously.

'Yeah,' he said, his eyes meeting hers, that high colour appearing in his cheeks. Selling in the lie, like he had in court.

'But straight away I could tell something was off. Your car was here and hers was gone.' He slapped a meaty hand to his chin. 'I mean, I was angry, like, because she wasn't properly speaking to me, but I knew I couldn't do anything stupid. If I . . . if I lost my temper . . . So I had to keep calm.'

'What did you do?'

'I had the key, so I just . . . I peeped inside. I didn't come in this room,' he added quickly, in the face of Fiona's dawning horror, the memory of being woken in the night by the sounds of someone in the house. 'I didn't come in the bedroom, I swear, I could see through the window. I just saw you asleep, your face like, because the moon was out. It was really bright. And I didn't understand, 'cos this was Mads' bed and she told me you'd be staying upstairs when you arrived.' He shrugged

again, a big, theatrical gesture – *so what would you do if you were me?*
'I just nipped up the stairs, to look for her. And of course there
was no sign. Bed was stripped. All her shower things gone.
None of her clothes there. Then I think I heard a noise down-
stairs, so I just left.' He sniffed, added by way of afterthought,
'Sorry if I frightened you, like.'

You aren't sorry, she thought. *You despise me.*

But she did believe, unrepentant and committed liar though
he was, that he was telling her the truth about that night.

She believed Madison had sent him away on Sunday because
she'd been expecting Fiona to come, then, after Wednesday,
Madison's texts had started to arrive.

And unlike Fiona, Dominic Tate had known, with the restless, obsessive ear of an infatuated, narcissistic lover, that he
was no longer communicating with the real Madison. As Fiona
should have known, but didn't – because she was too caught up
in her own drama, her own sense of martyrdom at having to
drop everything and come up here.

Her shame was complete. Dom had known Madison better
than she had.

Of course Dom had come back to Orkney, looking for her,
to demand an explanation.

But did he find her in the end? And where?

Did he do something to her?

'What did you think had happened?' asked Fiona, forcing
herself to sound neutral, unthreatening. 'When you found she
wasn't here yesterday?'

'I dunno.' He scratched his head, looked shifty now. 'How
should I know?'

'But you must have thought something, Dominic.' She sat
forward, met his gaze. 'Did you think she was with another
man, perhaps?'

'No!' His eyes widened. She'd hit a nerve. 'But maybe I . . .

I thought maybe she'd given you her phone, told you to pretend to be her, like.'

'What are you talking about?' Fiona asked, mystified.

'Well, you've got involved before. I've got to tell you, Fiona, me and Mads used to talk all the time about how very interfering you are.' His words were tight now, bitten off. That surge of underlying rage was visible again. 'I mean, it was you that persuaded her to put up those cameras in her flat and get me into trouble. It was you that made her take me to court. You wouldn't even *talk* to her for me. If you hadn't gotten all mixed up in things that are none of your business, Madison and me would have sorted things out months ago and things would never have . . . wouldn't have come to this.'

She stared at him. *So, was it me that stalked her? Slashed her tyres? Me that posted messages saying she ought to be raped and have her head cut off?*

'Dom, you need to go to the police.'

'I . . . I dunno.'

'What else are you going to do?'

He glanced at her then, and his gaze was flat, expressionless. It seemed to Fiona, in a moment of pure horror, that a thought, just now a mere seedling, had begun to grow in his mind.

Fiona was an inconvenience.

It would be good if Fiona was not here.

She needed to stamp on this seed, before it blossomed into action.

'Dom, this is serious. You need to . . .'

'I didn't do anything wrong! I'm not lying!' He was growing red again. 'I have all the texts, all the messages!'

'Yes, I know. I'm sure you do,' she said, dropping her voice so it was silky, honeyed – the voice Madison had doubtless used on him. 'But you have to go to them, Dom. You have to show them the messages . . .'

'But they won't know I've ever been here . . . not if you don't tell them.'

'Of course they know you're here. They know that right now. You're the very first person they will look for,' she said, trying to keep her voice soft, light. 'They know there was a restraining order. They'll have CCTV – they'll know you were on the ferry, they'll know you were on the island . . .'

'But . . .'

'You and I both know she *never* gave you a key to this place.'

'No, she did,' he interrupted, almost stammering. 'She . . .'

'No, she *didn't*,' said Fiona, with such decisiveness that he fell silent. 'I'd bet a thousand pounds on it. You borrowed hers and had one cut for yourself. And in a tiny place like this, someone is going to remember that. Don't you want to be the one that tells the police what you did and why, rather than them finding out?'

'I . . .'

'It's only a little island. There's nowhere to hide even if you wanted to, and no way to get off without being caught. You don't want to be caught, do you? You want to volunteer.' She fought to find the right words, the ones that would appeal to him. 'You want to walk in a like a *man*.'

He was mute, pale. She had made an impression upon him.

'You need to go and explain everything to them, the way you explained it to me. You need to give that key . . .'

'STOP NAGGING ME!' he yelled. His face was screwed up in an agony of indecision. 'Stop going on! I get it! I get it!'

Outside, there was the sudden purr of Iris's Taurus approaching.

His face whipped from her to the window and back again.

'Who's that?' he snarled. That menace was back.

She opened her mouth to speak, to deny, but suddenly his hard, furious fist was curled in her sweater, jerking her towards him. His breath was hot and stinking in her face.

'You fucking bitch. Did you tell anyone I was here?'

'No . . . *I* didn't know you were here!'

'Who is it?'

'Madison's boss. She's taking me back to Stromness . . .'

He glared at her for long seconds, while she held her breath. His frantic desperation was a palpable, living thing.

Then he flung her back against the floor. 'Get rid of her. Get rid of her or I will.'

28

Grangeholm, Orkney, January 2020

'Urgh, God, sorry, I thought I'd never get away from them. Why is it that people think asking you the same question a dozen times in different ways will magic the answer out of thin air? Never mind. I suppose it was a lot for them to take in. Did you manage to . . . Fiona, are you all right?'

Iris had emerged from the porch into the hallway, kicking her boots off and talking brusquely, her face fresh from the cold.

Fiona did not reply. She was still breathing hard, her heart pounding, her clothes and possessions strewn over the bed.

'Fiona?' asked Iris, peering up the stairs before coming into the bedroom.

'I . . .' Fiona looked up at Iris, swallowing against her dust-dry mouth.

Iris frowned. 'What is it?' she asked. 'Has something happened?'

Behind Iris, in the shadows of the hallway, a stray flicker of moonlight licked against Dominic Tate's sweat-damp brow. His eyes gleamed, like a feral wolf.

'Um, no.' Fiona was shaking now. 'No. I just got . . . I haven't packed. I . . . sorry, I think we just need to get out of here.'

Iris patted her shoulder, coming into the bedroom. 'No, I can see you're upset. It's all right. Is there anything I can do to . . . oh my, what happened to the wardrobe?'

She had stilled, her hand on Fiona's arm, staring at the broken mirrored door. 'What is *that*?'

'Oh . . . that?'

Oh, for God's sake, Iris, let's go.

'Uh, it happened before Mads went missing. Jack said the Fletts already knew about it . . .'

'Madison told us she'd just *cracked* the glass!' Iris stepped up to it, her hand to her chin, amazed. 'Fiona, somebody's *head* has gone into that.' She pointed at it. 'And is that *blood*?'

'Um, yeah, a little bit, I think so . . .' She swallowed again, desperate to get Iris out of here, get them both into the car.

Her eyes flickered to the darkened hallway, despite herself.

He was gone.

Where had he gone? Not out of the front door, they'd have seen him. Nor had she heard him on the stairs.

Weren't the knives in the kitchen?

'The Fletts said Madison told them she fell against the mirror getting out of bed,' Fiona said, desperate to placate Iris, desperate to get her to *go*.

'Fell? From where? *Upstairs*? The bed's only a couple of feet away. Whatever this was, it happened with real force.' She put her hands on her narrow hips, her dark ponytail twitching. 'Fuck,' she said. She turned to Fiona. 'Do the police know about this?'

'Um, yeah, I think so . . .' She wasn't even sure they did. She just needed Iris to . . .

Iris paused for a second, then simply sighed, pulling open the wardrobe door. 'Come on,' she said. 'I'll help you pack. Let's get out of here. The sooner the better, frankly.'

Oh, thank God, she thought. *Let's get out. Get out now.*

The hallway remained dark and empty.

Fiona packed her suitcase, her fingers trembling, her heart pounding, while Iris rooted through drawers, the wardrobe.

She was just forcing the suitcase lid down when she looked up and saw that Iris had vanished.

'Iris?'

There was no answer, merely a determined, quick tread heading up the stairs.

'Iris?' she shouted again, her voice growing louder, cracking with fear.

'I'm just going up. These toiletries, are they yours?' Iris called back down.

'We can always get those later . . .'

'Don't be silly. We're here now . . .'

Despite herself, Fiona darted forward, into the kitchen.

It was now empty.

Was he upstairs?

'Iris,' she said again, barely able to raise her voice above a squeak. 'Iris, I think we should . . .'

'What?' She'd appeared again on the stairs, her arms full of plastic bottles and deodorant. 'I think I got everything . . . oh, there's a draught in here. Can you just pull that window in the kitchen shut?'

Shaking, Fiona moved over to the window to close it, and saw a key lying on the kitchen table.

It must be Dominic's. Her own was in her pocket.

She quickly swept it up.

Iris offered her a smile. 'Is that it? Are we ready to go?'

* * *

'Iris . . .' Fiona could hear how small her own voice sounded.

'Yes?' Iris was heading back to Stromness. Over the dark sea the lighthouse on Helly Holm flashed and was still.

'Iris, Madison's ex was just at the cottage.'

Iris stilled. 'What?'

'Dominic. He was here. He said Madison invited him up. He had a key cut.'

Fiona held it up in her fingers, and the brass gleamed in the interior lights of the car.

'He did *what*?' Iris appeared stunned. 'Why didn't you say anything?'

'I thought he'd hurt us.' Haltingly, Fiona explained all that had happened since Iris had gone up to the Fletts'.

Iris did not interrupt, but at the end, sighed.

For a long moment she was silent, thinking. Then she looked up, into the rear-view mirror, and Fiona had the sense that, for a second, Iris was thinking of heading back there.

How like Madison she was, Fiona thought, with a sense of wonder. She was a warrior, like Madison. Nothing scared her.

'Iris, he's a very dangerous man, and . . .'

'Fiona,' Iris said, with a certain tactful delicacy. 'Have you considered that he just told you a pack of lies?'

'I . . .'

'You said yourself that he's an expert in mobile phones. Perhaps he tricked Madison into believing somebody else was pursuing her on Orkney, inveigled himself into "helping" her, somehow . . .'

'I don't know, Iris. He was very convincing. He'd definitely been in the room for a conversation I'd had with her last week. I mean, I . . .'

'Of course he's convincing,' said Iris contemptuously. 'These people always are. He could easily have bugged her. My point is, he's on the island and now Madison's car is in the sea and she's missing. As for the rest, I think that's for the police to unravel and that can start with us telling them all about him. Right now.'

Fiona nodded.

'You promised to help Madison, didn't you?' Iris had grown firm, her jaw set. She was punching a number into her phone, which she then held out to Fiona. A tiny voice – 'Police, Fire, or Ambulance?' issued out of it.

'Yes.'

Iris handed her the phone.

'Then go on. Keep your promise.'

Monday

29

Nordskaill, Stromness, Orkney, January 2020

When Fiona woke, cramped and exhausted, from her nest of blankets on the sofa, it was a beautiful winter's day outside. The smattering of snow from last night had held, and the sun glittered over it. The sea was a sparkling dark blue.

By the time they'd returned from Langmire and discussed all of these new developments with the others, it was too late for Fiona to sort out a hotel room, and the others would not hear of it anyway.

She was glad, in a way. A hotel room would have been very lonely.

And who knew who could find her there?

The archaeologists were in the kitchen, getting coffee and snatched breakfast prior to heading out to Helly Holm. Today was the big push, the attempt to remove the bones before the storm blew in.

There was a strained kind of earnestness at work in everyone, and she noticed that nobody spoke of Madison, seemingly determined to pretend that nothing was wrong. The removal of the human remains from the dig still had to be attempted today before all was potentially lost.

This embarrassed them all, she saw, but it was not enough to stop them.

And after all, what did she expect them to do? Sit at home, drink tea, weep?

Nevertheless, she felt a flicker of irrational rage. Her world was falling apart, and there was something hot and galling in the way other people's continued to turn, unchanged.

The first thing she did was phone the police again.

'And did you have some information you wanted to share?' asked the woman on the phone.

'No,' said Fiona, rubbing her tired eyes against her sleeve, 'not since last night. I was hoping Inspector Linklater would share some information with me. About the case. I'm coming into Kirkwall now anyway because I left my car there . . .'

'Well, it's under investigation at the moment, and if you're not one of the immediate family . . .'

'The family aren't here – her mother's had a heart attack with the shock, and I think Mads' brother is over there looking after her.'

'I know, love, but . . .'

'Look,' she said with sudden force. 'I came all the way up here to see Madison and I was the one who discovered she was missing! My whole life is on hold right now. I'm not asking for all the ins and outs – I know there are things that you can't tell me – I'd just like someone to give me the basic facts. At the moment I'm living on rumours and speculation, and it's driving me mad. Where the fuck is she?'

If she had surprised herself, she seemed to have shocked the policewoman. There was a moment of silence – she had the sense that the phone was being held to someone's chest, to mute it, and some lengthy conversation seemed to be taking place.

Fiona let her head drop into her hands. She had to try not to antagonise the police. For starters. Her mind was drifting now, and to miserable and depressing places. Would they send divers out to the car today? Tomorrow? What if they all had to wait till summer to find out if Madison was down there?

Surely not. Surely the sea could not be that cruel.

'Hello? Are you still there?'

The policewoman's voice startled Fiona.

'Yes, sorry, it's just that . . .' But she wasn't sure she was sorry. So far, being apologetic wasn't getting her anywhere.

'I'm sure,' said the woman, with professional sympathy. 'So, just so you know, the investigation will be handled from Inverness now.'

'Inverness? Why?'

'We're not set up to handle an inquiry of this type here. But anyway, they've arrived this morning and they'll be wanting to speak to you. They can explain the process to you themselves. Fiona Grey, is it?'

'Yes . . .' They must have been talking about her.

'You came up from Cambridge, aye?'

'I did . . .'

'And you're still on Orkney?'

'Yes. I'm staying with Madison's team at Nordskaill House, near Stromness . . . I haven't got the postcode on me.'

'Don't worry about that. We know it. We've got your mobile, it says here.'

'Yes.'

'Lovely. Don't worry. I know they mean to speak to you.' Her voice was soothing now, and Fiona sensed that in that hidden conversation, there had been a sea change. 'They'll be in touch very soon.'

* * *

'What're your plans, then?'

Jack stood next to her as she switched the kettle on.

At the kitchen table behind her, Iris was murmuring instructions to Callum, final remarks on the digging strategy, while Callum nodded wisely, his chin resting in his hand.

Becky, who was walking by, slowed, paused by the table to listen.

Iris did not look up at her. 'Are the lunches ready, Becks?' she asked shortly.

Becky, with a long-suffering sigh, moved away towards the fridge.

'Who, me?' asked Fiona.

'Yes, you,' said Jack, who appeared to be making an effort not to notice Iris and Becky.

'Um, I need to get my car,' said Fiona, distracted by what she had just witnessed. Obnoxious as Becky was, she seemed to get landed with the lion's share of the menial tasks at the dig – cooking, housework, taxi service . . . this, she knew, had not been Madison's experience. According to Mads, Iris had liked her, encouraged her.

Dominic Tate had told her that Madison thought her stalker was someone that was jealous of her.

With a slight crawling feeling, Fiona realised that Becky fit the bill perfectly.

'I realised I forgot something at Langmire,' she said. 'Madison's hat. It fell off the bed in the confusion and Iris didn't pack it. I don't want to lose it. And I still have the key . . .'

'Oh, you're heading back that way? You want to come see Helly Holm? We can give you the tour of the dig.'

'Won't you be busy?'

'Busier than a one-eyed cat watching three mouse holes.' Jack smiled. 'But you should still come. It's an amazing site.' He offered her a tentative shrug. 'It might be good to see what Mads was working on, yeah?'

Fiona had had it in her head to refuse, but after the night's long, tossing, turning thoughts, she had realised something – Mads had wanted to show her something.

Maybe it was time to start looking.

Other than the police, she would have little else to do. It

seemed unlikely, with Judy in hospital and Hugo with her, that she would be required to wait for her any more.

I should go home, Fiona thought. Adi was waiting. Work was waiting. She was accomplishing nothing here.

I will not go home until Madison is found.

She stilled, surprised at the steely resolve in this internal voice. Because that was the answer. Madison had called her up here because she was in trouble, and Fiona was going to answer that call through to the end.

She was going nowhere.

'Yeah,' she said, and heard the determination in her voice. 'I'd love to.'

'Are you good to go now? We'll drive you up to get your car . . .'

'Oh, there's no need to do that,' said Fiona. 'You're busy.'

'Not at all, it's partly on our way. You can follow us back.'

* * *

She drove her recovered car behind their white van, towards the road that would take them to Langmire, where the archaeologists would board the boat to Helly Holm. The fields were snowy, empty, and that vast sky was full of scooting, turbulent clouds. The lighthouse flashed against them.

On the fence lining the road there was movement, black flapping – a raven that had been resting on the wire lifted itself up with a harsh cry and moved off inland. Fiona watched it go out of the corner of her eye. Ravens, she thought, the feasters on the battlefield, the scavengers of the dead. It felt like an evil omen to her, and her heart sank within her.

Yet, according to the Vikings, also Odin's birds.

That was the legend, wasn't it? Odin, the Norse king of the gods, had two ravens called Huginn and Muninn, Thought and Memory, that he sent out into the world every day and who brought him back news of all that transpired.

And it seemed to her, for a second, that its black wings were like a fluttering banner, calling her to act, but to do what, she didn't yet know.

She was so tired she might have imagined it, but she thought she heard it calling after her, long after she had driven past it.

* * *

She said her goodbyes to the others at the tiny private jetty by Langmire, as they began loading the boat. Fiona would cross over to Helly Holm on foot in a little while to join them, once the tide sank.

The boat jostled the tyres nailed to the side of the quay, making her feel queasy and nervous. She was glad to leave them and set off on the day's errands.

First things first. She had to pick up Mads' hat and give the missing key, the one Dom had had cut, back to Douggie and Maggie. The bottles of Prosecco she had brought for her arrival dinner with Madison were still in the house, and she had resolved to give them to the Fletts as a thank you gift for letting her stay at the cottage.

She would certainly never drink them now.

* * *

The house itself looked vacant, bereft. The windows reflected the cloudy snow, and they appeared opaque, like shuttered eyes.

She yawned, caught sight of herself in the glass in the front door as she opened it. She was sallow, her hair sticking out like red straw, her eyes black-shadowed and tragic, like a banshee.

On the porch carpet lay a courier's note that had fallen through the letterbox – a package had arrived. It had been left in the shed around the back. She scowled at this, squinting.

There was no sign of a sender or an addressee on the note. This would be the books for review that her boss, Maude, had threatened to send. She hadn't thought Maude would follow through on it. She should have known better.

She tucked the note into the back pocket of her jeans.

On a peg in the porch hung Mads' furry wolf hat. She picked it up, wondering. She was sure she had had it with her in the bedroom. How peculiar. The Fletts must have come by this morning.

Surely it couldn't have been Dom. He no longer had his key and she'd shut the window last night.

Back here again, to this house. She sighed, closed her eyes. It was like she couldn't escape it, there was always one more thing. She wondered if she should go up to the house, ask them before coming into the cottage, but it was just a waste of everybody's time. She would nip in quickly, seize Madison's hat, and then take the key up there.

After that she would be done. She would never return.

Somewhere between her ears, it seemed to her that the raven was still croaking, an insistent message that she could not interpret.

Within, the house was as she had left it last night, except for a cold atmosphere that seemed unaffected by the heating. Dom had gone, she was sure, but still she checked upstairs, in the bathrooms, even in the cupboards.

She wondered where he was. Had he handed himself in? The police had refused to be drawn on the subject this morning.

It occurred to her that she was possibly standing in the middle of a crime scene, and that something might have happened here, or begun here, that had ended very badly for Madison. It might even have been happening while she was in Inverness at the Premier Inn, muttering and complaining to Adi about how inconvenient this all was.

A cold flush of shame was moving over her. Her whole attitude, from the very beginning, was that Madison was being selfish and dramatic. She could see that now. And while she hadn't said it out loud, she'd not stopped Adi or any of her other friends from expressing this opinion, not really. While Adi had been sniffing about Mads' lack of mutuality, and Maude had been shaking her head at the peremptory nature of Fiona's summons, had Fiona herself actually been not-so-secretly basking in the projection of herself as suffering martyr, willing to do so much and go so far for a friend?

Wasn't that the way they had always cast themselves – herself as the sensible one, the long-suffering one, the weak one from the broken home with the tragic past, and Madison as her confident, wealthy, thoughtless antithesis? And wasn't the truth more fluid, more complicated, and more difficult than that?

Yes, Madison had lied to her. It was undoubtedly true. But it was also true that she had been desperate for Fiona to come here.

She stood in the middle of the kitchen and she wanted to weep in regret.

Well, she thought, brushing a hand across her burning face, *that will all change.*

There must be something I can do.

The Prosecco was lying in the fridge. She had not even taken it out of the plastic bag when she put it in there, so she just lifted it all out, set it on the kitchen table. Other than that, the fridge was empty.

In the bedroom something was different.

The broken panel of mirrored glass in the wardrobe was gone, leaving only the wooden underlay behind, like a blind eye. Douggie must have come in and done it this morning.

That was fast, she thought, feeling an unreasoning, rising anger. What was the hurry?

Stop it. You're overreacting, she told herself, as her eyelids began to burn, her hands to shake, *because you've had this shock, and they've found, they've found* . . .

Madison, where are you?

'Hello?' came a familiar voice from the front of the house.

'Hello?' she called back, trying to compose herself into some semblance of normality. 'Douggie, is that you?'

What is it with them? she thought for a moment, filled with annoyance. *The minute something so much as moves here, they appear.*

They must have driven Madison mad.

'It is, it is.' He stood at the front door and was peering at her as he came into the hallway, and she had the unusual sense that he was not entirely sure what to expect from her.

She schooled her tiredness, her temper, away from her face.

'I saw you were here, and I thought, you know, I'll come down and see her . . .'

'They found Madison's car in the sea,' she said, not able to meet his eyes, aware that if someone was kind to her now, she would not be able to hold it together.

'I know,' he said, sounding gruff. His gaze was also kept low. 'Professor Barclay told me.' He let out a long, deep breath, shook his head. 'A very bad do. But no point fearing the worst till it's on ye, hen.' His hands went tentatively to his pockets, then out again, and she realised he wasn't sure whether to touch her or not.

'Thanks, Douggie,' she said. 'You're right. We don't know if . . . we don't know anything yet.' She took a breath, tried to pull herself together. 'Do we?'

'No,' said Douggie, with equal stoicism. 'Not at all. Anyway, I just wanted to say goodbye to you, and I wish you could have seen the place in happier circumstances.'

'Oh, how I wish that too.' She could feel it again, rising up within her, clamping her throat shut, compressing her breathing. 'I . . . I have some wine to give you both.'

He looked almost offended. 'No, you don't have to do that. You were barely here.'

'I know. I only stayed one night in the end.'

'So, you werenae here early this morning?' His blue eyes were wide, surprised. 'Maggie was sure someone was.'

'No. Not after we locked up the house last night. But it was so kind of you to offer it to me. You've both been so good.'

'Ah. Well. That's nothing,' he said, blushing. 'Anyway, you're very welcome. I know Maggie wanted to wish ye the best. She couldnae be here as she's working on Stronsay today.' He walked forward, let his rough fingers caress the blameless wood of the wardrobe panel. 'You know, you didnae have to take the glass out.' He gestured towards it. 'I would have been happy to do that. You might have cut yerself.'

In her tiredness, her grief, it took her a second or two to understand him.

'Me? I didn't touch the glass. I thought you did it this morning.'

'What? No, not at all.' He seemed surprised at the idea.

'But . . . you're quite sure? You didn't do this?'

'No, I did not.'

They blinked at one another, then at the wardrobe, with its new freight of sinister mystery.

'And Maggie . . . ?' Fiona asked. 'Could she have . . . ?'

'No. She'd have known better. I was going to patch it up after you left, you know, for the next guests. Put some tape over it for safety. The new panel is probably going to get held up on the mainland now, you know, with the bad weather we're expecting.'

'But that's so strange.' Fiona stared at the wardrobe, their figures reflected in the glass flanking the central missing panel, their faces filled with a mutual bafflement. 'Why would anyone do that?'

'I dinnae – I dinnae like to ask,' said Douggie, his words stumbling in embarrassment, 'but did you give the key to anyone else?'

She felt her face flush all the way up to the hairline. She hesitated. This was the moment she should tell him about the events of last night.

But if Dom Tate was telling the truth, and he wasn't Madison's stalker here, then who was?

Could she trust Douggie?

Or any of them?

Bloody hell, Mads. Why couldn't you just once, just when it mattered, have been straight with me?

Would it have killed you?

Douggie had stilled, aware that something was up.

She sighed, thrust her hands into her pockets. Well, this part he was going to find out anyway.

'You probably ought to know – Madison might have had a guest here for a couple of days. I think he had a key cut for his own purposes.'

Douggie didn't move. 'A guest?'

'Yes. A man.' Fiona looked away. 'I found out yesterday.'

Douggie shook his head. 'She's allowed guests, God knows. Cutting keys for them, well, that's . . .'

'I can guarantee you that she didn't know about it.'

He huffed out a heavy sigh.

'Anyway,' he said, 'it doesn't explain why anyone would come in here and smash the glass and tidy it away.' He shoved his hands in his pockets, peering at it. 'That is bizarre, to say the least.'

But Fiona suddenly understood and fell silent, chilled by the hugeness of it, the scope.

'There was blood in it,' she said.

'What? Blood? What do you mean, blood?'

'There was blood in the cracks in the glass. I saw it when I first arrived, before you and Maggie showed up, and it scared the hell out of me.' She turned to Douggie. 'You said Mads had had an accident with it, remember? When you came to the house to measure it and Jack was here with her.'

'Oh – oh aye. But she never said it was anything sinister. She told me it was her fault. She offered to pay for it.'

Fiona's mind was suddenly racing. 'Blood can be tested for DNA.'

Douggie merely stared at her, then at the wood.

'I – I suppose it could be tested, aye, if you say it like that. But now, think, your friend said it was her blood. And I remember her knuckles were cut.' He was shaking his head. 'Why would she say that, if it wasn't true?'

Because Madison was lying to you. She does that. She lies, when she has to.

'Could it have been the boyfriend's blood?' asked Douggie, pondering.

'Boyfriend?'

'Yeah, big blond fellow with the shaved head. He was with her. Mind, I didn't see any cuts on him.'

'Jack?' Fiona shrugged this off. 'Oh, he told me all about that. He said that it was a misunderstanding. They were just friends.'

Douggie's lips compressed. 'Does he say that, now?' he said tightly.

An unpleasant, crawling feeling had started between Fiona's shoulder blades. 'Yeah.'

Douggie's brows lowered, grew bushy and dangerous.

'Um, he said he was going to call you, explain that nothing was going on between them . . .'

'Is that so?' Douggie had grown gruff. 'If those two were friends, they were very, very good friends, let's put it like that.'

He folded his arms pugnaciously. 'And he certainly did *not* call here to deny it at any point.'

'Oh,' she said. 'Oh.' *He's mistaken Dominic for Jack*, she thought. *Oh, dear God, I hope he has.* 'Well, you know, about this mirror, I hate to suggest this, but, I think, well, we need to . . .'

'Call the police.' Douggie pronounced it po-liss as he glowered at the walls, as though they had personally betrayed him.

'Yeah,' said Fiona.

She gazed into the wood where the mirror had been.

It had been a clue all along, and yet she had not realised it.

I need to show you something, Madison had said.

And yet Fiona kept failing to see.

Someone had been in here, had been in this space, and now whatever secret the mirror had kept was gone for good, wiped away.

But who had done this? Dominic Tate? Jack? Perhaps even Douggie – he'd had the key, after all.

It could only be someone who knew what had happened to Madison.

She was sure of it.

30

Grangeholm, Orkney, January 2020

Fiona emerged from Langmire with Douggie, who looked saggy and lost, the ragged wind worrying at his blue woollen hat as he locked the door behind him.

'Are you all right?' she found herself asking, and he responded with a surprised glance, as though, like herself, he was amazed at this reversal of their situations, where she was comforting him.

'Oh, I'm fine, hen. It's just – it's a lot more than we're used to around here. It's a lot to take in.'

Fiona nodded. 'Yeah.'

'There's never any trouble here.' He shrugged himself deeper into his jacket. 'Not serious trouble.'

The sea had grown lively while they had been indoors, the waves now topped with white horses, and he paused for a moment, assessing it. 'If your pals are out on Helly Holm I wouldnae hang about if I were them.'

Fiona frowned. If anything, the weather looked more pleasant than it had in a while, though the wind had picked up. The sun was out, and the sea a brighter blue.

'It seems nice to me. An improvement.'

'Nah, this sun will be gone in an hour or two. And that sea . . . nah.' Douggie was shaking his head, peering suspiciously at the blue swells as though they were a gang of antisocial youths hanging around the front of his house. 'I would be safe indoors and have nothing to do with any of it, if I was you. Where will you stay tonight?'

'Nordskaill House,' she said. She did not add that Madison's 'boyfriend' would also be there, but Douggie gave her a shrewd look.

'I see. Well,' he said, offering his big hand in farewell. 'Watch yerself.'

* * *

Fiona threw open the boot of her little car. The wind tugged at its contents – her maps, her travel blanket – like a mischievous kitten, and before she could stop it, a plastic Waitrose bag was snatched up out of one of the side pockets and floating away towards the sea.

'Shit,' she said, confronted with sudden images of it sailing away into the water and going on to choke a whale. 'Oh no, no, no.'

She pursued it across the short, wind-blasted grass, grabbing it just before it could take flight from the tiny escarpment above Langmire's pebbly little stretch of beach.

'Gotcha!'

'Hello there. Not disturbing you, am I?'

She stumbled, nearly fell off the escarpment on to the beach below, in her surprise.

A man was approaching her, clad in a heavy jacket and black trousers, wearing a navy jumper over a shirt and tie. His silver Audi S3 had pulled in next to her own car and she had not even heard it.

'No,' she said, attempting to pull her flying hair to order under Madison's hat. 'Sorry. Are you the new guest for the cottage?' He didn't look like someone on holiday.

'No, I'm not a guest,' he said. His face was red and rough. 'I'm Detective Inspector Gillespie. I'm up from Inverness to look into the disappearance of Madison Kowalczyk from this address. Are you Fiona Grey?'

Of course. 'Yes, I am.'

'I think you called the station this morning, wanting to speak to me.'

'Yes. I did. You see, I don't know what to believe . . .'

'No?'

'I came up to see Madison about . . . I dunno, it was three days ago and she'd vanished. And then . . .'

She could hear the desperation in her voice, her desire to tell this story, to be believed, but instead he held up his hands as though to calm her down.

'All right – I was hoping to ask you some questions this afternoon. At the station – about three-thirty, if you can get over? Something I want to show you.'

She nodded furiously. Yes, that would be all right.

'I just . . . I wanted someone to tell me . . . You see, her team, her co-workers at the house, said you'd told them you'd found her car.' Fiona was aware of herself as huge-eyed, stammering, desperate. 'Is it definitely true? Is she in it?'

'Now, I'm afraid I can't tell you anything about the investigation that . . .'

'Can't you? I mean, I heard it was in the papers, so you must know something.'

He paused then, the wind blowing his short salt-and-pepper hair into tiny animated flickers.

'So,' he said. 'There's very little to say at this point that you haven't already read, then. A car has been found at the bottom of the cliffs on the west of the island, that's certainly true.'

'What kind of car?'

'A gold Peugeot.'

'Oh my God, that's what she was driving!'

'Yes,' he said patiently. 'It resembles a car that was reported missing three days ago. But beyond that, I can tell you very little. We don't know if anyone's in the car, and we won't be able to find out until sometime next week. It's too dangerous for divers to go down there, or even for us to send an ROV.' He shrugged at her. 'For the moment, at least.'

'I see.' She swallowed. 'But, I mean, I know it looks bad, but it doesn't necessarily follow, does it, that Mads is in it? I mean, she could be anywhere, couldn't she?' Her hands were shaking. 'She could have left the island, right?'

His gaze was very cool. 'What I *can* tell you, because we are about to tell the media this, is that we are fairly confident that Madison never left Orkney.'

'You are?' She felt cold, suddenly. 'How?'

'We've reviewed all of the CCTV footage for the ports and airports – there's no sign of her getting on a plane, or a boat. We even checked the cruise ships in case she'd stowed away for some reason – but nothing.'

'Oh,' said Fiona, with a violent exhale, as though he had just punched her in the face. '*Oh.* But . . . she could still be here but alive, couldn't she?' She could hear the ratcheting desperation in her voice. 'She could sail a boat. She piloted the archaeologists' boat. She had lessons. She was in the Sea Scouts when she was a teenager . . .'

Because it was one thing to suspect that the worst had happened, and quite another to hear all of those other doors swinging shut behind you, until the worst that could happen was the only thing left in the room with you.

'Possibly,' he conceded, but there was a reluctant edge to it.

'I mean,' Fiona continued, 'I know it doesn't look good, I mean, I know that,' she was jabbering, 'but she may have been kidnapped and held hostage somewhere . . . She had this stalker, you know, Dominic Tate . . .'

'Possibly,' he said, with a touch of astringent gentleness.

Fiona did not know what to say, so she said nothing, biting her lip, looking out towards the sea, because she could not bear to see that chilly compassion in his face any more.

'Did Dominic Tate hand himself in?'

'No.'

'Oh God . . . I should have, I don't know . . .'

'Don't blame yourself. You were potentially in danger. You did what you could to defuse the situation.'

Her mind was racing. She had a thousand questions.

'And what about Caspar? Have you heard from him?'

'Caspar Schmidt? Yes, he never left Sierra Leone. We did talk a little more with him, but he couldn't tell us much more than you did. Have you been in touch with Miss Kowalczyk's brother?'

'Hugo? Recently?'

'Yes.'

She wondered if he could see her flinch.

'No. Wait, yes,' she corrected herself. 'Briefly. It was him that told me about Judy's heart attack.'

'Well, she must be feeling better, as he's flying in this afternoon.' He put his hands in his jacket pockets, and Fiona tried to school her expression into neutrality, but already a racing panic had gripped her guts. 'We're picking him up from the airport. How well do you know each other?'

'A little.' Fiona glanced sharply at him. Did the police know about the money? The fighting? The power of attorney?

Would they know, if Judy didn't tell them? She couldn't see Hugo volunteering that information.

'I saw more of him when we were all kids,' she said. 'I think he and Mads . . . they grew apart.'

'I see,' he said. 'What about you? Do you have any family coming up here to join you?'

Her mouth snapped shut. The implication of this was

unmistakable, in the implacable way he had told her about the ports, the hotels. Fiona would need support, because he thought she was shortly going to hear some very bad news.

'No,' she said softly. 'I don't. My boyfriend is in Zurich at the moment. On business. I don't – I don't have any . . .'

Her eyes were burning. She was realising, now, the truth of it all. 'Madison was my family.'

31

The Strand, London, September 2019

'All right,' said Madison. 'What's the big deal? What are we celebrating?'

She was leaning back in the booth in their favourite bar, clad in a vivid red dress, her fake fur coat lying over her very real Burberry bag, a gift from Caspar.

Fiona grinned down at her, shaking the rain off her coat.

'Hello, Mads, let's get some drinks first. What are you having?'

Madison gestured negligently with her painted nails. 'Oh, I'm not bothered.' Her face was slightly strained, her jaw set. Fiona had the first sense then that this might not go well. 'What are *you* having?'

'I was thinking of getting some champagne in,' Fiona said, but already she could feel her enthusiasm draining away.

No, she thought with a sudden flash of insight, *being drained away.*

'Oh, champagne's so boring. Do you know what I fancy?' said Madison, gazing out of the window as huddled Londoners hurried past in the rain. 'Just a plain Chardonnay.'

'You're sure that's all you want?'

'Yeah, yeah. I can't drink too much tonight. Caspar is taking me to Prague for the weekend.'

'That's nice,' said Fiona.

Madison shrugged.

'So, just a Chardonnay, yeah?' asked Fiona. 'You're sure?'

'Yeah. But you can get champagne if you want.'

The bar was empty, the barman a little bearded hipster in a waistcoat whose smile seemed almost sympathetic, as though he guessed at the turn her evening was taking.

It would be impossible to drink champagne alone, as Madison must have known, so she ordered a large gin and tonic. Something told her she would need it. Almost pre-emptively, the bite of disappointment had shut its jaws in her heart.

No, she told herself. *Stop this. You're being selfish. Madison doesn't have to drink champagne if she doesn't want. And she doesn't know your news yet. People don't necessarily have to follow your script, you know.*

She carried the drinks over. Madison was buried in her mobile phone but put it down the minute Fiona reappeared and offered her a tight little smile.

'So how are you?' asked Fiona.

'Well, Hugo came round to mine last night. "Oh, Madison, I was just in town, let's go to dinner. I have reservations at Hawksmoor . . ." Like I'm going to go sit in a restaurant with him.'

'Yeah?' Fiona made a sympathetic face. 'What was it about?'

'What do you think?' Madison growled. 'Same as always. He wants my mum to give him power of attorney and "retire". I said, "She is retired, Hugo. She lives in a big house in Majorca and spends all day on the beach." Then it was, "Yes, but what if something happens to her? You know her *heart* . . ." And he has these big tragic eyes while he says it. "Aren't you worried about what will happen to her if she gets sick?"'

'I just said, "I'm very worried about what will happen to all her money and her house if you get your greedy fists on it and don't even have to ask permission to spend it any more. So no, I won't be hassling her to do whatever you want. Don't ask."'

Fiona shook her head. 'And?'

'He was despicable, Fee. Actually trying to bribe me at one

247

point. "You know, it has been so unfair that you've not felt the benefit of Dad's money. I could help you get a deposit for your own place, if I had access to the funds."'

Fiona did a double-take. 'He must be desperate if he's offering to give any money to you.'

'So, what do you think is happening?' Madison asked, taking a sip.

'He's in trouble. Big trouble this time, and he needs a lot of money in a hurry, and if your mum finds out she's going to go crazy.'

'My thoughts exactly, my dear Watson.' She smacked her lips. 'Anyway, he got no joy. Would like to think it's the end of the matter, but something tells me not.'

'Probably not,' Fiona agreed.

'So, are you going to keep me in suspense?' Madison asked. 'What did you invite me out for?'

'They've offered me the senior lecturer position.' Fiona was flushed, breathless. It felt faintly unreal, and now she was here, she could hardly believe she was saying it out loud. 'Senior lecturer. I'm only twenty-nine!'

'Fee, that's amazing news!' Madison grinned broadly, but her smile didn't touch her eyes. 'Congratulations!'

'Thanks.'

'This is that new university out in the north-east, right?' asked Madison.

'No, no. It's Cambridge. That's the great thing. I'd stay where I am, I'm just being promoted.'

Madison went very still. 'You'll be a senior lecturer at Cambridge?'

'Yeah.'

'You never said there was a job there.' There was a flat tone to her voice, as though Fiona had been concealing something important from her.

'No, Maude approached me . . . six weeks ago. Asked me why I hadn't applied.'

'You told me,' said Madison evenly, 'that if you wanted to get a promotion you would have to leave Cambridge.'

'I know, that's the amazing thing. Barbara is going to Harvard and I didn't even think of applying for her job. But Maude suggested it and . . .' Fiona shrugged, smiled. 'I got it. Starting in January.'

Madison frowned. 'That's all very quick. Didn't they advertise it?' She sipped at her wine, not meeting Fiona's eyes. 'I don't remember seeing an ad for it.'

'Yes, they advertised it.' Fiona could feel herself bridling. She was being subtly accused of something, she saw, some kind of underhand dealing. 'And then they suggested I apply for it and I got it.' Her cheeks were burning. 'Is there a problem?'

'No, no. God, you're so fucking *sensitive*.' Madison picked up her glass, and she wasn't sipping any more, but taking a big gulp.

'Yeah, maybe,' Fiona said, biting back a retort. Maybe Madison was right. Even though Fiona had never thought of applying for the job initially, once it had been suggested that she should, she had spent the last couple of weeks on tenterhooks. 'Waiting to hear has completely fried me.'

'Hmm,' said Madison, still not meeting her eyes. 'It's great how you managed to get lucky with that one research paper,' she said, taking another big gulp of her wine. 'You've spun a whole career out of it. It's the gift that keeps on giving.'

'What do you mean? I've written lots of papers.' Fiona was colouring again. 'I've worked really hard.'

'Yeah, but they're all the same thing, aren't they? *Technical information exchange in ferrous metallurgy*, it just rolls off the tongue.'

'Well, that is my specialty,' said Fiona, putting her own glass down. She didn't want to drink any more. 'What's got into you?'

'What are you talking about?'

'This is huge for me, and you don't seem very happy.'

Madison shrugged. 'Of course I'm happy for you. But they were always going to push you up on the fast track.' She drained her glass. 'You play their games and say the things they want to hear. You're their *type*.'

Fiona's blush was turning into a true hot rage. 'You're always doing this.'

'Doing what?' Madison still wasn't looking at her.

'This. Whenever I achieve something, it's like it doesn't matter or I didn't deserve it or I did something sneaky for it. Only you don't come out and say it, you just make these snide, snarky asides and don't look at me while you say them.' Fiona seized her coat. 'I worked my arse off for the last five years and now I'm finally getting recognised, and all you can do is sit there and undermine me.'

'I didn't say that or anything like it. Now you're just being paranoid.' Madison's eyes were hard. 'You never even mentioned to me that you were applying for this thing . . .'

'What was the point? I didn't think I was going to get it.'

'Hmm,' said Madison. 'Didn't you?'

'Whatever,' snapped Fiona, jerking to her feet. 'Enjoy Prague.'

32

Grangeholm, Orkney, January 2020

After DI Gillespie left, pressing his card into her hands with the request to call him if she thought of anything else in the meantime, Fiona let herself back into her car. She should, she realised, be heading over to the dig on Helly Holm and the causeway was at low tide now. It was an amazing, once-in-a-lifetime opportunity to see a spectacular site being unearthed.

However, no matter how she tried, she could work up no enthusiasm for the prospect. She had all the proximity to death she could possibly want; right here, right now. She felt trapped in this liminal space where her world was about to change forever, and for the worse, and the one person that she would rely upon to support her through such changes was no longer here.

Nor could she even begin mourning Madison. She was waiting for that most elusive of boons – closure. She let her head fall on to the steering wheel for a moment, while the cries of seabirds, like squeaky joints, floated in from over the ocean. *No man is an island* – was it Donne that had said that? Well, now she was an island – a rock alone in freezing, pounding waters.

She sat up once more and felt the pinch of cardboard in her jeans pocket. Oh yes, the package. Maude's books. She'd better get them before she drove away, as she had no plans to ever return to this house again.

The shed was unlocked but the wooden door latched shut. The package was bigger than she expected, sitting on top of the green recycling bin, and when she picked it up, heavy.

She carried it back to the car and was in the process of ripping it open when she noticed, with a flutter of horror, that it was actually addressed to Madison. She dropped it back on the seat, with a little cry of fright.

Where the box had been torn open, silver glinted within from a secondary covering of bubble-wrap.

'Shit.'

She was so crushed, so stressed, she was making stupid mistakes. She turned the box over and saw that the sender was actually a computer repair company. She stilled, her thoughts bubbling, then crystallising – of course, Callum had told her that Mads had blown up her own laptop and borrowed a company one.

And hadn't she thought that was strange at the time? It was brand-new, after all. Madison had bought it in her presence.

At least she hadn't opened the whole box, she thought ruefully, starting the engine. She would give it to the police this afternoon, try to explain herself, but a little lump of dread was forming in her throat at the mere idea.

She took a deep breath, tried to clear her head, fight off the incipient tears. For now, she would head over to Helly Holm and see what all the fuss was about.

* * *

Careless talk may cost lives, but it had drawn a tiny crowd. About half a dozen people and two dogs were milling about at the foot of the causeway, chatting amongst themselves, peering under shading hands towards the islet. Above them, clouds raced across the sky.

On the island itself, rising out of the sparkling sea with its lacing of froth, Helly Holm was once again distant and imperious, its lighthouse a pale spike. The archaeologists' boat was tied up by a little spit of land that jutted out at the side of the islet.

A large white tent had been erected somewhere over the central trench, and it was billowing angrily against its poles.

Someone had emerged from it, but it was too far away to see who it was.

'What d'you think it is?' a man was asking a couple with a Cairn Terrier nosing around their feet. 'Think they've found something?'

'I dunno,' said the woman, sporting a bright pink anorak and an Orcadian accent. 'We were going to walk over and ask them, but the causeway doesn't look too good this morning.'

Fiona threaded her way past them and instantly understood what was meant. The first morning she had attempted the walk, the low tide had exposed rock pools and algae but the sea had not been much in evidence.

This was very different. She could see it now, much closer, and every so often it sent forth forceful, slapping wavelets that in places looked likely to wet her ankles.

She wanted to turn around and go. The sea frightened her. The sky was blue, but what cloud there was, was in brisk, sulky motion.

Do this, she told herself.

She wanted you to look at something.

Go and look.

About halfway across the causeway she paused, anxious, aware that she did not want to be trapped here, but up towards the tent she saw Jack and Callum emerge, notice her. Jack gave her a big wave, while Callum turned on his heel and went back into the tent, presumably to tell Iris she was coming.

Fiona realised she was committed.

She managed to reach the steps without incident, ascended the dried yellow grass. Patches of snow still remained in places where the sun could not touch them, in ditches and nooks in the flanks of the islet. As she gained the top Jack reached over and hauled her up by the hand, so she would avoid standing on the open trench that yawned before her like a grave.

'Are you all right?' he asked. His eyes were kind but tired.

'I'm . . . the same.' Looking at him, his easy compassion, the way he was always the one who asked how she was, who betrayed any interest in her quest without being remotely pressing, it was hard to believe that he was lying about his relationship with Madison.

'How's the morning gone?' she asked.

'Good. The email with the licence was here first thing. We'd prepped the burial chamber beforehand so we're going to try and get as much of the work done today as we can.'

'Exciting,' she said, trying to inject some enthusiasm into it.

'Yeah,' he said, as Becky stomped out, heading past them, up the hill. 'The weather is going to be rotten tonight and absolutely bollocks starting from tomorrow, so we want to get the first skeleton out and ready to ship, if we can. It's in danger otherwise.'

The wind ruffled her hair, as if to underscore the point.

'Come in,' he said, gesturing at the tent, over Callum's head, who was kneeling down to grab a mess of small plastic bags out of one of the big storage lockers. He appeared to be studiously ignoring her. 'You can see for yourself.'

* * *

'This is the centre of the boat, with the burial chamber,' said Jack, as they stood inside the tent. 'Most of the stern has been excavated already.'

Within, three big spotlights were turned on to the grave, being run by the mobile generator which she could hear chugging happily away to itself.

Iris kneeled near the top, wielding a trowel with extreme care around the exposed dome of a human skull. Her expression was one of utmost concentration. She glanced up at Fiona and offered her a short nod before returning to her work.

Everything smelled of freshly turned earth.

'Wow,' said Fiona. 'How far back does the boat go?'

Jack gestured forward to the front of the tent, past Iris's head, to the outside. 'The prow is out there somewhere. We haven't even touched it yet. It's got more soil coverage, so it's less endangered than the rest. But the stern was already exposed by the time we started digging, with the cliff erosion and the bad weather. You were practically climbing over it to get up here.'

'A nice big boat.'

'Oh yeah.' He nodded. 'We're very lucky.'

The trench itself was square, about eighteen inches deep. Besides the skull, Fiona could see the end of a long bone poking up, and the shadow of what must have been a beam of wood at some point, now reduced to little more than a stain.

'Is there anything I can do?' she asked.

He shook his head. 'Not really. We've all got our orders. You're not insured to do any delicate excavation anyway.' He shrugged. 'I don't see how we're going to do this by the contract end, to be honest. Iris has been in touch with Historic Environment Scotland, to see if we can get more resources. Today will be busy, though – the county archaeologist will come through, HES will come through, and I think, once they do, things will start to really take off.'

Fiona nodded. 'It's a great site.'

'Iris thinks we might even be able to get a production company on board.' He grinned. 'I think we'd need to be a lot more sexy before we could depend on that. You'd want big, glamorous finds – something photogenic.'

'Yeah,' said Fiona, trying to nod, to be interested, but as her gaze lowered to the skull, its single exposed eyehole packed with soil, as though blinding it, she felt nothing but horror. The dirt looked like a brown bath, with this skeleton drowning in it, its jaw half open in a scream.

The similarity to what could be happening to Madison was suddenly unbearable.

'I have to get out,' she said.

'What?' asked Jack.

'I have to get out,' said Fiona, trying to master her panic, her fear. Even Iris had looked up again, peering hard at her. 'I have to . . . give me a minute.'

And suddenly she was outside and striding through the wind, to the edge of the islet, where the sea was, and she was breathing, trying to inhale that biting wind and take some sustenance from it while the lighthouse flashed at her every twenty seconds, like a warning. She should not have come here.

She should not have come here.

'Is something up?'

Someone was there, holding a mug of hot tea in her hand.

It was Becky.

'I'm . . . I'm . . . I'll be fine,' said Fiona. 'I was just looking at the lighthouse.'

This would have seemed patently untrue to Fiona, but Becky accepted it without demur. Fiona again had the sense of Becky as someone who didn't quite know how to handle herself around humans.

'Yeah, it's cool. It just runs on solar power.' Becky shrugged at her, held her gaze, appeared almost friendly.

Fiona glanced at her. She didn't want to deal with Becky's moods now, but somehow, today, there was a change, something almost hungry at work in the other girl.

'Sorry,' said Fiona, and noticed again that she was always doing this. What was she apologising for? 'It's just that . . .'

'It's Madison, isn't it?' Becky asked.

Cautiously, Fiona nodded. 'I shouldn't have come here. To the dig.'

Becky sat down heavily on a nearby boulder. 'I know. It's just so wrong, just carrying on as normal while . . .'

'While what?'

Becky fixed her with a glowering brow. 'They're all so *economical* with the truth, you know.'

'They . . . ?'

'Callum. Jack. And Iris. Especially Iris.' She snorted. 'It's disgusting, when you think about it. Obviously, something bad has happened to Madison, but everyone's so fucking desperate and ambitious that they're pretending it's not happening. It might interfere with their precious careers. Like, she just "went away".' Becky gestured parodically. 'As *if*.'

'What do you think happened?'

Becky blinked at her, those small eyes hugely magnified by her glasses. For a moment Fiona thought she was about to bark something out, but then she shut her mouth with a snap. 'I've no idea,' she said after a moment, shrugging dismissively, her eyes closed. In that instant, she looked like a mulish little girl.

More than one person was being economical with the truth, obviously. Becky definitely had some notion of what it might be.

Perhaps it could be drawn out of her, somehow.

'See,' Fiona said, 'I just can't shake the idea that Madison was in some kind of trouble. And I can't go home until I find out what it was.'

Becky shrugged again. 'Well, she might be down there in the car in the sea, she might not. But I do know one thing – no way did Madison just wake up and bugger off one day.'

Fiona looked at her. 'What makes you say that?'

Becky rolled her eyes. 'Common sense. Why should she? She was getting loads of great site experience on a really exciting dig; a fucked-up dig, yeah, but a career-making, important dig. She was filling in for Iris half the time, even helping out with research for *Discovering the Past* – doing stuff well beyond her pay grade. It would look great on her CV.'

'You think?'

'I don't have to think,' Becky said contemptuously. 'She knew it would. We talked about it for hours. We knew that not all of us have the advantages of dreaming spires to back us up – we have to graft.' She threw Fiona an arch look and crossed her thick legs angrily, her huge, muddy boots spattering her jeans cuff as she did so. 'If anyone was going to quit this shit-hole first, it was me.'

Fiona felt a low heat rising in her cheeks. Who did this girl think she was? Becky didn't know anything about Fiona, and how she'd worked and . . .

We knew that not all of us have the advantages of dreaming spires . . .

Maybe Becky *thought* she knew something about Fiona. Fiona remembered Madison's joyless congratulations when she'd told her about her promotion at the department to senior lecturer, her backhanded compliments about Fiona's research work.

Maybe, she thought uncomfortably, Madison had been saying something along these lines to Becky. The thought made her feel nauseous.

Stop it, she thought. *You don't know that.*

Stick to the task at hand.

'You know, Iris implied to me that you two didn't get on.'

'Me and Iris?'

'No. You and Mads.'

'That's completely ridiculous.' Becky made an annoyed har-rumphing noise. 'We're digging in the most challenging, fraught conditions, a person down a lot of the time, and carrying quite a few of the others too, the idle bastards.' She let out an arch little sniff. 'It's not like Callum's much use. Running around with your camera taking pictures for Instagram isn't exactly hard labour.'

Fiona crossed her arms. 'I suppose not . . .'

She had guessed that Becky and Callum were probably rivals. Had Madison and Callum been rivals, though?

Dominic Tate had said that Madison thought she was being stalked by someone jealous of her . . .

'You try staying all upbeat and happy-go-lucky with that going on in the background,' Becky muttered. 'And the foreground. And around the sides.' She folded her arms. 'Felt like we two and Jack were the only ones getting our hands dirty.'

'It must have been insanely stressful,' said Fiona, wondering at this recasting of the past. 'So much pressure to get everything right. You know, Iris mentioned that Mads had messed up some C14 samples . . .'

'Did she?' snarled Becky, with an impressively sarcastic swoop in her voice. 'Did she really? You'd have to prove that one to me.'

'What do you mean?'

Becky flicked a dismissive hand. 'Madison always looked to be doing everything right when she and I were processing the finds. Jack has been stretched six ways to Sunday, and Iris – she has no idea what's going on. She's barely here.'

'But she says there's only been a couple of trips . . .'

'Let's just say,' said Becky, stealing a quick look around the empty site before turning back to Fiona, 'that I've come into the tent and found Iris asleep over the laptop before today. Found her that way more than once, in fact.'

'You think Iris was tired with all the travelling, and she messed up and blamed . . .'

'I don't know,' said Becky, snorting again. 'I'm just saying what I saw.'

Yes, you keep doing that, thought Fiona. *You insinuate, loudly, then never have the courage of your convictions and state your conclusion. You are perhaps the most overtly angry passive-aggressive person I've ever met.*

Fiona kept her voice calm, soothing. 'It does sound very stressful.'

'You've no idea,' Becky grunted.

'The thing that gets me is why would Mads invite me up here and then . . .' She sighed. 'I just don't get it.'

Becky scowled at her.

'I'm sure it wasn't deliberate. She was counting the days until you came.'

Fiona glanced up in surprise. 'Really?'

'Yeah, *really*. It was all she could talk about in the days before you arrived. How you and she were going to go visit the other islands and she'd booked you in for a night's stay somewhere as a surprise.' Becky rolled her shoulders. 'I forget where it was. Somewhere nice.'

Fiona was stunned, as though, without meaning to, Becky had buried a knife in her heart, not with malice, but with kindness. Had flighty, difficult Madison really been that excited to see her?

Oh, Mads. I wanted to see you too.

'She kept banging on and on about it.' Becky's lips pinched together, grew white. Her voice was getting louder. 'It was very *annoying* after a while.'

Of course it was. Because you weren't invited, realised Fiona, with a lightning strike of insight, followed by the bite of pity.

After weeks spent elbow-deep in mud and bitching together about the rest of the team, and probably about me too, you thought that she'd bring you along with us. You thought that you two were friends. All this talk about arrangements did was prove to you that Madison only thought you were colleagues.

Something told Fiona that sullen, furious, undermined Becky didn't have many friends of her own. She fetched and she carried, but nobody took her seriously, not even Iris, her PhD supervisor. These plans, this excited anticipation of Fiona's visit, would have thrown all this into sharp relief for her.

Would she be angry enough at Madison over it to hurt her?

Fiona stole a glance at Becky, who was affecting to retie her bootlaces, her lips still compressed and pale.

Surely not, thought Fiona, horrified. But . . .

'She didn't do any of that for her brother,' said Becky. 'When he came . . .'

'Becky?' sang out Iris's clear voice from the dig site. 'Can we borrow you for a moment?'

Becky huffed out an aggrieved sigh and rolled to her feet. 'Her Majesty calls,' she muttered, forcing her hands back into her gloves. 'I should be glad she's actually here for once, I suppose.' She peered at Fiona over the top of her glasses, and her expression was suddenly unreadable, flinty. 'Are you going to help out or not?'

'No,' Fiona said, and felt a tiny measure of satisfaction in doing so. She put her hands in her pockets. 'I need to head back before the causeway gets any worse.'

'You could get the boat back with us later.'

'No. I'm frightened of boats. I don't like being on the sea.'

Becky narrowed her eyes at her, as if this was a ruse so Fiona could shirk some hard work, and with a little snort, turned and hurried back to the tent, nearly colliding with Callum, who had emerged from it to look for her.

He turned back – but not before he had paused for a moment, his eyes seeking out Fiona, settling on her, and then moving back into the tent after Becky.

33

A965, Orkney, January 2020

It took Fiona a long time to get over her conversation with Becky.

Madison had been excited, she thought, as she drove towards Kirkwall. Madison had been making plans for them both. And now Madison was gone and Fiona knew, deep in her heart, that she was never coming back. All the doors had closed behind her now. She was left alone in the room with the worst news in the world.

But she found she couldn't cry.

She needed to find out why.

Why would anyone kill Madison?

And suddenly Fiona was confronted with every phone call, every drunken wine bar therapy session, every night sat in the car next to her while she lurked, trying to catch her inamorato coming out of another woman's house.

Above her the sky was a fleece of shining white clouds, breaking apart every so often to reveal a tantalising blue, as she pulled into the police station. Her lip curled. It was beautiful, and it was wrong and ugly and obscene that today should be beautiful, with Madison at the bottom of the sea and the waves crashing so hard above her nobody could reach her.

By the time Fiona appeared in the station, approaching the glass windows separating the staff from visitors, the box containing Madison's laptop in her arms, her eyes were red and wet but she did not weep.

'I'm here to see . . .'

'Of course, just a minute,' said the woman at the desk, who'd clearly been expecting her. Behind her DI Gillespie hove into view.

'Good morning,' he said. He seemed reservedly compassionate and yet just a little suspicious of her. 'One moment while I get this now . . .' He vanished towards the back, while the woman at the desk watched her closely through spectacles low on her nose.

He reappeared beside her, at the interrogation room door, with a small plastic bag about the size of a postcard dangling from his fingers. Within it, something glinted gold.

'If you'd just follow me this way, Dr Grey.'

When had she become Dr Grey to him? she wondered, as he led her into the interrogation room. It was oddly jarring, and she felt uncomfortable as well as wretched as she took the seat he offered her.

'This came,' she said. Her voice sounded thin and scratched to her own ears. 'I thought it was for me. It's Mads' laptop.'

'It came to you? Where from?'

'Some computer repairs place. It was delivered to Langmire this morning. I found it after you left. In the shed. There was a card . . .' She swallowed. 'You should probably take it.'

He glanced at it. 'You opened it?'

She shrugged. 'I thought it was books. From work.'

He lifted the box out of her hands, put it on the empty chair next to him. She noticed he was careful not to touch it unduly.

'So,' he said. 'How are you doing?'

Fiona opened her mouth to speak, shut it again. She didn't know how she was doing. There were a thousand questions she could ask, but none of them were going to change anything. Her best friend was gone and she had been supposed to be helping her, which she'd failed at, and had spent the last few days hating her, and suspecting her of all kinds of treachery.

And all that while, she'd been most likely trapped in a car, dead.

'I . . . I don't . . .'

Her words tailed off. She had nothing to say.

'I'm very sorry. I'm sure this is very distressing and I won't keep you long.' He seemed relieved to drop the discussion of feelings, to cut to the chase, and he punched the buttons on the recording device. Something about his rough red face suggested to her that the processing of Gillespie's feelings had a distinctly liquid character.

'I'd like to ask you about an object that might have a bearing on the investigation, if I may.'

Fiona could not conceal her surprise. She had not been expecting this. 'An object?'

'Yes, can you identify it as Madison's?'

'Um . . . yes, if it will help,' she said, but at the same time, a sudden terror was at work in her. Was she going to be shown bloodstained clothing, broken possessions, some evidence of cruelty or suffering?

'It's nothing to worry about,' he said, as though he had guessed her feelings. 'Are you all right with this being taped?'

Fiona shrugged. 'Yes, of course.'

He nodded, pressed some buttons that clicked loudly.

'This is Detective Inspector Mark Gillespie interviewing Dr Fiona Grey in Kirkwall Police Station in regards to evidence sample number MG/YE01/01 . . . So, Dr Grey, I just need you to look at something and see if you can tell us anything about it. All right?'

She nodded slowly, intimidated by the machine, by these proceedings. 'Yes. If it will help.'

'It will be enormously helpful, yes, thank you.' He picked up the small packet, and without opening it, passed it across the scarred table surface to her. 'Do you recognise this at all?' He turned to the machine. 'I am now showing Dr Grey the evidence.'

It was a gold pendant, and Fiona frowned, disappointed and yet also relieved. She had never seen it before. For her own part, she could tell in an instant that it was the sort of thing Madison, who rarely wore necklaces, would have passed over.

She shook her head at him.

'No. Sorry.'

'Are you sure?'

She was aware of herself then, appearing to have barely glanced at it, to be dismissing it. She turned her attention back to it, wanting to appear cooperative.

It was a figurine of a woman with wings and a sword, strung on a yellow chain. Its long hair was tied in a knot at the top and it was through this that the thong had been threaded.

She bent to it again, and something about it struck her.

The pendant itself was roughly the size of a small lipstick, but gleamed with a dull but undeniable lustre, a warm yellow that she recognised from things she'd analysed in the lab.

Her heart quickened. Could it be?

'Can I pick it up?' she asked.

'You can,' he said, looking a little uncomfortable. 'But I would have to ask you not to open the bag.'

'Oh, sure.' She lifted it into her palm, feeling its weight. *Oh yes. Oh, you beauty* . . .

'You know, I think this is gold,' she said, peering at it. 'I mean, *pure gold*. You don't often see a lump that size of it out in the wild, especially in modern jewel . . . oh. Oh my. It has hammer marks. On the base. This was handmade.' She glanced up at him. 'Where did you *find* this?'

'I'm afraid I can't tell you that.'

'Hmm. Well, I don't think it's jewellery – well, not jewellery Madison owned and wore, 'cos it's not the kind of thing she liked, but . . . I wouldn't like to say too much without a proper analysis, so don't hold me to this, but this might be an archaeological find.'

She had been so engaged in studying it – the lines of its hair, the tiny places where it had been worn smooth, as though it had been handled, thousands and thousands of times before it had been lost or buried, so that when she looked up and saw Gillespie's face intent upon her, she nearly dropped the packet. His eyes were alight.

She had said something remarkable, it seemed.

'An *archaeological find*?' he repeated.

'Um, well, obviously I could be wrong, but yes.'

'And what makes you say that?'

Fiona felt herself flushing under the pressure of his attention. 'I . . . first of all, even more than the style, which could be a modern reproduction of an ancient piece, but we'll get back to that . . . I guess it's the weight and condition. The way it's scratched in some places and smooth in others – see here? Pure gold is a soft metal, and very hard to keep pristine. Modern gold, like, say, in your . . .' She had looked to his hands, as she often did when having this speech, but his fingers were bare. 'Gold in wedding rings tends to be mixed with copper alloys to keep it harder. Otherwise you wouldn't be able to wear them all the time without scratching them.

'Ancient gold on the whole tends to be purer, around the twenty-four-carat mark. You can dint it with your teeth.' She held the packet towards him, pointing out these features with her thumbnail. 'But it's the colour that's the giveaway. Pure gold just looks a certain way – the shade can change, but the lustre . . . Every culture in the world that has exposure to it has valued it as a high-status commodity.

266

'Gold's not like silver – it doesn't react with anything, so when you find gold objects it's always astonishing, breathtaking – they mostly look just as beautiful as the day they were made, hundreds or thousands of years ago. It's like – it's a direct encounter with the ancient past, because it looks to us just as it would have looked to them.'

He didn't answer her straight away, simply watching her, before remarking: 'I understand you know a lot about this, Dr Grey . . .'

'Oh, I suppose so. Ancient metallurgy is my specialty. Mostly steel, weapons in the main.'

'So have you seen something like this before?'

She turned the packet over in her hands, trying to see through the reflective glaze of the plastic, a building excitement in her. 'Personally? No. But I'm pretty sure it's early medieval Norse, at least in style. I think it's a goddess – no, scratch that.' Realisation blossomed within her. 'It's a Valkyrie.'

'A Valkyrie?'

'Yeah. You know? Like *The Ride of the Valkyries*? The opera? By Wagner?'

'Let's assume I'm not an archaeologist or an opera buff.' He was terse. 'Explain it to me, for the purposes of the tape.'

'Oh, right. Of course. Well, a Valkyrie is a female mythological figure.' She leaned forward, warming to her theme. 'To the pre-Christian Norse, the highest honour you could have was to die bravely with a sword in your hand. Valkyries were sent by Odin to choose the best from the dead on the battlefield and give them a lift to Valhalla, one of the Viking heavens. When they arrived, they would spend eternity fighting during the day and then feasting and drinking at night. Valkyries would serve the warriors their mead – they're dream girls, if you like, a fantasy figure to both men and women.'

'And you think that's what this is meant to be? A Valkyrie?'

'Well, I don't know. She's got a sword and shield, and wings. The style is early medieval Norse, and I'm betting that if you're showing it to me you found it here on Orkney, where there is a lot of Norse archaeology.' She glanced up at him again, searching for clues, but his face had frozen.

'And if it is a Valkyrie,' she continued, 'it's quite a unique piece. There aren't that many Valkyrie pendants, and they are usually made of silver and very rarely in gold.' She squinted at it. 'I've never seen one like this in gold, actually. It's amazingly detailed. But again, I'd need my lab to make anything of it, or tell you if it's genuine.'

'So you think this has come from an archaeological dig? Here in Orkney?'

'I've no way of proving that just by looking at it, I'm afraid,' she said, hearing the note of apology in her words. 'Especially since it looks like it's been cleaned.'

'Cleaned?'

'Yes, I mean, a find like this wouldn't be processed on site, usually. They'd ship this off to a specialist, probably someone at the British Museum, or the National Museum of Scotland in this case, and they'd do the cleaning, the analysis, you know. It looks like treasure, so you'd have to notify the coroner as well . . .' She thought for a long moment.

'I don't know where this came from. Certainly the chain is modern. You can see how thin and cheap the links are, even though the metal is harder. That said, it's not scratched the gold, so it must have been put on very recently. It *could* have come from the dig. You'd have to ask to see their finds records.'

She nudged it with her finger through the plastic, while the tiny woman regarded her with blank, saucer-like eyes. 'I mean, on the weight of the gold alone, this is probably worth thousands of pounds. When you factor in what a rare and unusual find it is . . .'

She trailed off, the implications of it all becoming clearer and clearer. If this had been brought in with links to Madison, then she might have been up to something much more obviously shady than cheating on Caspar with Jack.

They said Iris Barclay had a magic touch for finding rich, important sites. The ship grave at Helly Holm had already yielded an impressive little coin hoard, according to Jack. Who knew what else might turn up?

Could Madison have stolen this and been in the process of selling it?

Could she have been killed over it? Could there have been a rendezvous somewhere, and whoever it was had decided it was cheaper to murder Madison than pay her?

Would Madison really do something so immoral, so stupid? Fiona wanted to dismiss the idea, but still, burning like a hot coal in her memory, was Madison telling her that Dom Tate had anonymously contacted Rachel, her old boss in the London unit, and accused Madison of selling artefacts on the black market. Then Iris telling her the exact same thing, only a couple of nights ago.

She dropped her hands to her lap.

'I'm sorry,' she said to Gillespie. 'But this is all conjecture. Without being able to analyse it properly, I couldn't say much more.'

'That's fine,' he said. 'You have been more than helpful, Dr Grey.' He rose to his feet, switching off the tape. His face was grave, thoughtful. 'More than helpful, indeed.'

* * *

She couldn't face returning to her car, decided to go into town, sit somewhere where there were people. Everything felt very quiet, as though a bomb had gone off in her head.

She wandered past the grey stone buildings, allowing herself to feel a little lost. Eventually she found herself in a busy coffee shop on the high street, the front part given over to knitted garments and gourmet foods with romantic names like 'traditional tablet' and 'beremeal flour'. She ordered a pot of tea from a busy teenage girl with lilac hair. Around her was a cacophony of foreign voices, as tourists and Orcadians alike crowded around the tables, their voices high, excited, sharing gossip and news.

Her loneliness was sudden and crushing.

Had Madison stolen a find?

And, in her taped testimony in the police station, had Fiona dropped her in it?

But the police must think Madison had had the necklace. Fiona had been asked to come in and identify whether it was hers. If only they would tell her where they had found it! In the drowned car, in the cottage, on the site?

The only person she could think to discuss these allegations with was possibly at the bottom of the sea.

'Oh, Madison,' she murmured aloud, causing the old ladies on the next table to turn and glance curiously at her. 'You silly, silly mare. What on earth have you done now?'

And then her phone rang.

34

Judith Glue Café, High Street, Kirkwall, January 2020

'Hello?' Fiona hadn't recognised the number.

'Hello?'

The voice was male, peremptory, and sounded as though whoever it was, Fiona had called him rather than the other way around, perhaps at three o'clock in the morning, and woken him out of bed.

Even in the warmth and bustle of this Kirkwall café, she felt a sharp pang of melancholy, of dread.

'Hello?' she asked again. 'Who is this?'

'Who do you think it is?' he answered.

Her heart sank.

'Hugo.' She swallowed. *His sister is missing. Try to make allowances.* 'When did you arrive?'

'What difference does that make?'

'No difference,' said Fiona, scratching her cheek in discomfort. 'I was just asking.'

'Well, I suppose we better meet,' he said, as though Fiona had strong-armed him into this concession. 'I'm staying at the Lynnewood. When can you get over here?'

There was no way on earth she was going to be in a hotel room alone with him.

'I'm in Kirkwall right now ... perhaps we can catch a coffee ...'

'That's no good for me. I have to go in and see the police in five minutes. What about later?'

'Sure,' said Fiona.

He gave her the name of a café on Harbour Street, and the injunction to be there at six and not be late.

* * *

'Hi, Hugo,' she said, appearing at the door.

He was not exactly how she remembered him. It had only been six months since that awful holiday on Cala Llombards, and already his jowls seemed pouchier and cheeks slightly ruddier with broken veins, his belly straining against his too tight belt, his mouth now sprouting the beginnings of straggling wrinkles from being constantly pursed.

She saw instantly that he was now a haunted man, though what was haunting him was anyone's guess.

It was not clear whether he would hug her or shake her hand, but in the end, he did neither, instead crossing his arms at her and glowering as she approached him in the tiny café.

She took a seat in the wooden chair opposite him.

Within her was a mixture of surprise and relief at the idea of not having to touch him as she sat down.

'Hi,' she said again.

He did not respond, instead continuing to glare at her. He was clad in smart trousers and a rugby shirt and had not even removed his coat. Undrunk coffee sat in front of him in a tiny espresso cup.

She supposed he intended this to be a very short conversation.

Some good news at last.

She was, despite the dreadful circumstances, overcome with the sudden, desperate desire to let out a nervous giggle at his stagey posture, the pantomime drawing down of his brows.

'Did you speak to the police today?' she asked, deciding to forge ahead, talk anyway. 'I saw them this afternoon. They wanted me to identify a . . . a piece of art for them. They wouldn't say where they found it . . .'

'How long are you going to keep this up?' he snapped.

Fiona froze. 'Keep what up?'

'I know you and Madison are in this together, somehow,' he said, stabbing the table with his finger, very near her hand. She had the startling sense of how much he would have liked to hit her just then. 'You might have persuaded PC Plod up here in the middle of nowhere that it's an accident, you showing up on the very evening she "disappears", but you don't fool me, you dirty little *scrubber*.'

There was some sense of deep satisfaction in him as he called her a scrubber, she saw. Her first instinct was to get up, leave.

No. Do this for Mads.

'I don't know what you mean, Hugo.'

'Oh, come off it,' he snarled. 'I know she was texting you all the way up from Cambridge. The police told me.'

'Of course they did,' she said, and she realised she was shaking, both with fear, that residual fear she had of him, and now with something else, something alien, something like rage. 'Who do you think told *them* that?'

'Well, I can tell you what they *did* tell me – Madison's phone hadn't been used since Wednesday night and is probably in the sea. So God knows where these texts you had came from. If they ever existed. Did she get another phone? Is that how you're in touch with her?'

She couldn't speak for a moment – she was too stunned. She had not believed for a while that the texts came from Madison, but she knew they came from her phone number.

What else had the police told him?

Was Fiona some kind of suspect now?

'Hugo, what exactly is it you are accusing me of? Do you seriously think that Madison and I are running some kind of scam to . . . I don't know what – get you to miss your weekend at the golf club?' She could hear her own, ratcheting anger. 'Give your mother a heart attack? What's our plan supposed to be?'

'Maybe it's a plan to go on the run with a backpack full of gold doubloons or whatever the fuck they found out on that rock.' His eyes blazed. 'And maybe you're in for a cut of it. After all, you're the expert. You'd know where to sell it.'

It was as if he'd punched her.

Of course, she thought, he would immediately gravitate to where the money in this would be.

'Who told you about the Valkyrie?'

He didn't answer, merely smiled, that unpleasant, gloating smile he'd had since being a boy, the one that seemed to bisect his face.

'Okay, firstly, that's crazy, and secondly, that's completely crazy.'

'Is it? It's right up her street – she's always been a failure,' he snarled. 'She was never able to hold on to a man, or any kind of proper job – just these endless studenty "gigs" digging with sweaty hippies in the back of beyond . . .'

Something vast, and cold, and furious opened up in Fiona then.

'Listen, you fatuous imbecile. Mads paid her own bills. She wasn't the one being bankrolled by her mother while playing Fantasy Financial Advisor!' She snatched herself up to her feet. 'She was worth ten of *you*.'

'How dare you, you little . . .'

'Hugo, I did not come here to trade insults with you. I came here so we could try to work out what's happened to your sister . . .'

'Well, that's just you all over, isn't it?' He was no longer looking at her, but his voice was raised, as though he wanted the room to hear him. 'Always worming your way in to everything. You never change.'

Fiona felt herself reddening. 'What are you on about?'

'I remember you,' he said, his big round face gleaming with a malicious smile. 'Always trying to get Mum and Dad to take you with us on holiday, angling to get invited to stay for dinner, trying to feed off us like a tick.'

'What? You're talking about this *now*?'

'Poor little Fiona with her drunk father and her shithole stinky house and her school uniform so tight you can see her tits because she can't afford to buy a new one . . .'

Fiona picked up the coffee in front of him and threw it into his face.

It made a tiny splashing noise, that somehow dwarfed every other sound in the café. Even as she did it she couldn't quite believe it was happening.

Her palm tingled, as though it longed to make contact with his pampered, ruddy cheek.

Hugo didn't seem to believe it had happened either. He simply stared at her, one hand coming up to his face in disbelief, as dark liquid dripped from his chin, his nose.

'Take that,' she said. 'You're owed it on account.'

'Fucking hell,' he said. 'You threw boiling coffee at me!'

Fortunately, or unfortunately, it had been little more than lukewarm.

And furthermore, she could not even repent of it.

'You're mad!' he shouted, growing more and more agitated. 'You've assaulted me! You're *violent*. Just like your fucking crazy mother.'

'Yeah, and you're just a sordid bully, as usual. Does your mother know you were here bothering Mads two weeks ago, angling for power of attorney over her, like the disgusting ghoul you are? And that Mads sent you away with her boot in your fat arse?'

Under the streaming coffee he paled, then reddened.

'Because I'll be happy to tell her. She deserves to know what you're really like. And what happened in the cellar. It would be my *pleasure*.'

'I should call the police, you . . .' he said, but the power had gone out of it, and mere bluster remained. His eyes became huge, wounded, and he glanced around the room, appealing for sympathy. 'My mother is very *ill* . . .'

'If you think I'm in it with Mads, tell the police that. If not, stop wasting my time.'

The café door slammed shut behind her.

35

Nordskaill, Stromness, Orkney, January 2020

'You think she stole it?' Adi let out a long, slow breath. 'That's . . . *wow.*'

'I don't know if she stole anything. But this thing, Adi – this is very serious.' Fiona leaned into her phone, huddled in her icy car, trying to keep her voice down. She didn't want to be overheard.

And she absolutely didn't want to have this conversation back at the house with the other archaeologists around.

'I mean, I suppose I could understand it,' Adi said.

'What?'

'Look, Fiona, perhaps she got desperate. You told me yourself that the money in archaeology is terrible. It sounds like she has a taste for the good life. She kicked Caspar into touch – he was the one paying for all the little luxuries. If you were digging and found something like that, just lying in the ground – you have to admit, it must be tempting.'

'Tempting?'

'You know, pick it up, stick it in your pocket. It's been lying there for a thousand years. It's not like anybody's going to miss it anytime soon.'

'Except it isn't tempting,' said Fiona, taken aback by Adi's attitude. 'It's actually a really stupid thing to do, especially for an archaeologist. And she would know this.'

'How do you mean?'

'It's treasure.'

'Well, obviously it's valuable . . .'

'No, I mean it's *treasure* – that's the legal name for it. And you don't get to just keep any treasure you find. There are all these laws to stop our cultural heritage being sold off to private collectors abroad. You've got to tell the coroner in the first instance, and straight away. The minute you don't, what you have in your hands is stolen goods.'

He laughed then, and again she was disturbed by his attitude. 'Stolen from who?'

'From *us*.' She could hear the rising anger in her voice. 'From the people.'

'If I'm the people, I already own it. What's to stop me from having it?'

'Because something that belongs to everybody should be accessible to everybody! And not just sitting in the collections of Swiss banking fat cats like you go drinking with, which is where everything would end up if nobody stopped it!'

'Hey, hey,' said Adi, taken aback. 'Easy, Fee . . .'

'Sorry,' said Fiona instantly, but something was growing inside her. She wasn't sure she was sorry. But she said again, 'Sorry. I'm just so worried. What was Madison thinking?'

'As I was saying,' said Adi, with a slight drawl, and she had the sense that her apology might not have gone far enough for him, and this too made her prickle with annoyance. 'It could have been worth it to Madison. I was watching something on TV the other night where someone found all this gold with their metal detector, just out in a field, and it was worth hundreds of thousands of . . .'

'It might be, but that's money they've received *after* they've reported it and been paid for the find, and the objects end up in the British Museum or wherever. They didn't *steal* that money, they had it legitimately.' Fiona sighed, tried to sound conciliatory. 'I mean, it's all moot in Madison's case. She wouldn't get money for something that she found on a dig. Whoever is running the dig is responsible. But even then, it's such an insane thing to do.'

'Well, I could think of a few hundred thousand reasons to do it . . .'

'But that's just it. She'd never get anything *like* that, even if she did steal it. I did some consultation work a few months ago on some coins someone was trying to sell in the US. The finders never make the real money – the dealers do. They come up with the fake provenance and the pseudo-respectability. People don't want to buy something that can be seized back from them by the government at any time.

'And here's the thing that really bothers me – that pendant is worth more to her professionally, to the power of ten, than she could earn selling it on the black market. If that came out of Helly Holm, then what with the boat and the bodies it's a massively important discovery. She can be publishing things and writing papers on that, in partnership with Iris. Maybe get into Iris's media work. It could be just the boost she needs.'

'Fiona,' he said, 'listen to me. I think it's time you came home.'

She fell silent, shocked.

'I can't just *leave* . . .'

'Yes, you can. You absolutely can. And you should. Her family are there now, and the police can get in touch with you whenever they want.'

'Adi, I can't . . .'

'What are you achieving there? What's happening, except that you're being hurt and exposed to all these things you can't fix, and on your own? I can see how this is affecting you. So I'm flying back home tomorrow . . .'

'I thought you were there another two days . . .'

'Nah, I don't need to be. I'm just here to present and answer questions.'

'But they expect . . .'

'I don't give a shit what they expect. I've been thinking about this all afternoon. I know I've not been there for you. I might not have had a lot of time for Madison, but I know she was a huge part of your life and you're destroyed right now, running off the rails, doing and saying crazy things . . .'

A mulish rebellion flickered within Fiona then – *how do you know that I'm crazy?*

'Adi – I don't . . . I feel like this is something I have to do.'

Silence fell between them, except that she could hear his breathing, very quiet, very light. It filled her with a longing and a homesickness that hurt like toothache.

But still, when she thought about it, imagined booking that ferry ticket, packing her things into her car – she felt a jangling sense of wrongness, of desertion.

She had unfinished business here. It was that simple.

Her silence was answer enough, it seemed.

'Okay,' he said. 'I have to go now, there's another dinner tonight. But I want you to think about this, Fee. I would really love you to come home.'

There was a lump in her throat. 'I would love to come home too,' she said, and her voice was thick, stuffed with all the words they never spoke. 'I just have to wait until they bring her up. Once I know she's gone . . .' It was hard to breathe, suddenly. 'I'll come. I promise.'

'Are you sure? Because I would love to see you.'

And the thought flashed through her mind then, *ask him to come to you. Admit you are exhausted and grief-stricken and don't want to do this alone.*

Her mouth opened for a second, then closed.

It seemed too much, suddenly. He might downplay it now,

but this trip of his was so important for his firm, his career. She just couldn't ask it of him.

She bit her lip. The moment was gone.

'Me too,' was all she said.

A pause. 'Okay. Sleep well.' Another pause, and then, to her astonishment, he said, 'I love you.'

36

Nordskaill, Stromness, Orkney, January 2020

Fiona emerged into the living room at Nordskaill House with a beer in her hand and was somewhat surprised and a little alarmed to find Jack sitting on the couch, his own beer at his elbow, his vaper caught between his fingers.

The rest of the house seemed oddly empty.

He offered her a grin, but there were dark shadows under his eyes.

'Hello there,' he murmured. 'You missed the expedition to the pub. If you hurry, you might catch them.'

'Um, no thanks. I'm not really in the mood.' Fiona looked around the room in alarm. 'Why didn't you go?'

He shook his head. 'Not in the mood either. I'm knackered. Tomorrow will be worse. Big gale coming, and we need to run in and secure the site first thing. It's going to be a free-for-all.'

'I see,' she said, anxious. 'So, how did the dig go?'

Jack shrugged. 'Just the two skeletons, in the end. We didn't get a real good look, because we were in a rush. Ended up excavating things and packing them up in their soil. The bone people will pick it all apart. But very interesting. Iris was right again. We think the primary burial was a woman.'

'The primary burial?'

'Yeah. The person the grave was dug for.'

'But you said it was a warrior grave.'

'Yep. But it's also *her* grave. She's laid out on her back, and the grave goods — the sword, what we think is a bow and arrows, the helmet and armour, the coins – we're pretty sure it's all around her. The man is lying curled up, behind her head, along with the sacrificed horse. Iris reckons the second, male burial is a thrall – her slave. We couldn't get a really good look, but it seems like there's a peri-mortem slice injury to the vertebra in his neck.'

'So he's a sacrifice? He's been killed to accompany her into the afterlife?'

'We don't know,' he said. 'But that's how it looked.'

Fiona paused, stunned. 'That's amazing.'

'Well, there is precedent. The Birka warrior burial was genetically proven to be female, but it doesn't necessarily make the woman in the grave a warrior. I wouldn't get too excited,' Jack said, with a rueful sigh. 'As I keep trying to tell Iris.'

'Still,' said Fiona, considering this, 'it's all very suggestive.'

Jack snorted. 'Just because the warrior grave goods are lying in there with this woman proves precisely zilch. It implies she owns it, certainly, and has a right to it, not necessarily that she's using it in anger.'

'I suppose not,' she said, steeped in doubt for a long moment. 'You don't seem convinced.'

'Well,' she sighed. 'I'm a scientist. I go for the interpretation that makes fewest assumptions. And yet, here we are, presented with fairly straightforward evidence of a warrior grave with a woman in it, and somehow, all of these more abstract theories are suddenly more likely.'

'And I would say,' he replied, resting his hands behind his head, shutting his eyes, leaving his tattoos and the pale undersides of his arms exposed, 'things are not always what they seem.'

'They would have been what they seemed if the man had been the primary burial.' Fiona shrugged, her voice hardened. 'When we dig, after all, all we ever find is ourselves. Our own assumptions, our own prejudices. But you know, sometimes things are exactly how they look.'

He opened his eyes then, alerted to this change in her tone.

'What do you mean?' he asked, and she knew he didn't mean the burial.

'Douggie Flett was absolutely convinced that you and Madison were seeing each other.' She folded her arms, faced him. 'He's right, isn't he?'

His blue gaze settled on her and he hesitated, taking her in. For a second, neither moved, and then he sighed, looked away.

'You asked the wrong question, Fiona,' he said. 'When you came up here you were looking for Madison's secret boyfriend. I was *never* her boyfriend, secret or otherwise.'

'Really?'

'We may, however, have had a fumble or two.'

'Why didn't you tell me?'

'Because, in the nicest possible way, it was none of your business. And it's most certainly none of Douggie Flett's business.'

'How could you say that?' she asked, appalled at his disingenuousness. 'I came all the way up here . . .'

'I can say that *very* easily, Fiona. If it had been any of your business, Madison would have told you.'

Her mouth dropped open. 'For fuck's sake, Jack!'

'Ohhhh, I wouldn't feel too abused,' he said, with a snort. 'I was a spectator, not a player. We talked about this, Madison and me. She'd already made up her mind to leave Caspar, she just didn't know how to tell him.'

'And why would she want that?' asked Fiona, trying to stay angry, but feeling herself on increasingly shaky ground.

'I dunno.' He lifted his own bottle. 'You knew her better. But I reckon that it was just all too sedate for her. Madison wasn't into settling down. She was an agent of chaos. Everything had to be on fire and falling off a cliff in order to really matter. This was why she and I could never be a thing.' He took a swig from the bottle. 'I know her type, believe me.'

Fiona stilled, and it was as if Mads' ghost was in the room with them. She *recognised* Madison from this description.

'That was how I saw it then, at any rate. I don't have to explain everything to you. She is entitled to her privacy. Just as I'm entitled to mine. Anyway, this was all before her car showed up in the sea and everything turned on its head.'

'Have you told the police about this yet?' she asked, her anger fizzling out, to be replaced by a kind of bleak understanding.

'Yeah.'

'What will they do to you?'

He lowered his blond brows at her, cocked his head. 'What do you mean?'

'You didn't mention in the first place that you and Madison had had this ... this "fumble". Won't they think you have something to hide now?'

'I think you're not understanding me, Fiona,' he replied with a certain cool forbearance. 'I didn't tell *you* about that, or Douggie Bloody Flett, who somehow has become Orkney's Sex Police. I did, however, tell the actual cops in Kirkwall the day she was reported missing.' He put the bottle down. 'You may not believe this, but I'm not a complete idiot.'

Fiona fought to hold on to her anger, her suspicion, but there was no escaping it – he was right. It was none of her business, nothing to do with her. How was she to extort confidences from him, when even Mads had not seen fit to share this secret with her?

She licked her lips. 'Did Iris know about you and Madison, or is that also none of my business?'

'I don't ... I don't talk about that stuff with Iris any more.' He gave her a rueful look. 'She owns enough of me as it is.'

'What's she like to work for?' asked Fiona, intrigued by this unguarded response.

He fell silent, and she wondered if he would answer her.

'So,' he said, 'this is the thing to remember about Iris.' He let his head fall back as he sprawled against the sofa. 'Either you're in, or you're out. And if you're out, you're gone.'

He turned to look at her. 'I mean, don't get me wrong. She's amazing at what she does. She doesn't just have a magic touch with choosing digs, but with people too. If you have something going on, some talent, some bright idea – then no matter what the world says, she'll fight your corner. But if you disappoint her enough times – you're history. Or prehistory, if you prefer.' He offered her a quick grin and raised his bottle to his lips. 'She might have this cosy girly affect from time to time, but she really missed her metier. She would have made an amazing CEO. Or general.'

Fiona considered this, cold condensation from her own bottle chilling her hand.

'So I'm guessing Becky is "out".' She glanced at him. 'Right?'

His head twitched into a single reluctant nod. 'Poor Becks. Her PhD idea was amazing, right up Iris's street.' He shrugged. 'But she's not . . . she's not mentally flexible, she's not imaginative. And she's difficult. Wading-through-concrete difficult. She isn't long for the dig, to be honest. If we get an extension after next week . . .' he lowered his voice, glanced towards the door, even though they were alone. 'Becky is going to be replaced. It will *not* go down well.'

Fiona swallowed, that stab of pity back again. Kicked off a dig like that, on the eve of the media attention on it too.

'Wow – that's . . . Is it common in this team?'

Jack's lips thinned. 'It's more common than I would like.' He twisted his mouth downwards. 'But I'm not in charge.'

Fiona fell silent. Did Becky know, or suspect? She might. It would explain her bitterness, her rage. Had someone said something to her?

Or, more likely, had she watched it happen before, and recognised the signs of her own impending execution?

'Iris hinted to me Mads and Becky didn't get on. But Becky seems to think they were best buds . . .'

'Both things are true,' rumbled Jack. 'In their way. Becks resented Madison when she first joined. Becks wanted to be Finds Manager on this dig, though why she'd want that I've no idea. We can never keep a Finds Manager. It's like the job's got an ancient curse on it or something. We've been through three in two years.

'And also, Madison was Madison. You know. Vibrant, attractive. Smart as a whip.' He smiled at happy memories. 'Smart enough to put some effort into cultivating Becks rather than just putting her down. Listening to her while she pissed and moaned. Becks never has a good word to say about anybody.'

'Mads is generous when she wants to be,' said Fiona, and her grief was a wraith that wrapped around her heart. 'Very generous, or very mean. It's all or nothing.'

'Oh yeah,' said Jack, with some hidden feeling.

She glanced over at him. 'So was Madison "in"?'

'Absolutely,' said Jack, meeting her gaze. 'She was in, all right. I remember Iris talking about her when she hired her. "I just met the most extraordinary girl at the bar at this conference," she said. '"With more confidence, she could be incredible."'

'Madison, lacking confidence?' Fiona snorted out a laugh.

Jack did not laugh back. 'She didn't mean social confidence – obviously Madison had that in spades. She meant *intellectual* confidence. She meant that ability to have big ideas and to hold on to them and follow them, and then the courage to throw them away when they don't work. It's actually much rarer than you think.'

Fiona was about to laugh again, paused. You know, maybe it was true. She herself had grown so used to academic success she had started to believe that perhaps Madison just wasn't cut out for it.

She remembered Madison's cold eyes that day in the bar on the Strand – her spite. Her jealousy.

Perhaps Madison *had* been cut out for it, but just couldn't catch a break, unlike Fiona had with Maude. Perhaps Madison had just needed someone to believe in her.

Iris had.

With a flicker of shame, Fiona realised that she hadn't.

'Iris recognised some kindred spirit in Madison, I reckon,' Jack continued. 'She went to bat for her, even with the mistakes in the sampling and recording, some of which were quite serious. I mean,' and he shut his eyes, 'I don't know what was happening with Madison, but she was definitely taking her eye off the ball a little in the last ten days or so . . .'

Yes, thought Fiona, *she would be. She was being threatened on social media and her previous stalker had invited himself up to her cottage. Since she was already juggling her boyfriend with you, she had a lot on her plate.*

And she hadn't seen fit to tell Fiona about any of it.

She slumped down into the armchair at right angles to the couch, conscious of herself as deceived again, as taken in.

Bloody hell. *Madison.*

'You know, Fiona, you shouldn't feel bad.' Jack seemed to see straight through her. It was impressive, she had to admit. 'Madison would have told you everything anyway, if she'd been here when you arrived. She was looking forward to seeing you, to having a good long chat. She said as much.' He rubbed his eyes. 'She talked about you all the time. Whatever they find when they finally get that car up,' he twitched his shoulders, picked up the vaper again. 'You should know you did a good thing when you said you'd come up here.' His mouth tightened. 'Even if it didn't make a difference in the end.'

'Thanks,' she said hollowly.

He shrugged. 'You're welcome.'

'But I don't know what I'm supposed to do now.' She could hear the quaver in her voice, the defeat.

'No?'

'No.' She shut her eyes. 'I had a massive fight with Madison's brother in a café in Kirkwall.' She bit her lip. 'I chucked a cup of coffee over him.'

Jack was silent for a moment. 'Interesting,' he said eventually. 'Did he deserve it?'

'Not at that moment. Though he was being a complete prick.' She kicked her boots off, let them fall on to the carpet. 'But he . . . he did something unpleasant a little while ago which deserved worse than coffee, so I guess he had it coming to him.'

'I'm sorry to hear that. Still, it's a statement gesture. I can respect that. Delightfully retro and oddly feminine and yet still hitting all the whistles and bells of interpersonal violence.'

'Isn't it?' Fiona laughed, despite herself. 'I was shaking after, but I felt . . . I felt so good.'

'Yeah?'

There was a long pause, as he puffed in silence, blue light gleaming along the vaper, along with the lively bubbling of liquid.

'Adi thinks I'm going "off the rails" and should come home.'

He told you he loved you.

Jack nodded, as though in thought. 'And you?' he asked, his gaze assessing. 'What do you think?'

'I feel, very strongly, that I can't leave yet.' She rested her chin on her hand. 'Not until I know she's down there.'

37

Nordskaill, Stromness, Orkney, January 2020

'Ah! There you are!' Iris cried.

Fiona glanced up as the door opened. She and Jack had been sitting in the living room, and together they'd made inroads into the beer stacked in the fridge. Dead soldiers were racked near their feet.

In the midst of her unresolved grief, her loss, it was some comfort to just sit on the couch with someone who had also known Madison, someone else who had liked her. It didn't make her feel any better, but also, it didn't make her feel any worse. And Jack was very easy to get on with.

Iris had a taut expression as she opened the door, like a woman spotting trouble up ahead. Behind her, Becky seemed to freeze for a second.

Fiona suddenly felt uncomfortable, as though she had been discovered doing something sleazy. Callum seemed oblivious, and rather drunk. He threw himself on to the couch next to Jack and from the armchair Fiona could feel the cold radiating off him.

'How was the pub?' Jack asked them.

'Freezing, then all right once we were there and thawed out, then freezing again,' Callum said.

'I told you not to go,' said Jack mildly. 'It's miserable out.'

Becky stormed past them all, vanishing into the kitchen. There was a moment's eddying discomfort, everyone aware of her transparent unhappiness, and determined to ignore it.

She's in love with Jack, of course, Fiona thought. Jesus, what would Becky have done if she'd discovered he was sleeping with Mads?

'When did you get in, Fiona?' Iris asked loudly, hanging her coat up by the back door, as though enforcing normality again.

'About sevenish,' said Fiona.

'Oh, I should have asked you to the pub,' she said.

'Thanks, but it's all right,' said Fiona. 'To be honest, I probably wouldn't have braved the pub anyway. It was . . . it was kind of a challenging day.'

'I would have advised you not to go to the pub, anyway,' said Jack to her. 'Because it's miserable out.'

'You said,' remarked Iris. 'If it makes you happier, Jack darling, you were right about that.'

'Yes. I expect I was. I made this derivation through the high-tech solution of Looking Out Of The Window.'

'Lightweight,' said Iris, plopping down next to him. She raised a dark eyebrow at Fiona. Her cheeks were still pink with the cold.

She seemed to be thinking, and then coming to a decision.

'Come with me.' She rose to her feet, beckoned imperiously at Fiona. 'I have something to show you.'

* * *

Iris led her back up the stairs, not speaking, but there was some hidden, coiled feeling in her, something that made her hurry, for Fiona to have to rush to catch up.

'In here,' she said, opening a door.

Fiona found herself in Iris's room. It must be the master bedroom, judging from the size, and had a picture window with a view down the hill towards Stromness Harbour. It contained its own fireplace, no longer in use and with a board over it, an antique wardrobe, a scratched dresser and a large pine sleigh bed.

'Oh,' said Fiona, pausing, taking in the view, with the twinkling harbour lights, the massive glassy sea spread out in darkness. 'That's gorgeous.' But still, it made her sad. She wished Madison was here, to say these things to, rather than Iris. And if you followed that thought, she understood, you would realise that Madison would probably never be here again, to say anything to, and . . .

Iris, who had bent to the fireplace, craned back at her over her shoulder. 'Oh yes, it is a nice view, isn't it? But it's not why you're here.'

To Fiona's surprise, Iris was kneeling on the hearth, unscrewing the painted wooden board in front of the disused fireplace with her Swiss Army knife.

'This is off to Edinburgh this week,' Iris said, as the screw on the left popped out and she quickly captured it with her long fingers, placed it carefully on the mantelpiece. 'Providing the planes are flying with the bad weather that's coming in, of course. It doesn't look very exciting at the moment, since it's not been cleaned and sorted yet, but still . . . I think as a professional you'll get a kick out of it. I did.'

The other screw quickly came out, and Fiona drew nearer, curious.

'After all,' continued Iris, sliding her short fingernails under the board, lifting it away to expose the fireplace proper, 'it's not something you see every day.'

Within was a plastic storage tub, about the size of a large sewing box. With great care Iris lifted it out, the tendons in her wrists visibly straining – the box was heavy.

'Come here,' she said. 'Have a look.'

Fiona approached, with a strange reluctance building within her that she couldn't quite explain.

'What is it?' she asked, kneeling down next to Iris.

Iris merely smiled, a wolfish expression full of appetite and enthusiasm, and popped open the lid. 'It's not very glamorous right now. This is how the bag came out of the ground. But there might be something nice in it, once they sort through it.'

Within, there looked to be nothing more than soil and rags, perhaps pebbles or sea-smoothed glass shards, and dirty black discs. It took a few moments for it to resolve into what Fiona then realised to be a rotting leather bag, filled with silver coins, now tarnished, and here and there, peeking through the mud that still clung to everything, the tiny bright glint of gold.

Fiona did not know what she had been expecting – the bones from the burial, perhaps, though this box was too small for that, or some other find from the excavation. Whatever it was, it was not this.

'This is the silver hoard from the dig?' Fiona's eyes roved over it, taking in the designs on the coins, etched with whirling stylized animals and the heads of bearded men.

'Yes.'

Fiona blinked. 'You keep this in the *house*?'

'Just for a couple of days,' said Iris. 'Until we can fly it out to Edinburgh. I have to head back for another round of filming on Wednesday, and I'll be killing two birds with one stone.'

'But still, wouldn't the police have taken this into the station for a few nights? If you'd asked?'

Iris glanced at her, as if noticing her unease for the first time. 'Well, probably. We never asked.'

'But you must have asked. They must know this exists. When you told the coroner . . .'

'They do. But they never asked where we were keeping it, and I . . . well, I might have neglected to tell them.' Iris sighed.

Fiona stared at her.

'It's not that I don't trust them, or think they might steal any or anything that stupid – though you never know.' She tucked a lock of her dark hair behind her ear, very deliberately not meeting Fiona's shocked gaze. 'It's just that, well, people talk. And I don't think we'll be wrapping up on Helly Holm any time soon.'

'I know . . . but *Iris* . . .' Fiona began, scandalised. 'What if someone *stole* it?'

'That's hardly likely,' she said, waving this idea away as if it was a bothersome fly. 'Here's the thing – I don't know what else is up there on Helly Holm, and I am desperate, and I mean desperate, to control the news of this find until we're sure we have the scientific data. Otherwise, we're going to be inundated with amateur treasure hunters, tearing through the site with their metal detectors, destroying evidence . . .'

'Perhaps you're right,' said Fiona. 'Though I have to tell you, that this coin here – see it?' She let her fingertip rest just above, but not on, a tiny dark disc half-buried under the mud-coloured leather fragments. On it was a little triangular representation of a banner, surrounded by etched runes. 'That there is a triquetra penny from the reign of Anlaf Guthfrithsson, minted in Harrogate in the tenth century. That's worth nearly thirty thousand pounds to a collector, just on its own.' She looked hard at Iris. 'You can't . . . you can't just *keep* this stuff here!'

'I know, I know. It's so against protocol. But I trust you.' She turned to Fiona, and her face seemed to shine with passion. 'Did Jack tell you about the burial?'

'The primary burial being a woman? Yes, he did . . . it's amazing to think, isn't it?'

'You know, you wait your whole life to find something like that.' For a second Iris seemed too overcome to speak, on the verge of tears. 'I feel like this woman, whoever she is – I feel like she has *chosen* me.' She offered a tiny half-laugh of embarrassment, as though remembering where she was.

'I sound like a madwoman, don't I? No, don't answer, I know I do. But this could be so huge, Fiona. Not just for our views on women's roles in the past, but also on the careers of women in archaeology, right now.'

'Absolutely.' Fiona nodded. 'It's a great find.'

'And maybe there is something in this for you, too.'

'Me?' Fiona was taken aback. 'I don't understand. I'm just a bystander.'

'There are no bystanders in life, Fiona. But I've been thinking about this. There will be media opportunities in this discovery, and it should be the women on this dig that take advantage of that fact, and promote that message. Madison and I talked a lot – she would have been wonderful at this.'

Fiona felt a tug of loss at these words. Yes. Madison would have been good at this.

'But you know, perhaps you coming up here was fated.'

'How do you mean?'

'I know your work. You're presentable, articulate, you're on the ground here now, as they say – there could be opportunities here for you too.' She reached forward, closed the lid of the box. 'I'm already in talks with a production company. I could put you in the mix right now.'

'I . . . thanks, Iris, I don't know what to say. I'm very flattered, but I'm afraid I can't possibly think of this right now, with Madison . . .'

'Of course,' said Iris, blushing. 'I'm sorry, I'm letting all of this run away with me. Naturally you have much more important things on your mind.' Her arm came about Fiona's shoulders. 'But in due time, have a think about this. Come on. Help me put this stuff back. Most of the others don't know it's here.'

Quickly they replaced the box, and Iris screwed the wooden plate back on, concealing it, while Fiona's attention travelled the room, fell on the dresser. There were three photos, ones that Iris must have felt important enough to bring up with her. The first was of herself with her arms around a fat chocolate

Labrador, the second of two little girls dressed as Disney princesses, and finally, one of her and Jack taken at Stonehenge, before the Altar Stone, and from some time before the first sprigs of grey had appeared in his temples.

Through the window, Stromness was quiet, still.

With a flicker of unease, she wondered if Dominic Tate was out there somewhere.

'There we go,' said Iris, running a possessive hand over the sealed fireplace. 'All tucked away.'

Fiona felt anxious, suddenly, burdened with the knowledge of this treasure secreted within. What if something happened to it?

They returned downstairs, Iris chatting away about the day's work. Fiona merely nodded amiably along as they re-emerged into the living room.

So Iris felt chosen. *Choosers of the slain* – that was another name, a *kenning*, for a Valkyrie.

She was so keyed up on this, so obsessed – and the DNA results weren't even back yet. They might not even get DNA. This dream of hers might yet tumble away to nothing.

What would Iris do if she thought that Madison had stolen something so precious, so apparently personally meaningful, from the dig on Helly Holm?

And something else occurred to Fiona then – if this dig was such a huge opportunity for the women on it, then it was striking, and a testament to Jack's truthfulness earlier that evening, that Iris hadn't mentioned Becky once.

Tuesday

38

Nordskaill, Stromness, Orkney, January 2020

That night, on the sofa in Nordskaill, Fiona dreamt of Madison.

She dreamt she was back at Langmire again, having been led there by a vague sense she had forgotten something.

When she reached her journey's end and opened the unlocked door she already half-knew what she would find.

Sitting in the kitchen, her knees crossed under the table, was Madison, her large green eyes fixed on her.

'You're late,' was all she said. 'I've been waiting ages.'

Fiona wasn't even surprised, merely vaguely uncomfortable.

'Everyone's looking for you,' she said. 'They think you're dead.'

Madison merely half-shrugged and smiled, as though Fiona was overreacting and should worry less.

'Your mother is sick,' said Fiona. 'She had a heart attack.'

The shrug again.

'Don't you care?'

'I didn't say that. Did you forge your sword?'

'Wha . . .'

'A sword, Sword Lady,' repeated Madison, with that sharp, exaggerated diction that masqueraded as patience, and yet signalled its absolute opposite. 'Did you bring it?'

'No . . .'

'Well, that's no good. How will you fight your blood feud, then?'

'My . . . my what?' Her fear was suddenly huge, overwhelming. 'Madison, we have to go.' She reached out to grab her sleeve. 'Your family is coming, we have to tell them . . .'

Madison didn't move and didn't look away from her face.

'You're my family,' was all she said.

Fiona woke up.

* * *

She was sweating, and her T-shirt clung to her damp skin. The living room was a sauna, condensation sparkling on the double-glazed windowpanes. The heating was turned up way too high.

She fumbled for the lamp switch, blinked in the resulting light. What a weird, weird dream. When she closed her eyes she could see Madison's direct, unpanicked green gaze . . .

And why had Madison asked after a sword? A blood feud . . . what on earth had she meant? Why had she dreamt of that? Was that what was stirring in the depths of her subconscious, some antiquated notion of Viking revenge, a revenge that was almost always at blade point?

Vikings . . . the Valkyrie . . . Choosers of the Slain.

Something stirred within her, some flash of . . . no, it was gone. It was all moot, anyway. All hopeless.

She burst into rasping sobs, surprising herself and she stifled them with her hands and the thin bedsheets, so as not to wake the others.

The one person that she could talk to about this, that she wanted to talk to about this, was Madison herself.

How will you fight your blood feud, then?

What did it mean?

* * *

'Fiona,' Jack whispered. 'What are you doing up?'

'Sorry, I couldn't sleep.' Fiona rubbed at her red eyes, her tears dried to a salty crust. She'd come to the kitchen to get a drink of water, had not expected anyone to be awake.

'D'you want a cup of tea?'

She was confused, unsure. 'It's the middle of the night.'

'No, it's gone six.' He grinned at her. 'You're up north now.'

She looked down at her phone: it read 6:04.

'Oh my God,' she said. 'Sorry.'

'Tea?'

Fiona scratched her head. She felt wide awake now and would have liked to talk to someone.

'Um, yes. Yes, please.'

In the kitchen she became aware of her T-shirt and its bralessness, but Jack paid it no mind as he pottered about, switching on the steaming kettle.

'Why are you up so early?' she asked.

'We need to get out there as soon as possible. Iris was listening to the forecast last night, and everything is going to be earlier and worse.' He reached over, scratched his shoulder. 'We need to get everything tied down and storm-ready before mid-morning. Which means we need to be on the boat in an hour.' He shook his head. 'Not going to be a popular decision.'

'I'm sure,' she said, as Jack placed the cup in front of her. Two half-drunk ones were on the table. One was Iris's, presumably.

'I don't suppose,' Jack said, 'you could see your way clear to helping us out for an hour or two? It's not digging, just helping us throw everything on the boat.'

'Um,' she said, aware of Jack's hopeful face, his gift of tea. She would rather have done anything else in the world but was conscious that she had no good excuse to refuse. It was a vitally important dig.

Fiona had a strong sense that this was where her duty lay.

'Sure,' she said. 'I have to make some phone calls this

morning – I need to check in with the police. But yeah, I'll come over. Shall I drive . . .'

'Sorry, no. Low tide's not till eight-thirty today and it's just too late. We're going across in the boat in . . .' He checked his phone. 'Forty minutes. Can they wait until this afternoon?'

Say no. Say you can't go to Helly Holm today, and it was as though Mads was talking to her. *There is nothing good waiting for you there.*

His gaze on her was intent, unwavering, and she felt a second's chill.

There was no way. The dig was so important – unique. She had to help them protect it. To refuse was to fly in the face of everything that she believed was valuable, important.

But the thought of the boat, especially in this weather, made her blood run cold.

'I suppose I could always make those calls now,' she said. She picked up her cup of tea. 'I'll be back soon.'

39

Nordskaill, Stromness, Orkney, January 2020

Sprawled on the sofa, Fiona opened her laptop to check her email. It was mostly department circulars and invitations to present papers to international conferences, but also a few imaginative excuses from students as to why their essays were late. She was about to shut off the browser when she saw a text had arrived in iMessage, the little red icon glowing.

Could it be? Her heart leapt. Had Madison got in touch?

She clicked eagerly on it.

TONI&GUY HAIR – Take advantage of our winter bargains! 30% off until the end of February . . .

Disgusted, she moved to delete it, saw it stacked against all the other texts she'd received, including the ones from Madison.

She clicked on these. There were hundreds and hundreds of them, a record of their friendship through the years, a collection of candid pictures, links, emojis . . . but nothing new. The last four she'd received were there too. Read against the others, Fiona was quietly furious that she hadn't spotted straight away how different they were.

How self-absorbed she'd been, how selfish. It made her numb and nauseous.

Hugo had told her during their fight that the police could find no records of Madison texting after Wednesday, yet here they were, indistinguishable from all the other texts she'd ever sent Fiona – from the same contact, and with the same avatar – Madison in big sunglasses, vivid lipstick and red-spotted bikini top, grinning brightly at the camera like an escaped fifties pin-up.

A white flash of understanding came over Fiona.

Whoever had texted, pretending to be Mads, would not necessarily need her phone to do it.

If they could get into her laptop, log in as her, they could text anyone from that. From there it would be easy to send texts to Fiona purporting to be from Madison.

Fiona sat on the sofa, completely frozen. In the kitchen, she could hear Iris marshalling the others for their unexpected early start.

The more she thought about it, the more it made sense, the pieces clicking into place.

She researched it quickly on her computer. Texts sent through the laptop app did not go through the mobile network. They were sent through the internet. This was why they hadn't appeared on Mads' phone records.

She saw, instantly, how it had played out.

Whoever had sent those final texts had had access to Mads' *computer*, not necessarily her phone. Her phone was probably in the sea with her, and Fiona brutally crushed down the spike of anguish this thought gave her. Even now, Madison could still be down there, in the icy pounding depths. Even now, while the freezing snow beat against the glass.

However, Fiona still didn't know why the texts had been sent in the first place. Why would they lure Fiona of all people up here? What could it possibly achieve? Why invite that kind of trouble?

But it was starting to become clearer, as she let herself fall back against the cushion.

If the killer texts me, she thought, *and tells me to turn back when I've already set off from Cambridge, what is the first thing that will happen?*

I will demand to speak to Madison in person.

Whoever it was would need time to destroy evidence . . . to get rid of the phone, the car, the mirror glass from the cottage – which, in his panic, he probably forgot about and came back for.

Somehow, whoever this person was, they had access to Madison's laptop.

But not Mads' actual laptop, surely? Her laptop was in Kirkwall police station now – Fiona had given it to DI Gillespie yesterday, when she'd gone in, given her statement on the Valkyrie.

Previous to that, Mads' laptop went off to the mainland for repairs for at least a week. Nobody had had access to it. How could anyone have sent texts, genuine or otherwise, from it?

* * *

'Hi, I just got my laptop back from you and I wanted to check something.' Fiona's voice felt tight – she supposed what she was doing was technically fraud. Well, not technically fraud. Absolutely fraud. Her nails drifted up to her mouth as she nervously chewed on the skin bordering her thumbnail.

The man on the other end of the phone sounded polite but bored. 'Sure. What's the reference number?'

'I don't know, sorry – I threw the paper away.'

'It don't matter,' he said. 'I can search for you by postcode.'

Fiona reeled off Madison's details while the man on the other end clacked away on a keyboard, occasionally asking her to repeat things.

'Ah yes, Miss Ko-wow-allchick.' The man cleared his throat, as though attempting to say Madison's name had physically irritated it. 'I see it now. It says on our system that we repaired it, but as it was out of cover you were liable for the repair costs.'

Fiona frowned. She had been with Madison when she'd bought it, mere months ago. It had been a beautiful autumn day in Cambridge, and the students had just returned in a flurry of shopping and busywork. They'd both laughed at the anxious, self-conscious confusion of the freshers gazing owlishly about themselves as the pair of them drank coffee in King's Parade.

'Remember when that was you?' asked Madison, sprawled on one of the squashy sofas, a flat white perched in her hand.

'I still feel like that,' said Fiona, and Mads had snorted.

This memory made Fiona ache, distracted her for a moment from her purpose.

'Out of cover, you say?' she asked the man, gripping the phone, coming back to herself. 'But that laptop was practically brand new.'

'Yeah, but it had been accidentally damaged, see? Your warranty don't cover that.'

'What do you mean, accidentally damaged?'

'It says on our system,' said the man, clearly determined to keep any possible recriminations tied to this self-same system rather than himself, 'that when the technicians opened it they found water inside. It says they talked to you, and you said to go ahead and repair it anyway.'

'*Water* inside it?'

'Yeah. Quite a lot of water inside it. Like a glass of water had been spilled over the keyboard.' He sounded nervous, as though expecting trouble from Fiona. 'Any liquid inside it counts as accidental damage – we discussed this with you, according to our records. Twice. We recommended you replace it on your home insurance.'

'Oh yeah,' lied Fiona, hearing a suspicious hitch in the man's voice now, conscious once more that what she was doing was deceitful. 'I remember now. And the stuff on the laptop?'

'Have you switched it on yet? Can you see it?'

'Um, no. No, I can't.'

'Sorry, but it's probably gone then. You might find someone good with computers who can try recovering the hard drive, but to be honest, I wouldn't be hopeful.' He let out a little chuckle. 'They don't swim well, I'm afraid.'

'Ah well. Never mind. I'll look into that, thank you.'

'No problem, thanks Miss Kow . . . Madison.'

'Bye now.'

Fiona stood there for a long while, staring out of the window at the sea.

It might have been an accident. Say Madison had been at the house with the other archaeologists, one of them might have, in a well-oiled moment, spilled some beer over it and this had gone undetected till the next day.

Possibly the person who had done it would have noticed it at the time, then neglected to mention it. It was an expensive laptop.

But beer would have smelled – the man on the phone would probably have said 'liquid' rather than 'water'. And the guy had said it went over the keyboard. *Quite a bit of water.* Madison could be careless about her possessions, but she would have shut the lid of her nearly new laptop if not using it. It had been a substantial purchase for her – she was still paying it off.

Fiona gnawed on her nail again. She didn't know what she thought.

No, she realised, *it's not that. I know exactly what I think. It's just that it feels crazy saying it out loud.*

I think it was sabotaged.

But why?

Had it been Dom, perhaps?

But no, this had happened two weeks ago. Dom had only come up on Sunday. Though Dom was a liar, and . . .

Wait . . . thought Fiona, the hairs on her arms starting to rise in cold realisation.

Hadn't Callum told her he'd loaned Madison a company laptop when her own went off for repairs?

40

Grangeholm, Orkney, January 2020

The fat sideways snow had changed to sleet as they emerged on the driveway, and the freezing mud had sucked at their feet as they'd trudged from the van. Fiona had clung, feeling faintly sick, to the dirty seat in the back, while the others, silent and sleepy, had been shaken up and down by the van's cantankerous shock absorbers.

She'd abandoned her own car at the Helly Holm car park on the way to the quay at Langmire – she'd be coming back via the causeway. There was no need, she thought with a shudder, to risk two boat journeys in one day.

The sea was grey, agitated, nipping at the van's treads as they rolled up next to the little jetty at Langmire.

Terrified but determined, Fiona followed them out of the van.

Nobody knows you know anything, she told herself. *You just need to get on the boat, help them out, and then go.*

Come on. You can do this.

'We ready then?' asked Iris, leaping out. It was now seven in the morning, and the red pennants of dawn were starting to vanish behind tumultuous grey clouds. Unlike the others, she looked brimming with life and enthusiasm, her cheeks glowing.

She threw a questioning look at Jack.

He was gazing upwards towards Helly Holm, then at the boat, shivering against the icy wind. 'That doesn't look good.'

The tips of the waves were trimmed with little bursts of

white foam, springing into existence, vanishing again. Fiona didn't know much about the sea, but it definitely looked angrier than it had yesterday. She had been told the boat trip was very short from here to Helly Holm. She hoped so. Already her heart was starting to hammer.

The boat, about thirty feet (the size of the buried Viking boat, she realised), stirred, plunging up and down against the quay like a nervous horse. Its ropes and fittings jingled with a shrill ringing in the high wind, the prow battered by the choppy seas.

Fiona merely stared at it, while gulls criss-crossed over and above it.

'All right, everybody, start loading up,' shouted Iris. 'Come on, we need to get off.'

Fiona didn't move, hypnotised by the way the boat surged and bumped against the small quay, the slap of the waves against its fibreglass sides.

'Fiona . . . ?' Jack had stopped next to her on his way to the van, was searching her face. 'Are you okay?'

'I can't get on that,' she said. Her chest felt tight, as though no matter how hard she tried, she couldn't squeeze any breath in.

'What do you mean?'

'That boat. I can't get on it. It's too small. The sea's too rough. Just looking at it tied up to the quay is making me feel sick.'

Iris, aware there was a problem, was striding towards them both. She looked impatient, her lips thin, a few strands of escaped hair whipping her red cheeks below her woollen hat.

'Come on, you two! We're on a clock here.'

'I can't,' said Fiona, the words sticking in her throat.

'What?'

'I get seasick and I'm frightened of the ocean.' She was trembling now, and not just with the cold. 'I can't . . .'

'Oh, don't be ridiculous . . .' Something hard had appeared in Iris's face.

'No,' Fiona said. 'I told you, I can't.' She sucked in a great breath. 'I *can't.*'

'Wait,' said Jack, holding up a quelling hand. 'Iris, wait. She's scared.'

Iris rolled her eyes at Fiona. 'For Christ's sake, the journey's only *ten minute*s . . .'

Fiona felt herself then, being chivvied like a spoiled child, and suddenly something turned over in her chest.

She would not be treated this way, not for a second longer.

'I said,' and she could hear the ring of steel in her own words, 'I am *not* getting on that boat.'

There was a moment of silence, and she realised that, even though she had not raised her voice, had not sworn, somehow they had been profoundly unsettled, even shocked.

In a flash of insight, she understood that none of them refused Iris anything, ever.

'Listen, it's simple. Fiona can go over the causeway,' said Callum suddenly.

'The tide won't be out for ages . . .' Iris was scowling, but Fiona caught a flicker of surprise there.

You thought you had the measure of me.

'It's out in forty-five minutes,' corrected Jack. He tapped Iris brusquely on the shoulder. 'Come on. If she can't do it, she can't do it. We'll see her in a little while. But we have to hurry *now.*'

Iris sighed, careless of all else except her precious dig, and Fiona had a glimpse of that famous focus at work. 'It's going to take you forever to walk to the start of the causeway in this weather. If it's even crossable by the time you get there.'

'I can drive her,' Callum said quickly. 'It's only a few minutes in the van. I'll come straight back.'

'Fine,' said Iris, her eyes dark, folding her arms and turning her back on them both, striding back to the kit on the quay.

Fiona watched her go, surprised at this sudden turn of events. Why was Callum of all people coming to her aid?

Because you are holding things up, she realised. *And he is all about solving problems for Iris.*

Anyway, it was an opportunity for her, and she would be foolish not to seize it.

Callum handled the IT for the group. If anyone knew about Madison's loaned laptop, it would be him.

'Come on,' said Callum, not looking at Fiona. 'I'll run you up there.'

* * *

'Sorry about that,' said Fiona, as Callum started the van. The others had already boarded the boat, and its rocking movement still managed to unsettle her from the passenger seat. She trembled on the cold leather. 'I just couldn't . . .'

'It's all right, don't apologise.' There was a chilly pause. 'Iris is . . . she just, she cares so passionately, you know.' His voice took on a defensive edge. 'And she doesn't always get the support she needs from the others. She's under such huge pressure . . .'

'Yeah,' said Fiona, as he gunned the engine. 'I'm sure she is.'

The Helly Holm car park was only five minutes away, but she was grateful not to have to negotiate her way up the road, over the icy verges. It seemed only moments before they were in the car park, the van pulling to a halt in the space next to her car.

'Right,' Callum said, 'I better get back . . .'

'Of course – it's a big day for you all. Actually, could I very quickly ask you something? If that's okay?'

'Sure,' said Callum, his mouth a thin, flat line, as though *okay* was the very last thing in the world it was.

She was conscious of Iris like a magnet, or like the lighthouse on Helly Holm, guiding him back to her through the irresistible force of her personality.

You are her thrall, she thought, as his glance twitched towards Helly Holm. *A thousand years ago, if she fell in battle, it's your throat they would cut before they threw you into her grave.*

'You do the IT support here, don't you? For the team?' she asked.

'Yeah – well, after a fashion. It's not like any official title . . .'

'Isn't it always the way?' Fiona laughed coquettishly and was gratified to see Callum offer her a faint smile. 'I wanted to ask you about Madison's laptop.'

'Me?'

'Yes. Her own got damaged, and you lent her one . . .'

'Oh yes, that's right.' Callum rubbed his sharp nose, nodded. 'Not me personally, she had one of the team laptops. We always have about three with us. We can't account for who'll be entering what data on any given day, so we share them.'

She searched his face, but could see no trace of guilt or guile in it.

How would he respond to a direct question?

'I guess I'm wondering whether anyone could have got into her mail and texts. Do you think it could have been hacked?'

Callum rolled his shoulder up in a sceptical shrug. 'Well, yes, I suppose,' he said. 'They have antivirus and firewalls on them, but if people switch that stuff off – for instance, if they need to install something or update the software, and then don't switch it back on again – of course they can be hacked.'

'Risky,' said Fiona, nodding wisely.

'Yes. And to be honest . . .' he paused, and Fiona felt the tension in that moment – the fact he didn't trust her, and yet, despite himself, could not give up an opportunity to cast Madison in a bad light. 'You know, Madison was never good that way. She had no common sense with computers.'

'No,' Fiona said. 'She was never very techy.'

He grinned conspiratorially, his large white teeth very visible. Once again Fiona had the sense that criticising Madison made him very happy in a way he couldn't openly own, even to himself. *Iris must have really liked her.* 'She just, you know – it wasn't her fault, I suppose. She clearly had things on her mind.'

'So everyone tells me,' said Fiona, letting a little mournful note enter her voice, as if this was something she was being forced to admit was true after all.

It was bait, and she was astonished at how quickly he took it, snapping at it with those big teeth.

'See, the team laptops are only for team use, but this laptop was a loan to replace a personal one.' He let out a deep, theatrical sigh. 'We probably shouldn't have done it because it was company property, but it would have been pretty mean to deny Madison a laptop while she was working here.'

'I suppose.'

'No, it really would have been.' He gestured out towards the islands. 'The locals aren't doing without the internet, I can tell you that, especially in this weather. People need to stave the long winter nights off, and I don't know if you've noticed, but some of the team can be . . . um, kind of prickly.'

Fiona offered him a half-smile, an invitation towards complicity. 'I'll take your word for it.'

He laughed then, though she noticed he was already becoming a little more anxious, glancing at his watch. Relentless Iris would be waiting on the quay for him. 'Yes,' he said, with a smug little snort. 'It would be hard to miss.'

'But none of that explains how anyone could have got hold of Mads' account details. In fact, it makes it even stranger.'

'Did they? Is that what happened?' He blinked at her, and his surprise seemed visceral, genuine.

Was he surprised it had happened, or surprised someone had found out about it?

Fiona twisted a curl of her windblown hair around one finger. 'Um, well, the police asked me about it . . .' she lied.

Callum blushed then, his high cheekbones turning scarlet.

'Ah. *Ah*. Yes. So, what you probably need to know about our company laptops is that they all have a keylogger installed on them.' He knotted his hands together, his large, bony knuckles prominent. 'It's policy.'

'What's that?' Fiona recognised the word, wondered for a minute from where.

'A keylogger records all the keystrokes on our computers. It's so we can tell what you're browsing, who you're emailing, that kind of thing.' He made a little typing mime with his hands. 'Which means it also collects your passwords too.'

'Collects passwords?' asked Fiona, astounded.

'Yes.'

She found herself astonished by his flat reaction to this question.

'Isn't that illegal?'

'Not at all,' he said. 'Those laptops are company property, and it clearly states in our contract, the one everyone has to sign, that you can only use your computer for work and its use can be monitored. There's to be no personal information on there. I mean, obviously people do use them that way, but strictly speaking, you're not allowed to.'

'Why would you do that?' Fiona was horrified.

'Do what?'

'Spy on their computer use like that? Isn't that an invasion of privacy?'

'No.'

'It seems very hardcore.' Fiona's thoughts flicked to her own machine in the office, which she frequently used to email scandalous work gossip to Mads and check her bank balance on. 'Is it usual?'

'In archaeology? No. It's the first I'd heard of it. But basically, there was . . .' he paused, then stammered, as though he'd been led down a conversational avenue that constituted a distinctly wrong turn. 'Anyway, there was this scandal. If you could call it that. More of a nano-scandal.'

'Oh yeah?' asked Fiona, playing her wide-eyed, breathy surprise just a bit more than was natural. Madison would have laughed at her. But then Madison would have done it all better. 'What kind of scandal?'

'Hmm, well . . .' Callum blushed again, and this time the very tips of his ears went pink as well as his neck. 'Uh, we're not supposed to talk about it, but I suppose . . . you know, considering what's happened, it would be okay to tell you. Just don't say you heard it from me, okay?'

'I promise,' said Fiona. She would have promised him her firstborn child at that point.

'Yeah. So. We worked on a teaching dig on Lewis last summer. It's an early medieval Celtic settlement with graveyard . . . It's a big, big project – three different universities sending students, been running for eight years. Each year there's about thirty undergraduates, and then the supervisors on top.'

'Oh yeah, I think I've seen papers presented on the metalwork finds. It sounds great. They found some amazing goldwork there one year, didn't they?'

Callum nodded.

'Yes – that said, it was a shit season last year – one of those where you're digging in all the wrong places and don't find out till two days before you pack up.' He sighed. 'And it pissed down. Every day.'

Fiona nodded. She knew about those kinds of digs.

'Anyway,' said Callum, who, having decided to tell the story, had abandoned his reluctance and was doing so with salacious relish. 'They thought someone was using one of the laptops to harass this female student, Mara Miller. You know, to, well, to send her, um, pictures of a gentleman's anatomy, shall we say.'

'You're kidding.'

'Nope. Anyway, Ms Miller is not impressed, and there was an investigation – it was a student dig and, you know, political correctness and universities and it's all very #MeToo at the moment, so people at the top want a paper trail.' He frowned. 'Or at least a virtual paper trail.'

'And what did they find?'

'Someone had sent them from the team's email account – we normally left Outlook open on the laptop because not everyone knew the password for it, which was a teeny bit stupid but you live and learn, I suppose.'

'That does sound like asking for trouble.'

'One of the other students pranking her, most likely. Much ado about nothing. But anyway, she gets these emails and there was so much noise that Iris just said to me, do what you have to do, but I won't tolerate a repeat of this. I want this stuff tracked on all the laptops from now on.' He sighed. 'So it was left up to me to sort it out, and this is the solution I chose.'

Fiona was astonished by this revelation, by his language in describing it. She was also thinking of Mads' tweets, the sexual nature of her bullying.

'So you're telling me that there was an incident of sexual harassment on a dig six months ago?'

Callum looked shifty, as though sensing the switch in Fiona's mood.

'Well, if you could call it that. I never understood why the silly cow didn't just delete the pictures if she was that upset,' he said. 'She was hardly a saint. She was all over Jack Bergmann like a rash that summer. Since she was an undergraduate, we could have ended up in trouble, so we had to look tough on this kind of thing. Some girls just like to get upset over nothing. They love the attention; the drama, you know?'

'You think she shouldn't have complained?' asked Fiona, trying to keep the sharpness out of her voice, only partially succeeding.

He shrugged, defensive now, not meeting her eyes. 'No. Not at all.' He glanced at his smartwatch. 'Look, I have to get back . . .'

Now Fiona was at a wrong conversational turn, and she could feel how her ploy to get into his confidence had backfired on her, made him feel comfortable saying these things to her. She wanted to go on, to explain how undermining and alarming it would be to receive an official email from the dig team and to open it and find ugly, obscene images of someone's genitalia, and then be unable to trace them, to learn who had done this to her. Was it a student? One of the supervisors? A teacher?

How would that affect how you looked at them all when you turned up for work in the morning? What would it do to your level of engagement, your trust in your colleagues, when you're a young woman on your first dig?

And when it started to show, and affect your work, how quickly would you be written off as a shirker, a casual, a part-timer?

She realised, looking at Callum's stubborn expression, that this would all be wasted effort to explain. It sounded as though Iris had already tried and failed.

And if the Divine Iris couldn't get through to him, Fiona would have no chance.

It didn't matter, ultimately. She was here on Madison's behalf. She needed to stick to the programme.

'Sorry – I interrupted you.' She leaned in again. 'You were telling me how these keyloggers work . . .'

'Oh yeah,' he said, also seemingly glad to drop the subject. 'Nothing easier. You install it on the laptop, and whenever that machine comes online, it sends every keystroke you enter to a log file. Then your sys admin or whoever just accesses the log file.'

'And who would have access to that?'

'Um, well, the sys admin,' said Callum.

'Who would be . . .'

'Me, usually. But to be honest, we're a small team so we all log in as admin from time to time. It's one thing to have this locked-down security when there are dozens of overly hormonal undergraduates under your feet, sending each other dirty pictures, but when there's just half a dozen of you, it's starting to get ridiculous.'

'So, anyone on the team could read those log files?'

Callum looked uncomfortable again. 'I suppose so. That said, I'm not sure where they are. Once it was done and dusted, we never bothered reading the log files. Nobody has the time to sit there and monitor what everybody else is doing on their company laptops.'

'No,' said Fiona, her thoughts a million miles away. 'I suppose not.'

She had discovered so much more than she had bargained for, she realised. Potentially any of the archaeologists could have accessed Madison's passwords at any point.

Any one of them could be Mads' murderer, and she was contemplating joining them on a tiny remote island, far from aid.

'Thanks for the lift,' she said, opening the van door. 'See you at the dig.'

41

Helly Holm Car Park, Orkney, January 2020

The minute Callum pulled away Fiona was on the phone, letting herself into her car, pushing down Madison's trapper hat to control her wind-whipped hair. This close to Helly Holm she was down to a mere couple of bars of signal.

In the distance, against the louring sky, storm clouds roiled towards Helly Holm.

'Hi, I'd like to talk to DI Gillespie. This is Fiona Grey. I just found something out about Madison's laptop . . .'

'I'm afraid he's not here yet.' It was the woman she'd spoken to yesterday morning. 'But I can get him to call you back.'

'Um, that's no good to me,' Fiona clutched her phone tight to her ear, gazing all around her. 'I'm about to head off to Helly Holm soon. There's no phone reception out there.'

'Ah. Well, I can certainly take a message. Is this in connection to the missing persons case?'

* * *

There was one more thing she could do, she reflected as she opened up her phone.

She could check Madison's email account. She knew the password was Rhub4rb1. It had used to be Rhubarb, until Fiona had persuaded her, and not without encountering some resistance, to add the numbers in.

Madison was a hacker's dream.

It had, up till now, seemed an unforgivable breach between

them, even if Madison was dead, but Fiona's thoughts had changed in the aftermath of her conversation with Callum. It was very likely Madison's enemy had been hacking her online life constantly.

Maybe it was time one of her friends did. There might be something in there that would help.

She logged in on her phone, entered Madison's details.

At first, when the email portal came up, she thought she'd typed something wrong.

The second time, her heart started to pound.

Everything in Madison's inbox had been deleted from before she went missing. There were the eight emails Fiona had written; enthusiastic, suspicious and then desperate. There was a welter of promotional spam and newsletters, none older than Wednesday. There was an email from a Sam Hardwick, someone Fiona didn't know, titled *Greetings!* which she didn't want to click on, as she realised it would then show as read . . .

Oh, of course. How stupid she was.

She realised that the mere act of looking at this page altered the evidence on it – that the police would be able to tell when it was last accessed, and her imagination embarked on a car crash scenario where the police saw it had been opened, and gave up searching for Madison, abandoning her to her fate.

She was going to have to explain that she'd done it, and she wasn't sure, but she suspected it might be illegal, even though Madison had told her the password. What with tearing open the box with the laptop, she was starting to rack up her Interfering With Evidence Miles – throw in the assault on Hugo and she wondered if she was looking at actual prison time.

Maybe she should blow out Helly Holm and head back to the mainland, explain herself, throw herself on DI Gillespie's mercy.

'I am so stupid,' she said to herself, and once again had that hot, squeezing sensation of wanting to cry, of longing for the relief of tears, and being unable to satisfy it. 'I'm sorry, Mads. I'm so sorry. I keep fucking everything up.'

She was about to close the browser, when she thought she would just briefly look at the other folders. Perhaps not all was lost – there was Mads' Sent folder – no, that was completely empty, everything in it deleted, and this gave her a pang of pure fury. Mads had been silenced within her own account, the central repository of her funny, touching, spiky, rambling missives gone, and it struck Fiona as yet another violence against her.

The other folders were empty too – Spam, Junk, Trash, and in Drafts there was only a handful of things Mads had started but never sent: an email to her landlord about the stinking drains, a note to Fiona about a play they were off to see at the Donmar that night, and finally, an email addressed to her, dated January 12th that year. Whoever had gone through, systematically deleting the contents, must have missed this folder.

They had probably had a lot on their mind at the time.

Eagerly, she clicked on it to open it.

There was no text, and she ached with disappointment. It seemed just an empty email, before she realised it was not empty – it was just a single large attachment: SMAIDEN*NOV*19.mov.

Before she could stop herself, before she could think, she had hit Send. It blinked for a moment, then vanished out of the folder, on its way to her.

Ah well. In for a penny, in for a pound. Mads had been in the process of sending it to her, after all, right?

Sometimes the ends justified the means.

It would take a while to arrive, with such a large attachment (a video – what could it be?) and she probably wouldn't get to watch it till she was off Helly Holm.

Now she had done it, so impulsively, so spur of the moment, anxiety and guilt suddenly assailed her. Was she mad? What if she'd destroyed something important, committed some computer faux pas that would keep Mads' killer out of prison?

What if she'd committed an actual crime? Would she be fired from work? Would she go to jail?

Stop it, she told herself.

Calm down. You need to think.

Her fingers tapped lightly on the steering wheel.

She had been right. It *was* one of them. Whoever it was had faked being Mads from a computer. She knew now that they had access to all her passwords – they had the means to pretend to be her.

But why? She still had no idea why.

And what was she going to do? She couldn't go over to Helly Holm now, surely?

A cold chill stole over her. Her tapping fingers ceased.

You know, I think I have to.

If she didn't go, whoever it was would know that she knew. If she just ghosted them now, they'd ask Callum when he'd last seen her, perhaps even ask him what they'd been talking about. From there whoever it was could destroy evidence, run away, or even hurt someone else.

And whoever they were, they couldn't get away with this.

Her teeth gritted, and she felt wild, almost feral. *I will not allow it. I owe it to Madison.*

She had to go. She had to get herself to Helly Holm once the way was clear. She must give them no reason whatsoever to suspect anything was wrong. Callum wasn't the threat – he would never in a million years have told her what he did if he'd thought it mattered.

She wouldn't be in any danger, they weren't on alert. She just needed to make sure she wasn't alone with any of them.

Just cover up that boat burial and get off the island, and then run, not walk, back to Kirkwall.

She had already packed her belongings into her little suitcase, thrown it into the back of her car that morning.

She would not spend another night in Nordskaill House.

There was every chance one of them was a killer.

42

Helly Holm, Orkney, January 2020

Fiona stood on the edge of the causeway leading out to Helly Holm. Before her, the islet rose out of the sea, the straight concrete road to it wet and grey before her. The smell of the ocean, briny and organic, blew all around.

She dropped her chin into the collar of her coat, the wind already tugging at Madison's hat, and started walking.

The sky behind the islet was an icy blue-grey and swirled dangerously with fast moving clouds as she picked her way over the slippery causeway. A growing smudgy line of darkness stretched across the horizon, and from far away came the first rumbling of thunder.

On Helly Holm itself, the boat bobbed next to the little shingle spit they had tethered it to. The archaeologists were on the islet, hurrying about their tasks. The tent they had erected over the burial lay to one side, the poles splayed, like a grounded jellyfish, and someone, probably Callum, though it was hard to be sure at this distance, was standing over it, rubbing at his head.

Beyond, the white stub of the lighthouse flashed in the gathering darkness.

She had the sense then that she should go no further – that she should turn around, flee.

Someone on that island had very likely murdered Madison. Yes, Dominic Tate and Hugo had motives, it was true, but it could only be one of the archaeologists who had the means. It was one of them that had got hold of Madison's account details, who had pretended to be her, all the while knowing she was gone.

But why? She just didn't understand *why* . . .

The fact that she didn't understand why put her in a very dangerous position.

Surely whoever it was wouldn't attempt anything against her – they had no reason to suppose she knew anything suspicious.

She would be in the open, in public. She would be perfectly safe, so long as she was careful.

But all of this opened up the burning, gnawing question – who had killed Madison? Was it Jack, who'd lied about sleeping with her? Was it Becky, who she'd befriended then dropped? Callum, who'd envied her Iris's favour? Or even Iris herself for some strange, hidden reason?

All of these motives seemed tenuous to Fiona, though; barely enough to trigger a quarrel, never mind a murder.

There's something you're not seeing. You were brought up here to look.

As she hesitated, her steps slowing, she saw them noticing her on the islet, calling to one another as they rushed between the storage boxes. Iris waved at her.

Don't be a fool, she told herself. *Don't tip them off.* She'd help them pack the site up, wave goodbye, cross this causeway back to land, get in her car and never look back. She'd tell the police all she knew and then, the minute she could, head on home.

She'd call Adi, when she was done here, and tell him she was coming back.

So, though the skies churned and the sea roared, she walked on, the water lapping at her new, creaking boots, as though it wished to drag her down and claim her.

* * *

She arrived into a typhoon of activity, whipped on by the darkening skies. The three big storage boxes were being pulled into a circle by the men, as if they were cowboys defending a wagon train about to be attacked by Indians.

'Fuck me,' snapped Callum. 'Where's the key for this? It's so *heavy*. Is there a body in . . . Fiona!'

'Hey, Fiona!' Jack called out with a grin. He and Becky were now wrestling with big rolls of black plastic sheeting. 'There's gardening gloves in the storage locker, the one on the end.'

'Thanks!' she shouted back. From here, at the top of the dig, the wind was already strong and gusty enough to make standing feel unsteady. It had blown down the tent protecting the main chamber of the burial. Pools of water collected in the waterproof fabric, gently vibrating as if to the footsteps of monsters.

Iris was at one of the storage boxes, kneeling to examine the lock. She looked up as Fiona approached and smiled. Now Fiona was here and ready to work, it seemed all was forgiven.

'What are you after?' she said, half-shouting over the wind, the far away crash of thunder.

'Gloves,' said Fiona.

Iris pulled off her own. 'Take these, they're dry. I've a pair in my coat. We're going to pack the tent up next and take it down to the boat, yeah?'

Fiona responded with a nod.

* * *

It took the best part of an hour. All activity – even something as simple as rolling up the tent fabric – took far longer than normal as everyone was hampered by the wind and the driving sleet that came up out of nowhere. Holding things up to pour the gathered rainwater out of them caused it to spray into faces and over coats. Aluminium poles thrummed as though they had independent life, and at one point one was knocked into Callum's chin, grazing it.

Fiona was pink-faced with effort, the inside of her coat hot and damp in spite of the weather. Her ears stung, and her hair was soaked.

On the horizon, lightning arced across the clouds, down into the gunmetal sea. The storm was drawing nearer.

She was dispatched with Jack to the boat, each gripping heavy, sweat-damp, folded tent fabric.

'Watch your step on the way down!' shouted Iris, carrying big whorls of twine and coloured pegs in a wheelbarrow. 'Becky, no, leave the big tools, the spades and mattocks! And don't forget, we need to get the wheelbarrows on board too, so save space for them!'

Fiona turned, looked back towards the mainland. Already the water looked nearer to the causeway, the rock pools fuller.

'I need to go soon!' she shouted to Jack, pointing.

He nodded. 'Yep. Just this load and I think we all need to go. The sea's not looking too clever.'

They now began marching down the slippery, sodden turf, with its pockets of ice and snow, to the spit at the bottom of Helly Holm.

Fiona regarded the boat with dread and suspicion.

'Are you all right getting on it while it's tied up?' shouted Jack over the wind.

'Yeah,' she said, her heart in her mouth. Already she was alone with one of them. How had that happened? 'I think so.'

Jack flashed her a smile. 'Let's do it, then! Are you all right? You look pale . . .'

'I'm fine.'

They carried the poles and sticks down three steep steps, piled them in the cabin. Within, crates and stray boxes had begun to mount up. The deck lurched beneath her feet.

'Here, Fiona, give me that,' said Jack. 'We can put that across the stuff at the back, keep the rain off it.' He lifted the tarpaulin out of her hands. 'You're soaked,' he said. 'I'm going to run back up. You stay down here, and clear spaces for the buckets and smaller tools.'

'Right,' said Fiona, conscious this would leave her alone. 'But I n-need to get off soon . . .'

'Yep, just do this for me now and we can all take care of the rest. See you back at the house later for a beer, yeah?'

She hesitated, barely able to meet his frank, friendly gaze. 'Um, yeah. I've got an errand in Kirkwall, but . . .' she stammered, aware of herself as evasive, shifty. 'Of course.'

'Great,' he said, but his face was cloudy, and she felt he had guessed something was up. 'Catch you later.'

Then he was gone.

She quickly moved various things into a more stable order, tidying up fallen measuring tapes, stacking the poles against the walls, but nobody else came. Anxious, she popped her head out.

Up on the top of the islet, she could see them manipulating full wheelbarrows down the steep path, moving slowly, Iris at the front, acting as a guide. It would take them a little while to reach her. Becky and Callum followed her. There was no sign of Jack.

Idly, she pulled out her phone, rubbed the condensation and water off the front with her bare hand. Her mail was open, and she saw that the file from Madison's account had downloaded.

It was, indeed, a video.

She looked out again. The others were still quite far away, and in fact had stopped, as Becky's barrow had tipped over, and some trowels and short shovels had fallen out.

Fiona swiped through her phone, while rain pattered once

more against the cabin roof, the tapping of a thousand fingers – a few at first, then a driving tempo of them.

The video, SMAIDEN*NOV*19.mov, opened instantly. It must have downloaded while she crossed the causeway.

It was short, a mere three minutes. Numbers ran along the bottom, showing the running time. It opened on Iris, peering into a display case, containing a golden necklace that Fiona instantly recognised as the Jesmond Hill torc. This must be the British Museum. Iris leaned in towards it, her face glowing with soft wonder, one hand drifting up to her chest. Then she stood up, faced the camera. Her brightly coloured geometric top was of a piece with her painted lips, the vivid dark mass of her hair. A thin leather thong went around her neck, vanished down into the front of her shirt.

It was film, an outtake, perhaps, from *Discovering the Past*. It was some kind of pre-production footage – with the date, it must have been made in the past couple of weeks.

'And this is one of my favourite objects – both historically, and also in a personal context. The torc is made out of nearly pure gold.' The camera now concentrated on the object itself, a solid golden necklace, open at the front with lavishly ornamented ends. It was sumptuous and beautiful.

The archaeologist in Fiona lingered, fascinated, as Iris went on to describe its construction.

It was an interesting enough video, she supposed – but why had Madison thought of sending it to her?

'Fiona! Are you in there? Give us a hand!' shouted Iris from outside, her voice more shrill and urgent than the velvety narration she'd been delivering in the video.

Shocked, Fiona hit pause on the video and shoved the phone in her pocket, then hurried out on deck. Iris was there, and the others, and soon she found herself helping to carry the wheelbarrows down the steps into the hold.

'Right, that's it,' said Iris, smoothing her damp hair out of her eyes and heading for the wheelhouse. 'You guys take a seat.'

'Did we get the total station?' asked Jack, poking his head through the door.

'Did we . . . oh shit, no.' Becky looked around. 'Callum, did you?'

'No.'

'Jack, where did we leave it?' barked Iris.

'Up by Trench C.' He pulled up his hood. 'I think. Should I get it?'

'Well, we can't leave it here,' snapped Iris. 'It's a brand-new piece of surveying kit and cost me nearly ten grand.'

'It's all right,' said Fiona, realising this was her chance to leave, now they were all gathered together. 'I'll get it. I have to go anyway. I'll get it back to you later.'

'Perfect,' said Jack. 'If you're sure.'

'Yep,' said Fiona. 'See you later!'

'Thanks, Fiona!' called Iris. 'Be very careful on that causeway! Now, let's get off this rock and find ourselves a pub!'

The others let out a cheer, as Iris guided Fiona over the deck and back on to the spit, holding on to her arm until both feet were safely on dry land.

'I wouldn't linger, if I was you,' she said, nearly shouting against the whipping weather. 'That sea is rough. You get one bad wave while you're out on that causeway and . . .' She made a shooting, slipping gesture.

'Thanks, Iris. See you later!'

And she was away from them, hurrying up the steep path. A couple of times the wind nearly knocked her down, pushing at her back, the stray grass around her susurrating and whistling as she grabbed at it, used it to hold her steady till she reached the top once more.

The sky was transformed into a swirling dark grey of clashing clouds. The dig was before her, with the three storage chests in a circle in a little natural depression, all locked up tight with padlocks, the mattocks and spades lying in the middle, like captured spears, and the trenches all covered now with black plastic sheeting, nailed down with iron tent pegs and weighted with old tyres.

Trench C, Trench C – that was the one on the lighthouse side, wasn't it? She hurried towards it, and there was the total station theodolite in its green plastic case, sitting upright on the edge.

What a strange place to leave it.

She bent down to pick it up, glanced over her shoulder. She was completely alone, able to think, able to wonder.

Why had Madison wanted to send that video?

It wasn't a YouTube link, or something online. It was raw, unfinished – it had the running time printed along the bottom. It had been obtained from somewhere.

Hadn't Becky told her that Mads had been doing unpaid research work for *Discovering the Past*?

Why send it? What did it mean?

Carrying the theodolite with her back to the path, she paused.

Watch it. There's only a minute left.

Madison wanted to show you something.

The storage cases came to thigh height, and she sat down heavily on one, the one with the loose hasp that now rattled in the wind, hunching her back against the gale.

The video on the phone was paused as she lifted it out, but impossible to hear over the noise of the wind. She popped her earbuds in and listened, the total station resting next to her on the case.

'. . . the most spectacular find from the Bronze Age burial

discovered at Jesmond Hill by myself and the team in 2015. You can see the tiny scratches of wear at the front here . . .'

The camera was back on Iris, and she was talking directly to it.

Then, like a crash of thunder, Fiona understood what was going on.

She was so mesmerised, so stunned at its enormity, that she didn't realise that someone had picked up the green plastic case next to her until they smashed it into her head.

43

Helly Holm, Orkney, January 2020

When Fiona woke up she was freezing, blind and stiff – everything hurt, especially her head. It sent out waves of sharp pain, like a radio signal. And . . .

She couldn't move.

She was curled into a foetal ball and crammed into a tiny space, only big enough to contain her. All was total darkness. The only sound was the wind, howling mournfully, all around the outside of wherever she was.

Her fear was vast, all-embracing – she could not even scream, shocked into muteness. She was trapped in what seemed to be a locked box or a coffin, with only the buffeting wind and her own fast, shallow breathing for company.

And something else – a faint rattling, of metal against metal, happening somewhere close to her head.

She tried to stretch her chilled legs, heard her boots clang against steel. Her frozen hands pressed against the icy walls of her prison – yes, it was a metal box. She pushed upwards against the lid, and it seemed to rise a couple of millimetres before stopping dead, and the air instantly grew even colder, the wind howled louder, and the rattling from outside grew momentarily heavier then ceased altogether.

Silent with horror, she realised that she knew where she was – she was in one of the site's all-weather storage boxes. The rattling was the padlock, trembling as the wind buffeted the box.

She had been locked inside it.

A surge of sheer panic moved through her, and she couldn't breathe with it, and it seemed to her that there wasn't enough air in the box, there wasn't enough *air*, she was going to suffocate, she was going to . . .

No. You are not going to suffocate. If the wind can get in, air can. Stop this. Concentrate. Think.

But she couldn't, not for a long while, as she tried to calm her gasping breath, her racing heart, to control her ratcheting claustrophobia – *I can't be in here I can't move what if I never get out and I am stuck here forever I can't move I can't . . .*

Be calm. *Breathe.*

Eventually she was able to recover herself enough to realise that she was lying on top of some kind of bulky weatherproof fabric and what seemed to be aluminium rods – one of the smaller wind shelters for digging delicate finds, she suspected. Everything – the material, the box walls, her coat – was covered in a faint mist of dampness; the condensation she had breathed against her prison walls. Her numb hands, crabbed with cold, travelled over the rods beneath her, but they were nearly exactly as long as the box and she couldn't lift or move them.

I was so stupid. I couldn't wait to watch the end . . .

But there was something else in here with her, pressing into her thigh through her wet jeans. It had a wooden handle, and as her hand fell on it, she recognised its diamond-shaped blade. It was a garden trowel, of the type the archaeologists used, the edges still crusty with compacted mud.

She drew it out. The blade felt fragile, thin, but she had no choice.

Bracing the lid above her with her feet, she once again felt the freezing bite of the wind as she inserted the blade into where the gap between lid and box must be – she couldn't see it, so had to feel with her cold fingers.

At first it merely scratched along the inside of the steel, with a horrible squeak as the tip moved over the metal, then, just as she was despairing, it disappeared easily into the gap.

But when she tried to lever up the lid, the padlock held firm in its hasp. Her fingers moved to the place where the blade was, while her legs shook with the strain of pushing. There was a gap, and it felt at least half an inch wide, but would go no wider. And something else – the weather bit her fingers – and there was a sudden flash of blazing white light.

For a second she could see it – the gap – and then it was gone. It didn't matter, though – it would be back, she knew.

It was the Helly Holm lighthouse. The fact that it was the only light she could perceive told her something else too – night must have fallen. If it was still daylight, that would be getting in the box too.

It doesn't matter about the dark, she told herself, while her heart pounded again and her fear seemed to overwhelm her once more. *If you can get out of this box, you can cope with the dark.*

First things first. You need to get out of this box.

No amount of kicking or pushing at the lid with her legs made any difference, and now her legs were growing tired, the muscles in them trembling. Her feet were so cold she could no longer feel them.

Maybe she could break the hasp.

The rattling, the way the lid rose up – the padlock was threaded through it, but the hasp was loose, she could tell. She had noticed it earlier that day. If she levered her trowel through and used her feet to push near it rather than straight up, she might be able to get it to break off.

A sudden upwelling of hope grew in her then, and all the

inevitable dangers she would face afterwards – the cold, the darkness, the lack of heat or shelter, her isolation, suddenly counted as nothing. If she could only open the box.

She couldn't get the angle right. There wasn't enough room to get her legs to bend high enough to truly push, the trowel needed gripping with both hands, and even then she couldn't properly bring all her strength to bear in the cramped, shuttered space.

I bet you're sorry you didn't stick with the yoga now, a voice like Madison's seemed to murmur in her head, and when this happened – either memory or hallucination or concussion or visitation from the unquiet dead – whatever it was, Fiona's panic calmed for a moment, and with a deep breath, she shut her eyes and simultaneously pushed with her legs and pulled down on the trowel handle.

Without warning the lid of the box flew upward, and a swirl of icy sleet descended upon her, the wind driving it into her face.

With a huge sucking breath, as though she had been under-water, Fiona jerked upright, her frozen hands gripping the edges of her would-be coffin, and she was clambering out into the darkness, her feet splashing as they contacted the ground, the back of her head aching, pierced with the icy cold. When she lifted Madison's hat to touch her hand to her scalp it was wet, and it came away slicked with some warm liquid.

All was soaked, muddy and slimy, and so, so cold.

In the background, the sea roared, like a furious crowd bearing down on her.

She gazed about the abandoned site, shivering. The other two storage boxes lay locked nearby, and tarpaulin and old tyres neatly covered the open ground of the dig.

Then all was darkness once more, and there was only the tiny, painful kiss of the sleet on her face, stinging her with cold.

I'm going to freeze to death up here.

She sucked in a deep breath.

You can't think like this. You need to get off this island. You need to . . .

Call the coastguard. Yes, call the coastguard, like it said to do on the safety signs. Of course! Burly men would come in a red helicopter and she could tell them everything – all about Madison and the Valkyrie . . .

Her hand felt in her pockets – her coat, her jeans – searching helplessly.

There was no sign of either her phone or her car keys.

She let out a little cry of disappointment, bent back over the box, tearing out the fabric and poles as the lighthouse slowly lit her up, then cast her into darkness, then lit her up, but her phone and keys were not there either.

Fiona raised her naked hands to her face and howled. She had no way of telling what time it was, as the clouds were thick and fast, moving and combining like oil in water, and the lighthouse lit them in ugly orange and sulphuric yellow as it passed over them, and then blinked off.

The only shelter she had was the box and windbreak inside it. The thought of climbing into it again horrified her, and as for the windbreak, there was no way it would stand upright in this angry wind.

As she stumbled over to where she thought the tyres and tarpaulin might be, her arms wrapped around her sodden coat, she wondered if it was worth trying to shelter under them somehow. Perhaps . . .

Again, the light.

Only this time, with it, an idea.

It took a few more flashes of the lighthouse for her to find the trowel, and one of the short poles that acted as ribbing for the windbreak.

This last she shoved under her arm.

* * *

She was freezing, really freezing, and wherever she put her feet she seemed to be ankle-deep in rushing rainwater, as though it was springing like a fountain out of the spongy ground. It made the going slimy and treacherous.

It didn't help that she couldn't see – the blazing world of the lantern, every twenty seconds, made it impossible to adapt her eyes to the darkness in between flares.

She could only force herself on towards it, and hope.

She was climbing the slope towards the lighthouse, the angle growing sharper as she staggered upwards, the rain driving into her face, and overhead, just once, the crack of seething lightning, like jagged teeth in the inky sky. Surely, if lightning were to strike, it would strike the lighthouse first?

But say it did? The ground was so wet. She was so wet. And she was exposed . . .

Exposed as she was, she was starting to feel warmer, and with a slice of panic, realised that this was the beginning of hypothermia. She needed to get indoors soon, or there would be no way she would be able to check its racing progress.

Gritting her chattering teeth, she started to climb.

* * *

Fiona yanked down on the steel door handle to the lighthouse, and to her surprise it scraped freely, uselessly up and down, and here, sheltered a little out of the wind, she could hear something on the other side rattle at the same time, as if in sympathy.

The lock was broken. Burglars or vandals perhaps, encouraged by the lonely location.

Excitement bloomed within her, galvanised her in her frozen misery.

She pulled the door towards herself, and it flew open for an inch or two before holding fast with a metallic ring. A tiny whiff of warm, fetid human scent, one with a familiar tinge, whipped past her nose and was gone, as completely as if she had imagined it.

She tugged again, hard, driven with new adrenaline. But the door held – something inside was catching it, stopping it from opening.

No, this couldn't be. She had to get inside. She had to get out of this weather or she would die in it.

And then she remembered the short pole she had brought from the chest, its weight jostling against her thigh in the deep, sodden pocket of her anorak.

She could use it to lever the door open.

If she didn't, she thought it unlikely she would make it back to the site and the box alive.

The end of the pipe was hammered flat, and Fiona rammed it between the door and the jamb, using it as a crowbar. She pulled.

Some wild thing had woken in her now, and her teeth gritted and she strained, groaning as there was a sudden tearing noise, and then the metallic ping of something falling to the concrete floor. The door, its lock still in place but redundant, swung out wide, nearly striking her.

The darkness within yawned wide.

It was the loveliest thing she'd seen all evening.

She had then a moment of clarity. It was not that she stopped being cold and terrified, but that her own will leapt to the fore.

If she died out here, in this terrible, endless night, then she would effectively be the victim of a perfect murder.

It would be easy enough to explain Fiona's death away as an accident, a terrible consequence of mixed messages and poor comms. 'We were so sure she had gone back over the causeway,' they would say, weeping. 'We were all on the boat, we'd already set off. And we were all so distracted in the wake of Madison's death . . .'

Madison's death.

One of them had killed Madison.

And with a rush of certainty, Fiona knew who. And she was not going to let them get away with it.

44

Helly Holm Lighthouse, Orkney, January 2020

The first thing that struck Fiona as she stumbled into the darkness of the lighthouse was the smell – stale, sour – the odour of sweat, concentrated urine, and just a metallic hint of blood.

Suddenly the lights, moved by some sensor, flickered into fluorescent life with a click.

What the hell?

She was blinking in the sudden illumination, her hand wrapped around the short pole, knuckles whitening.

She stood in a small, windowless, L-shaped room – furnished with cabinets, a counter, and a narrow interior door lying open, leading to a chemical toilet and a sink. It must have at one point been a neat, compact space, but it was now utterly dishevelled, as if it had been looted at some point.

Probably just vandals, she told herself, while she wrapped her arms around herself and shivered, *kids using the place as a drinking den.*

On the floor at her feet lay a single screwdriver, now slightly bent. She reached down, picked it up. If Fiona could guess, this was what had been rammed through the door handle and into the broken lock in the frame to secure it.

'Hello?' she called out, hearing the quaver in her voice.

Nothing. There was nothing to see and no one here, only mess and disorder – spilled medical supplies, discarded waterproof clothes piled around a small, freestanding oil radiator, and an upended green box with a white cross painted on it.

She sighed, pulled off Madison's wolf hat, now soaked, ran her fingers through her tangled hair.

It was still better than nothing. Whoever these vandals were, by bursting open the lock they had probably saved her life.

She pushed the screwdriver back into the door, threading it through the handle, back into the gap left in the frame, hammering it home as well as she could with her frozen palm.

There.

For the first time she let herself sag after her long labours, draw a deep breath, try to think.

There would be no leaving the island tonight, not unless she found a radio in here somewhere.

But this was a lighthouse, she realised. There *must* be a radio.

And there was some form of electricity, at least, enough for interior lights, and therefore a chance to switch on the radiator, perhaps even boil the tiny kettle for a hot drink if she could find a tea bag.

She wandered over to the radiator, moving aside the upended medical box with her hand.

On the concrete floor in front of her, dark red smears and drops of dried blood trailed a thin, ragged pattern.

Fiona's breath caught in her throat.

Her gaze tracked the smeared blood to a corner, where a pile of discarded clothes and blankets huddled around the radiator.

Her heart froze.

Poking out of this pile, palm upwards, fingers slightly curled, was a single human hand.

Fastened around the icy-white wrist was the rose-gold Ted Baker watch she had bought Madison for her birthday.

Fiona's hands drifted up to her mouth in horror.

Oh no, no, no . . .

'Mads? *Madison!*'

And she was kneeling down by the hand, as if in a nightmare, and the storm and the cold and her own danger were all forgotten.

The smell intensified as she lifted the blanket up. Yes, there was Mads curled up into a foetal huddle, in her indigo Anthropologie jumper and dark jeans stained with blood. Her right leg was so badly broken that it appeared to have two knees, the foot in its workboot twisted around at an unnatural angle.

Madison's spilled hair lay over the concrete, her cheek resting on her other hand. She was utterly still, almost peaceful, though the white hand beneath her was laced with dried blood. Her face was hidden.

'Mads?' breathed Fiona, reaching forward to move her hair away. 'Mads?'

And then she felt it – a tiny puff of breath against her fingers.

'Oh God,' said Fiona. 'Mads! *Mads?* Can you hear me?'

No answer.

She's freezing, Fiona thought. *She needs warmth. And water.*

The radiator was already plugged in, and when Fiona snapped on the button, a kind of low ticking began, and almost immediately it started to warm up.

It was stuck on a two-hour timer, presumably to limit the electricity it used. The lighthouse ran on solar power, and most of that must go to the lantern.

She would have to stay awake to keep pressing it on.

With a start, she realised that this was what Madison had failed to do. Madison, with her snow-pale skin and motionlessness – Madison was dying of the cold.

'Shit,' she said. 'Mads, can you hear me?'

The only reply was silence. A silent Madison was somehow more horrifying, more unnatural, than a dead one.

'It's going to be okay.' Fiona ignored the internal voice that wondered how she knew this and reached down for the full cup of water next to her. An abandoned bottle of it, half-drunk, had been lying upended nearby. 'You'll see.'

The quiet mocked her, interrupted only by the purring tick of the radiator timer.

Fiona shivered, aware that she too was freezing, was possibly in danger.

She was beginning to guess what had happened.

Madison had broken in here somehow, crippled and desperate. Perhaps she had been trapped on the islet like Fiona. She'd been wet, soaked – the coat she'd worn lay nearby and was still sopping, the pockets full of the sea. Her jeans and jumper were damp.

Perhaps she'd been waiting for some opportunity to go for help, but slowly, over the next four, maybe five days, the cold and her injuries had overtaken her. Perhaps she'd tried to get out, leaving those bloody smears on the floor, found that with her swollen, shattered leg she could no longer reach the screwdriver to remove it?

Perhaps it was easier to huddle up, to try to sleep, clicking on the radiator every two hours to drive the cold away, waiting for her strength to return, but growing weaker and weaker, the ice creeping ever deeper and deeper into her . . .

How long had she been here? Fiona felt her face harden. Had she been here the whole time that Fiona had been drinking and flirting with Jack, moaning about her to Adi, cursing her with every new revelation?

It was pointless to think of this now.

'Mads,' said Fiona, trying to keep her voice cheerful, upbeat, despite the horrified tears that kept threatening to break through. 'I'm going to try to give you a little water, okay?'

Nothing.

'You have to drink something. I might have to move you. Tell me if it hurts.'

344

Madison's head was surprisingly heavy as Fiona wrested it on to her thigh – a dead weight. This thought came unbidden and unwelcome. Brushing aside her hair, Fiona nearly choked.

Madison's face was a mass of clotted blood, her lips horribly swollen, a gash in one. Stuck to it were pieces of medical dressing, sticky and filthy.

'Oh God! Mads . . . '

Pull yourself together, she told herself sternly, as the frightened tears rolled down her cheeks. *This is not helping.*

Gently Fiona pulled at the dressings with trembling fingers, which came away, revealing white, white skin beneath. Madison's beloved face was so cold – like her silence, this coldness terrified Fiona. Apart from the slash in her lip, Fiona could see no other wound, though there was a larger piece of bandage crushed inside her mouth, almost like a gag.

'I'm going to take this out, babes,' she said, and gave one end of it a delicate tug.

It didn't move, having dried against Madison's mouth.

She tried again, a little more forcefully, wincing all the while, and two things happened almost immediately.

The first was that a blood-darkened spool of bandage emerged from Madison's torn lips.

And the second was that Madison gave a little choking cough and opened her eyes.

They were mere slits, cloudy and lost, with no hint of recognition in them.

Through dint of tender trying and patience, Fiona managed to persuade Madison to let her wet her lips with the water, and at one point to even take a tiny sip, her throat trembling with the effort of swallowing.

But Madison would accept no more. She did not resist even as Fiona stripped off her damp jumper and bra, gently forcing her arms inside one of the yellow waterproof jackets she was lying on top of, trying to lever her off the cold floor as far as possible. As for her jeans ... Fiona could not bring herself to touch that twisted, bulging leg, could barely bring herself to look at it.

Madison must have been in agony. Perhaps it was a mercy that she was unconscious now.

Once Madison's top half was curled around but not touching the radiator, as dry as Fiona could make her, her head pillowed with a fire blanket, Fiona sighed, sat back on her haunches, shivering with exhaustion and ringing cold.

She swallowed, forcing herself to face facts.

Madison could die – was probably near death even now.

Somehow, Fiona had to get back in contact with the outside world.

She couldn't walk or swim off here to fetch help. But it was a lighthouse. There must be a radio in here, to contact the coastguard, to contact ships ...

She stood up, trying to ignore the tiny internal voice that said, *but if there was, surely Mads would have found it.*

Rubbing her cold hands against her wet jeans, she surveyed the room. There were cupboards and cabinets, all lying open and jumbled, but nothing that looked like ...

Wait.

In the far corner, almost in the crook of the L-shaped room, a small wooden desk was pushed up against the wall, with a flimsy plastic chair nearby. A pair of yellow waterproof trousers lay over it.

Why else would you need a desk in here?

She pulled the trousers off, and saw it then – a squat black box, the handheld microphone attached to it by a coiled plastic cord.

It was silent, but the light on the dial glowed red in invitation as Fiona reached for it.

'It won't work.'

Her voice was slow, quiet, hideously muffled and slurred, but within Fiona could hear the essential Madison.

'What?' Fiona turned to her. 'But it's got power. There's a light . . .'

A long, breathy sigh from the blankets. 'The antenna on the roof's broken.'

'But . . .'

'No antenna means no signal.' That sigh again, as though Fiona was being deliberately obtuse. 'Try, if it makes you feel better. I already have.'

Fiona didn't. Of the two of them, Madison was the sailor, the one most likely to know.

Instead she came back to the radiator, sat down next to Madison. A paltry amount of heat glowed out from it as she raised her hands towards it.

'Maybe I could fix the antenna,' she said, trying to ignore the doubt and dread that crept into her voice at the mere idea of going outside again.

Madison lay on her side, anchored in that position by her broken leg. Her chest rose and fell gently, and Fiona thought she might have drifted off again, until she said, after a long moment, 'Don't be daft, Fee.' A weak chuckle. 'You wouldn't know where to begin.'

Fiona bit her lip. 'I suppose not.'

Silence, then another weak, bruised chuckle.

'Morning can't be long. And if you fall off and break your neck, what will happen to me?'

'Well, you can't be that hurt,' said Fiona drily. 'Your priorities are back to normal.'

Again that ghost of slurred laughter, drifting into the echoing quiet.

'How did you end up in here?' Fiona asked, glancing down at Madison's pale cheek. 'Did you break in?'

Madison moved her chin, the shadow of a nod. 'I was thrown off the boat.'

'*What?*' asked Fiona, horrified.

'I went into the sea.' A pause, as though Madison was considering making a joke, but somehow couldn't bring herself to. 'I should have died. But the waves threw me on to some rocks. Climbed back up . . .'

'With a broken leg?'

'Not broken then. I broke it when I slipped going up the hill.' She winced, licked her sore lips. 'If it had been broken when I was in the sea, I wouldn't be alive.' A pause, then, in a high, distressed voice, 'Does it look very bad?' She swallowed, the tiny noise echoing in the concrete room. 'You don't think they'll cut it off, do you?'

Fiona realised, with a little start, that this had probably been tormenting Mads for days, perhaps even more than the idea of her impending death.

Yep, your priorities are just like normal, she thought, this time with a tiny burst of affectionate anguish. *You silly, silly mare.*

'No. Well, I mean, your leg looks broken. Which it is,' prevaricated Fiona. 'I mean, they can sew on legs that have been severed nowadays. A broken one is just . . .' She shrugged, trying to sound nonchalant, to swallow her own numb terror. 'Neither here nor there.'

It was a lie, she knew – she still could not bring herself to look at the mangled leg, to remember how swollen yet cold it had felt as her fingers brushed it, but Madison seemed to accept this as truth.

'Right,' she said.

Silence fell, while both worked to hide their fear from one another.

'Mads,' Fiona said, trying to master her grief, her anger, 'why didn't you tell me anything about what was going on here? About Dom and Jack and . . .'

'I couldn't,' she said instantly, as though this was a question she'd been expecting, one she'd prepared for, as though for an exam. 'I just *couldn't*. I couldn't tell you anything. I couldn't tell you about Jack because you'd just go off on one about Caspar and how I deliberately screw everything up. I couldn't tell you about Dom because you just would have gone mental and you'd've been right. And you might have called the police and I absolutely couldn't have you do that right then. I needed everything to look normal. I just needed you to come.'

Fiona was stunned. 'What are you talking about? You're not making any sense. Was Dom . . . ?'

'Forget about him.' Madison flicked one cold hand with a weak but undeniably contemptuous gesture. Her nails were a pale blue. 'I couldn't tell you why I needed you up here. I couldn't tell anyone. I didn't even believe it myself. It was insane. It *is* insane.' She turned her stiff head, despite her obvious pain, and that cat-like green gaze blazed. 'Fee, it's . . . it's just so *huge*. I thought, if I said anything and got it wrong, it would all be over for me.' She licked her mashed, cut lips again with a dry tongue. 'And it would have been over for you too, if people thought you were mixed up with me. You'd have been ruined.' Her voice ratcheted upwards. 'I had to be absolutely sure before I said anything. You work so hard – it's going so well for you. I couldn't have borne it if I brought you down. I'm so sorry, Fee. You have to believe me . . .'

'But Mads, I *do* believe you.'

Her eyes narrowed, confused. 'What do you mean?'

'I believe you.' Fiona shrugged. She ran her hand through

Madison's damp hair, brushing it out of her face. 'So stop wriggling and try to relax.'

'What . . . how?'

Fiona leaned down and whispered, even though they were both alone and miles from any other human: 'I did what you wanted. I looked.'

'And?' asked Madison, her eyes huge, the question tight despite her blurred speech.

Fiona smiled at her. 'And I saw the Valkyrie.'

Wednesday

45

Helly Holm Lighthouse, Orkney, January 2020

Fiona would have thought it impossible, what with the broken door that banged ever more furiously as the wind rose, gusting freezing wind in at her, but eventually she napped next to the sleeping Madison, wrapped in the damp plastic grip of the waterproofs, her body lying semi-curled around the radiator, like a dog before a fire.

It was relentlessly uncomfortable, and she kept shivering herself awake to restart the timer – her head aching, her throat parched. Every so often she would urge Madison to drink more water, move a tentative hand above her mouth and nose to check if she was still breathing.

As Fiona lay there on her back, staring at the water-stained ceiling, she let her mind wander, drift over the nightmarish last hours.

The archaeologists – surely they must know she was missing. The police would have been expecting her at Kirkwall Police Station. They would know that someone had tried to do her harm . . .

Wouldn't they?

After all, she had taken all her clothes and effects from Nordskaill House. With her keys, it would be a simple matter to move her car, perhaps send it crashing into the sea too. Perhaps everyone would think that she, like Madison, had chosen to vanish. Jack had guessed that she had no plans to return there and would doubtless tell the others that.

And Hugo would not have hesitated to share his theory of her and Madison as artefact thieves with the police.

Fiona sat upright, her head aching, finding any more sleep impossible.

She felt like a boat lost on the breast of a trackless ocean. Somehow she was here with Madison, trying not to freeze to death in an unmanned lighthouse on a rocky, uninhabited island, because somebody had found a Valkyrie.

And with that, the lights in the room clicked off, and she nearly screamed, flinching against the radiator.

Something had changed. Instead of the utter blackness, there was now a kind of thin, cool daylight, in a pale pinkish-grey. The sensors had reacted to it, had shut off.

What time was it?

Impossible to say without her phone, but probably no earlier than seven o'clock.

It would be low tide eventually. She wasn't injured, other than the crack on the back of her head. If she was lucky, and brave, she might be able to walk out of here the way she'd come in.

It wouldn't hurt to get up and look.

She glanced over at Madison, who was still locked in sleep. There was no question of Madison walking anywhere.

Fiona fought her way back to her feet in slow increments – her head had worsened in the night, and if she moved too fast she felt sick, dizzy, her skull full of throwing knives. She was in the waterproof coat and trousers she had found, which were made for somebody larger and didn't fit her particularly well, but at least were dry.

Her new boots rubbed against her feet, welts of forming blisters stabbing her as she pulled them on.

'Where are you going?'

Madison sounded faint, muzzled, but as though she'd been awake for hours.

'Just to look.'

'Is there a plan?'

'Yeah,' said Fiona. 'It's not a good one, but all I can think of without a phone. The minute the causeway is clear I run, as fast as I can, to the Fletts' farmhouse and get every ambulance and policeman in the world up here. If I can flag someone down on the way there, so much the better.'

'How long will that take?'

'I don't know,' said Fiona. 'It's what, maybe one, two miles . . . ?'

'It's five miles to Grangeholm if it's a minute,' said Madison.

Fiona's heart was sinking. Madison was right, of course. 'I'll hurry,' she said.

'I hope so,' said Madison. 'Because I can't stand up and seal that door after you.'

'I'll prop something up against it. That chair, maybe. Nobody will think of coming up here anyway.'

'Are you sure?' asked Madison.

The question hung there.

'I won't be long,' was all Fiona said, since the things she did want to say were too portentous, too alarming. Too final. 'Try not to worry.'

Before her, the broken door shook violently against the improvised bolt she had made for it. Despite the tenuous dawn, the weather had become no less aggressive.

Don't go out there empty-handed.

She searched through the tumbled contents of the room, but could find nothing helpful. She didn't need the big electric torch. Even the first aid pack on the wall contained only a tiny pair of bandage scissors, which she stuffed into her pocket anyway.

'You should keep this. You know, just in case.'

She pressed the screwdriver into Mads' cold hand, trying to

355

hide the way her own hand trembled as she did so, trying not to notice the way Madison's did as she took it.

'I'm just going to look at the causeway,' she said, trying to sound upbeat, confident. 'If it's underwater I'll be right back.' She bit her lip. 'If not . . .'

'Fee,' said Madison, her voice only hitching a little. 'I'll see you soon. And mind that slope on the way down.'

The screwdriver vanished under the blankets.

* * *

The sleet had stopped, but the minute she put her foot on to the concrete step, it nearly shot away from under her.

All was ice. The steps were ice, the thin, short grass rustled together like so many blades of glass. The very ground, so wet last night, had set into hummocks and ruts, spanned by frozen little pools of water.

The wind sang and the sea roared.

She would have loved nothing better than to go back indoors to Madison, but something stirred within her, some intimation of peril. They were not safe here. They would not be safe until they were back on the mainland.

Carefully she blocked the door behind her as well as she could with the chair, and navigated the steps, her heart sinking at how slippery everything was. She was protected by the building from the worst of the wind at the moment, and the minute she was out of its shelter there was every chance she could be blown flat and slide all the way down to the edge of the island.

Wasn't that how Mads had broken her leg?

That said, the clouds were little more than fast-moving banners, and the sky was a vivid pink and blue. The rain, at least, had stopped.

She hobbled to the top of the rise, bracing herself against the tearing wind, heading for the three storage cases below, one lying open and half full of slate-grey ice. It occurred to her then, with a lurch of terror, that if she had stayed there and tried to shelter in it, she would almost certainly have frozen to death.

For a long moment she could do nothing but stare at it, this box that would have been her tomb.

Beyond the dig site, at the foot of the turf steps, there was no sign of the causeway – it was buried under frothy white water.

Still, it was early. It was probably not long until low tide. If she could just hold on until . . .

That's when she spotted it.

The boat was approaching from the east, with the ragged dawn behind it. If it had appeared unsteady, terrifying before, now it seemed to buck and roll in the frenzied ocean like an unbroken horse.

There was no mistake. It was the boat the archaeologists had been using, the *Samarkand*.

Fiona's heart was in her mouth.

Her purloined waterproofs were bright yellow. Very soon there would be no missing her as she stood here, exposed, on the bald, frozen brow of Helly Holm.

She had to get to cover, *now*. She had to get back to the light-house, barricade them both in, wait for the coast to clear . . .

She turned, ungainly, heedless in her fear, and slipped hard on the frozen grass, and then she was rolling, rolling down the hill towards the dig site, gaining speed and shrieking in panic, until with a thump that took the air out of her lungs she was sprawled in a mess of ice and tyres and black tarpaulin.

Fiona was lying on her back, on top of the warrior woman's grave.

She staggered to her feet, sucking in the cold air, delirious with fear. She had knocked out one of the foot-long spikes holding the tarp down and it had gashed her hand and wrist. The scarlet was shocking against her ice-white skin, and drops of it fell on to the frozen grass as she scrambled towards the nearest storage case, ducked behind it, peered out.

The boat had vanished, but Fiona was not fooled. The spit they lashed the boats to was just out of her line of sight, where the turf path came down over the buried stern of the Viking boat, and headed down towards the sea.

She looked down at the tent spike in her hand.

Run back to the lighthouse, she thought. *Go NOW.*

But at the same time she realised she would never make it. She would only succeed in luring her enemy to where Madison lay, helpless.

And as if to prove this, she saw the crown of Iris's dark head appear, saw her moving up the path. Her face was pale, livid, and her eyes glittered as they roved over the beach, turned towards the dig site.

Iris would not be cut and bruised and nursing a concussion.

It struck Fiona like a baseball bat to the ribs. She would never be able to outrun her. All she could hope to do was find some piece of cliff to hide against, or, failing that, chance herself with the sea and try to swim to the mainland.

Which would be nothing short of suicide, she realised, watching the vast, foaming breakers rise and fall beyond Iris's approaching figure.

Somehow, she would have to face her.

46

'Fiona! Fiona!'

Iris was waving, hiking up the path, stalking carefully over the sea-blown kelp and shells the storm had racked up from the sea.

The ocean was still lively, and she could see the waves bashing against Iris's ankles in their steel-toed boots, pursuing her up from the beach.

Fiona merely stared, paralysed with terror. *She's mad.* One high wave could knock her into the sea at any moment.

Of course.

She's mad.

And quite, quite desperate.

* * *

It's about Jack, Fiona realised. Or at least, that was how it started.

Jack who is unfaithful, who flits from woman to woman. Jack who is sleeping with Madison, flirting with Fiona.

Even so, Iris was in love with him. Iris suspects Jack knows her great secret, but so far, he has done nothing. Thinking back to how he was – with Fiona, with Madison, the barmaid – and that girl on the dig on Lewis last summer (what had been her name? Mara Miller?), Iris can't, or won't, surrender the digging to Jack while she pursues her media and academic career. She has to keep an eye on him. She has to be *there*.

Of course Iris didn't try to kill Madison over *Jack*. Not at all. That would be absurd. And anyway, she has other ways to get rid of her rivals; sneaky, underhand ways, that she carries through under the cloak of her mentorship and has perfected through the years, and until now they have always worked. Mara Miller finds herself receiving obscene pictures from a works computer, and clever Iris manages to turn that into an opportunity to up her surveillance, even while appearing to be tough on the perpetrators.

Madison finds her stalker is once again pursuing her, that the C14 samples she is putting together are somehow incorrect or contaminated, that she is considered impaired and unreliable. Iris seems to support her, but probably does nothing to stop their murmurs, perhaps quietly encourages them under the guise of appearing concerned.

And then Madison, who is nobody's fool and who has suspicions – perhaps through listening to Becky's sulky insinuations, perhaps having Jack whisper his worries in her ear during those snatched moments in Langmire – sees Iris hiding something at the dig site and puts two and two together.

Madison, who is an agent of chaos, and now holds Iris's life in her hands.

Perhaps even considers wearing it around her neck.

* * *

'Oh my God, I can't believe it,' Iris cried, her voice carrying over the sound of the waves. 'We were so worried!'

Then why are you the only one here?

Fiona had always needed Madison to think the unthinkable, to say the unsayable. But Madison was not here now.

It would be down to Fiona to think the unthinkable.

To do the impossible.

As Iris scrambled up the exposed rocks and icy grass towards the dig, Fiona realised she had mere moments to choose – to run, or to pretend to suspect nothing.

She tried to tell herself that having failed to kill her through head injury, and then exposure, Iris might still believe that Fiona didn't know who her attacker was.

Because of course it was impossible that Professor Iris Barclay, respectable academic and media figure, would have sailed through such dreadful seas alone to murder her here on this uninhabited, inhospitable islet. The mere thought was absurd, must be some kind of massive misunderstanding.

In any case, they were not necessarily alone here. They were outdoors, and any birdwatcher or dog walker could happen along at any moment, see them from the mainland coast. A gale would not necessarily put the locals off here.

Iris's eyes were huge, her pupils dilated. No doubt about it – she was mad. Her colourful passions, her imaginative impulses – they were not affectation. She was actually insane and hiding in plain sight.

But neither of them needed to hide any more.

'It was you that tried to kill Madison.' The wind had dropped, or perhaps the import of these words, their power, was enough to carry them across the broken ground. They erupted out of Fiona, despite her terror, which anchored her there, froze her on the spot. 'You tried because she guessed. I think she's not the only one that guessed, but she was the only one that confronted you.' Fiona breathed in, felt the power in her words, the words that could not be taken back. 'She knew you were a fake.'

The silence that followed was like the silence after a gun goes off – solid and full of echoes.

It was Iris that broke it.

'Fiona, I don't know what you're talking about . . .' Iris cocked her head to one side, her gaze soft, a picture of compassionate forbearance. 'You're delirious and freezing, and need to come back to the boat . . .' She moved forward, to lay a hand on Fiona's shoulder.

Fiona snatched herself backwards, nearly stumbling on the icy ground.

'You made the Jesmond Hill torc yourself. By hand.'

Iris froze.

'That's . . . that's not rational, Fiona . . .'

'No, it isn't, but you did it anyway. It's the only thing that makes sense. You were going nowhere in your career, tired of being undermined, unappreciated. And then you had an idea. A big, bold idea. You're good at those. You had a background in metallurgy. You made your own jewellery and sold it at festivals when you were a student. Jack told me. You probably still make your own.

'And the thing was, you could afford to buy the gold for it – the right kind of gold, Irish gold, that has the right chemical signature so it wouldn't look suspicious when the museum analysed it – it was probably what, about ten thousand pounds in bullion? And the torc is valued now at, I dunno, about three-quarters of a million pounds? It was a big gamble, yes, but you came from money and could afford to take it – and you've never been frightened of risk.'

'Fiona, I think you've hit your head and . . .'

'Well, you'd know I had, wouldn't you?' Fiona shouted, aware of the spittle landing on her frozen chapped lips, how desperate, how unhinged she must appear. 'It was so perfect, such a great story! The last hour of the last day of this nowhere little dig, one they're going to throw a supermarket up on top of, and suddenly you have the world's attention with this amazing golden treasure! Just pulled it out of the ground! And they accept it as real!' She let out a burst of shrill, hysterical laughter. 'They put it in the British Museum!'

'Fiona . . .' Iris's hand was still outstretched, but her eyes – Fiona had never seen eyes so cold. For a moment her fear threatened to smother her, to stop her breath.

But she owed things. She owed things to Madison – Madison who was lying there, utterly broken and vulnerable, in the lighthouse. Madison was paying the price for her own courage.

It was time for Fiona to pay for hers.

'And this is the thing I'll never understand, Iris. You'd got away with it. It was all over. Forever. They'll probably never test that torc again in our lifetimes. There is absolutely nobody that wants to find out it's a fake now, for an international institution like that to be embarrassed in front of the world. You got everything you could have wished for out of it, and more. Ten grand well spent.

'But somehow, for some reason, you just couldn't stop. You can't *stop* . . .'

'Fiona . . .'

'You made the Valkyrie. You've probably made other things too, like that goldwork in the training dig at Lewis. Other places too, just little things. But you know, it's something they say about frauds and killers. If you get away with it once, it becomes an addiction.'

Iris appeared to have turned to marble. Her outstretched hand dropped to her side.

'You probably planted the Valkyrie here on Helly Holm, ready to be discovered the next day, by one of the others, and she saw you do it. Madison. So she took it.'

The beautiful golden Valkyrie. Small but exquisite. Smoothed and scratched with wear, having been lovingly worn and handled by unknown ancient hands; a gleaming talisman standing for a warrior woman.

How had Iris got those authentic wear marks? She'd worn it herself, probably, for months, underneath her shirt, waiting for its opportunity to come, for just the right contract.

She'd been wearing it in the video. Perhaps Madison had recognised the thong.

'It's all over, Iris.' Her fear was smothering her, and yet somehow the words were coming out. 'Don't even think about trying to hurt us.'

Us.

That was a mistake. She should not have said *us*.

Already Iris's gaze was flickering up to the white tower of the lighthouse – because of course, if Madison was here and had somehow lived after being cast into the ocean, where else could she be?

'Fiona,' she said, facing her, her arms crossed over her breasts, and with only the slightest shadow of a tremor in her hands, 'I think you have had a terrible experience, and you're not thinking clearly . . .'

'I'll tell you what I'm thinking. I think it was you that took the glass out of the wardrobe door at Langmire, because it was your blood in it. You fought with her there on the Monday, a couple of days before you came back to finish the job. Was it over Jack? Did you turn up and find him there with her?'

Something in Iris's face flinched.

'In bed with her?' asked Fiona, with a lightning flash of insight. 'Was that it? Was that when she lost it, and told you *she* was the one that had taken the Valkyrie, had seen you plant it?'

That flinching again.

'That's it, isn't it?' snarled Fiona, realising through her pounding terror, her rage, that this was the truth. 'I know Madison. She could never be ruled. She told you if you came after her again – if you sabotaged her work again and blamed her – if you pretended to be Dom fucking Tate and threatened her online again, she would ruin you!'

Iris appeared to have turned to stone.

'Was Jack there? Did he hear?' Fiona tilted her head, curious. 'Or did all this wait till he left?'

It happened so fast. No wonder poor Madison had been

overwhelmed. In an instant Iris's face transformed in rage — her mouth a red maw of gritted teeth, her eyes wide and her pupils bottomless.

Out of her open coat appeared a glint of silver — a monkey wrench. She must have taken it from the boat. Her knuckles were blue-white around its handle.

Fiona had that crushing yet bewildering revelation, borne in on a tidal wave of indescribable fear, that these were to be her final moments, as Iris's arm was flung back, the wrench ascending into the air.

Yet, somewhere at the back of it all, was a familiar, beloved voice, and it was saying: *it's you that needs to be the warrior woman now.*

And as the blow tumbled down towards her, Fiona lunged forward; the tent spike from the dig, the one she had shoved into her pocket, clutched and cutting into her frozen fingers.

With a dire, trembling strength she had never known she possessed, she buried it in Iris's heart.

47

'It happened exactly like you guessed. All of it. Including the fight I had with Iris at Langmire.'

Madison lay back on her hospital pillows, her torn lip closed with tiny sutures, the bruises around her mouth starting to settle – or at least until she spoke. Then the black hole where her left incisor should be gaped, and she whistled softly if she said her 's's too loud.

Fiona slouched in the chair next to Madison's bed.

Everything seemed gauzy, unreal somehow.

Two hours ago Adi had bailed her out of Kirkwall Police Station, led her out blinking into the thin winter sunshine. He had come straight to Orkney from Zurich immediately after their last phone call, looking for her, aware that something was very wrong, and arrived twenty-four hours later to find her missing and raise the alarm.

Even he had seemed to flicker before her, like an illusion – or at least until he had grabbed her, hugged her so fiercely that the breath flew out of her, buried his face in her tangled hair.

This too had seemed unreal, like something out of a dream, even as her hands had drifted up his warm back, under his leather jacket, closed around him.

She knows they have problems. He does not always listen to her, and sometimes, she has realised, he thinks she is least like herself when she is being her most true.

She does not know what she is going to do about Adi.

'That cow,' muttered Madison venomously. 'I should have . . .' She paused. 'Are you all right?'

Fiona glanced back at her; at the bandage across the back of her hand where the IV had been, the angry red grazes along her arm where the rocks had cut her in her fall, the blue-black shadows under her eyes, the elaborate pulleys and braces supporting her smashed leg.

'Me?' she asked, surprised.

'Yes, *you*, you daft mare,' Madison said, but her face was concerned. 'Are you all right?'

'I don't . . . I don't know,' Fiona answered truthfully.

Silence fell over them, weak and thin, like the afternoon sunshine through the window, and tiny motes drifted in it, trapped.

'Hugo was here,' said Madison. She didn't look at Fiona.

Fiona nodded. 'I know.'

He'd passed her in the corridor, as she'd sat outside Madison's room, waiting for him to go. Their eyes, despite both of their best efforts, met.

She'd watched him try to muster up some kind of smug, petulant remark, some expression of his old contempt, and fail. Instead he'd merely given the tiniest nod as she met him gaze for gaze, and walked past her.

Well, she thought. *I am a killer now, I suppose. And Hugo has always had an unerring sense of his own self-preservation.*

'He brought me Percy Pigs,' said Madison, weakly shaking the little bag of sweets in her hand. 'I suppose I must have given him a real fright.'

Fiona smiled at her. She might despise him, but he was still Mads' brother. It would be good if those two could come to some sort of understanding.

'When did you know something was up?' she asked. 'You know, at the dig?'

'Straight away.'

Fiona raised an eyebrow. 'You never said anything to me about it.'

Mads looked at her for a long moment.

'I didn't want to admit it.' Her bruised mouth turned down, as though this admission tasted sour. 'Getting this job was the most exciting thing that ever happened to me.' She offered Fiona a crooked, secretive smile. 'I could tell *you* were impressed.'

'I was. Of course I was. But Mads, you don't need to impress me . . .'

'I know I don't,' she said, flicking the idea away. 'It's me, not you. I get it. But see, the thing is, you've never understood how intimidating you are. You think you're still that little girl from the estate, from the bad home. But it's not true. It's not been true for years and years now and it makes me absolutely crazy when you pretend it is.

'You're like . . . like this machine, that people just promote and praise and admire. It's not your fault, but I don't think you've ever appreciated what it feels like to constantly be playing catch-up.'

'Mads . . .'

'No, no, let's be real.' Madison held up a quelling hand. 'I know you work hard and are super-smart and blah blah blah. I get it. I do. But you know . . . we started out at the same time, and, well,' she looked away, her cut mouth twisting with restrained emotions. 'Sometimes it's hard to watch.'

'Mads . . .'

'It doesn't mean I don't love you.' She scowled, sniffed. 'It *may* mean it's difficult to cope with you when you rub it in with impromptu celebration drinks in London with no warning . . .'

Fiona flushed. 'I'm sorry, Mads. But if I can't share my good news with you – I mean, what are we doing?'

Madison shrugged. Her green eyes were shining, and wouldn't

quite meet Fiona's. 'I dunno. I suppose that's true. It's just . . . hard to process that news sometimes, you know?' She swiped at her face with the back of her hand. 'And maybe . . . maybe I could be less of a jealous cow.' Madison sniffed again. 'I'm sorry. I know I hurt your feelings that day, and I never apologised.' She half-smiled. 'If it makes you feel better, it totally ruined Prague for me.'

Fiona was amazed and touched. This was the most frank she'd ever heard Madison be about this; this massive white elephant that had stood between them. 'All right,' she said, softening. 'If Prague was left in ruins, I consider myself avenged.'

Madison let her head fall back on the pillow and began to chuckle, before bursting out a gasp of pain. 'Ow, these fucking ribs! Ow . . . ow. I hate my life.'

'Do you think Jack knew Iris was planting these finds, then?' asked Fiona eventually.

'Yeah.' Madison scratched behind her ear. 'Or at least he suspected. I don't think he was ever actively part of it. But he knew all right.' She dropped her hand, sighed in weary disgust. 'They all knew. It was just that they didn't dare say anything.'

'Why didn't he tell anyone, though?' asked Fiona. She was surprised at how much it hurt, realising this about him. She blew out softly, thinking. 'Probably because they'd have looked at him too. Even if he was found not guilty, everyone would always have wondered . . .'

'That's part of it.' Madison fell silent for a moment. 'Personally, I think he didn't say anything because, deep down, as much as he resented all her efforts to control him, he loved her.'

'Really?' Fiona frowned.

Would you call that love? Iris had systematically run off all his other lovers through threat, manipulation and deceit, while pretending their relationship was platonic.

If that was love, it was from the same family as Dom Tate's

369

love for Madison – a dire, toxic, controlling emotion that cared nothing for its object; something better exorcised than indulged.

'Oh yeah.' Madison gave a wise nod, her head only slightly stiff. 'This was the thing with Iris, the crazy, stupid thing. If she'd only ever faked the Jesmond Hill torc, she would have got away with it. If she'd been able to love Jack without trying to own him, they would have ended up together. Even this dig now – you say they found this gorgeous little silver hoard, a woman warrior grave everyone's going to be analysing and talking about for years, the TV stuff, the academic success – it should have been enough. But, somehow it just wasn't.' She made a helpless gesture. 'It was just the way she was built.'

Silence fell. Fiona was remembering that last moment, that gritted-teeth rage, the falling silver of the wrench, the way Iris's chest had resisted then yielded as Fiona drove the spike into her heart.

She was remembering it every few minutes, with the steady, remorseless predictability of Helly Holm's lantern. Then, after a little while, she remembered it again. Then again.

Without being told, she knew that she would be remembering it, at greater and shorter intervals, for the rest of her life.

'You're right about one thing, I reckon,' Madison said. 'They'll all take the fall along with Iris, guilty or not.' A pause. 'It's a shame. I really liked Jack.'

'So I hear.' Fiona raised an eyebrow.

'Don't start.'

Fiona didn't reply, instead gazing at her own broken nails.

'And what about Dominic Tate?'

Madison blinked at her. 'Are you serious?'

'He told me at Langmire that you two were "back how you always were" . . .'

'He's a liar,' snarled Madison. 'I thought we'd established this.'

'So you didn't ask him to help you?'

'No!'

Fiona waited, silently.

'Of course I didn't ask him for help,' said Madison, rolling her eyes. 'I *may* have pointed out that someone was pretending to be him to spook me and it was in his interest to look into it – remotely. I certainly didn't invite him up to Langmire, if that's what you're thinking.'

'He had a key cut while he was there . . .'

'Did he?' Madison's fist clenched, making the bandage strain against her skin. 'Fee, he was in the house for just twelve hours. He pitched up in the middle of the night with some story about how his hotel had let him down. I could have died of shock when I opened the door and there he was, complete with stupid grin and a fistful of petrol station flowers.'

'But you took him in . . .'

She waved this away. 'I did. I had to. He slept on the couch and he took a lot of persuading to keep on it, too, the cheeky bastard. The next day I told him the Fletts had seen him and he needed to bugger off. In fairness to him, he went.'

'He's a dangerous man.'

'*You* always thought so. The police caught him trying to sneak on to the ferry home, you know. Tail between his legs. They told me this morning. Didn't surprise me. I always thought he was all talk. Talk, and spiteful little acts of vandalism.' She let her head fall back. 'I keep telling you this, but you won't listen. I never *once* thought it was him when the harassment started up again here. He has things to lose.' She rolled her eyes. 'And he didn't like me *that* much.'

Fiona couldn't help herself – they should agree to disagree, she supposed, but it was just so ridiculous – why couldn't Mads see?

She growled in frustration.

'It's not about him *liking* you! Mads, the things he threatened to do to you – the things he's already done – he's a fucking nutter that respects no boundaries, no matter how much you try to minimise him away. Why didn't you just call the police and have them sort it out?'

'Because I couldn't. Don't you get it?' Madison was growing angry, even while appealing to her. 'I was gathering all this evidence for this gigantic archaeological fraud, trying to keep a lid on everything – I couldn't have Dom arrested in the middle of sodding Orkney while I'm trying to prove that he's nothing to do with it all . . .' she petered out, as though struck by something.

'You know,' she said, turning to Fiona, her expression suddenly wondering, 'I was so terrified, Fee, but of all the wrong things. I knew Iris was storing up trouble, big, big trouble for me, and that she was a bad enemy, but I never thought she'd plot to *kill* me. That's just . . . I mean . . .'

She shrugged helplessly, as though at the sheer absurdity of it all, but her mouth was turning down now and she had begun to shake, the burden of her bravado becoming, suddenly, too much for her to bear.

'Mads,' said Fiona, moved nearly to tears herself in pity, and also because she saw in Madison's shock and anguish the mirror of her own. She reached over to take her clenched hand. 'Mads, don't. It's okay. We're safe now. It's going to be okay . . .'

Madison shook her head wildly, as though denying anything was wrong, but her bruised face was scrunching up, and ugly, hoarse sobs were issuing out of her. Those thin fingers hurt as they dug back into Fiona's hand.

'I-I can't help it. I keep *thinking* about it, Fee. It was this nightmare and it just went on and on and on . . .' She swiped at her face with her hand. 'I don't . . .'

'Madison,' asked Fiona gently. 'What happened with Iris and you? At the end? Did you go to Helly Holm and meet her . . . ?'

'No!' Her response was explosive, her cheeks wet. 'Not at all . . . she came round to Langmire on Monday night after Jack left.'

'And you fought?' Fiona asked. 'And broke the mirror?'

'Oh yeah. Proper fisticuffs. She knocked on my door at midnight – I thought it was Dom come back again so I didn't answer, and she was supposed to be on a plane to Edinburgh anyway. Then I heard her voice and I just knew.' Madison rolled her eyes. 'I had to let her in, didn't I? I didn't want to. After all, I had her fake Valkyrie hidden in the sugar jar and the house still smelled of sex.'

'Mads,' said Fiona, disgusted. *'Please.'*

'Well,' said Madison, with a slight blush. 'It did. And it had a bearing on how things went, I think. She didn't directly threaten me, but it was this . . . I dunno how to describe it – concern trolling.'

'Concern trolling? What's that?'

Madison rolled her eyes heavenward, in a parody of piety, joining her hands as though in prayer. '"I'm so *worried* about you, Madison." Talking about my stalker. About more problems with the samples, which somehow justifies her driving out here at fucking midnight while she's supposed to be off filming. And oh no, what can she do to *help* me . . .' Madison snarled, despite it clearly hurting her. 'Gaslighting me – no, not gaslighting me. Just clearly laying down that I'm in her power.' She dabbed at her torn lip, where a tiny spot of blood had sprung up. 'Just so there's no mistake.'

Fiona considered this. 'Hmm.' Once again that silver wrench was falling, and her arm was drawing back, the spike gripped in her cold hand. *Oh God, will this ever stop?*

Madison did not appear to have noticed. 'I knew by then she

was deliberately contaminating some of the samples I sent to the lab. You know, to throw off the C14 dating, that kind of thing.'

Fiona was distracted, surprised at the pettiness of this, though really, why should she be? 'She sabotaged you?'

'Oh yeah,' said Mads, licking more of the blood on her lip away. 'But you know, looking back, I don't think screwing up my dating samples was personal at all. I think it was part of the whole plan.'

Fiona threw her a sharp glance. 'What makes you say that?'

Madison gave her a crooked smile. 'It's smart. Very smart. Because when she plants her Valkyrie, she's probably been very careful but she can't guarantee there's not something on it, some DNA or chemical which might give her away. If, for some reason, it's hard to get a good reading out of that soil, or something is screwy, or the Finds Manager is having personal problems and is just a blubbering wreck, it covers her if something inconsistent turns up on the object, do you know what I mean?'

Fiona gave a little gasp of understanding. 'So she was always going to throw you under the bus?'

Madison thought. 'I dunno. Maybe. I'm not sure. I think she would have taken me with her, if I'd kept my mouth shut and played ball and seemed properly grateful for all the compassion she had over my sample-screwing personal issues. And kept my hands off Jack, of course.' Again that half-smile. 'That goes without saying.'

She stretched, shifted on the bed, wincing around her bound leg.

'Or maybe she would have booted me just like she meant to boot Becky. But the contaminated samples always seemed to come from Trench C, where I found her little smoking gun, so I guess I was consistent in my "incompetence".' She made little air quotes. 'It was how I knew to look in there first. Speaking of smoking, they're not going to let me vape in here, are they?'

'No. Absolutely not.'

'Brilliant.' Madison scowled, adjusting her pillow with impatient little tugs. 'Anyway, she's stood there, saying these things, and I just – I just saw red. I was so sick of everything by then. Sick of keeping secrets. Sick of lying and being two-faced. Sick of being controlled. I tried to walk away. I went into the bedroom, but she followed me, so I told her she was a fraud. She went ballistic, Fee. She went to slap me, and I threw her backwards into the mirror hard and it broke. The crash kind of snapped us both out of it.'

'So what happened?'

'After the fight?'

'Yeah.'

'After the fight, we calmed down and talked.'

'Talked?' Fiona squinted at her, mystified. 'What about?'

'Well . . .' Madison was looking away, her expression bleak, not able to meet Fiona's gaze. 'After I found the Valkyrie on Saturday, I got to thinking some more.'

Something about Madison's evasiveness impressed itself on Fiona. 'And?'

'I started to wonder,' she paused, as though considering how to proceed. 'I started to wonder how useful it was to turn Iris in.'

'How useful it was to turn Iris in?' repeated Fiona.

'Yes.'

'Turn her in, for perpetrating a series of massive and criminal archaeological frauds?' Fiona persisted. 'Is that what you mean?'

Madison blushed, a purplish colour under her thin, bruised cheeks. 'Um, yes.' She glanced at Fiona. 'You know, I knew you'd be like this about it all. I just *knew* it.'

Fiona regarded her thoughtfully. 'I guess I'm waiting to hear why I shouldn't be.'

'Right,' conceded Madison, her attention sinking to her orange hospital blanket. 'I will admit it does look very bad at first glance.'

Fiona was silent. 'I'm waiting,' she said eventually.

'No – right – I'm just saying that if you take Iris down, it's true, Iris is stopped. And that's a good thing. But also, I thought of all the damage this would cause. That torc is going to be declared a fake, right, and no one will thank you for that. And all the people that work with her, all the archaeologists that ever dug with her, everyone at her production company, the millions of people that watch her show, and . . .'

'Jack,' inserted Fiona with crisp emphasis. 'You forgot Jack in that list.'

Madison had the grace to look embarrassed.

'Yeah. I admit. As much as I would have loved to have taken Iris down publicly, I couldn't do it to Jack. Because, you know, it would have been the end for him.'

She raised her head, and their eyes met.

'You really liked him, didn't you?' Fiona asked quietly.

Madison didn't reply to this, affected not to have heard. 'All that other stuff is true too, you know,' she said. She sighed, and it was like a sob. 'I thought if I could just get her to stop, you know, *scare* her, then – well, maybe that would be as good as handing her over and not ruining all these lives. It seemed the most, I dunno, the most . . .'

'Humane option,' supplied Fiona.

'Yes,' hissed Madison, though with an element of surprise, as though she hadn't expected Fiona to see it that way. 'Exactly that. I told her I'd give her back the Valkyrie after the dig, but I had pictures of where and how I found it, and if she ever pulled anything like this again, anywhere in the world, I'd go straight to the authorities . . . and she was shocked. Absolutely shocked, Fee. Like, huge levels of denial. She couldn't believe I was accusing her of this, despite the fact that I'd basically caught her red-handed. It was so weird.'

Madison blinked, as though the strangeness of it all was once again nonplussing her.

'At first I thought it was bluster, but I think she just – she just couldn't cope with the idea of herself as someone who does something like that, even though she must have been making and prepping the artefact for ages . . .'

'Cognitive dissonance,' said Fiona, remembering their final conversation, and once again that spike was plunging towards Iris's heart – the resistance, the giving in . . .

. . . The unbelieving shock in Iris's dark eyes as she'd sunk on to the icy grass.

. . . The way she'd looked up at Fiona, and her final expression – that terror, that despair, as she realised she was dying.

Behind her, the sea had roared.

It took her a moment to focus her attention on Madison again.

'Yeah!' Madison was saying. 'Cognitive dissonance. And to be honest, it gave me a bad feeling. But I told myself . . . I don't know what I told myself. I told myself she was not an apologiser. That she was probably mortified at being caught – after all, she lived in this world where nobody ever confronted her. That for all her female empowerment talk, the person that Iris was interested in empowering was herself.' Madison spread her palms helplessly.

'And you wanted to do the right thing,' said Fiona slowly. 'I bet you even thought she'd be grateful to escape public humiliation.'

'Yeah.' Madison's face was bitter. 'No good deed goes unpunished.'

'No, it doesn't,' agreed Fiona, thinking. 'It was a lovely idea but it would never have worked, Mads.'

'But . . .'

Fiona shook her head. 'If Iris had submitted, she would have been in your power.'

'You think I'd blackmail her? I wouldn't do that!' Madison's anger was awl-sharp, her head lifting.

'It's not about who you are,' said Fiona, trying to find the words that would make Madison understand. And once again, that wrench was rising, about to fall, and . . . 'It's about who Iris is. And she's the dominator. She rules Jack. She rules the dig. She rules you. You think that by offering her mercy she'll reassess, seize the second chance, but nah, nah. She can't be in your power or in your debt. And you know things about her now.' Fiona tipped her head at Madison. 'You had to go.'

Madison swallowed. 'So it seems.'

'What happened?' asked Fiona gently.

Madison twitched at the little bag of sweets again. 'I got a text from Jack. I mean, I thought it was Jack. Had he left his wallet on the boat? Could I look? So I went out there, I think – I can't remember it. They say it's the concussion and it might not come back. The next thing I knew I was on the boat with a chain around my ankles and she was . . . anyway.' She wiped at her chin, the cuts on her knuckles standing proud. 'The rest you know.'

'Mads,' Fiona shook her head. 'You're lucky to be alive.'

'I'm alive because of you, babes.' Madison's face was deadly serious. 'Luck had nothing to do with it.'

Fiona reached over, wordlessly squeezed her hand again.

The silence lay between them, growing in weight, in substance.

'I . . .' Fiona began. She swiped at her eyes, feeling she was sinking, sinking, and might never get up again. 'I just stabbed that woman through the heart, you know?' She looked at Madison, and her throat was clenching, full of tears – tears of horror – horror and unavoidable regret. 'I don't – I don't really know how I feel about that.'

Madison looked back at her.

'You did. But we're both alive.' Madison offered her a crooked smile. 'So I know how *I* feel about it, Sword Lady.'

48

Grangeholm, Orkney, January 2020

It takes Madison about five minutes to pile on her outdoor clothes. When she turns off the cheerful noise of the television, the stillness is mournful, sinister somehow.

She is hopeful that perhaps the strange light over on Helly Holm will have vanished by the time she braves the fresh outdoors and darkness, and heads out of the cottage to her little gold rented Peugeot, but no such luck. The wind batters at her as she opens the car door, the sea murmuring nearby, as though telling secrets.

She can see the Helly Holm car park in the distance as she putters along the road in the Peugeot, her coat and hat and a heavy industrial torch thrown on the seat next to her. Normally there are at least a couple of cars or caravans parked here at night – when it's clear, she's told, there's often a chance of seeing the Northern Lights.

But now there is only one vehicle – the white van the archaeologists use. Someone must have cocked up – dropped or forgotten something important, and she hopes it isn't her.

Ah well. She should swing by, make sure they're all right out there in the dark.

She's braking, just before she turns off towards the car park, when she glimpses someone walking back from Helly Holm along the causeway.

In an instant, even at this distance, she recognises Iris – her long, lean figure, her rolling walk, the torchlight jiggling over the wet concrete path before her, and before she realises, consciously, what she's doing, she's driving on, past the turn-off for the car park, along the road, accelerating as fast as she dares.

What the hell did she just see?

She cannot account for her kneejerk reaction to this. Something about it, the oddness of it, set her off – Iris driving the van up here, and not in the plush embrace of her white Taurus in which she could be recognised; the lateness of the hour, her aloneness – she has a bevy of attendants she can send in her stead – why has she come alone, in so dark, so dangerous an hour?

And hot on the heels of all this, a thousand chance remarks, intercepted glances, and the whirling sparks of Madison's own intuition. There's something about all this *gold* – this brilliant, unlikely and constant outpouring of good fortune.

Fool's gold.

Something not right.

Madison's fingers tap on the steering wheel as she speeds along the winding road to Finstown under the ink-black sky. In the rear-view mirror, the van has appeared – far away now, but gaining in speed. Iris must be hammering the accelerator.

Madison turns down a farm lane shaded by boulders, waits.

Nothing about this is right.

You know what you think.

And they all think it. All of them. Everyone must think it. But nobody is saying it, at least not out loud.

So, go to Helly Holm and look. If you're right, whatever it is will be in one of the trenches – C, probably, as that's the one Iris was working in today. If you look now, the soil will be fresh, disturbed.

Go look. Now. *While the tide is still out.*

Tomorrow may be too late.

Even while she tells herself it's too dark to see anything, she's wasting her time, imagine what would happen if the tide goes out and she's stuck there, what if Iris comes back? the white van is passing her hiding place now, and is it her imagination, but is the van slowing slightly, as though Iris is looking for her?

Madison sits absolutely still.

She waits for what feels like hours but is probably no more than ten minutes.

The van does not return.

She fires the car up, heading back the way she'd come, as though drawn by the white lantern of the lighthouse, blinking on and off, away out to sea.

And each time the light flashes alive, Madison briefly sees the rising bulge of Helly Holm, and the cloudy pale road cutting through the sea, leading to its foot.

When she climbs out of the car the sea is returning to the causeway – it glimmers briefly on the edge of her vision in the predictable shuttered pattern of the lighthouse lantern.

This is madness, she realises. She will be lucky to get up there, find what she's looking for, unseen – if there even *is* anything to see – and get back in time without being stranded.

And if she is stranded, what will she tell the archaeologists? She cannot shake the sense that Iris spotted her speeding away tonight.

She stands at the foot of the causeway, her torch pointing at it. It shines slickly.

You could just go back to Langmire, you know. Go home and say nothing – see no evil, et cetera. Pretend to be delighted when whatever it is turns up tomorrow. If anything turns up tomorrow. Pose for the pictures. Smile for the local press. Look pleased.

Besides, what good would trying to stop it do? Madison knows she's being sabotaged, undermined at the dig already, because of her relationship with Jack. It will be easy to paint her as a crazy person, unstable, difficult after the fact. She can see Iris mournfully explaining – 'Poor Madison. She was under so much *stress* with her stalker. She's imagining things.'

Iris is famous, celebrated, on her way to becoming a national treasure. The others will follow her lead.

You could just go with it, she thinks to herself, as the wind buffets her back.

It could be good for you. Good for your career.

Fiona would be impressed. It might finally put you on an even footing with her.

And something hardens within her.

No.

It's a lie.

And if you roll with it, it will be a lie you'll be living with all your life.

She understands that it will own her, utterly. She'll forever be waiting for Iris's fall, for it to take her down with her. This is what she sees in Jack's gritted smile whenever he talks about her, in Callum's fawning adoration.

And why am I even doing this, enduring this life – this freezing digging, these stupid politics, these thousand thankless tasks – if I am not even contributing truth?

It's not what I signed up for.

She stands there, determined but intimidated by the vastness of what she is contemplating.

She wants to call Fiona suddenly. She wants to get her advice. But she already has the sense of what Fiona's advice will be.

Sometimes it is simply time to act.

Before she realises it, she is already walking, stray strands of seaweed squelching between her boots and the concrete, as ahead of her, lit for a moment by the tower with its blazing electric lantern, Helly Holm looms like a dark mountain against the starless sky.

Acknowledgements

This novel, more than anything I've ever written, was helped enormously by the kindness of strangers.

I'd like to thank Julie Gibson, the County Archaeologist for Orkney, for taking valuable time out from her day to describe how rescue digging works on Orkney. It was she that observed early on that archaeological fraud would be a more compelling and likely motive than antiquities theft. The book is so much richer for her input – and as for the rest, any errors, exaggerations, dramatic licenses and outright inventions are all down to me.

Thanks are also due to the Cambridge Archaeological Unit, who let me dig alongside other volunteers at the Northstowe site as a refresher, and finally to Professor Marie-Louise Stig Sørenson, who taught me archaeology when I first came to Cambridge. It has remained a lifelong fascination.

I've been going to Orkney for years on a writing retreat, and I've long wanted to write a novel set there. I'd like to thank Ann and Alan Stevenson, the owners of Peedie Hoose, in Burness. A fictionalised version of this house appears as Langmire in the book, though Ann and Alan are far more congenial hosts than Douggie and Maggie, having nothing in common with them except for their friendliness, and I am extremely grateful to them.

It would be wrong to overlook other Orcadians that came to my aid during the writing of this book, including Robert Bruce at Drive Orkney Car Hire, who helped me with my missing hire car questions; the guides at the UNESCO World Heritage sites, who were unanimously friendly and well-informed; and

Sarah Bailey, local writer and Novelry member, who invited me to lunch at Helgi's and pointed out the merits of a mince roll to me.

I'd like to acknowledge my debt to Andrew Cowan, legal advisor, and PC Andy Kay of Greater Manchester Police, who both assisted with my questions around restraining orders. My biggest thanks must go to Julie Revell, court usher and home-girl, who not only set up my visit to Manchester Magistrates' Court but who came to my rescue when I broke my arm on the morning I was supposed to be in the visitors' gallery. Love you lots, babes.

I'm likewise grateful to Louise Dean of the Novelry for her helpful advice when I was stuck in the first draft.

Massive thanks must go to Joel Richardson, my editor at Michael Joseph, for his unfailing support and fantastic suggestions; as well as to Grace Long, Maxine Hitchcock, Tilda McDonald, Nick Lowndes and Sarah Bance.

As always, words can't express all I owe to my fabulous agent Judith Murray, and to all the crew at Greene and Heaton.

I've been hugely lucky to have benefited from the friendship of other writers and their families. I'd like to thank Gordon Fraser, Melanie Garret (who also opened my eyes to the beauty of Orkney scallops, fresh out of the sea), KD Grace – mistress of fresh air and perspective, Lucia Graves, Sumit Paul-Choudhury, Dave Gullen and Gaie Sebold for their constant support and encouragement. I couldn't have done it without you.

Finally, all my love always to my Mum and Dad, to John and Atsuko, to Joe, Darla, Aiden, Arcadia, Aiden, Arcadia, Finn, Rain, Remy and Oliver, and to Jackie and Lance. Sometimes it's your family that is your family.